PHANTOM BETRAYAL

HAVOC IN HARRIS PART ONE

E ABRAHAM

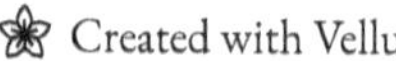 Created with Vellum

To my religious trauma for saving me time on research.

And for you who enjoy watching the emotional drama of finding love again.

One

Ghost

A sharp wind whistles through the trees, sending them shivering. It creates a cacophony of voices like phantoms weaving their way through the night. They're a perfect companion for our members. A chill rolls down my spine as I glance over my shoulders at the trees standing guard at our backs.

Tonight shouldn't have any surprises. It's a run we've made a thousand times before. Yet something is different. I can smell it in the shadows, in the ice flooding my veins, in the song dancing in the breeze. It sets my nerves on edge and my heart racing.

I keep my reservations to myself. No use bringing up what I can't explain. As President of the Phantoms MC, I need to be strong—confident. If I'm second-guessing my decisions without proof, it'll weaken my position. And while I'd like to think all the members of the Phantoms are loyal, I know it's not true. There's always someone waiting in the wings, thinking they can do better.

"What's wrong, Ghost?" Storm mutters as he sidles up next to me.

I should have known he'd notice I was off. He's not just my vice president, but my best friend. Has been since we were in diapers, running around the small headquarters like we owned the place. And we've become so much more since then. If anyone would notice shit was off with me, he would. There are few people who know me like he does.

"Nothing." There are too many people around to adequately convey what I'm worried about. "Let's just get this over with."

"There a reason we have our whole crew out here?"

"We could use the extra hands. With the prospects tagging along, we need the protection." It's the best explanation I have, though it's not the real reason. I should tell him, but we don't have time. My only hope is the Disciples don't show up. I have no idea how Storm will react, and I can't risk shit falling apart right now.

He steps in front of me, blocking my view of the road. I raise an eyebrow as he studies my face. His hair is a touch too long, the blue-black strands fluttering in the breeze. He refuses to get a haircut no matter how much I tell him he needs it. I could pull rank on him, but I've never done that before and I'm not about to start with his fucking hair.

"We're talking about this when we get home." He steps next to me once more and shoves his hands in the pockets of his jeans.

I roll my eyes, then glance around once more. "You're worse than Rivet."

"I'll take that as a compliment. They'd better get here soon. My balls are fucking freezing. Riding back isn't going to help either."

"Quit your bitching. You're getting too soft if you think this is cold."

Widow, an enforcer, steps next to Storm and gestures toward the empty road. "You smell that?"

Storm sniffs the air, and I hold back a heavy sigh. Widow and Storm start whispering to each other and I tune them out. I pull my phone from my pocket and text our contact. If the supply doesn't get here soon, I'm pulling us. They were supposed to be here almost an hour ago. We normally wouldn't wait. In fact, this would be the end of any type of relationship we had with another club in any other circumstance.

Except this is the Reapers. We've had an alliance with them for years. They're good allies. So much so, most of my club went all the way to Rima to help them stop the Guild from taking over the city a year ago. We would have gone anyway, since the Guild was an abhorrent operation, intent on stealing the lives of innocent people and selling them for rich people's sick pleasures. Most of the members were more than willing to volunteer to bring them down.

My phone buzzes and several heads turn toward me. I keep my face blank as I glance at the screen, not letting my confusion show. Eyes follow me as I make my way through the men waiting around the trucks. When I'm far enough away, I brace myself before answering.

"Griggs. What the fuck?" I say by way of greeting.

He grunts, then clears his throat. "Change of plans. We're moving to the southpoint."

"That wasn't the agreement. Either we meet here, or the deal is off."

He doesn't answer, merely hangs up instead. I don't blame him. He's just the middleman between the Reapers and us. We usually don't have to use one since Helms takes the opportunity to visit. He didn't elaborate why we'd be using Jackal and his crew this time around, and I didn't question it. Now, I'm regretting that decision.

I pull up Helms's number and wait for him to answer. "Helms, I'm not doing this again."

"What the fuck are you talking about?" Helms growls, and the beeping of machines in the background gives me pause.

I'm not about to ask him where the hell he is. I already know it's a hospital. I've seen the inside of them more often than I'd like. All of us have. If Helms wants me to know why he's there now, he'll tell me. Otherwise, it's none of my damn business.

"Uh, Griggs is over an hour late. When he finally called, he wanted to move the drop to the southpoint. I know you've got shit going on, but I'm about ready to call the whole thing off."

"Do it. If Griggs wants to pull some bullshit, then call it and let me know. Hawk will deal with them." There's a pause and I wonder if he'll hang up on me as well. "What? No, it's fine. You don't need to talk to him."

It takes me a minute to figure out he's not talking to me. I assume it's Mac, though I can barely hear the other person. I don't have time to wait for them to work shit out. I'm about to say something when he huffs.

"She wants to talk to you," he says.

"Ghost? It's Mac. There should be some of our guys coming, too. Ryker's texting them to figure out what the hell is going on." She pauses, a low whine ringing down the line. "Sorry. Willow was with them, but they might have turned back."

"Why?" If Griggs is supposed to have the Reapers escort him, there's no reason they should have left until the job was done. It's not like them.

"Well, I'm kind of, maybe, might be...in labor."

My mind blanks and I desperately search for what the hell I'm supposed to say in this situation. It's not like we haven't had members have babies, but I'm not usually involved in any way. I'm only brought in when it's time to give them money or rearrange places to live. And even then, it's mostly Rebel who handles the details.

"Congrats?"

She chuckles, then groans. "Yeah. So, I may have texted Willow, and she *may* have freaked out and insisted on coming back. Not entirely sure, but I'd put my money on that. Which means Griggs no longer wants to drive the extra miles to get to you."

"Well, seems like you've got more important things to worry about other than the drop. We'll make a trip down there when you…uh, when it's over?" I run my hand through my hair and shoot Storm a wide-eyed look.

"How about we just call you, hmm?" She's still laughing when she hands the phone back to Helms.

"Cancel the drop, Ghost. I'm not fucking dealing with his bitchy ass right now."

"I got it handled. I'll work with Hawk while you…do whatever it is fathers do when their wives are—"

"I wouldn't finish that sentence if I were you."

He hangs up, and I'm left clutching my phone, feeling like a complete fool. I text Rebel, our resident mother figure, to send a basket of some kind. She'll know what to do. Griggs name flashes across the screen and I brace myself.

"What'd your keeper decide, Griggs?"

He doesn't acknowledge the slight, merely jumps into a long-winded explanation of a bunch of bullshit that doesn't matter. I give the signal to move out and the men grumble.

"We're leaving, Griggs. Either you're here in the next three minutes or you'll be hearing from Hawk next."

I hang up and set an alarm. There's no way he'll be here in time. It'll put us back a little, but it doesn't matter. We have plenty of guns to move on to the next stop. It won't be easy to find someone to take their spot, but that's the least of my worries.

"How long are we waiting?" Storm asks. Several others turn to look at me expectantly.

"Three minutes. Then we roll out."

Storm raises an eyebrow, and I saunter away toward my bike.

"What's the problem?"

"Mac is having a baby. Reaper escort turned back to Synd and Griggs is trying to call the shots because of it. I need you to alert Fuse of any possible retaliations on their part. He'll get the word out." I brush my hand over the seat of my bike, wishing I could just take off. We try to create time for us to just ride, but it's not easy with an empire to build.

Storm wanders up, his face buried in his phone. "We have three more drops with Jackal in the next two weeks. We rerouting those as well?"

Another shiver rolls down my spine and I glance toward the road. Fog floats over the gravel, giving the scene an ethereal appearance. I thought the pit in my stomach would go away after we called off the drop. It hasn't. If anything, my unease has grown. It claws at my throat, threatening to shred me from the inside out. We need to get out of here.

"Ghost. What do you want me to do?"

My gaze narrows, eyeing the end of the road. A light flickers through the mist, and I suck in a sharp breath. There's no way Griggs had enough time to get here. Not from where he called me unless he lied. Griggs is a lot of things, but a liar isn't one of them. Storm makes a noise of disgust in the back of his throat, and it snaps me out of my haze.

"Scatter," I bellow and shove Storm toward his bike.

We have protocols for this. What should be a chaotic scene is quiet and orderly as men hurry to their bikes and the trucks. They'll abandon the latter if need be, but we should have enough time to get away. I chose this area specifically because it looks like it only has one exit. A deep rumble takes over the night as dozens of motorcycles start. Two at a time, my men take off for the trees, slipping between them like wraiths.

The box trucks won't make it on the paths the bikers are taking. They'll have to go another route and they'll be on their own. I throw my leg over my own bike and start it, then wait. Storm should be leading the others, but he's next to me. No matter how many times I tell him to follow protocol, he refuses. Apparently, we're supposed to die together or some bullshit.

The headlights waver as the vehicle bumps along the potholes. A large, black box truck splits the fog a second before the lights cut out, plunging us into darkness. We should go—ride as fast as we can away from this. But only a fraction of my men are safe. I slip my gun from my waistband and catch Storm doing the same. Hopefully we don't need to fight our way out of here.

I glance over my shoulder and my chest tightens. We still have at least forty guys left, nervously waiting their turn to take the narrow path to freedom.

"Get them out of here, Storm," I call before I start my bike.

He shouts something, but I don't hear as I circle around him and head toward the truck. If it is Griggs, he'll stop and bitch some more. He won't fucking shoot me if he knows what's good for him. If it's not him...well, they might try to run me over. At least I'll provide a distraction for my men to retreat.

The truck rumbles closer and my headlight illuminates the driver's gaunt face. Recognition floods through me as his eyes meet mine. I lift my gun as I slow down. Before I can think twice, I empty the magazine, aiming for the tires and windows. He wrenches the wheel and sends the box tumbling toward me, the whole thing tipping over. I swerve and circle back from where I came, barely missing the wreck. If he didn't die in the crash, he'll be close.

"Ghost! Get out of there," Storm screams and I glance over my shoulder.

The box of the truck crumples as it hits the ground, and the back doors pop open. Barrels topple out and explode as they hit the ground. One rolls closer, spilling its contents. A sickly green liquid splatters across the gravel, and a billowing smoke fills the air. I don't know what was in the drums, but I'd rather not find out. Especially if it's Oracle. We've been fighting to keep the drug out of our territory. From the looks of it, we've failed.

As much as I want to follow my men, I have to make sure the driver is dead. He'll keep coming after me, hurting the club in his quest to get to me. I glance over my shoulder again, intent on turning around if need be. My front tire hits a soft spot, and I ease off the throttle, hoping the gravel doesn't put me on the ground. Storm's yells echo through the air, but I can't understand him. He won't be able to get to me before I crash. I wouldn't want him to.

Time slows to a crawl as the pressure around me drops and the ground rumbles seconds before a thunderous explosion rattles through the air. Heat sears across my back, and I swear the smell of burning leather wafts around me. I tuck my chin to my chest as the blast sends me flying over my handlebars. Blackness takes over my vision before I hit the ground and I tumble into a pit of nothingness devoid of life.

Two

I shouldn't be here. Running away from the Phantoms was the smartest fucking thing I ever did. At least that's what I've been telling myself for the last six years. I don't regret leaving after I was banished, but being back here is stirring up memories I thought I'd buried deep.

Huffing, I hitch my backpack higher and wince. Slowly, I trudge my way toward Phantom territory on the north end of Harris. I glance back at the tiny train station and my muscles relax when I find it empty. The last thing I need is someone following me. Not that I'm worried about that. I'm not important enough for someone to chase. At least not in Harris. Most of the cities I've been to in the last few years, I haven't stuck around long enough to make friends, much less enemies.

And now I'm home. Except it doesn't feel like home anymore. The streets may be the same, but the changes stand out. The hardware store on Main is gone, replaced with a florist. The old chop shop looks like it's actually running a legit business now. A row of apartment buildings has taken over what used to be a park. With each step, I'm reminded of how out of place I am in a city I used to know like the back of my hand. I used to roam these streets with Ghost and Storm, pretending we were grown and in charge.

I shake my head as I skirt around an abandoned block filled with warehouses. Graffiti covers the bricks and boarded-up windows. At least the sigils are familiar. I've tried to keep up on what's happening in Harris for times just like these. I don't know if Ghost got my message or if he even cares. If he wants to be stubborn and hold a grudge, I can't change his mind. But I also can't let him walk into a shitstorm without a warning. If any of them got hurt because I didn't say something, the guilt would eat me alive.

Then two days ago, I got the text. Two simple words that flipped my life upside down: *come home.*

Storm hadn't texted me in six years. Not when I left him drunk voicemails. Not when Ghost won his bid for presidency. Not when Storm's mom died. It took me an hour to craft a response which only ended up as one word: *why?* He never answered. Because of course he didn't. He made it very clear all those years ago I would never hear from him again. I was dead to them both. His last message echoes in my head.

It would be better if you were actually dead.

I shake my head, shoving the memory away. It doesn't matter what happened in the past. I can't afford the distraction right now. For the next two days, I'm stuck here and then I can leave again. The train tickets I bought before I left Stowe are burning a hole in my pocket. They're non-refundable, too. I wasn't particularly attached to Stowe. It was a quirky little town and I never fit in, but it was a nice change from the cities I've been to. My tickets aren't for a return trip. I forget where I picked to go after facing the demons of my past.

"This is going to be a shitshow," I mumble as I limp into Phantom territory.

Black flags hang in windows with the crowned skull of the Phantom's emblem emblazoned on them. I remember asking my father when I was five why the flames were blue when fire was orange. Instead of an answer, I got a nice new bruise I couldn't hide from Ghost. He used to make grand promises back then—

vowing to protect me. Ghost would probably turn a blind eye if it happened today.

The deeper I get into Phantom territory, the more I realize this area is largely unchanged. Same buildings with a fresh coat of paint line the streets. The same rumble of motorcycles splits the night. The same shadows stretch far into the alleyways, sending a chill down my spine. A somberness has spread through the area. It was never a cheery place before, necessarily. Except now there's a layer of bleakness as if this slice of the world is holding its breath.

I slide between two houses, a soft glow from the windows lighting my way. Headquarters lies straight ahead across a gravel parking lot. I won't be able to sneak up on them. Not only are there floodlights everywhere, but cameras, too. They'd know within seconds of me stepping onto the street. Actually, I wouldn't be surprised if they already know I'm here.

"Psst," a voice hisses behind me, and my heart clenches.

I turn slowly, a smirk dancing on my face. "Well, well. Didn't expect to see you here still."

"Where the hell else would I be, bitch?" Lexi steps from the shadows, then leans against the house. "Not all of us can swan-dive off the face of the damn planet without a word."

"And I'd still be gone if I had a choice." I cross my arms, waiting.

Her face splits into a grin, and she jumps toward me to wrap her arms around me. Tears fill my eyes, but I blink them back as I return the hug gingerly. She smells exactly the same as she did all those years ago. My breath hitches, a bolt of pain lancing through me as she squeezes, and I dig my fingers into her sides. She shrieks, ripping her body away.

"Sorry," I chuckle. "Forgot how ticklish you are."

She shivers, wrinkling her nose, and she tries to reach behind her. "Dammit. My arms are too damn short. Scratch."

She spins and I run my nails down her back. She shudders and grumbles under her breath. After all this time, I was nervous we wouldn't be the same as we once were. It's like no time has passed and we just saw each other yesterday. When she faces me, her cheeks are wet. I sober as she swipes at her tears.

"My bad. I'm just happy you're back." She clears her throat. "Except you're not staying, are you?"

I shake my head, pressing my lips together. She nods once, then glances away. Our relationship was always a little bit like being on a seesaw. At fifteen she breezed into town, claiming she was Ghost's sister and would be staying in Harris. I always got the feeling she wanted a family so badly she'd do anything to make it happen. Avery, Ghost's other sister, was wary of her at first, but I was just happy to expand our family.

Lexi never was one to try to talk me out of things. If anything, she was the one encouraging me to take a risk. She dared me to skip class six months after she got here. She double dared me to steal Ghost's bike when she was sixteen. She triple-dog dared me to drink an entire bottle of vodka right after I graduated. That last one was the worst, and I swore I'd never do it again, which was a lie.

I purse my lips when she clears her throat again. "Caught a frog?"

She sighs as our gazes meet. "Anyone tell you what's going on?"

"No. Just got a text saying come home." My voice catches on the last word, but she doesn't comment. "I doubt it's to repeat that night we went skinny dipping in the middle of winter."

She smiles, but it doesn't quite reach her eyes. "It was October. Hardly the middle of winter."

"Still fucking cold as fuck," I mumble and glance over my shoulder as a bike turns into the parking lot. I don't recognize the man who climbs off and stalks through the double doors. He doesn't hesitate to walk into the dark interior and no alarms ring through the night.

"I wouldn't know since I was too chickenshit to actually take my clothes off in front of the boys." Bitterness weaves its way through her tone. Lexi used to care what others thought of her, but by the time she graduated high school, she said she didn't give a shit anymore.

I bite my tongue, not wanting to bring up hurt feelings. "You going to tell me what's going on, then?"

She runs her hand through her jet-black hair and tips her head back. "Better you figure it out yourself. Mostly because I'm not willing to poke the bear."

A jolt of nerves hits me square in the chest. "What the fuck does that mean?"

Her nostrils flare as she studies my face. "You're not sticking around anyway, so it probably won't matter. Let's just say a lot of things have changed, but not enough. Just go."

My jaw drops as she stomps off into the dark. I didn't think she'd throw a welcome home party for me, but the sudden change in her demeanor has me stunned. I shouldn't have assumed neither of us had changed. Or that she'd be perfectly okay with me just breezing back into town. It was naive hope on my part. Plus, she's right. I'll be leaving soon enough, and it'll be like I was never here. Most of the members won't even know I was back at all. Hell, I didn't plan on seeing Lexi, either.

I hitch my backpack up once more, wincing as a nerve pinches in my shoulder. I skirt around the house, attempting to keep in the shadows. The longer I stay hidden, the easier this trip will be. Avoiding Ghost would be ideal. I won't get away with dodging Storm since he sent the text. I doubt I'll get as warm of a welcome from him as I did from Lexi. Maybe I'll get lucky and he won't give a shit. Indifference would be far preferable to the other possibilities.

I slip into the trees and run along the side of headquarters, making my way to the back. Hopefully the side entrance isn't locked. Before they would put a guy on the door when there was a threat. My entire journey here it's been quiet, so I doubt the Phantoms are under attack. No one should be there to catch me.

When I dash across the gravel alley, it occurs to me I have no plan. My hand rests on the metal handle and I gnaw on my bottom lip. I thought I'd just sneak into headquarters and find a friendly face. Except that wouldn't work. I only have two days. No matter how much I want to avoid Storm, he's the one who texted me. I'll have to face him sooner rather than later. Getting it over with is better than waiting for him to ambush me.

Biting the inside of my cheek, I yank on the handle and the door pops open. The move isn't as silent as I'd hoped, but the entire room is dark and hopefully empty. I slide along the wall, hoping they haven't made major changes to the furniture placement. Crashing into a table isn't on my bucket list. It takes me a lot longer to reach the bar built along the far wall. For a split second, I contemplate stopping for a shot. I might need the liquid courage. I decide against it and make my way to the hallway.

I'll have to sneak past the rooms for the other members, go all the way up the stairs to the second floor, then back down the hallway to Storm's room. It'll be a miracle if no one finds me, except this place is dead. No one stirs. No snores echo through the air. No light filters from the gaps. It's as if the place is deserted, though I know at least one guy is in here.

By the time I'm standing in front of Storm's room, I'm completely confused. I could knock, but I run the risk of having a gun shoved in my face. Instead, I turn the knob and swing open the heavy wood.

"What the fuck?" I mutter into the empty space.

I pivot and stomp back the way I came, then down the stairs, and into the main area. I use the flashlight on my phone to light the large room and weave through the tables to the front doors. The biker's motorcycle is gone, and I'm starting to think I've lost my mind. He was definitely parked here before, and I didn't hear him leave.

I shouldn't be surprised Storm isn't here. Most of the time they didn't use their rooms at headquarters. It was foolish to think he was randomly waiting here for me. It would have made shit a lot easier, though. Now I run the risk of finding both of them. Together. At the same time.

When I take off across the parking lot, my backpack thuds against my body, keeping time with my steps. Running is a bad idea, but I can deal with the fallout later. The wind picks up, sending a blast of cold air into me. I'm wheezing by the time I skid to a stop in front of Ghost's house. At least, I hope it's still his house. He grew up here and he kept it when his dad died. He always said he wouldn't move into the official president's house when he took over the Phantoms.

One lamp lights the front window, but curtains block my view of the inside. I don't bother to muffle my steps as I clomp up the stairs to the front porch. The door swings open before I can knock, and I drop my hand. Storm's scowling face greets me, and his dark eyes scan me up and down.

"What the fuck are you doing here?" he growls, and I grit my teeth.

I cross my arms, then drop them to my sides, scowling right back at him. "You said come home. I came home."

"Phantom territory isn't your home. You've got five minutes to get the fuck out of town before I send Bones after you. And we both know how much she'd *love* getting her hands on you. She's still salty you crashed into her bike."

He goes to slam the door shut, and I shove my foot in the way. He growls and slowly opens it again. I smile when he glares at me. Little bitch doesn't get to summon me whenever he wants for no goddamn reason. If he wants to play this game, so be it.

"Tell me why you texted me and what the hell is going on here and then I'll be gone."

He leans forward until his face is inches from mine. His scent washes over me, and an ache blooms in my chest. The notes are foreign—bitter and antiseptic. Just when I think all of the man I once knew was gone, I catch a hint of cedar. My heart skips a beat as nostalgia overtakes me. I swallow hard, reminding myself why I'm here.

"I didn't fucking text you, *sweets*," he snarls. "Move your foot or I'll do it for you."

"Go right ahead, Storm. I'd love to see you try."

We glare at each other, neither one willing to back down. The longer I stare at him, the more I have to fight against my emotions. Regret. Shame. Guilt. They swirl together, then crawl up my throat, threatening to choke me. Rage washes them away. Or maybe it merely shoves the rest deep down within me. My fingers curl into a fist at my side and I resist the urge to slam it into his perfect fucking nose. His insipid little smirk almost puts me over the edge.

There's a grunt from behind him and I freeze.

"Let her in, Storm. I need answers only she can give me."

Three

I barely stop myself from strangling Siren. She's sitting across from me, her body sinking into the old couch as if she belongs. She doesn't. If she were anyone else, she would have been shot on sight. My hand twitches, wondering if I could get away with it still. From the exhausted look on Ghost's face, I'm thinking no.

Her gaze flits around the room, probably cataloging all the changes. There aren't many, except for a few of my things scattered around. She probably isn't even fazed by my jacket thrown over the chair, but the painting might give her pause. I don't fucking care what she thinks. Or why she's here. I just want her gone. We've been perfectly fine without her.

"You look like shit," she says, breaking the silence.

I narrow my gaze at her, but she's focused on Ghost. No shit he looks like he does. He was blown up not even a week ago and refuses to slow down more than the three days it took for him to be conscious for more than ten minutes. Not that she knows any of that. I doubt she's kept track of what's happening here. She washed her hands of us long ago.

"And you look like you've been whoring yourself out to every MC within a hundred-mile radius," I spit out when Ghost doesn't say anything.

Her gaze snaps to mine and hurt flashes through her eyes. It's gone with the next blink, and she's back to staring at Ghost. He warned me to keep my mouth shut, but I won't sit here and let her dictate the way this goes. When we finally get rid of her, we'll be having a confrontation. Him texting her from my phone is just an extra layer of bullshit.

Ghost huffs, wincing as he twists in his chair. "What contact have you had with the Disciples?"

My head whips around. He subtly shakes his head, though I'm sure Siren caught it, too. I don't give a flying fuck if he doesn't want me to mention anything. Or pretend like I know what the hell he's talking about. If he had questions, he should have come to me. If he had theories, he should have brought them up. If he wanted to know what they're doing, he should have leaned on me. Instead, he brought the one person we swore we'd never mention again, no matter how much her absence hurt. We kept that promise for six years, not once saying her name.

Siren's face shutters. "In the last five years? I don't know. Anything else?"

"We both know that's not true, Siren," Ghost murmurs.

She doesn't give anything away. None of her usual tells come through. No lip twitch or flush across her cheeks. Her arms stay firmly folded across her chest. Hell, she still has her goddamn backpack on. I wonder where she's been all this time. Once she left Harris, I refused to keep tabs on her. I thought Ghost did the same, but apparently not.

"What exactly do you want, Ghost?"

"Already told you. I won't ask again." He crosses his arms and his shoulders tighten. It's the only indication he's in pain.

She huffs, her fingers digging into her bare skin. "Bold of you to assume—"

"Why aren't you wearing more clothes?" I blurt out, immediately regretting my outburst.

"You gave up the right to comment on my clothes, or lack

thereof. I suggest you keep your mouth shut during this particular conversation. It's clear you have no idea what's going on."

Ghost kicks me when I open my mouth to respond. I'd walk away if I could, but I'm not about to leave Ghost by himself with this viper. She's fucked us over before. I won't allow her to do it again. Especially with Ghost being injured.

Ghost leans forward and rests his elbows on his knees. "Tell me what I want to know, and then you can flit off into the night again. You can do whatever the fuck you want."

"You want to know when I last had *contact* with the Disciples? Fine. A week ago. And seven weeks before that. And four months before that. Not to mention six months before that. Would you like me to continue?" Her cheeks flush and her chin trembles. It's the first sign of, well, anything from her. She's been a blank mask for the most part.

I glance at Ghost and stiffen. Beads of blood have seeped into his shirt, dotting the fabric. The explosion from the barrels in the back of the truck hit him the worst. Most of our men were on their way out. We'd all be dead if it wasn't for him stopping the truck. He's been pushing himself too hard and he won't listen to me. I can run shit while he heals, yet he brushes me off every time.

"What type of contact?" he finally asks.

Siren glances away and waves a hand. "Oh, we're best buds. We just had a lovely little sleepover a month ago. Real humdinger of a time."

"Who the fuck says humdinger?" I mutter, and Ghost sniffs. I'm not sure if it's amusement or an admonishment.

She pushes to her feet and hitches her backpack higher. "I don't know what the hell is going on, but whatever is happening between the Phantoms and the Disciples has nothing to do with me. I can't help you. Not that I wanted to in the first place."

Her words are hollow, devoid of any inflection. She swallows, then pivots and makes her way to the front door.

"You owe us," Ghost snarls, jumping to his feet.

She spins back and thrusts a finger at him. "I owe you *nothing.*"

She runs from the house, slamming the door behind her. I have no idea where she's staying or how she got here. Fuck, I don't know a damn thing about any of this. Ghost collapses into the chair again and drops his head in his hands.

"What the fuck was all that? Why the hell would you text her? And from my goddamn phone." My nostrils flare as I pace in front of him, needing somewhere for this energy to go.

"I needed to know."

"Know what?" I cry, sinking onto the couch. Siren's scent wafts around me and an ache settles in my chest. I shake my head, refusing to let myself fall into the myriad of memories it evokes.

Ghost leans against the chair and stares at the ceiling. "The guy behind the wheel of the truck was a Disciple. Held a grudge against me personally."

"What the hell did you do to him?"

Our gazes me and he smirks. "Killed his brother. Dick deserved it, but apparently the brother found out it was me."

"What'd his brother do?" Because of course the brother did something. All the Disciples are scum—some of them worse than others.

Ghost sobers and his jaw twitches. "Raped his girlfriend. She ran here. I took care of it. Driver knew his brother was a piece of shit, but I couldn't figure out if he knew specifically what I'd done. Which is the only reason I left him alive. He played the long game, though. I wasn't expecting that."

"When? When did all this happen and why the fuck didn't you tell me?" I can't believe how much shit he's kept from me. I'm his fucking VP. We're best friends—more than that. Yet he's been lying to me.

"Right before Siren left. She...she helped me take care of the body." He runs his hand through his hair and winces. "You were on a run."

I could keep pushing him for more answers. A run only took a few hours back then. He could have told me when I got back. Hell, Siren could have told me, too. Nothing I say will change the past, no matter how much I bitch about it.

"What does any of this have to do with *her*?"

"If she's still in contact with them, she probably knows whether the attempted hit was personal or a coordinated attack on behalf of the Disciples. If they're targeting us, we need to be prepared."

I know all this. It's why I put everyone into lockdown after Ghost got hurt. With my rank, I was able to pull it off, though some of the members weren't very happy about it. Some of the ones who were here years ago wanted to retaliate against Jackel immediately. I wasn't about to start a war while our president was high as a fucking kite. We didn't have enough info. Once Ghost was back on his feet, we lifted the lockdown, but we're still on high alert.

He clears his throat. "You still have her number."

I push off the couch and make my way to the kitchen. As I dig around for the meds our doctor gave Ghost, I glance at him. He's staring into space, his profile a blank mask. Maybe he's just tired. We had a meeting earlier. With Siren showing up in the middle of the fucking night, he's probably exhausted.

I shove the pills and a glass of water at him. "Take these. Now."

He takes them and some of the tension leaves me.

"Why do you still have her number?"

"I still have your dad's number in there, too. Stop avoiding the fact you brought her here. And fucking lied about it."

He shakes his head and won't meet my eyes. "She's the only connection we have to the Disciples. I'm not about to start a war with them, where hundreds of our men might die, on a hunch. Until we know whether it was the guy working alone or an order from Prophet, we can't make any decisions. I thought she..."

"You thought you could exploit her, catch her off guard into revealing something?"

"Sure," he sighs as his eyes flutter shut.

"Stop fucking lying to me, Ghost. We don't lie to each other," I snarl.

"Fine. I thought she might feel guilty. I thought she might slip up—give us some indication which way it goes. I thought she'd make the right choice."

I snort, though my stomach flips. "She fucked us over once, Ghost. Don't let her do it again. Even if she knew something, she'd never tell us. That woman doesn't give two shits about us, and she never did."

His jaw twitches and I expect him to agree, but he doesn't. Usually, I have no problem following Ghost's lead. He worked hard to become president of the Phantoms. I stood by him every step of the way. I didn't care about being his second. If he would have chosen someone else, I still would have stayed, helping in any way he saw fit. Because it was more than just the Phantoms for me. We were always more than the MC. Once upon a time, Siren was part of us.

"Maybe..." He swallows hard. "Never mind. I'm going to bed. Do *not* let me sleep in. We've got shit to do."

"Shit you won't be able to do if you're still fucking hurt."

He walks away without responding. There's nothing else to say, anyway. He'll do whatever the fuck he wants. I'm not foolish enough to think he shares everything with me, but I thought he'd tell me the important bits. Hell, the night of the drop, he knew something was up and barely said shit. I usually don't have to guess whether he's telling me the truth and I don't have to pull it from him.

Until now.

I don't know what the fuck is going on with him, but summoning Siren back into our lives isn't right. We made the decision together to throw her out. Her betrayal wasn't something we could get over. I don't care if it's been six years. She fucked us over and I won't allow her the opportunity to do it again. She can't be trusted.

Ghost might think she has an ounce of shame inside her, but I know better. I know she played us. Maybe when we were kids, things were different. At some point she chose herself over us—over everything we could have been. I wonder what the Disciples gave her for her to throw away our future.

I pull my phone from my pocket and text Widow. He'll keep watch while I go searching for answers. I might not trust Siren's words, but her movements won't lie. If she runs to the Disciples, we'll know she's in their pocket. The sooner I figure this out, the quicker she'll be gone. Then we can go back to pretending she doesn't exist.

Four

Siren

Phantom territory is the wrong place to be right now. Sure, Ghost may have texted me to come home, but I should have left immediately once he interrogated me. Except I'm safer here. If I leave, even to somewhere else in Harris, I'll be a target. They'll come after me and I don't think I'll be able to run fast enough to get away. Not with the wound in my side. Plus, I'm tired of running. No matter how far I go, they're always there.

I shiver rolls through me, and I glance around before dropping my backpack. I only have one sweatshirt, and it has holes in it. Pulling it over my head, I brace myself for the influx of memories I always get when I wear it. Storm would have ripped it from my body without a second thought if he saw me right now. I suppose he has the right since the sweatshirt was his. But he gave it to me. It was a gift. He probably didn't think I'd hang onto it for all these years. Pain stabs at my heart, and I dig my knuckles into the spot.

Sniffing, I throw my backpack on again. I thought I'd find an abandoned store and hide out there until the sun rises. Which doesn't explain why my feet are taking me to my old house. It's small and might be occupied, but it's better than sleeping under a bridge. Or the old fort in the forest behind Ghost's house.

I trip over a crack in the sidewalk and barely keep my feet under me. My breath catches in my throat as my childhood home comes into view. It doesn't look like anyone took it over. The porch swing hangs off one chain and leaves are scattered across the steps. It needs a fresh coat of paint and one of the windows needs to be replaced. Actually, all the windows need fixing. If I was staying...

I shake my head and slip around the side. Being on the edge of town was always a bittersweet thing. When I was a kid, it terrified me. I always thought someone was hiding in the trees behind the house. When I was a teenager, though, it allowed me to come and go without a trace. Not that there was anyone to sneak away from. Mom was long gone by then and Dad didn't remember he had a kid. I suppose that's what I get for being born a girl. Or maybe my father just forgot he was supposed to be a parent.

The back door creaks open and dust wafts around me. My nose wrinkles when I step inside. From the look and smell of things, no one's been here since I left. Hell, I wasn't spending much time here either before Dad skipped town. He was always out getting high or gambling. It was lonely and I preferred to stay with Ghost and Storm. They'd sneak me into headquarters sometimes, too.

"Doubt they'd let me stay there now," I mutter and kick the door shut. The glass rattles, and the knob falls to the ground.

I wander around the place, taking in the broken dishes in the kitchen and the ripped-up cushions scattered in the living room. Whoever came through here didn't seem to be searching for anything. This was rage and retaliation. The pain in my chest throbs again, and I suck in a deep breath, only to get a lungful of dust. I clutch the railing to the upstairs as I double over and cough. My eyes water, and I convince myself it's from the musty smell in the air and not my heart breaking all over again.

Going upstairs isn't an option. Not only do I not trust the steps, but it'll bring with it a whole host of memories I'm not willing to face. Being back in Harris could very well be the death of me. All the work I did of shoving down my feelings is quickly crumbling under the weight of the past. And it won't stop until I leave. At least with the Disciples constantly two steps behind me, I don't have time to linger on what went wrong.

It'd be nice to know *why* the Disciples care so much about me. I haven't been part of the Phantoms in years. No matter how far I run or how deep I go, they're always popping up, intent on bringing me back. It's not like I have any insider secrets to share with them. I'm the worst fucking candidate for the role of a mole. Yet they won't give up.

One of these days, I might just let them take me. I'd get answers then. Eventually, they'd kill me, but at least this would be over. I just want to be done. I'm desperately trying not to spiral after seeing Storm and Ghost. Is it healthy to contemplate Prophet sending more of his men after me in the hopes I won't have to face them again? No. Except I'm in pain and exhausted and done. I'm just so done with fighting every minute to survive. Doesn't mean I actually want Prophet to come for me. I'd like if they just all left me the hell alone.

The blankets in the closet are still tucked away in plastic totes. They're musty, yet warm. I make my bed in the corner of the living room facing the large windows overlooking the front yard. I should secure the back door before I sleep. Exhaustion washes over me, and I decide to take the risk. No one will be following me. If someone does, well, I'll just deal with it. Just like I always do. It'd be really nice if someone was there to protect me for once.

I don't know what wakes me, but suddenly I'm staring wide-eyed at the ceiling. The wind whistles through the gaps of the windows. It'll probably start raining any minute, which will make it harder to run if I need to.

Slowly, I unravel myself from the piles of blankets and grip my dagger. My knife is never far from me. I learned the hard way to always have a weapon nearby. Being in Phantom territory lulled me into a false sense of security, but not enough to abandon all my good sense.

I shove my feet into my flip-flops as I squint out the window. Branches from the large tree out front lash through the air, the wind ripping off leaves. At least I'm not out there in the cold. A thump echoes around me and my head whips toward the back. I can't see the kitchen door I came in from where I am. It could just be the broken knob.

My stomach flips and I shove down the nerves as I push to my feet. I'm kicking myself for not dealing with the knob before I slept. Or buying tennis shoes before I came here. It's only been a couple hours since I fell asleep. Grumbling under my breath, I make my way down the hallway to the kitchen. I don't have any tools to fix the door, but I might be able to rig up something to keep it from banging open.

I grab the metal knob and straighten, only to drop it when a shadow flits across the window embedded in the door. The wavy glass distorts the figure, but it's definitely a man. Thunder rolls overhead, hopefully covering my mistake. I inch backward, then crouch as he paces back and forth. Maybe staying here wasn't a good idea. I didn't think the Disciples would follow me into Phantom territory. Maybe I was wrong.

He reaches for the door, and I sprint away. I can't afford to lose my flip-flops, but they're the worst for running. My complacency will be the death of me. Footsteps echo after me and I head for the stairs, praying they'll hold my weight. I don't dare look back.

A muffled sob leaves me when a large hand wraps around my ankle when I'm only halfway up the stairs. I barely get my arm over my face before I smash into the wood and my knife goes tumbling through the rails. Panic swamps me until instinct and training take over.

I kick back, my heel hitting something hard, most likely a shoulder since he doesn't react. I twist my ankle, trying to break his grip and get my balance back. A growl erupts from me, and I grab one of the spindles. When I yank at the wood, it rips free from the banister and sends me slipping toward him.

My elbow catches the edge of the stair, and my arm goes numb. My face slams down and blood flies from my nose. I swallow a scream, needing to keep silent. If he has anyone waiting outside, I'd rather not give myself away. Killing this guy and running is my best bet to getting away. I have no idea where I'll go but anywhere is better than with the Disciples. With Prophet.

An arm wraps around my waist and hauls me upright. I kick at the stairs, the spindles, anything I can reach. I throw my elbow into his stomach, and he grunts. He growls in my ear, and I freeze, then renew my efforts. Just because I know him doesn't mean I'll take it easy on him.

"Knock it the fuck off, Siren. You're bleeding all over me." Storm's voice rumbles through me.

"Put me down," I yell, and he snorts, probably at the muffled tone from my stuffy nose.

Storm stomps down the stairs with me kicking the entire way. I don't want to end up breaking something because he loses his footing, but he was chasing me. I don't think he'd hurt me regardless of how he feels about me. Nothing is ever for sure, though. He clearly stalked me here for whatever reason. I don't think I'd be able to kill him if it came down to it. A wave of exhaustion crashes over me and I slump against him. His arm tightens and a flash of heat hits me. I bury the feelings, reminding myself how much I hate him. My body doesn't listen.

He makes a noise in the back of his throat and drops me onto my nest of blankets. I catch myself with my hand and my wrist gives out. A whimper escapes me. Thankfully, he doesn't notice. He's too busy pacing back and forth. I tip my head back and grab one of the covers to staunch the flow of tears and blood. Bastard could have kept me from hurting myself. He doesn't fucking care.

"What the hell are you doing here?" he snarls.

"I was fucking sleeping, asshat. This is technically still my house."

He leans over me and I force myself to stay still. "You're in Phantom territory, if you'll remember."

"Back the fuck up." It's not as intimidating as I'd like, but it's hard with a busted face, numb arm, and a twisted wrist. Not to mention all the other injuries I'm hiding under my clothes. I drop the blanket and sniff.

"Get out. You have ten minutes to leave, or I'll put a bullet in your head." He straightens, then tilts his head as he scans my face. "Why the fuck did you run?"

My mouth drops open. "Because you were chasing me, asshole. How the fuck was I supposed to know it was you? And even if I did, I'd still fucking run."

He scoffs, throwing up his hands. "Why the hell—"

"You said you'd put a bullet in my head. Excuse me if I thought you were fucking serious." Bitterness weaves through my tone and I squeeze my eyes shut.

I don't want him to have anything to use against me later. It's why I kept my emotions in check while I was at Ghost's place. From the look of things, I'm pretty sure they both live there, which isn't surprising. It was always their plan to share. At one point, I was part of that. Not so much anymore. Nausea bubbles in my stomach and I press my lips together. If I puke on him...on second thought, maybe I do want to throw up on him. It might get him to back off.

"What the fuck is wrong with you?"

"Nothing," I mumble, searching for my knife so I don't have to meet his gaze.

"Doesn't look like nothing."

"Well," I snap as I stand and grab my backpack, "turns out you slammed my face into the step and probably broke my nose and I'm now covered in blood. Now get the hell out of my way."

He steps closer and I plant my feet, which isn't easy standing on blankets. "Oh, I'm not letting you out of my sight until you're far away from Phantom territory. The last thing Ghost needs is you hanging around and fucking shit up for us. Again."

I grit my teeth and throw my backpack around. The bag smacks into him and forces him to back up. My vision goes blurry when I swing the straps over my shoulders, and I teeter to the side. Storm's hand shoots out, but he snatches it away before he touches me. I didn't expect him to actually help. Not after he was the one who hurt me in the first place.

"You have to move," I mumble as my head pounds. I need to find the meds I stuffed in the bottom of my bag. There's only a few left, but I won't make it through the night without something to stop the pain coursing through my body.

He steps back, eyeing me warily. I roll my eyes, which does nothing for the myriad of injuries ailing me. I swallow down another bout of nausea and slip around him. My knife fell over the side of the stairs, and I refuse to leave without it. He'll probably throw a fucking fit about it, but whatever. It's not like I'm going to stab him even if he deserves it.

I thought I'd have enough guts to take them out. My fickle heart got in the way. I love them as much as I hate them. Or maybe I just love the memory of who they once were to me. Either way, it all comes to the same conclusion. I can't kill them.

Trying to keep him in sight while searching for my knife isn't easy. Apparently, it's more important to sit there and glare at me than do, well, anything else. I squint into the dark, trying to use the lightning flashing outside to find my dagger. I refuse to leave a weapon behind. I only have a couple as it is, and I can't afford to lose this one. Plus, it was a gift.

"Hurry the fuck up, Siren," he growls from right behind me.

I shuffle forward and the side of my foot brushes against the blade. Immediately it stings like a paper cut, and I hiss. It's the least of my injuries at this point. I grab the dagger and slip it into the sheath tucked in my waistband. When I glance over my shoulder, I jolt. Storm is practically up my ass. I mumble a string of curses under my breath as I shove past him.

The back door swings open, then shut. Over and over, it bangs against the counter as the storm continues to build. It feels apropos to be escorted out into a veritable gale with a man named for such things. I grab the straps of my backpack and hope I don't need to use it as a shield. A blast of wind hits me square in the face as I trip down the back stairs. My guts gurgle and my wrist aches and my nose throbs, but I keep moving forward. I'll have to find another place to crash until the train station opens in the morning.

"Where are you going?" Storm bellows over the wind, and he grabs my upper arm.

I turn my face away and rip from his grasp. "You told me to leave, so I'm leaving."

"And where the fuck you think you're going to go?"

"Not really any of your business, Storm. Why the hell do you care?"

It doesn't make sense. I'm too tired to figure it out, though. I've been on the run for years and I don't know how much longer I can hold out. I could try to find Lexi. Even if she's pissed at me, she'll let me stay with her. Except with Storm following me like a lost puppy, she won't open the door. Or rather, she'll open the door, let him in, and leave my ass outside to be swept away. Lexi is loyal to the Phantoms to a fault. Once upon a time I was too, and then they broke every promise they made. Every single one of the bastards in the Phantoms.

I stomp around the side of the house with my foot stinging the entire way. If I move fast enough, Storm will leave me alone. He'll follow me to the edge of Phantom territory and let me go. I'll be back on the train to wherever the hell I'm hiding next. Eventually I'll forget I was ever here. I'll be too busy trying to stay alive to remember how far I've fallen.

Five

Storm

As I track Siren's movements, I realize she's stumbling. It's more than the storm and her busted face. I can't read her expressions with her hood pulled over her head. If she trips, I refuse to catch her. I've been trying to keep my hands off her as much as possible. Mostly because I don't know what I'll do if I touch her. I'm not in control of my emotions right now.

This entire night has thrown me off. Between Ghost keeping shit from me and Siren bursting back into our lives, I'm off-kilter. My head pounds with the effort to organize my thoughts. I'll have to talk to Ghost more when I get home. I haven't wanted to push him about the Disciples with him being hurt. Hopefully, I won't have to worry about Siren after tonight. It'll take a lot off my plate, and I'll be able to focus on what matters.

"Don't think you can sneak back in," I yell over the screaming of the wind. I need to get home soon or I'll get stuck in a downpour.

"Don't worry, I won't."

I barely catch her words as they're ripped away from her. I'd set one of the prospects on her tail if I trusted them enough. Ghost and I promised we wouldn't kill her, but we never thought she'd come back. I'm not about to explain the whole situation to someone else. As soon as the words *betrayal* and *Disciples* came out of my mouth, they'd shoot her. Or maybe torture her. Ghost could stop them, but I'm not entirely sure they'll listen to me. I haven't thrown my weight around as VP enough to know whether or not they'd follow those particular orders.

Most of them have lost someone to the Disciples over the years. Not to mention the businesses burned down or the jobs we've lost to them. Everyone has a reason to hate the Disciples. Our members would love to take a pound of flesh from a former Phantom who betrayed us.

"Where are you going to go?" I snarl as we weave between closed businesses. At least it blocks some of the wind.

She spins around and I almost run into her. "Why the fuck do you care as long as I'm not here?"

I don't care. I really don't fucking care. She means less to me than anyone else. I'd do more for a stranger than I'd do for her. I can't force the words out, though. She's clearly hurt and doesn't have anywhere else to go. If she's anywhere close to who she used to be, she wouldn't have chosen to go back to her dad's house. She raises an eyebrow when I don't say anything.

"Just walk." I curl my hand into a fist when she doesn't listen. "Where's your bike?"

It was one of the few things we let her take when we threw her out. I told Ghost not to advocate for her to have it. Technically, her bike belonged to the Phantoms. With her father's previous standing in the club, they allowed it. If she sold it, it'd be a slap in the face to everything Ghost did for her despite her betrayal. He gave her more concessions than she deserved.

"None of your business," she snaps. The streetlight highlights a flash of pain in her eyes before she turns and starts walking again.

"You crash it? That why you're walking around looking like death?"

"Would you shut the fuck up?"

We walk five more steps before I fall into step next to her.

"You'd think Prophet would give you another bike as a reward for all your hard work."

"Ooh, you think so? Maybe I'll ask him the next time I see him." The sarcasm is a bit much.

I don't know why Ghost thought she'd tell us anything. She played us so thoroughly when we were younger. I used to make excuses for her. I tried to find any way I could around what she did to us. There must have been something, even if it was a sign she didn't truly love us.

I grab her arm despite my better judgment and haul her into a secluded alley. "Why the hell are you wearing leggings and flip-flops? It's practically winter and you're running around like you have a death wish. And where the hell is your bike? And why'd you come here?"

Her jaw twitches as she grinds her teeth. "I'm no longer—"

"Don't give me any of that bullshit about it not being my business. You're in our territory, you answer to us."

"Well, if you'd let me go"—she rips her arm away once more —"I wouldn't *be* in *your* territory anymore. Besides, *your* president was the one who summoned me here. Why the hell don't you go ask him instead of harassing me?"

I'm not about to admit to her I haven't really talked to Ghost. And it's all her fault. We were perfectly fucking fine until she showed up. Sure, he got blown up a little. But we were dealing with it. Just like we always do. We've dealt with every problem life has thrown at us together. When Siren left, we raged together. When our respective parents died, we rejoiced together. When Ghost threw his bid in to be president and fought to the death, we succeeded together. In the span of just a few hours, I feel like I'm losing him. Maybe I have been for a long time and was merely too blind to notice.

I step back, struggling to keep my emotions from my face. Whatever Siren does is none of my concern. She's not the reason shit is falling apart. She's merely the catalyst—highlighting all the cracks in our relationship. I need her out of our lives so I can fix what's broken. Siren will only complicate things.

"Ghost isn't going to have answers when it comes to you. The only reason he has any interest in you is because of your connection to the Disciples," I sneer.

She throws up her hands and cries, "I don't have a fucking connection to them, you asshat. I'm wearing flip-flops because I lost my damn shoes in the last fucking town I was in. I don't have my bike because it got blown up. Any other fucking questions or are you finished prying into my goddamn life?"

My heart clenches, but I can't allow her to suck me back in. At one point, I would have cared. I can't afford to now. She'll use everything I give her against me, even my pity. She shoves past me and stomps toward the mouth of the alley, jostling me out of my stupor. I follow her reluctantly. Regardless of the push and pull of my emotions, I still have to make sure she leaves.

My phone buzzes and I pull it from my pocket. The wind has died down, though that doesn't mean much around here. The moon could reappear and ten minutes later a rainstorm could sweep through. Ghost's text sits on the screen, demanding to know where I am. I didn't think he'd wake up and notice I was gone.

When I glance up, Siren is gone. Panic spears me, then fizzles out. Or rather, I douse it with my anger. The only reason I'm worried is because she might have slipped deeper into Phantom territory. If I keep telling myself I hate her, maybe that small part of my brain that still cares about her will finally let go. Maybe my body will stop reacting to her being near.

"Siren," I bellow as I take off down the alley. When I reach the street, I whip my head back and forth, searching for her.

"Would you stop yelling? For fuck's sake." Her voice floats through the dark from the left.

I hurry toward her, then skid to a stop. She's standing on the corner, arms crossed and foot tapping away. At first glance, she seems pissed, confident, and two seconds away from biting my head off. The longer we stare at each other, the more I realize she's barely hanging on. Her chin trembles and I swear she's paler than she was just a minute before. She rolls her eyes and spins around. She's not quite quick enough to hide the wince.

I follow her in silence, watching her gait as her flip-flops snap in time with her steps. Except she's shuffling and listing to the left. She keeps ducking her head, though there's no wind to brace herself against anymore. When she stumbles, I instinctively reach for her. I tug her toward me and her body molds to mine. Her back presses into my chest, her ass grinding into me. I swear my cock thinks it's my birthday, standing at attention and waiting for his present. Fucking traitor.

"I'm fine," she snaps, shuddering in my arms.

"Yeah, fucking right." I need to let go. Having her this close fucks with my mind, yet my fingers dig into her hip and my arm tightens around her stomach.

"Let me go." She drops her chin to her chest but doesn't attempt to pull away. I don't think she's able to stand on her own.

I could just drop her—let her flounder on her own. Taking her back home and figuring out what's wrong with her would be the humane thing to do. Ghost doesn't want her hanging around and she's made it this far by herself. I'm sure she'll be perfectly fine. If she's not, then she can do something about it herself.

It takes me another ten seconds to make up my mind, and I drop my hold on her. She crumples to the ground with a yelp. It takes her longer than I thought it would to get back to her feet and my resolve wavers. She doesn't deserve my sympathy. She doesn't *want* my sympathy. Nothing would bring her more joy than to throw it back in my face.

"Get the fuck away from me, Storm," she snarls as she stomps away. "Fuck. I knew this was a mistake. I knew I should have just left well enough alone."

She's close enough to the border that I let her go. Her voice fades away as she slips into the shadows. I should call someone to trail her and find where she lands. Even if it's just for tonight.

She'll probably take off tomorrow morning. She'll be gone from our lives once more. Unless Ghost tries to reel her back in with some other ridiculous excuse.

I pivot and make my way back home. Hopefully Ghost fell back asleep and I can slip into bed without him noticing. After everything tonight, I doubt I'll sleep much. I'm too wound up to go home, but I don't have it in me to do anything else. And I don't want to leave Ghost alone any longer. I'm probably babying him. At least, he's been saying I am. I can't help it. He'll run himself into the ground if I'm not there to pull him back.

When I step into the house, I close my eyes and breathe in the familiar scents of home. It's hard to describe what it smells like, but it's comforting. Everywhere else, I have to be on high alert. A lead ball of anxiety sits in my stomach, waiting for the other shoe to drop. There's always someone lurking in the shadows, hoping for our downfall.

I step into the living room and the light clicks on. I jump, my hand fumbling for my gun. Ghost glares at me from the couch. My mouth waters as my gaze travels from his mussed-up hair, down to his bare chest, and on to his boxer briefs. My weapon slips from my fingers, and I snatch at it once more before setting it on the coffee table.

"Settle the fuck down, Storm. Where the hell were you?"

I deflate, all the energy coursing through me fizzling out. "Can we not tonight? Why aren't you sleeping?"

Ghost leans forward and props his elbows on his knees. "Maybe because not even ten minutes after she left, so did you. Maybe because she was the last hope I had at getting info on the Disciples. Maybe because my back fucking itches like a thousand fucking fire ants have taken up residence under my skin. So answer the damn question, Storm."

"I went to make sure she wasn't hanging around. I can't handle her being here."

"I needed answers," he growls.

"At what cost?" I bellow, throwing up my hands.

I drop next to him and stab my fingers into my hair. I grip the strands, tugging as hard as I can to center myself. This is why I never wanted to see her again. She has the unique ability of stirring up feelings and emotions I wish would die. Every once in a while, she'd crop up in my memories, forcing me to relive the loss and betrayal all over again. For a long time after she left, something would remind me of her, and Ghost's gaze would meet my own. We rarely commented, but we both knew. She was such a large part of our lives that she left a hole in her wake. I've been trying to fill it ever since.

"We can't keep doing this, Storm," he finally says. "There's shit we need to talk about and plan for. And I don't have it in me to fight over Siren."

He sits back and his hand lands on my thigh. My muscles relax and my cock strains against my jeans. The nervous energy I'd buried under my exhaustion resurfaces, and a shiver of anticipation rolls through me. I grit my teeth and fight against my desire. I'm not ready to forget all the shit he kept from me. Except I need the release as much as he does.

Between Siren showing up again and Ghost being hurt, I'm losing all sense of control. I feel like I've been running on high alert with no break. It's going to be a long night if all it takes is Ghost's touch to make me come. A long fucking night.

Six

Ghost

Storm practically vibrates the more I dig my fingers into his thigh. Usually, the move helps calm him down. Now, it's as if my touch has only served to overload his senses. His heavy breath fills the room, his chest rising and falling rapidly. He runs his trembling fingers through his hair, mussing it up even more.

I want to ask if he found Siren. Where was she hiding? Did she leave? Is she hurt? I shake my head and force the questions from my mind. It's not important right now. Opening that can of worms will only end in another fight. We'll have to talk, and I'll let him bitch me out. Just not right now. I don't have it in me to talk about Siren or the Disciples or the future of the Phantoms.

"I should have talked to you," I murmur. It's the closest we get to apologizing. The last time either of us said we're sorry was when Siren betrayed us.

"You going to tell me the real reason why you didn't?"

I sigh, running my nails up and down his leg. "I thought you'd talk me out of it."

"I would have." His nostrils flare and his jaw twitches.

If I don't distract him, he'll end up freaking out more. I wouldn't put it past him to sneak off into the night again just to make sure Siren isn't hanging around. I don't care whether or not she is. It's not like she can do much damage if she's here. In fact, I'd almost prefer her in Phantom territory. Storm probably shoved her straight back into Prophet's arms. As the leader of the Disciples, Prophet will probably try to use her against us. I opened the door by contacting her. Which is another thing Storm and I will have to talk about. But not right now. I need him calm and levelheaded.

I push to my feet and step in front of him. "Except you forgot."

He tips his head back and meets my gaze. "Forgot what?"

A smirk pulls at my lips as I cross my arms. "I outrank you."

His fingers dig into his thighs and I step back, then look pointedly to the ground. His throat bobs and he shakes his head.

"You're still—"

"Don't use my injuries as an excuse. You've been doing that the last week. On your knees, Storm."

He slides from the couch and sinks onto his knees. "You're not—"

"Take out my cock."

A shudder rolls through him and his pupils dilate. When his thumbs hook in the waistband of my boxers, my cock hardens, and I bite back a moan. Being confined to a bed and not being able to fuck has been a special kind of torture. My length springs free as he pushes the fabric down and grips my thighs. His tongue darts out to run along his bottom lip. He glances up at me, a promise and a plea resting in their dark depths.

My hand slides to his cheek, then into his hair. I grip the strands and force his face closer. Without a word, he opens his mouth, and I slip my tip in. My groan ripples through the air as heat flashes over my body before settling between my legs. He pulls back and laps at the precum leaking from me.

My eyes flutter closed, and my head drops back when his hand grips the base of my cock. Then his mouth is on me again, teeth scraping against the sensitive skin with each pass. I can't bring myself to watch or I'll end up coming too quickly. Storm needs this almost more than I do. Not only to remember who he belongs to, but to relieve the tension riding him. My knees grow weak when he takes me deep and sucks hard.

A growl leaves me, and I tug at his hair. "This what you needed? What you craved?"

I punch my hips forward and he chokes, then swallows. It's more than I can handle. Going slow, making him work for it, isn't an option anymore. To his credit, he takes me with ease. Each thrust is harder, faster than the last. He hums and I focus on my cock disappearing into his mouth. It's always mesmerizing to watch his pleasure dance across his face. When he glances up at me through his lashes, my release spills from me, and I groan as he swallows every drop.

I cup his jaw and brush my thumb over his cheek. "Such a good boy. Do you feel better?"

His tongue swirls around the tip before he pulls back. My hand drops to my side as he swipes at the corner of his mouth. His chin drops to his chest, and my stomach flips. I didn't actually think this would make up for not talking to him. I blindsided him and it wasn't fair. One blowjob isn't going to magically fix anything. I tug my underwear up, my cock still hanging out, and drop in front of him, our knees pressed together.

Sliding my hand to his neck, I rest my forehead against his. We stay like that for several minutes as he works through whether or not to still be pissed at me.

"I need…" he breathes.

"I know," I murmur.

His fingers fumble with his zipper, and I slip my hand under his waistband to grip his cock. He sucks in a sharp gasp, which quickly turns to a moan. I stroke him once, then freeze.

He grits his teeth and glares at me. "Don't you dare fucking stop."

"Pants, Storm."

He shoves his jeans and boxer briefs down to his hips, then slides his hand around my neck. Our mouths fuse together as I brush my thumb over the tip of his cock. He tilts his head and deepens the kiss. We rarely show any affection outside of these private moments. Everyone knows we live together, but we keep things professional when we're around the men. Being tender isn't a choice we can make in our lives. Except for here.

I fall into him, giving myself over to the desire he stirs in me. I stroke him faster, the need to give him the relief he so desperately craves riding me hard. In a way, it's a plea—for forgiveness, for understanding, for faith. I need him to understand why I did the things I did. Because I don't have words right now. I can't explain the why behind my decisions. This is the best I can do for now.

I rip my mouth away from his and bury my face into his neck. The scuff along his jaw scrapes across my cheek. When I sink my teeth into his soft flesh, he lets out a moan. I drink in the sound, letting it feed my soul.

"O-ohh," he groans, and a smirk spreads across my face.

I push him back and lean down, taking him into my mouth. As soon as my lips wrap around the tip, his fingers spear into my hair and grip the strands tightly. It burns in the best way possible. This isn't the best angle, but he's close. Especially when I suck hard, hollowing out my cheeks. He grunts and his hips kick up, forcing his cock deeper. Seconds pass and his warm cum trickles down my throat. I stroke him gently as I ease back and take him in.

With him on his knees, head tipped back against the couch, and his eyes closed, he could be sleeping. Except for the satisfaction stamped across his face. I release him and brush away the dark hair that's fallen across his forehead. He blinks at me, pain still sitting in the dark depths. I knew it wouldn't fix everything, but I thought it would help a little.

"I want her gone," he whispers.

I nod, though I can't agree. I can't reassure him or hand out promises I'm not willing to keep. With anyone else, I could lie through my fucking teeth. Never with him. Not only would he see right through me, but it wouldn't be fair to him. He's stood by me all these years. He deserves more than a fucking blow job for this.

"I can't promise you she'll never come back."

He shoves my hand away and struggles to his feet. If he goes out again, it might break me. I'll know he's searching for her, putting himself at risk just to drive her away again. He's still too wired to cope with Siren's antics—her wrath. Clearly, she's been harboring resentment for us for a long time. Probably going back years into our childhood. I've often wondered how the Disciples got their claws into her. Was there something we did to push her further into their grasp?

"I'm not asking for promises, Ghost. But if you keep shutting me out..." He shakes his head, zipping up his pants.

"I can't promise that either. If I have any choice in the matter, I won't, but you know I can't make promises like that, Storm." There's no heat behind my words, but he explodes like I've mortally wounded him. "Go ahead and blame me for this shit, but I needed to know if she was behind the attack. And I couldn't have you—"

"Fucking it up?" he spits out.

I climb to my feet slowly, the half-healed wounds on my back stinging. I tuck my cock away, not willing to have this conversation while it's hanging out. It's going to be hard enough to get him to understand this isn't personal. I didn't do this to hurt him. It may not erase the pain he's feeling, but the least I can do is to be presentable for this.

"You know as well as I do I can't share everything with you, Storm. This isn't about *you* or your position in my life."

His mouth drops open, then he snaps his jaw shut. "*Position?*"

"As VP for the Phantoms, asshole. In some situations, I can't tell you shit." We've talked about this a hundred times before. He's never reacted like this. "Are you this pissed because it's Siren? Or is there other shit going on?"

He glares at me, and a flush splashes across his cheeks. "I've been running on fucking fumes. You were fucking unconscious, and I didn't know if you were going to live. And no one knew what the hell happened. Helms called and bitched me out while a goddamn newborn screamed in the background. Add in trying to hold back the members who are out for blood and yeah. I'd say there's other shit going on."

"This is what you signed up for," I say in a low tone.

I don't want to have to remind him of his duty to the Phantoms. He's not fucking hurt about dealing with the MC. This is about Siren more than anything—more than my keeping shit from him. This all goes back to Siren and the hurt he still harbors for her.

"I didn't sign up for that," he explodes, throwing out his hand to gesture at the front door. "I didn't sign up to have her flit back into our lives like nothing's changed. I didn't sign up for her to force me out of the house when you're hurt. And I sure as hell didn't sign up to save her from herself."

As his panting fills the room, my chest seizes. "What do you mean, *save her from herself*? What the fuck did you do?"

His chin trembles and he glances away. Little bitch isn't going to tell me anything. I assumed he just searched the area and didn't find her hanging around. No one she once knew here would take her in. None of the members still in Harris would shelter her. Even Lexi would turn her away. At least I think she would.

"Was she at Lexi's?" I spit out, crossing my arms.

He shakes his head, his gaze fixed on the front window. Not that he can see through the curtains. "She was at her house. Her old house. I made sure she left Phantom territory. Left her at the border."

"How in the hell would that be saving her from herself?"

"She didn't look good."

Mentally, I study the picture implanted in my mind from mere hours ago. I've been studiously ignoring every emotion seeing her again evoked. If I pretend like I don't care, then eventually I truly won't. Some may think six years was enough of a punishment for her betrayal. It doesn't work like that in clubs like ours. She's lucky she's not six feet under. It was the only mercy she was afforded. My loyalty lies with the MC and Storm, not with a woman who's part of my past. Still, it's hard to ignore the feelings still swirling around. Siren was a huge part of both our lives. Neither of us saw her betrayal coming.

"What do you mean not good?"

"Looked like she was hurt." He scoffs, squeezing his eyes shut, his profile outlined perfectly in the lamplight. "Good."

"Hurt? Like, injured?"

He shrugs. "Fuck if I know. And I wasn't about to ask her. She's dead to us already. Make it easier if she was dead for real, too."

"You fucking prat."

His head whips around and he glares at me. "First of all, who the hell says prat? And second of all, I'm just saying what both of us are thinking. It's not my fault I'm the only one who can admit it."

"You're a goddamn fool, Storm. If she has information, she sure as shit isn't going to give anything up if she's *dead*." I prowl to the chair and grab my shirt before shoving it over my head. My leathers are next, emblazoned with the Phantoms sigil and my name and title stitched on the front. It's not great if I'm going incognito, but it's an armor I'm afraid I'll need tonight.

"Where the fuck are you going?" Storm yells as I stomp toward the front door.

I slip my boots on and lace them up, ignoring his glare. When I'm finished, I stand and face him. "I may have fucked up by not telling you I texted her, but you fucking left her to die. I'm just as pissed as you are at her. I'm just smart enough not to let my pain and rage blind me to everything else. Get your shit together."

"Or what?" he jeers, though there's a layer of hurt beneath the anger.

"I don't know."

"You're not going to find her," he bellows as I step into the night.

Thunder rolls overhead and I brace myself for a very wet and extremely cold ride. I'm not about to run all over Harris searching for her.

"Seriously, Ghost, come back. She's not fucking worth it."

I spin on the front porch. "She's worth the information in her head. Nothing more, nothing less. And if you fucked this up because you're too fucking butthurt over shit that happened six years ago, then step the fuck back and let me handle her."

Fear flashes in his eyes, but I'm too fucking pissed to decipher it. I'll deal with it later, along with everything else. Right now, I have to make sure she hasn't fallen back in with the Disciples. She doesn't have anything to give them about the Phantoms, thank fuck. I ignore the voice inside telling me it's more than the information she harbors. I thought I'd smothered any desire, any love I had for her long ago. Now, I'm not so sure.

Seven

Siren

I had half a mind to sneak back into Phantom territory. I kept walking, though, not willing to deal with Storm for a third time tonight. It's questionable whether I'd make it all the way back to my old house. If Lexi knew I was injured and likely sick, she'd probably let me stay. I wouldn't put her in that position, though..

Which is why I'm huddled on a bench outside the train station. All I can do is beseech whatever god is controlling the weather to hold off on the rain. I thought the tides had turned for me and maybe my life wouldn't be a complete shitshow. Alas, it was not meant to be since the skies opened up and are currently pelting me with raindrops. Each one pierces my bare skin with pinpoint accuracy. I probably should have kept the sweatshirt on, but I didn't want it to get ruined. It's my only one, and I'd rather freeze for a little while rather than have it rip beyond repair. Besides, being numb helps me forget all the aches and pains currently assaulting my body.

Thunder rolls overhead and I whimper, covering my head with my backpack as best I can. There's a small awning over me. It's provided a little relief when the wind changes. I've just about made up my mind to crawl into an abandoned building when another rumble echoes through the air. It's different than the rest. I'd know it in my sleep.

To be fair, it's common to hear motorcycles in Harris. I shouldn't be surprised or worried. Except a biker out in this storm doesn't make sense. I doubt anyone would come looking for me. The only people who know I'm here are Storm, Ghost, and Lexi. None of them would care enough to be out in this. Except Storm. His ridiculous ass would definitely be on his bike, making sure I wasn't hanging around.

The only other bikers that would come find me are the Disciples. I wish I could figure out why they're so obsessed with me. It's not like I have any ties to the Phantoms anymore. And there's no reason to believe Prophet thinks I can find my way back into the fold. It wasn't highly publicized *why* I was gone, but once someone leaves, they're not allowed back. I'm lucky I made it out alive.

The sound grows louder, and I groan as I sit up. There aren't many places to hide out here. They built the train station on the edge of town refusing to let any other businesses near it. I think they were afraid someone would try to blow the place up and didn't want anyone else caught in the crossfire.

Still, I search for somewhere to hide. As soon as I push to my feet, my knees give out and I crumple to the ground. I gasp as the rain pounds into me, and I get a face full of water. I sputter and cough as I attempt to stand.

I end up crawling around the building where there's a little reprieve from the wind and rain. I slide the straps on my shoulders and my backpack settles into place. Since I won't be able to run, I slide my dagger from the side pocket. There's a gun resting among my few items, but I only have a couple bullets. I'd rather use them when I come face to face with Prophet. I doubt he'd be out searching for me right now. He prefers to send others to fetch me. Bitterness washes over me, and I shove it aside to deal with the current problem.

I've been so fucking lucky these last five years. The first year away from Harris, they let me be, though I never learned why. Unless they couldn't find me then. Even when they eventually caught me, I was always able to slip free.

It took me much longer than it should've, but I finally came to the conclusion they were doing it on purpose. Most of the men sent after me were practically prospects. Half of them didn't even realize their safeties were on when they were waving their guns in my face. Which is probably why I fucked up. I got too complacent and now I'm living with the consequences. If the biker really is a Disciple, I won't be able to fight them off.

"Siren," Ghost yells over the whistling wind, and I groan, knocking my head back into the concrete barrier.

My brain fractures, sending shockwaves of pain through my head. Each shattered piece slips through my fingers. I slam my eyes shut, hoping for a bit of relief. All I find is blood—crimson red and filling my vision. A memory flits through my mind, and I strain to catch it. It slips away into the shadows, another relic of a life forgotten. Each remaining fragment slices at my consciousness and drops, only to drown in the nothingness of regret.

"Shit." Ghost's voice spears through the darkness and a fragmented cry rings through the air.

Warmth envelops me and I shy away. His mumbled words wash away with each beat of my heart. He could be damning me or comforting me. Either way, I can't be near him. I can't allow myself to sink into him—rely on him. He didn't listen. He didn't care. All the years we had together—everything between us—none of it mattered. If I put even a little bit of trust in him again, I'll break completely. The only way I've survived this long is by staying as far away from them as possible.

I never should have come back. My downfall was that sliver of hope. That small voice whispering *it's time.* Yet nothing has changed. They're still the spiteful assholes they were when I left. Actually, they're worse now. Ghost could barely look at me and Storm...Storm left me out here in the cold. He *knew* I was hurt and he didn't give a shit. He'd rather wash his hands of me, content not to be at fault because he did nothing.

Ghost shakes my body and my head flops around. I can't hold it up anymore. The world spins as I open my eyes, a fuzzy grey reducing my view to pinpoints of muted light. I realize he's not shaking me, but we are moving. He won't be able to transport me anywhere on his bike. Which means he's only moving me away from the cameras surrounding the train station. I doubt he'll take me to Phantom territory.

"Stop screaming," he growls.

He wraps me in his leathers and a choked sob leaves me. My life and all that could have been rushes past me, and here he is, surrounding me with his scent without a care in the world. This isn't what it would have been like, though. I would've never been out here by myself. I'd never have left. I'd never have been in danger. At least not how we see things. Being in an MC like the Phantoms, there's always the threat, but there's also a sense of safety.

When they threw me out, I didn't know how to cope in the real world. It didn't matter anyway, since I've been running from the Disciples. I never experienced what other people would consider normal.

When the deafening drum of the rain subsides and I'm no longer being waterboarded, I peek through my lashes. My head still lolls from side to side, but at least my vision has cleared. A lone lightbulb clicks on overhead, and I shy away from the brightness. Ghost drops me onto a hard mattress on the floor. My muscles scream in protest, and I press my lips together. I doubt he'll kill me. He can't pull non-existent secrets from a dead woman.

"What do you want?" I wheeze, unable to keep my pain quiet.

"Right now, I want you to shut the fuck up." His gaze is fixed on his phone, fingers flying across the screen.

I push myself upright, pain lancing through my body, and I bite my tongue. Copper fills my mouth, and I grimace. We're in a one-room shack, probably a safe house. They're scattered throughout the city and used for all sorts of things. Sometimes, it's merely a safe haven for members. Other times it's for forcing truths from enemies. Two chairs sit across from my spot and chains are sunk into the concrete next to one. There are handcuffs attached to the wall next to my head, and I suppress a shiver.

"Why don't we get this over with."

His head snaps up at my tone. It wasn't a request, more of a statement given out of resignation. I don't have it in me to give sarcastic quips like I did earlier. Now, I just want to be left alone to die in peace. I've finally resigned myself to my fate. I fought long and hard, and I just don't give a shit anymore. Seeing them again just solidifies the thoughts and plans that've been swirling in my head for the past few months.

"Get *what* over with, exactly?"

I roll my eyes, then glance away as one starts twitching. "You won't believe me regardless of what I say, so why do all this?"

"I'm only here to make sure you don't die," he snarls.

"Too late," I mutter. He steps into my space and towers over me. When I jolt back, I hit my head on the wall and my vision swims. His gaze travels down my body, and I clench my hands into fists.

His focus settles on my face once more, and I hope I've schooled my expression into one of indifference. I don't have anything to tell him. The most I can offer is to let the Disciples take me and I'd gather all the intel I could. The chance of me getting back to tell him anything is slim. The chance he'll trust what I divulge is even slimmer. There's literally no way for me to win.

"You're not fucking dying. At least not on my watch and not in my city. Now, what the fuck is wrong with you?" He crosses his arms and glares at me.

"I have a cold." I refuse to mention the bruises and scrapes canvasing my body. Or my obviously broken ribs. Or my sprained ankle. And certainly not the stab wound in my side. I'm surprised neither of them noticed the faint marks circling my neck.

"Pneumonia, maybe, but this is more. Do you need a doctor?"

I swallow hard and shake my head. It does nothing to help my migraine. I close my eyes, and the potential scene plays out behind my lids. The Phantoms' doc, Bones, shows up, takes one look at me, and refuses to do a damn thing. The Hippocratic oath doesn't mean a fucking thing to her. She barely stitched me up the last time.

He opens his mouth as if he'll argue when the metal door flings open, revealing Storm. Because of course he's here. I should have expected it, but for some reason I thought he'd stay away. They probably split up to find me and now they're here to take me to task or some shit. Except Ghost is glaring at Storm again. Their dynamic is off. At least, from what I'm used to. I assume they're still together. Especially with Storm's painting hanging in Ghost's house.

"What?" Storm snaps as Ghost gestures to me.

"Are you fucking serious right now? For fuck's sake. She's pale as shit—"

"Hey," I cry out in a reedy voice.

"She's clearly had the shit beat out of her." Storm glances at me finally, and I turn my face away. "Ribs are sure as shit broken. Oh, and I'm pretty sure she's bleeding internally."

"Clearly not." I swing my head around and find them both glaring at me. "I was fine until *he* showed up."

"Fine?" Ghost explodes, throwing up his hands. "You're not fucking fine. And you—"

He rounds on Storm, who merely stares at him with a blank expression. "We're not doing this in front of her, Ghost. Either you want to use her for information, or you don't. Pick one and let's be done with this."

The indecision on Ghost's face pulls at my heart, and a new ache settles within. I assumed whatever feelings they had for me before were dead and buried. From the guilt sitting in his eyes, maybe it's just buried. I beat back the ember of hope that flickers to life. Guilt doesn't mean much. Especially when applied to our relationship. He probably feels guilty for not talking to Storm about texting me.

"He's not going to listen to anything I have to say. Or the fact I don't *have* anything to say. Because I don't know a damn thing about the Disciples. I've been gone for six fucking years. It's not like we were pen pals or something." I roll my eyes, though it still hurts to do so. It feels like the only way to convey my emotions without hurting myself further. At least with Storm showing up, I've got a shot of adrenaline to keep me going.

"I still have questions," Ghost growls.

Storm grabs Ghost's arm when he tries to advance on me. I don't react. There's no reason. Eventually they'll walk out of here, and I'll either get better or I won't. I swallow hard at the thought. I suppose I didn't have anything going in my life. I've just been running. And I'm sick of it. I'm sick of feeling like nothing matters—like *I* don't matter. There was a time I wanted to make my mark on the world. That dream died the day I left the Phantoms. Or rather, the day I was banished.

"Fine," Storm shouts over the thunder cracking across the sky outside. "Ask your fucking questions and then let's go."

Ghost rounds on me, a scowl on his face. I never was afraid of him. Either of them, really. No matter what's happened between us, there was a certainty they wouldn't physically hurt me. Earlier, I might have wondered if that still held true. I just don't seem to care anymore, which scares me more than the injuries spread across my body. If I don't find that stubborn resistance I've been carrying my whole life, I'll end up a shell of who I could have been. And that's no way to live.

Eight

Storm

The last twenty-four hours have been a complete shitshow. Usually, I can handle it just fine. Ghost might be the calm one out of the two of us, but I keep my deranged side under tight control. Ghost doesn't seem to mind wielding me within my position as he sees fit. We rarely disagree on how shit needs to be run anyway, and we both know our roles. We work together—a seamless team.

Until Siren showed up. Now, I'm stuck schlepping her broken-ass body back into Phantom territory after I worked so hard to get her out. I wasn't about to let Ghost carry her. He's pushed himself too hard today, both emotionally and physically. Once he gets his answers from Siren, she can fuck right off to wherever the hell she came from, and our lives will go back to normal.

Unless we're on the brink of war with the Disciples, then nothing will be normal for quite some time.

We've had enemies before. We've taken them all down and even helped others with a few. It's the way our world works. At least it gives us something to do other than running illegal shit from city to city. It took longer than expected to find some semblance of stability in Harris. Growing pains plagued us when we expanded the Phantoms to nearby cities. They mostly run under their own command now, ready to come when we call, but we don't have to do much for them to remember who calls the shots.

"Stop jostling her," Ghost growls, and I stop suddenly, the urge to drop her riding me hard. "Don't even fucking think about it."

"Where the hell are we taking her?" I ask instead of blasting him. He's acting like a protective prick and I'm fucking over it.

Ghost runs his fingers through his wet hair. Thankfully, the rain stopped before we left the safe house. We've been waiting on the corner for at least five minutes for the car to come since both of us brought our bikes. I wasn't going to follow him out here. If he wanted to run off and be a goddamn hero, it didn't matter to me. Except I couldn't. I'm desperately trying to hold on to my anger—at him, at Siren, at the situation. All I feel is emptiness and the sense that everything I know is slowly slipping away.

I hurry after Ghost as he calls over his shoulder. "The house. We can't trust anyone else. And who would take her in, anyway? No one."

Precisely. Stands to reason why we shouldn't be housing her either.

I doubt he'd see the irony of the situation he's put us in. I steal a glance at Siren, wondering why she hasn't bitched us out yet. I'm met with her sleeping face. Or she's passed out. Either way, it keeps her quiet. She wasn't happy when I was forced to carry her, yet didn't have the strength to protest much. I don't understand how she deteriorated so quickly. She might not have been healthy, but she was able to walk away from me.

"How'd you get her out of her house?" Ghost asks, pulling my thoughts away from the woman in my arms.

"What do you mean?"

He turns to me, something heavy resting in his eyes. "Did you hurt her? When you were getting her out of her house?"

I brace myself for his rage, then open my mouth, but nothing comes out. A car pulls up to the curb and he shakes his head.

He'll ask me again. He's just tallying up all the questions he has. As soon as he's ready, he'll blast me with them. We were fine before she showed up—before the failed run. I'm not entirely convinced she didn't have anything to do with it.

"Put her in the back seat, Storm," Bones says, an edge to her voice. I'm not surprised.

Bones grew up with us, always following us around. Siren and Bones got into it more than once when we were teenagers. Neither of them would tell us why, and it didn't matter anyway. When everything with Siren went down, Bones disappeared. For a while we thought she was in on the scheme Siren concocted, but she showed up a week later looking like shit. She never did tell us where she went. We just know she wasn't with the Disciples or Siren.

Ghost slides into the driver's seat as I shove her into the back. He glares at me in the rearview mirror, and I roll my eyes. If he wanted me to be gentle, he should have carried her himself. It's not like it's easy to put a body in the back seat of a car. I slam the back door and lean on the driver's window.

"How are we getting your bike home?" If I have to call someone, I'll need an alibi as to why we were out here.

"Bones is riding," he mutters, his eyes fixed forward.

I straighten and he rolls up the window, effectively cutting off our conversation. Not that it was one to begin with. With every decision, every thought, he's pulling away from me. I glare at the woman passed out behind him. Everything stems from her, and I have the irrational urge to rip her from the car. I'd put her on the first train in the morning and forget she existed. It didn't work last time, but I sure as hell would make sure it did this time.

"Don't read into it too much, Storm," Bones murmurs as Ghost drives away. "He just needs to get his bike home."

"Don't talk about shit you don't know, Bones."

I turn and stalk toward where I stashed my bike. In the fifteen years Ghost's had that bike, he's only let two other people ride it. Bones is not one of them. It's too personal among us. Most of our guys never even consider choosing a partner to ride with them, much less let them use their bike. It's broken up more than a couple relationships. The fact Ghost doesn't seem to have any problem with Bones taking his ride doesn't make sense. I doubt he'll reveal why later. The dissonance between us is throwing me off. There's an ever-widening gap growing and I don't know how to stop it.

"So, I'll follow you then?" Bones yells after me, and I flip her off over my shoulder.

It takes both too long and not long enough to get home. The car is already parked outside the house, the back door hanging open. I kick it shut as I pass and pound up the stairs. Regardless of whether or not I want Siren here, she's here. And she's not going anywhere until she's able to walk out on her own two feet. Which means I have to take over her care so Ghost can sleep. He's pushed himself too hard.

"Storm?" he calls from upstairs when I shut the door, and I take the stairs two at a time.

I groan as I turn toward my room. It doesn't matter if I rarely use it, preferring to sleep next to Ghost in the primary bedroom. He didn't have to put her in here. I stand in the doorway, watching Ghost fuss over Siren. Her pale skin stands out against the dark sheets. An ache forms in my chest, making my breath as ragged as hers. My nostrils flair when he brushes the hair away from her forehead and reveals a long gash along her hairline.

"She's burning up," he mutters, his brows pulled low when he glances at me.

I take an involuntary step forward. Then another one. "Any other injuries?"

He flips back the covers, and I press my lips together. He's stripped her down to her underwear. She's covered in bruises and cuts. Fingerprints ring her neck, and the imprint of a boot mars her side. I'm impressed she stayed upright as long as she did.

Heat floods my cheeks and I bite my tongue, hoping to get a grip on myself. Guilt and shame twist together and form a ball of lead in my stomach. How many of those bruises did I inflict upon her? How much am I to blame for her downward spiral? Is it because of me she's lying here?

"Storm," Ghost snaps as if this isn't the first time he's called my name. "Where's Bones?"

"I don't know. I didn't wait for her. Has she woken up?"

"Like you care," he snarls, turning to stare at her again.

I shuffle to the chair on the other side of the bed and drop onto it. Exhaustion washes over me, and I lean my elbows on my knees. Deep grooves line Ghost's face.

"Go to bed. I'll wait up for Bones." Nausea bubbles in my gut when he shakes his head. "Why do you care? I get you think she'll magically have all the answers and it's fucking with you whether to trust her or not, but fuck. You're acting like she's still important to us."

He shoves away from the bed and spears his hands through his hair, gripping the strands tightly as he paces. My last statement felt hollow even to me, but I won't take it back. Siren isn't staying. We can't afford to let her back into our lives. The sooner he remembers how she betrayed us, how much she hurt us, the better off we'll be. Bringing her back into the fold will only result in more deceit on her part, and I doubt we'd survive another round. It would break us beyond repair.

He collapses in the other chair and stares at Siren. "I don't know. There's just something in my gut, in the air, whatever, that's telling me she's the key in all of this. There's something we're missing, and it's fucking with my head."

"Are you sure it's not just because you got your ass blown up?"

He chuckles, though I wasn't entirely joking. "Maybe, but I felt it before shit went down."

I've learned over the years not to question his instincts. For some reason, he's more in tune with the universe or some shit. If he says something's off, then it is. The problem is, until shit goes down, he can't tell me anything. Not how bad it'll be or even what the disturbance actually is. It's annoying as shit and he usually keeps the feelings to himself until he's worked something out. Like the night the truck blew up. He got our people out.

"How long?" I finally ask.

"Couple months. Something isn't right. I'm wondering if all the small shit we've been chalking up to just normal issues is actually something bigger."

"And what? Siren's at the center of it?" I scoff, leaning back.

"I don't know. Which is why I need her here. I want to know what she's been doing the last six years. How she survived this long on her own. Why she's on the brink of fucking death. Oh, and who the fuck she's working with. Because there's no way in hell she got by at nineteen without someone helping her." He drops his face in his hands and my body tenses.

"That doesn't explain why you *care*."

His head snaps up, though my words were soft. "I don't fucking know, okay? You can't honestly say you don't feel anything for her. Look at her, for fuck's sake."

I swallow hard, refusing to move. "One of us has to keep a level head, Ghost. We can't all fall down the rabbit hole."

He scowls and Bones clears her throat from the doorway. "Sorry to interrupt...whatever this is, but I need to make sure she's not dead."

Ghost snarls at her, and she holds up her hands in surrender. I push to my feet and move the chair as she edges around the mattress. Bones drops a bag next to her and stares down at Siren.

"Who the hell used her as a punching bag? Where's her bike?" Bones asks, her hands hovering above Siren as if she's afraid to touch the other woman.

"You're asking questions we don't have answers to. Just fix her up enough to tell us something," I mutter. As soon as the words are out, I wince.

Bones glances at me over her shoulder and raises an eyebrow. "Perhaps you'd like to rephrase that?"

"Do your fucking job," I snap back.

Ghost's hand wraps around my forearm, and he yanks me from the room, closing the door behind us. "You want to explain why you're biting her head off? One might think I'm not the only one who cares."

I shake off his grip and glare at the window at the end of the hallway. Rain lashes against the glass and lightning flashes, illuminating the pictures lining the walls. Most of them are of bikes and various MC events. A couple are from our childhood, though there used to be more. Ghost took most of those down five years ago. It took him almost a year to finally erase her from our space. For a long time, I thought he'd thrown them out. Or burned them. I found them stuffed in the attic about a year ago.

My shoulders slump as I face him. "Go to bed, Ghost. I'll stay up. Make sure she doesn't die tonight."

He nods and steps around me, fingers brushing mine as he passes. I wait until his door closes before turning back to my own. It's going to be a long fucking night.

NINE

SIREN

I'm burning.

Flames ignite behind my lids and my whole world explodes. My bones disintegrate, becoming piles of ash within my skin, yet seconds later they fuse once more, only to crumble again. Someone brandishes a hot iron, pressing it to my flesh over and over. The smell infiltrates my nose and chokes off my breath. A scream ricochets in my head as I attempt to pull away, though I don't know how to escape.

"Stop," a familiar voice echoes through my psyche. "You have to stop, sweets."

Nostalgia hits me hard and I gasp. I'm rewarded with smoke and flames racing down my throat. A choked sob leaves me as Storm's familiar scent slips through the sulfur invading my lungs. Only one thought remains as pain continues to lance its way through my body:

He isn't real.

When I wake, the smoke and burning have vanished. The rawness of my throat convinces me whatever I went through was real. It's as if glass shards have taken up residence in my lungs and every breath corrodes away the tissue within. My bones ache and I feel like I've been skinned alive, then stitched back together.

There's a weight on my chest and I strain against it as I attempt to inhale deeply. My eyes fly open and dart around the dark room until my gaze lands on my backpack sitting on the chair next to the bed. My entire world has spilled out, and I assume the contents are scattered across the floor. It'll take me forever to repack everything with the pain still pulsing through my body.

I bite back a groan as I roll my head to the other side. I'm met with Storm's dark hair glittering in the light from the single lamp in the corner behind him. His palm rests on my chest, fingers spread along my side and covering my stomach. I try to lift my hand to dislodge his, but it won't move.

My toes wiggle and my hips twist, but my arm sits like dead weight at my side. Panic seizes me and I wheeze as my shoulders twitch. Tears streak from the corners of my eyes and gather in my hair. When a drop trickles into my ear, I shake my head back and forth. It doesn't help. If anything, it makes the pounding in my temples worse.

"Breathe, Siren. No use freaking out. Ain't going to fix any of your injuries," Storm grumbles as he removes his hand.

I inhale, then cough, and nausea bubbles in my gut. I pray to whatever god will listen to please let me puke on him instead of myself. I'd rather not die asphyxiating on my own vomit. Not only would it be ridiculously embarrassing, but it's definitely not the way I want to go out. And having Storm here to witness it would just be the cherry on top of an already shitty demise. Maybe I can haunt him when I'm dead. The thought eases some of the panic.

"As if you'd get picked to be a fucking ghost," he mutters, and my gaze snaps to him. "Yeah, you said that out loud."

He straightens, then stands, his hands fluttering at his sides. I track his movements as he paces toward the door, then back to me. Pressing my lips together, I brace myself to take whatever the hell he'll throw at me. The sooner he gets it over with, the sooner I can leave. Then again, I can't move quite yet, which I'm dutifully ignoring so I don't freak out.

I tense when he swings around and glares at me. "What the fuck happened to you? Because I sure as shit didn't rough you up like that."

I shake my head and his nostrils flare. I'm not about to list all the bullshit I've been through the last few months. Hell, I wouldn't even reveal the last three days to him.

"If you don't tell me, you're just going to end up telling Ghost. And then he'll tell me, so you're fucked either way."

"Bold—" I only get out that one croaking word before my throat seizes.

He huffs and stomps to the side table. When he holds out a bottle of water, I stare at it longingly. I can imagine the cool liquid soothing the sharp burn. His eyes narrow and I blink away the tears. With a muttered curse, he tosses the water next to me. A protest springs to my lips when his knee hits the mattress. Whether to cuss him out for jostling me or to get him not to touch my battered body, I don't know.

When he leans close, a ringing starts in my ears until his mouth is moving, yet nothing comes out. Or maybe I just can't hear it. His pupils dilate, the black almost taking over completely. My body trembles and I still can't lift my arms.

He'll never believe me. Even if I told him my whole sordid story, he wouldn't believe me. I tried to talk to them when shit went down six years ago and neither of them would listen. They didn't give a shit. Whatever evidence they were given of my betrayal was enough to convince them. I didn't stand a chance. And now I'm right back where I was. He'll demand answers he won't listen to, then throw my ass out again. They'll rip the remainder of my heart from me, and I'll be a shell. I'll die on the streets of Harris, just minutes from my childhood home. Pain stabs at my heart, my gut, my head.

Storm's hand lands on my chest and he presses hard. It's as if he's cut off my senses and all my focus is on his touch. He pushes harder and my body sinks into the mattress. I can't breathe. I can't talk. My eyes plead with him to stop, but his gaze narrows.

"Come on," he says through gritted teeth. Seconds later, my lungs open up and I suck in a deep breath. "Finally."

"Stop," I gasp.

"No. You're having a panic attack. Surprised you didn't notice." He shakes his head, then ducks his chin to his chest.

I don't know why he thinks I'd notice I was having a panic attack. I've never had one before. Ghost used to have anxiety attacks, but I assume those are two different things. He used to fall deeper and deeper into himself until he'd fall off the edge of whatever cliff he was standing on. He'd end up in bed for three days with a migraine, refusing to see anyone except Storm.

And me.

I used to be there, lying with him in the dark. He'd cling to me, and I'd reassure him over and over I wasn't going anywhere. It was terrifying when we were younger, but I got used to it. The older we got, the less he had them. I wonder if they came back after I left. I wonder if only Storm fills the gaps I left behind. Then again, he probably wouldn't be leading the Phantoms if anyone else knew. Being the president of an MC is brutal, and the members wouldn't let Ghost in if they thought he'd disappear when shit got overwhelming. They'd needlessly judge his skills based on false pretenses and stigma.

Storm removes his hand, and my gaze darts to him. "Bones gave me a list of things for you to do. I'm supposed to take you to the hospital if you can't do them."

I blink away the wetness in my eyes, though I don't know when I started crying. "Fine."

He winces at the softness in my voice before his face hardens again. "Wiggle your toes. Pull up your knees. Follow my finger."

He pauses after each directive and waits, then moves on to the next. It's not until he tells me to lift my arms that I hesitate. He raises an eyebrow, and my gaze darts away. I haven't even tried to move my fingers, much less my arms again. I'm scared. A single tear slips down my cheek, and he catches the drop. His head tilts and his dark eyes soften the slightest bit.

"Okay," he whispers. "I'm going to sit you up. Then we'll figure it out."

I shake my head, but he doesn't pay me any mind. Heat seeps into me when he slides his arm under me. A hand slips to my neck and into my hair. For all the pain coursing through my body, I can't stop a grunt from escaping when he tightens his grip. At least I didn't moan from the contact with another human. Because that's all he is—another human. It has nothing to do with our past or how I felt about him. I was too caught off guard when Lexi hugged me earlier. It's been a long time since someone has treated me as gently as Storm is now.

I didn't realize how much I missed having someone take care of me. I've been running on fumes for the last six years, barely surviving from one day to the next. Between learning how to be in a world I never truly understood and isolating myself for my safety, I lost part of myself. Storm taking care of me like he used to fills in the shattered pieces of my heart.

The moment is over too soon, and I remember how precarious my place is here. I fight the urge to vomit on him. He grumbles under his breath, but I'm pretty sure the sentiment is the same. He holds the water to my mouth, and I slowly sip. It's not nearly as refreshing as I expected it to be. When I try to gulp it down, he pulls it away. A cry of protest rings around us, and tears fill my eyes once more. I need to get my shit together or I'll end up bawling in front of him. And while he may be gentle now, he'll use it against me later. I don't know how, but he will.

"You're not puking in my bed," he says gruffly as he sets down the bottle and grips my wrist. "Wiggle your fingers."

I squeeze my eyes shut and focus on my hand. I don't feel

anything, but I didn't really expect shit to magically work. There's no way I can function without the use of my limbs. Not in this world, not without anyone's help. The Disciples will come for me. They'll torture me, then leave me to rot. With no one to mourn me. The tears stream down my face and Storm grunts.

"None of that, sweets. Look." He nods, his gaze focused on my lap.

There's a tingling in my palm, and I let out another choked sob. This one of relief. I still can't lift my arms, but the needling pain in my wrist is a good sign I just have to be patient.

Storm drops my hand like he didn't realize he was holding it. "Bones mentioned you might have a pinched nerve in your back from the broken ribs. Take this."

He holds out a couple pills and the water again, then huffs. It's slightly humiliating since he has to physically put the meds in my mouth and has to wipe the dribble away. Actually, it's really fucking humiliating.

Once I've swallowed, he grabs a pillow from the floor and shoves it behind my back, then eases me down. He grabs another one and shoves it under my legs. I wince as the ache settles in my bones and I struggle to pull in a full breath. If the pain meds don't kick in soon, I'm going to lose it again. He throws a fluffy comforter over me and tucks it under my chin.

"Can you...go?" I understand this is his room and I doubt he'll listen, but I need space. I need to fall apart and then get my shit together. Having a breakdown in front of him would be a step too far.

"Nope." He drops into the chair and spreads his legs wide as he crosses his arms. "If you start choking on your own tongue, I'll have to actually save your ass. Then Ghost will be pissed off and I'll be left to deal with his whiny ass. So, no. I won't be going anywhere."

I shake my head, and another wave of nausea rolls through me. I'm not tired anymore. My mind might be fuzzy, but adrenaline zings through my body. I wish I could sink into the darkness.

Usually, I wake up every hour. Sometimes I have to run in the middle of the night. A good night's sleep hasn't happened in a long time. As shitty as Storm is, I feel safe here. I'd actually be able to fall into the void of nothingness without fear of someone coming for me. Yet my body won't settle.

"How'd you lose your bike?" he asks after a long while. It's a quiet question, no malice or vitriol hidden within his tone.

I swallow hard, then suck in a deep breath. "I was in a town up north. Had a job at a coffeeshop."

He snorts, sliding down in his chair more. "*You* had a job? Making fucking coffee for hippie bitches?"

I shoot him what is hopefully a withering look. "Turns out when you don't have access to MC funds, you need actual money to eat. So, yeah, I was working. And they weren't hippie bitches. Mostly it was businesspeople. Couple parents. You know, regular people living their normal lives. I'm sure that's a wild concept to you, but there are whole swaths of the population who—"

"Okay, fine. I fucking get it. I'm out of touch and don't know you at all. Just fucking tell me about the bike."

I roll my eyes and shuffle onto my side. It feels weird to be cuddled on my side under a blanket while he's just sitting there, but I can't lie on my back anymore. I sift through the memories he's wanting, picking and choosing which ones to share. I can't tell him the whole story. The short answer to his question is the Disciples happened. Everything ties back to them, but if I say that, Storm will jump all over me.

"Anyways, I was at the coffeeshop. I usually walked to work, but that day I rode my bike. When I got off, it was raining. Not ideal, obviously." I squeeze my eyes shut, then open them wide, trying to dispel the weird feeling sitting behind my eyeballs. "I got on anyway, thinking I'd just go slow. Once I got to a corner, though, something went wrong."

He leans forward and rests his elbows on his knees. "What went wrong?"

"Front tire wobbled. Then a car swerved into my lane. Didn't matter I wasn't going that fast. The whole front began to shake and the next thing I know I was waking up on the side of the road. Bike was gone, and I had more broken ribs."

I press my lips together and close my eyes once more. He doesn't say anything for a long while and I'm guessing he won't. He probably thinks I fell asleep. I even out my breathing to complete the ruse. He sighs and there's a rustling as he sits back.

While he's probably silently mocking me for wrecking my bike, I'm reliving the feel of hands grabbing me, a bag scratching my cheeks as it's shoved over my head, and the pain of being beaten when I tried to escape. While Storm is convinced of my ineptness, I'm wondering what I could have done differently to not be a target for men who think they own me.

Ten

Ghost

Storm clomps down the stairs, not even bothering to keep quiet. It's annoying, but I don't blame him. The last time I checked on Siren, Storm was propped up in the chair next to her bed. He didn't want to watch over her in the first place. Didn't want her in our house. I couldn't explain why it was important she stay here. Probably shouldn't have put her in his bed, though.

"She sleeping?" I ask, focusing on my plate of food. It tastes like ash, but I shovel in another mouthful.

"Yeah. I think the pain meds knocked her ass out." He dishes up hashbrowns and sausage links on his plate before collapsing in the chair across from me. He never did like eggs. They're probably cold now, anyway.

"She tell you anything?"

He nods, then tilts his head back and forth. "Lied about how she wrecked her bike a couple months ago. Said she worked in a coffeeshop. Almost had a freak out when she couldn't move her arms."

My head snaps up. "She can't move her arms?"

"Just a pinched nerve or something. Bones said it could happen with the ribs or back or something. I don't know. Bones

73

will come by later to check on her." He sets his fork down and levels me with a stare. "What the fuck are we doing here, Ghost?"

"What do you mean?" I thought I was perfectly clear why I needed her here. We don't have any other leads, and I'm not about to send a mole to infiltrate the Disciples. They rarely come back and if they do, they're in pieces. I won't put my people through that again.

A growl rips through air thick with tension. "Don't bullshit me. You've been off since the drop. I'm barely keeping shit together here. Then you go and bring her in without even talking to me. And when I told you it was a shit idea, you tried to distract me by sucking my cock."

I lean back in my chair and cross my arms. "Never been one to complain about that before."

His hand slams on the table, rattling the dishes. "For fuck's sake, Ghost. You're the fucking president. Start fucking acting like it."

Slowly, I push to my feet and rest my fists on the table as I lean toward him. "You're damn right I'm the president. And I am acting like it. Just because I'm not doing what *you* think is right doesn't mean it isn't what's happening. Fall in line or—"

"Or what? Get the fuck out? Is that where we're at now?"

The anger that gripped me moments ago leaches from me, and I drop into my chair once more. His face falls the slightest bit and his lips part as if he'll take back the words. Maybe he's right. Maybe I'm not acting like I should. Clearly, I've had other things on my mind while I was recovering. I don't understand why he doesn't get it. We're usually in sync, anticipating what the other will do before we've even made the conscious decision to do it.

"I wouldn't kick you out," I say wearily. "I was going to say fall in line or figure your shit out. If we're constantly at each other's throats, shit is going to get messed up a lot quicker. We need to be on the same side, Storm."

"Except I don't know which side that is. I can't be on *hers.*" He spits the last word out like it's a curse. Like *she's* a curse.

Before, I would have agreed with him. She put everything at risk when she sided with our enemies. Our lives, our futures, our everything. She marked us for death. We should have killed her back then.

"It isn't her side and ours, though. In fact, I don't think she has a side anymore."

"What the hell is that supposed to mean? You texted her to come here, thinking she had answers to questions you couldn't even understand. When she finally shows up, you're convinced she's lying when really she's just being a fucking brat like she always was. Then you somehow got it in your head you need to save her. From what? I don't fucking know because she's not going to tell us a damn thing and even if she did, we wouldn't believe her. So, why the fuck did you actually bring her here? You owe me an answer, at the very least." His chest heaves as he attempts to get his shit together.

I bite my tongue, knowing I'm about to piss him off even more. "For months, I've been having dreams. They're all of her. I didn't think much of it."

He holds up his hand, stopping me. "You're telling me you brought her back here based on a fucking dream?"

"No. I just said that's where it started. Shit here has been weird. Shipments delayed. Members going missing. The factions under us are restless, but no one can tell me why. If we were smaller, like the Reapers, it wouldn't be as hard to figure out. Here? Not so easy."

"None of this has to do with her. Phantom issues aside, I need to know about her."

I shake my head. "It's all jumbled in my head, though. Everything's tied together. Remember when I went down to Rima to help the others take care of the Guild? It wasn't just Raines dealing with that shit. The Guild was in Synd before that, and we didn't step in. They said they had their shit figured, but they didn't. Everything tied back to the Guild years before they even knew it."

"And you think that's happening here? Shit, Ghost. We don't have millionaires rolling into Harris looking to take over and start stealing our people." He glances over his shoulder down the hall. "She isn't going to be the catalyst for some major plot. The woman can barely hold her head up."

He always does this. He interjects a shitload of questions to process whatever is going on in my own head. I wish I could pluck out my thoughts and lay them in a nice little row so he'd understand. Unfortunately, magic doesn't exist in our world. Only shadows and death.

"Listen, I'm not saying she's directly involved in anything. But I'm not willing to take the risk. I'd rather have her here, where I know she can't influence outcomes. We have to clean up the ranks. With the different groups beneath us, we have to be careful we don't get too big, that everyone's staying in line, that no one tries to take me out, and we have to keep everything running smoothly." Exhaustion settles on me, though I just woke up.

"Is this what you've been worrying about for the last couple weeks? Just overanalyzing shit while you should have been sleeping?" He looks affronted, but I can't just turn off running the Phantoms because I got hurt. That's a disaster waiting to happen.

I glance over his shoulder as soft light filters down the stairs. "Even if things aren't connected, we still need to keep her here. Can you honestly say you'd be okay if she died? Especially if it was because we ran her off?"

He shakes his head, then sucks in a deep breath. "I don't know which bruises are mine," he whispers.

"What do you mean?"

His dark eyes are haunted when his gaze meets mine. "I was pissed. When I found her hiding in her old house, I was so fucking pissed. All I could think about was how she was ruining everything. We were fine. After so long without her, we were finally fine. And she thought she could just stick around in our territory after everything she did? I couldn't handle it."

"What did you do?" I struggle to keep my voice even.

"I busted in there and she ran. Up the stairs that were rickety ten years ago. I don't know if she tripped or I knocked her over, but the split lip was definitely me. She must have thought I was someone else. Or maybe she knew it was me and was fighting me, anyway." His hands curl into fists. "Her entire body is covered in bruises. She won't tell us where they came from."

"And we wouldn't know if she was telling the truth or not."

The wood above our heads creaks and we both look up. I doubt Siren is up and about. Her body was ready to give out when I got her home. She barely stirred when I carried her into the house last night. I've been shoving down all the emotions I felt —*feel*. The emotions currently assaulting me. We never fully dealt with her betrayal. It was easier to ignore them and throw myself into fixing what she broke around us.

"I never thought she'd come back here, but I also never thought about her dying. What the fuck are we supposed to do?" he murmurs.

"We could get cake." I smirk as confusion flashes in his eyes and then a reluctant grin stretches across his face.

I open my mouth to suggest some pie as well when there's a knock on the door. Storm's head snaps around and he reaches for his gun. I gesture for him to stay where he is. It's probably just Bones, but after the last couple of weeks, I'm not taking any chances. I grab my weapon from the table next to the door, then peer at my phone. There's a camera pointing straight at the door, but it's dark as if someone's covered the lens.

I glance over my shoulder at Storm, indicating he should get into position. Instead, he eases up the stairs, heading for his room. My eyebrows shoot up and I shake my head. For someone who doesn't want to have anything to do with her, he's sure eager to put himself between her and potential danger. I don't know how to feel about it.

Whoever's on the other side knocks again, and I slip into the living room. The front window won't have as clear of a view, but I might be able to figure out who it is at least.

"Open the fucking door, Ghost," Fuse bellows, and some of the tension leaves me.

I rip open the door and glare at my enforcer. He's technically not an enforcer anymore, but old habits die hard. Being my third isn't easy since he basically has to keep all the lower factions of the Phantoms in line.

Sometimes I wonder what life would have been like had Jag stuck around instead of moving to the Vipers in Rima. Dante needed a VP, and I respect both of them. Except I lost my sister in the process. Avery didn't want to stick around here, always being known as the president's little sister. I don't blame her. Still sucks, though.

Fuse pushes past me, and I swing the door shut. We haven't kept him in the loop when it comes to Siren being back. Unless Storm said something, but I doubt it. I wanted to play this close to the chest. The Phantoms are the center of my life, which makes keeping shit separate hard.

"Why don't you come in and make yourself at home," I grumble as he settles on the couch. An image of Storm leaning over that same couch flashes through my mind and I shove it away.

"Since you're refusing to set a meeting, I figured the easiest thing was to come to you. Where's Storm?" He tugs the elastic band from his blond hair, then gathers the strands again.

"Upstairs." I drop onto the chair opposite him. "What's so important we need a meeting? We just had one."

He rolls his eyes, and I suppress a grin. The move always looks a little off coming from a man who looks like a goddamn Viking. Most of the time he's scowling, playing up the role he's been shoved into. Over the last year, he's proved his loyalty. Not only to the Phantoms, but to myself as well. It was hard losing Jag, regardless of Fuse's presence.

"Some shit is going down with one of the factions."

"Which one?"

"Southside. Flame seems to think he's got a mole, though he

has absolutely no evidence to back that shit up. Venom's been on his shit again, too. Storm probably told you about his latest stunt?" He folds his arms and levels me with a stare.

I pull out my phone and text Storm to come down. I should have probably done it right away. He'll probably bitch about it. It doesn't matter in the grand scheme of things, but it matters to our relationship. Trying to figure out how to balance my personal life with what's essentially my professional life is hard. It's harder when my job takes over my existence. Being part of a motorcycle club like ours becomes your whole world. It's even worse because I'm the president. I don't have the luxury to put everything else off to fix my relationship with Storm.

"Why don't you give me your version of events when it comes to Venom?"

He huffs, shaking his head. He may not have been in the position long, but he knows me. Which means he definitely knows Storm didn't tell me shit. Fuse opens his mouth, then snaps it shut when Storm pounds down the stairs. I jump to my feet and spin as he skids into the living room.

"She's gone."

Eleven

Siren

A groan echoes through my head as light filters into the concrete room. It's not the first time I've been shoved into a hole like this with no idea how I got here. Actually, I do remember waking up to a set of startlingly blue eyes. They seemed otherworldly. I didn't have enough time to make sense of them before the prick of a needle sent me into dreamland.

My sluggish mind tries to piece together what the fuck happened, but it's all a disjointed mess. Ghost and Storm arguing. Pain raging through my body. Storm forcing pills into my mouth. The smell of sausage floating through the air. The sweet cloying scent of cinnamon and myrrh overriding all my other senses. And unfamiliar vibrant blue eyes that seemed to strip away all the defenses I put in place to merely stare into my soul.

A shiver rolls through me from both the memory and the cold. I thought I was safe in Phantom territory. As safe as I could be with two people who once loved me and now loathe me. It's why I let my guard down. Not that I could have fought back when the others came for me. I assume they're part of the Disciples. I don't know how they got into Ghost's house, though.

I shove my hands under my armpits, trying to get some feeling back in them. My toes are numb, but there's not much I can do about them. Hopefully, I won't have to run anytime soon. Every time before, I've waited for the right moment to slip from their grasp. I doubt I'll have that option this time around. And no one is coming for me. Even if Storm or Ghost knew where I was, they wouldn't come. Storm didn't want me around in the first place. As soon as Ghost finds out I'm with the Disciples...he'll think he was right. Every single doubt he has ever harbored over whether or not they made the right decision will vanish.

I'll have to save myself once more. I should be used to it by now, but I'm weak and tired. Just once, I'd like someone else to care enough to come for me. Except I never cultivated any relationships. I didn't want to get close to anyone else. No one deserved to be sucked into my shitty life. No one needed to get caught in the fallout. It's why I didn't keep in touch with Lexi. I don't know whether she would have helped me. I never wanted to find out.

"Perhaps you'd like a drink of water?" a calm voice asks from the doorway.

I lift my eyes slowly, expecting to see those same startling blue ones from before. I brace myself for it. Instead, I find dark brown ones. They're just as unsettling as the last ones except for the soullessness resting within their depths. A shiver rolls through me, and I scoot into the corner. The last thing I want is to be snatched from behind. My feet might be frozen, but they can still pack a punch if he gets too close.

"You remember who I am?" he asks, crouching and setting the bottle of water closer to me. When I nod, he continues, "Good. I've been waiting for you. I very much enjoyed our little game."

I always wondered what kind of man would name himself Prophet. Apparently a psychopath. He runs his hand through his dirty-blond hair and flashes me a brilliant smile with too much teeth. The energy radiating off him sets me on edge, threatening to overwhelm all my senses. Everything in me screams to run—to fight. I pull in a deep, calming breath.

I should ask questions, get as much information from him as possible. I know better, though. He'll reveal much more if I stay silent. Plus, I have no idea if I'll be able to get any words out. My throat is trying to close in on itself and my body vibrates with the effort to not attack him. If I could kill him right now, I would. Not only for myself, but for the Phantoms. I don't owe them anything, but I'd still do it for them.

"Nothing to say? Not surprising. I understand this might be jarring for you." He drops to the floor and leans against the wall. I pull back even more when he stretches his legs out and crosses his ankles.

Someone knocks on the door, and my gaze snaps away from him. There's something unsettling about his face. I thought it was his eyes, but now I'm convinced it's something else. Maybe it's the unassuming nature he exudes. He looks like he could be a fucking altar boy. Or one of those priests in a horror movie.

"If you're really not going to speak, I'll have to fill the silence. Perhaps you'd like to have a conversation about your friends?" He raises a perfectly manicured eyebrow. Apparently, he's ignoring whoever is knocking. "No, I suppose that's too personal. We'll talk about you instead, hmm?"

He nudges the bottle closer to me, taking the opportunity to move to the wall next to me. I wrap my arms around my knees and attempt to make myself as small as possible. This room isn't exactly large. My gaze darts to the ceiling, desperately searching for a way out. I won't be able to act on it until he leaves, but I'd rather be prepared.

"I'm sure you don't remember, which is fine, but we met several years ago. You were glowing. I believe that's what caught my eye. You may not be smiling now, yet I still remember how enchanting it was." He reaches out as if he's going to brush my hair away from my face or touch me in some way. I flinch, though, and he pulls back.

He tilts his head and sighs. "There's only so much time I can give you, Siren. We're on a bit of a deadline with what we're planning. You understand how it is. All the plans being put in place took a while. Now that we're in the final stages, things are moving much more quickly. So, what do I need from you?"

I bite my tongue. It takes everything in me not to grill him about these mysterious plans he's talking about. Clearly, it has something to do with the Phantoms. My first thought is I need to warn Ghost. Except he won't believe me. Or maybe he already knows. Either way, they all know how dangerous the Disciples are. They used to, at least. It's been so long since I've been home and even longer since I've been involved in things.

Actually, I was never in a position of power within the Phantoms. Snake, the previous president, didn't know I existed until my supposed betrayal. With Snake, I was just a kid, then I was a young woman. Neither one of those things helped me in the slightest when the informant came forward. Just like nothing will help me now.

"You see, little lamb, I need something from you. Something only you can give me. You're not ready to accept me yet, which is fine. Just remember, you can be part of this whenever you need."

Nausea bubbles in my gut. His hand twitches at his side as if he wants to touch me. If he does, he'll lose at least a finger, if not more. I have enough energy to break a few before he subdues me. He probably wouldn't expect it, even with all the evidence of what I'm capable of. I've sent his men back in body bags. He probably thinks I won't do anything in the condition I'm in. I'm sure looking like death warmed over doesn't help.

"Still don't have anything to say?" He pauses as if I'll actually answer him. It takes everything in me not to roll my eyes. "Well, a little more time in the hole might do you some good."

He pushes to his feet and steps closer, his feet almost brushing my bare toes. It didn't occur to me until he's towering over me how undressed I am. Just a ripped shirt and a pair of small shorts. I'm glad I put some on after I went to the bathroom. It took me a lot longer than usual to even get to the toilet, but it allowed me to overhear Ghost and Storm's conversation. Now I wish I would have put on sweatpants. Especially when Prophet's gaze slips down my body. My skin crawls when he licks his lips.

"You'll see soon enough, little lamb. This is where you're meant to be."

With that, he pivots on his heel and clicks out the room. The heavy door thuds shut, and a lock snaps into place. I glance up again, then my gaze slides to the corners of the room. A single lightbulb shines overhead. There's nothing else other than concrete walls and that one bulb. Obviously, they don't see the need for cameras in here. The Phantoms have a room just like this. I stayed in it after Snake dragged me from my house. I wonder how much Ghost uses it.

I lean my head against the wall, attempting to stay as warm as possible. When I turn my head, I catch a whiff of copper underneath the stench of must and urine. My ass is probably soaked in someone else's bodily fluids. If I had more energy, I'd probably care. My lids flutter shut, but I don't really sleep. When a small click echoes through the space, my eyes fly open and fix on the door. There's no handle on the inside, so I'm forced to wait for Prophet to enter.

As the door inches forward, I tense. My arms ache from holding my legs for so long. I probably won't be able to kick him now. I slowly untangle my fingers and ease my limbs out. A groan slips from me, and I clamp my lips shut.

Instead of Prophet's perfectly coiffed hair and soulless brown eyes, a petite woman with shockingly green hair and vibrant blue eyes appears. She glances over her shoulder, revealing a tattoo snaking up the side of her neck. For a minute, I swear I know her, yet I've never seen her before in my life. She doesn't look like she's going to threaten me.

She slips fully inside and eases the door shut. When she holds out a bread roll, I tuck my legs up again. The last thing I'm going to do is have them poison me...again. It took me a long time to figure out to not take food from someone. Even delivery was suspect. I had to learn a lot of things the hard way once I was on my own. I didn't realize how coddled I had been with the Phantoms. You'd think growing up in a motorcycle club would have prepared me. It really didn't.

"Hi," she whispers. "We don't have a lot of time. I need you to eat something. Drink the water. None of it is tainted. Then I can sneak you out of here."

Every few seconds, she glances at the door. I don't know if I can trust her, but I don't really have a choice. All I need to do is get out of this room and I can run. I'll go anywhere else, though getting out of Disciple territory in Rosewood might prove challenging. It's a problem for future me.

I use the wall to push to my feet. My knees have mostly forgotten how to work, but they keep me upright enough. I should ask her some questions. She's a Disciple, though. I can't trust any of them, even if she's helping me.

Maybe helping me, I remind myself. She could be walking me straight into a trap. If Prophet is waiting outside...nothing will change. Could still be a trap.

"I get what you're thinking. I'd be of the same mind. Don't have time to explain anything so just get your ass moving." She widens her eyes at me before inching toward the door.

She peeks through the crack and waves me forward. I use the wall to shuffle toward her. I'm afraid I won't be able to walk, but asking this woman for help isn't an option. I barely trust her to lead me away without getting me shot. She doesn't look like she could drag my ass out of here. Sometimes looks can be deceiving when it comes to women who grew up in an MC. Except I don't know if she spent her childhood in the Disciples or somewhere else.

"Stay quiet. They're in the next room." She grabs my hand and leads me out.

Her fingers grip me tightly and I sway. We shuffle along, the sounds of raucous laughter echoing from behind a closed door. She leads me down a dark hallway, then another one. I can't make out anything other than black walls and concrete under my feet.

The woman's green hair is a beacon in the night, leading me hopefully toward an exit. When she turns another corner, my mind freaks out and I rush forward. My ankle gives out as I swing after her and I crash into a wall.

Her fingers curl into my upper arm, nails digging into my skin as she hauls me upright. "None of that now. We need you, Siren. Whatever else happens, we need you. Don't give up now."

I use the wall to follow her, though my head swims with the beat of my heart. I don't know if my body will make it. Each breath has glass shredding my lungs. Each step has pain radiating through me. Each blink has my vision blurring. As soon as I'm about to pass out, cold air slaps me in the face and I gasp. The chill sends a zing of energy through me, and I cross my arms to ward off the freezing wind whipping around us.

She tugs me outdoors into the dark. She shoves a black sweatshirt over my head. For a moment, my mind freaks out, thinking I'm being taken yet again. The last thing I need is to be on my knees about to be executed in a dirty fucking alley in Disciple territory. Convincing myself it's not going to happen like that doesn't take long—about the time it takes for her to pull it down.

She throws some pants at me, scrunching up her nose. "The bottoms got wet. I doubt you care. Better than what you're wearing. Your feet are bigger than mine, so I got some flip-flops."

"Why—" I cough, trying to clear the dryness from my throat. "Why are you helping me?"

She rolls her eyes. "Told you. We need you. Just not yet."

She spins me around and pushes me toward the opening of the alley. These flip-flops will be a dead giveaway if I have to run. They're better than nothing, though. When I reach the main street, which doesn't look like much of anything, I glance over my shoulder. I need to ask her name at least.

"Go home, Siren," she whispers from the dark, then vanishes back inside.

Twelve

Storm

If we don't find her...

Ghost's threat rings in my ears, trailing after every step I take. I didn't think I'd be out searching for Siren for the third time in almost as many days, but here we are. Sharp pains ricochet through my chest, making it hard to breathe. I'm ignoring them and the reason why they're plaguing me. It doesn't matter anyway.

After we find her, we'll have answers. Ghost is convinced she was kidnapped, but he wouldn't explain how he knew that. I'm sure he had his strange sixth sense feeling or he went into worst-case scenario mode. Whatever it was, we won't know for sure until she's home.

Not home. Harris isn't her home anymore. With each passing second without her, it's getting harder to remember.

My phone buzzes and I snatch it from the pocket of my hoodie before slipping into an alley. I peer into the darkness, searching for anyone lurking in the shadows. There hasn't been much activity in Rosewood tonight. Part of me wishes I was back in Harris instead of here. I have more chance of finding her there. The likelihood of the Disciples sneaking onto Phantom territory, breaking into our house, and kidnapping her from right under our noses is unlikely. It's much more plausible she ran. Because that's what she's good at. Even with her injured, she's capable of escaping. In fact, she probably played up how she was truly feeling just to throw us off.

Even in my head my thinking sounds flawed. She wasn't faking. Her body was battered, bruised, almost completely unrecognizable. Getting out of the house in her condition wouldn't have been easy. We would have known. How they were able to grab her is a mystery we'll have to deal with later. Too many issues are piling on top of each other. Eventually, it'll bury us.

My phone buzzes again and I shake my head. Ghost's text sits on the screen, a warning. Maybe a threat. For a split second, I think about ignoring him. He doesn't deserve the added stress. I had hoped he found her already. Then I wouldn't have to be in this shitty town with enemies lurking around every corner. I hate Rosewood so fucking much. Even without the Disciples running this place, I'd hate it. I don't know if it's the dinginess or the asshole drivers, but there's just something about Rosewood that sets my nerves on edge. At this point, I can't separate the city from the MC, though.

"You okay, mister?"

I spin around, my gun in my hand before I register it was a tiny voice tucked behind a dumpster. The child's eyes widen as they press their small body farther into the shadows. I glance toward the mouth of the alley, then back at them. I crouch, trying to get a better look at them.

"Are you out here by yourself?" I murmur, trying not to scare them.

"No," they whisper. "My b-brother. H-h-he's coming. Soon. Don't..." A flash of light glints off a tiny blade as they brandish a small knife.

"Not going to hurt you, kid. What's your name?"

"A-Alex."

I narrow my eyes, though they probably can't tell in the dark. "Try again."

The kid huffs and the knife drops a little. "Oliver."

"I'm Storm."

He lets out a short laugh, the sound barely carrying through the air. "That's not a name."

"Sure is. Got it when I was young. You want to tell me why you're hanging out in an alley when it's this fucking cold out?" I wince, realizing a second too late I probably shouldn't swear around a kid. Then again, if he's living on the streets, he's probably heard worse than an f-bomb.

"Waiting for my brother," he mutters, then tips his tiny chin up. "None of your business, though, is it?"

"Not in the slightest. Except you're probably cold and your brother shouldn't leave you here without at least a jacket."

I don't really have time to help anyone. We don't have kids living on the streets in Harris. It was one of the things Ghost, Siren, and I vowed we'd never let happen when we were kids. There were too many children our age and younger fending for themselves when Snake was in charge of the Phantoms. We weren't really in a position to help them, but we still tried. Since Ghost became president, we've changed a lot.

"Don't have a choice, mister. You looking for something?" he asks, breaking into my thoughts.

Rage swirls through me at the thought of this kid dealing. It's not his fault, though. "Someone, actually. A woman."

"She got hair?"

"Uh, yes?"

"No, I mean like..." He gestures to his own hair, getting dangerously close to his eye with the knife. "Like hair. With colors."

"Like purple?"

He grins, his teeth practically glowing in the darkness. "Yeah. She got hair like that?"

"No. She used to, but not right now." I shake my head. "It doesn't matter."

"If she doesn't matter, why'd you ask about her?"

That's the question. It's one I don't have an answer to right now. "She's important. I meant it doesn't matter in regards to you. Right now, I'm more concerned with getting you a jacket."

"You're wearing a jacket." He tilts his head and scans the holes where the stitches used to be. I have several leather jackets, but I removed the patches from this one. I'm glad I did since it allows me to go unnoticed in other territories—especially here.

"Can't have my jacket, but if your brother comes back, I can get you someplace else. A place that would have jackets and food. A roof over your head. Just got to get there." I don't have time to escort them back myself. If they can get to Harris, we'll take care of them. If I'm caught sneaking them out of Rosewood, we'll all be killed.

He presses his lips together, and his eyes dart around the dark. I can practically see the gears turning in his mind. I doubt there's a brother. He's probably been sleeping in this alley for fuck knows how long. Now he needs to figure out whether or not I can be trusted.

In our world, it's not an easy thing either. Most of the time, this would be a trick—a scam to reel him in only to use him as a drug mule or a runner. It happens all the time, though I doubt others put in this type of effort to get them. Most kids are snatched off the streets and forced without a conversation. They don't care they're destroying lives. It's what the Disciples, in particular, thrive off of. Whoever survives the harsh childhood is inducted into their ranks. They're so beaten down and brainwashed by then, they don't even know how to fight back.

"He died," he whispers. "They killed him."

"Who?" I have my suspicions, but I'm not about to accuse the Disciples.

"I don't know. No one knew who he was. They smashed his

face in. 'Cept he had a tattoo. Wanted to give me one when I was older."

He sniffs, and the knife drops from his grip before he buries his head in his arms. His small shoulders shake and my hands twitch. I'm not the right person to give him comfort. Dealing with emotions, especially grief, isn't something I'm good at. I always thought Ghost was better at those things. Now I'm not so sure.

"I'm not going to make promises I can't keep, but if you come to Harris, you won't have to sleep on the ground."

His head pops up and he gazes at me. His tear-streaked face tugs at my heart, and I realize I can't let him go alone. If he takes me up on my offer, I'm going to end up taking him with me. Duchess will take him in, take care of him. As long as he follows the rules and doesn't cause trouble.

I glance toward the mouth of the alley, wondering how long I can wait for him to decide. My phone has been buzzing in my pocket the entire time and my nerves are balancing on a razor-thin wire. Hopefully Ghost has found Siren and my detour won't have mattered.

I jolt when Oliver's finger traces the tattoo on the side of my neck. It's a simplified version of the Phantom sigil. I turn back to him, and he drops his hand, then nods.

"Is it far?" he asks, his voice taking on a steely quality.

"If you're walking, yeah." I stand, intending to extend my hand. He lifts his arms instead, hope blooming on his face.

I sigh before I grab him and settle him on my hip. He's tiny, much smaller than I expected. He grips my neck, fingers digging into my jacket. I should have wrapped him in it before picking him up, but I doubt he'll let go of me now. I make my way toward the street.

"Oliver, how old are you?" I murmur.

"Eight. Is that too old? Or too young?" He drops his forehead onto my shoulder.

"Neither. Just wondering." I don't know if he's telling the truth. I doubt it, though.

"How old are you?"

"Older than eight," I mutter.

A shadow flits across the thick fog that's settled over the landscape. It's too dense to decipher whether the shape is a person or something else. I press us close to the wall and angle Oliver away from the bricks. There's a shuffle, then a snap. Over and over, the sound repeats like an omen echoing through the night. I ease my weapon out and grip it firmly. I glance at Oliver, and he shakes his head. His legs tighten around me as if he knows I want to put him down.

"Hide your face, little man."

He shakes his head again and peers into the haze, determination plastered across his face. His small knife appears in his hand, and he sticks it out in front of us. If I'm lucky, I won't lose an eye. The shadow detaches slightly from the fog and the cloudy light catches on long dark strands of hair. It takes my brain a minute to process the whole scene unfolding in front of me.

Oliver whimpers and the figure whips around. Something glints off the streetlamp overhead, and I ease us into the alley more. My boot scuffs across the pavement and I silently curse. It's clearly a person, though they're hunched over. The snapping sound speeds up as the figure bobs and weaves through the misty vapor. I can't place where I've heard the noise from before, familiar as it is.

Flip-flops.

I take one unconscious step before I realize what I'm doing and stop myself. Just because there's some other fool running around in ridiculous footwear doesn't mean it's Siren. I'm sure she's not the only one who has no regard for their safety. Besides, why would she be wandering around Rosewood? She wouldn't. If the Disciples snatched her, they wouldn't let her go so easily. And she wasn't in any condition to escape the last time I saw her. If someone helped her, they would have stayed with her. It's what I would have done. Then again, I let her walk off not too long ago without a second thought.

Actually, that's not true. She occupied every waking moment of my night until Ghost insisted we go out to find her once more. I never should have let her go in the first place. I'm not ready to examine why. It doesn't matter anyway. I have more pressing issues currently since the person stumbling around can't be Siren.

I step back again when a flip-flop snaps once, then stops. There's a scuffle followed by a thud, and a whimper floats through the air. Oliver strains in my arms, wiggling like he wants to be put down.

He leans close to my ear and whispers, "Put me down. They won't hurt me."

My instinct is to hold him closer. He's still too young to understand. Some people don't give a shit whether or not he's a child. They'll hurt him if they think they can. Even more if they believe he's a threat of some kind. Others will use a kid to lure their victims in. All of it is fucking ridiculous. I can't change the world, but I can stop Oliver from running headlong into danger.

Oliver wiggles in my arms, pushing with his small hands.

"Stop it. You're going to get yourself killed."

He doesn't stop, of course. Instead, he starts flailing until I practically drop him on his ass. His bare feet hit the pavement, and he scampers off into the darkness. My body sways, stuck between going after him and waiting to see if he succeeds. A whole minute passes while indecision swamps me. My phone buzzes again and I grit my teeth.

"Storm." Oliver's voice rings through the night, and I rush forward.

It takes me too long to find him in the fog. By the time I do, my heart hammers in my chest and I'm weirdly out of breath. I practically trip over him and a figure sprawled on the ground. Dropping to my knees next to the boy, my mind tries to process what I'm seeing. Even before I brush the hair away from her face, I know who it is.

Siren blinks up at me from dull eyes. Her tongue darts out and licks her cracked lips. Oliver shushes her when she tries to speak. He murmurs encouragement and promises to her. For a kid, he seems to know all the right things to say.

Her gaze locks on mine, and she sucks in a shuddering gasp. "Run."

Thirteen

Siren

I'm tired.

Tired of running. Tired of being in pain. Tired of life.

Every time I open my eyes, there's something else. I've fucked up my life so much, I doubt there's anything I can do to make things right. For the last six years, I've been meaning to get back on track. Except every time I try to begin anew, I'm thrust into another crisis. I'm fired or thrown out of town. One of the Disciples shows up and kidnaps me. It's as if fate intervenes, destroying my world. My path is fraught with peril—a destiny determined to come to pass whether I like it or not.

And at the center of it all are two men who threw me away without a second thought yet refuse to cut the ties between us. They ensnared me long ago, and I can't push them from my thoughts. From my dreams.

My eyes flutter open, and I stare at a familiar ceiling. I knew where I was long before I was awake. My body, my spirit, knew. I hate how safe and peaceful I feel being back in this house. All I wanted was to breeze into town and run away just as quickly and easily. I fucked that up, too. I thought Storm would have enough sense to heed my warning. I thought he'd run when I told him. I should have known better.

"You okay, lady?" a small voice from beside me whispers, and I roll my head to the side.

He looks familiar with his mop of brown curls and chubby cheeks just barely giving way to age. He props his elbows on the edge of the mattress and rests his chin in his hand. His arms are gangly, almost too long for him to pull off the move. I swallow hard when his dark eyes meet mine. A heaviness rests in their depths. He can't be more than six or seven, but he's clearly seen more in his short years than he should have. Growing up in a city like Rosewood, I'm not surprised. I was him, once.

"I'm fine," I croak.

He straightens and grabs a glass of water from the bedside table. "I got it myself."

My eyebrows shoot up, but he doesn't seem to notice my shock. I haven't spent a lot of time around kids. Not since I was one myself, which I don't think counts.

I struggle to sit up and his hand wavers like he can't decide whether to wait for me or help me. I take the glass when I'm steady, grateful my arms still work this time around. As soon as the rim hits my lips, I hesitate. While logically I know they wouldn't hurt me, my mind hasn't caught up to the fact I'm in Harris and not in Rosewood. Besides, poison isn't really the Phantoms go-to. Nor do I think they'd drug me. Then again, Storm would definitely slip something in if it would get me to sleep if only to shut me up. Bastard.

"It's not poisoned. I made sure," he whispers, and his gaze darts to the closed door.

I tip the glass, and the cold water soothes my parched throat. Once I drain every drop, I crave more despite the liquid sloshing in my stomach. The kid grabs it from me and sets it gently on the nightstand. A bottle of pain pills sits there, and I press my lips into a thin line. I need them, but I'll wait until I figure out who the hell this kid is.

"What's your name?" I ask, and he shushes me, his head whipping back and forth.

"They'll come back soon and they're loud." He turns pleading eyes back to me. "I'm Oliver, but the one keeps calling me little man."

"So—" I say, and he waves his hands. I lower my voice. "So, you don't know them?"

He shakes his head violently. "They didn't kidnap me. He was going to bring me here and said I'd have a bed. It sounded like a good deal."

His voice trails off, and I scramble for something to say that'll reassure him. "They will. They're good people."

He drops his head and mutters, "Bikers."

"I mean, yeah, but not like others. They take care of their own." I almost choke on the words. For almost anyone else, my statement was true. Especially for someone like Oliver. For me? Not so much. He doesn't need to know any of that, though.

"I'm not their own."

"Neither am I," I murmur, my heart clenching, and I clear my throat. "Yet here I am. And so are you."

We sit in silence while he processes what I said. I stare at the door, my gaze fixed on the knob. I'm surprised one of them isn't in here making sure I'm not escaping. It took me a while to work through what Ghost and Storm would assume.

With my disappearing act and Storm finding me wandering around Disciple territory, they probably figure I left on my own. Otherwise, this room would have been trashed. They would have heard the fighting or gunshots. Even with the drugs spreading through my system, I'd have known if they were coming to help me.

"Then why was he looking for you? When he found me, he said he was looking for a woman. Then when he found out I was by myself, there was something in his eyes. Like he needed to find you, but didn't want to leave me behind. If you're not one of them, why was he searching for you?"

"Storm? I don't...how old are you?"

His brows pull low. "Ten. Why?"

"No reason," I murmur, not believing him one bit. "I don't have an answer, though. They think I have information."

"You don't?"

"Nothing they want to know." I snap my mouth shut when he nods.

I have no idea who this kid is. He could have been lying to me the entire time. It wouldn't be the first time someone used a child to manipulate someone else. They're used as runners and bait without truly understanding what they're doing. Once they grow up, they don't know how to function as adults, if they grow up at all. This kid might be at the beginning of that journey.

I have no idea if Storm really did find Oliver in Rosewood. Or maybe he's a plant for the Disciples. I let his dark curls and soulful eyes lure me into a false sense of security. I forgot to keep my guard up. I forgot I'm not safe—even here.

I forgot my number one rule: trust no one.

"You should go. Doubt you're supposed to be in here." I nod to the door, hoping he'll take the hint.

"I'm supposed to watch you. They said to watch you to make sure you didn't go out the window. I don't know why you'd do that since it's a long way down and there's no trees nearby." He leans to gaze out said window. It's covered by thick curtains, though. Not surprising since Storm sleeps in pitch black. Like a fucking vampire.

"The back has bricks. Decorative bricks. Which means they stick out a little. Makes it easier to get down if you know the way."

Oliver tilts his head. "How you know that if you're not one of them?"

I wince. "I used to be one of them. I'm not anymore."

It takes everything in me not to choke on the words. I've never said them out loud. Sharing my past wasn't high on my priority list. Not that I had anyone to confide in. Everyone here knew what I'd done. They shunned me without hesitation.

Once I left, I never spoke of the Phantoms again. Whenever

someone would ask me where I was from, I'd lie. Occasionally someone would inquire into my childhood, and I'd make it up. No one knew, therefore it could never touch me. If I buried the pain deep enough, no one would ever know how much I hurt. Even I'd be ignorant of it after some time.

"Time to go, Oliver," Ghost says from the doorway.

I glance away, hoping he didn't see the tears swimming in my eyes. The last thing I need is for him to say something shitty. Or to pity me. I don't want his fucking pity any more than I want his forgiveness. If he didn't stick to his hatred for me, then I don't know him like I thought I did. Doesn't mean it doesn't hurt. Except I'm shoving that pain away until I no longer feel anything anymore. It's the only way I'll be able to survive here.

Oliver's fingers brush my arm before he hops off the chair. I'd think the kid was lying about his age if it wasn't for his gangly arms. He could be right on the cusp of preteen, even if he is on the skinny side. If someone takes him in, they'll be able to put some meat on his bones. I still can't figure out how he fits into the story here. Ghost and Storm never talked about how to fix things around here other than getting Snake out. Unless they just didn't tell me, which is much more likely. I doubt they implemented all the things we talked about when we were kids.

"You don't look like you're about to keel over this time. Want to tell me what happened?" Ghost asks, taking Oliver's vacated seat.

I grab the bottle of pain meds, and it slips from my numb fingers. Ghost sighs as he picks it up. I expect him to hand it back, but he opens it instead and gives me two pills.

Ghost holds out the glass, then scoffs when he finds it empty. He stomps off to the bathroom, and I wonder if he'll actually come back. He wouldn't leave me alone, though. His one question told me all I needed to know. Despite what Oliver said about Storm coming to find me, I get it. He wasn't coming to save me. They were more concerned with me revealing my supposed secrets. As soon as I tell him everything he wants to know, I'll be back on my own. Prophet will continue to send his men after me. Eventually he'll catch me for good, and I doubt my savior will be around to help then. I'll have to run faster, farther.

"How'd they get in, Siren?" Ghost asks, leaning back in his chair and folding his arms.

"Don't know," I mutter. I avoid his eyes, though they're boring two holes in me.

"How'd they get you out?"

"Dunno."

"Was it night or morning when they came?"

I huff and finally meet his gaze. "I. Don't. Know."

"You don't know much, do you?"

"Not surprising. I've been telling you since I got here, I don't know anything. You not believing me has no bearing on my reality. I can't force you. I never could." I glance around the floor, trying to find my backpack. I can't afford to lose what little clothes I have.

"What the hell are you looking for?"

"Pants. This seems like a pants type of conversation." I flip back the covers, intent on searching for my things.

Ghost's growl is the only warning I have. His hand wraps around my throat and he forces me onto my back. A thrill rolls down my spine as he looms over me. His fingers flex against my skin, then he freezes. I'm not naive enough to believe there's desire in his eyes despite my entire body coming alive under his touch.

"You'll rip your stitches," he says, then slowly releases me.

I swallow hard, trying to control my racing heart. His words sink into me gradually and I shake my head.

"Stitches?" I croak and pat at my chest as if they'll magically appear.

He bats my hand away. "Knock it off. You didn't have open heart surgery. They're in your side. Bones said she noticed it before but didn't think it was that big of a deal. Did you fall?"

I shake my head as I finally find where thread holds me together. As soon as I'm aware of it, my skin pulls and itches.

"They had a needle. I'm not going to be much help to you. If you give me my damn pants, I can leave. Then you can deal with whatever bullshit you've got going on with the Disciples."

He tilts his head, and the familiarity of the move sends a bolt of pain through my chest. "A needle?"

I sigh, resigning myself to at least telling him what I remember. Not that there's much in my muddled memories. It's as if a hazy film covers each one. Some parts are clear, with colors too vibrant for reality. Others are shadowy and muddy. I'm not willing to dissect every single one of them to make sure they're real.

I huff and push myself upright. Ghost leans forward as if he'll snatch me up once more. Part of me wants to try my luck. My rational brain keeps me in check, though, and I rest my back against the headboard.

"I don't remember much because they stuck me with a needle. Everything's a bit muddled. When I woke up, I was in a hole."

"Like, *the* hole?"

"Yeah. Like the one in the annex Snake used." I could ask him if they still use it, but I'm too chickenshit. "Prophet came in. Said a bunch of shit that didn't make sense, then left."

His eyebrows rise a little more with every revelation. It's hard to concentrate on what happened with him staring at me. I thread my fingers together and fix my gaze on the door, hoping I can get through this without him interrupting.

"What did he say, exactly?"

"Something about plans he's had for a while. He said they were in the final stages so things were moving quickly. He asked about my friends. I assume he was talking about you and Storm. I can't imagine he'd care about anyone else." I open my mouth to tell him about Prophet fucking with me—the game we've been playing without my knowledge. I stop myself just in time. He won't care about Prophet's obsession with me.

He rubs his fingers along his jaw, and I tuck my chin to my chest. My eyes feel heavy, and I close them before I keel over. I'm sure he'll wake me up whenever he figures out his next question. I need all the rest I can get before I leave. Just a few more hours and I'll be ready. Hopefully, they'll let me go when the time comes.

I just need a little more time.

FOURTEEN

GHOST

I catch Storm's gaze from the doorway. I doubt Siren noticed him before she fell silent. He widens his eyes, then gestures to her. He's right. No matter how much she needs sleep, we need answers first. She was missing for over twelve hours. She had to get more than just a vague reference to plans.

I clear my throat and her head snaps up. "What other friends could he be talking about?"

Confusion floods her face as her eyes snap open. "What?"

"You said he asked about your friends. Could he be talking about someone you've met since you...left?"

She snorts, then smothers the sound with a cough. Then again, the cough may be real. Her body is a mix of half-healed scars and fresh wounds. Add in the kaleidoscope of bruises littering her skin and she's almost unrecognizable. When she first showed up, I didn't allow myself to look too closely at her, afraid of what time had wrought upon her. I realize not much has changed other than the tapestry of pain etched into her flesh. She hides the weight of despair in her dark eyes well. Or maybe she's just good at avoiding my gaze when the world becomes too much. Otherwise, she's still the same girl she was all those years ago.

"Might be Lexi, but I doubt it. I've only seen her once and that was when I got back. I haven't spent much time in one place."

"Which means you don't have friends."

She turns her head and smirks. "So eager to know what I've been up to. Thought I was dead to you?"

"Don't do that," I growl. "Don't hide behind sarcasm and bullshit. Just answer my questions."

Her mouth twists, and she rests her head against the headboard. "No. I don't have friends. He was talking about you two. He said something about my needing the Disciples. Or maybe he needed me. I have no idea."

"When was the last time you saw him?" I hold my breath while she sighs.

"Eight, nine years? I don't know. Before I left. I don't remember it. He mentioned I was glowing. And smiling, so I assume it was before I left."

I don't know what the fuck she's talking about. If it was that long ago, I'm not surprised she doesn't remember. We were inseparable back then, which means we met Prophet, too.

I glance at Storm and a flash of a memory races through my mind. Some kind of party we'd all gone to. Someone mentioned there were Disciples there, but we didn't see them. At least, we didn't think we did. Prophet must have been at the warehouse watching us, though why he'd care about us back then doesn't make sense. Storm and I were technically only members, barely initiated.

It's not until I see the set of Storm's mouth that I realize he thinks she's lying. When I glance at Siren, her eyes are closed again. The longer she's here, the more my convictions waver. Storm wants her gone. The need to keep her close grows within me, and I'm starting to think it's more than just whatever info she can give us.

"What game are you playing at, Siren?" I murmur, the question slipping out before I can think better of it.

Her lids fly open and her body tenses. To the casual observer, they'd think she was caught. Except I notice the trembling in her hands and the fear in her eyes. Her gaze darts around the room and her breath comes out in short gasps, though she's trying to hide it.

Storm pushes off the wall in the hallway. He's not as unaffected by her as he pretends. We'll need to talk about it before long. We need to get on the same page and that requires us to open up to each other. Even if it's to confess we don't know what the fuck to do with her.

"I'm not a child anymore, Ghost. I don't play games. Especially ones I know I'll lose."

"How'd you get out?" Storm calls from the doorway, and Siren shudders.

"A...a woman helped me. I didn't know her." Her face blanks, though a heaviness remains in her eyes. "I wandered in the fog for a while, then you found me."

He takes another step into the room. "You told me to run."

She shakes her head. "I thought I heard voices. Like someone was stalking me through the mist. I thought...it doesn't matter. Obviously, it was just my imagination playing tricks on me."

"Why are you lying?"

I shove to my feet and Siren snaps her mouth shut. "We're not getting anywhere. Siren, I need you to rest. Then you can tell us whatever else comes to you. Hopefully by then you'll be ready to—"

"To reveal my deepest, darkest secrets?"

"To tell the truth."

"I'm not lying." She says it with such conviction, I almost believe her.

I sigh, the weight of everything pressing down on my shoulders. "Regardless of whether you're telling the truth or leading us on, we need answers."

"I can't give you answers I don't know. And you can't keep me here."

Storm laughs, though there's no mirth in it. "For someone who was so adamant to stay before, you're sure eager to fuck off now. Got someone waiting for you?"

"You know nothing about my life or what I've been through. You don't deserve to know anything. You lost that right when you threw my ass out without a goddamn—" She inhales sharply and curls her hands into fists. "You want to know what I'm *hiding*? Fine. The woman who helped me had green hair. She said they need me, just not yet, and to go home. I assume she meant here. I didn't correct her."

Storm opens his mouth, but she holds up her hand. "Prophet said we were playing a game and now it was over. Prophet's been fucking with me for years. Started a year after I left Harris. I don't know why or what he's after. No matter how far I run, his men always find me. The only reason I came this close to Rosewood was because of the text. Otherwise, I would have run again."

"So when I asked when the last time you met with the Disciples?" I murmur.

Her jaw tics as her gaze fixates on the end of the bed. "I took the cheeky route, but I didn't lie. I saw them not long ago. They nicked me in the side when I was escaping. Does that satisfy your curiosity?"

"No. Why would they go after *you*?" Storm snaps, then winces at Siren's expression.

She glances away. "Your guess is as good as mine. Unless they think I'm somehow still linked to you two. Which is why I shouldn't have come in the first place. If you let me go—"

"He'll still come after you," I interject.

"Why the fuck do you care?" she cries, throwing up her hands. She grimaces and jerks to the side as if protecting her wound. She sucks in a deep breath and presses her palm against it. "It doesn't matter. It's not like you guys have to deal with it."

"Except we are. You showed up and all fucking hell broke loose." Storm runs his hand through his hair, then grips the back of his neck.

He knows it's not her fault, but he's not willing to admit it. It's my fault. I brought her back here. I thought I was making the right decision. Instead, I fucked everything up. We were doing just fine without her. Then I threw a spark onto a powder keg. We'll be lucky if we get out alive, much less unscathed.

"Shit was bound to blow whether or not she showed up, Storm."

Siren snorts. "Defending me, Ghost? Well I'll be. I never thought I'd see the day."

"Stop being a brat, Siren. We don't have time for your antics," Storm growls.

Her nostrils flare, but she stops. The last thing I need is them bickering. My head hurts enough as it is these days. If Storm can't get his shit together when it comes to her, it'll make our lives a lot harder.

"Go to sleep, Siren," I say, exhaustion lining my voice. Being up all night and half the day while running solely off adrenaline didn't do me any favors.

She shakes her head, her fingers twisting in the sheets. "I need a shower."

"No." Storm pivots and heads for the door.

"You've got to be fucking kidding me," Siren whispers harshly, then turns to me. "Are you really going to deny me getting clean? If you're going to keep me here, the least you can do is let me shower."

I shake my head. "I'm not going to be a referee between you two. Until we figure out what Prophet wants, you're not going anywhere."

"So, you're kidnapping me. To prevent me from being kidnapped by them? Or is it just to gather more intel on the Disciples? I suppose it doesn't matter either way. You'll get what you want, and I'm just expected to go along with it. Fine. Do whatever the fuck you want. You always do."

Nothing I say will change her opinion of me. Not that I want her to. I don't give a shit what she thinks of me. Even to myself, the sentiment feels empty. I always cared what she thought of me. When our relationship evolved into something more than childhood friends, I realized my life was better with her in it. And then she shattered everything.

I thought that moment of betrayal would erase all those feelings. The love for her, the desire for her body, the want for her approval, I thought it all would vanish. I *hoped* it would. I *begged* whatever higher power who was listening to take it all away. It didn't happen, which only meant the pain was smothered in rage.

Her being back in our lives doesn't mean those emotions need to rise once more. They can stay hidden and life will eventually go back to normal. I have Storm. I have the Phantoms. I have everything I need.

As long as I keep reminding myself of the baggage and uncertainty that trails after her wherever she goes, we'll be fine. We'll get out of this mess and our world will right itself once more. Except every time I'm reminded of her existence, my mind goes off the rails. I'm lost in a fog for much longer than I should be. Storm is worse since he vacillates between silence and rage. He takes his shitty attitude out on everyone around him. I've usually been spared until recently.

"You and I both know you can't leave. The minute you step outside of Phantom territory, they'll snatch you again."

She snorts, yet her lids droop along with her shoulders. She knows I'm right, even if she's not willing to admit it. If I have to be the bad guy, then so be it. I'm probably the villain in her story, anyway. I can live with that.

"Get some sleep. I'll bring you food later."

I walk out of the room and pull the door shut behind me. Something thuds on the other side against the wood, and I grimace. When I glance up, I meet Storm's gaze.

"Is she sleeping?" he asks as he stops in front of me.

Another heavy object smacks into the door. "Not exactly."

He smirks, then wipes it away like it caught him off guard.

"Fuse called. Needs you at headquarters. Unless you need me to go."

From the look on his face, he doesn't want to leave. Whether it's to keep an eye on Siren or because he's feeling guilty, I don't know. For some reason, he thinks he should have known she was taken. He should have been able to prevent it. Which is ridiculous. He found her in the end, and that's what matters. He might not have gotten her out, but he brought her home.

I shake my head. Both because of my silent word choice and the expression on his face.

"I'll go. You make sure—" Another thud echoes through the door and the wood rattles at my back. "Make sure she doesn't destroy our house."

He grits his teeth and glances away. "If she keeps throwing a temper tantrum, I'll give her something to throw a fit about." His voice rises with each word until he's bellowing.

"I'd like to see you try, fucker," Siren yells.

I close my eyes, begging for patience. "Just figure your shit out with her. And make sure she doesn't rip her stitches."

I step aside, but Storm doesn't move. He just glares at the door, and I hurry away. I want to be as far away from here as possible before they explode. As long as the house is still standing when I get back, I don't care what happens. As I make my way down the stairs, I realize our world is shifting once more. Pulling Siren back into our lives will either redeem us or destroy us. She holds more power than she thinks. And I gave it to her.

Fifteen

Storm

As soon as the front door closes behind Ghost, some of the tension leaves me. It's hard enough having Siren in the house, but all of us together is a recipe for disaster. Unless we sit down with a mediator, we're going to be at each other's throats the entire time. The only way anything will change is if something gives. I didn't want it to be me, but Ghost doesn't know what the fuck he wants, and Siren's a stubborn fucking brat.

I reach for the knob, and a thud echoes from the other side. I grit my teeth as I slip inside, hoping she doesn't have another missile ready to launch at my head. She glares at me, her arms crossed over her shirt. *My shirt.* I put her in it without a second thought. I was too worried about her not breathing. Oliver kept telling me she was and not to worry. It was a particular low point in my life, being reassured by an eight-year-old. Or maybe he's ten. I have no idea.

"Where'd you send the kid?" she snarls as if I stuffed him in a closet or some shit.

"He's with Duchess." I give the bed a wide berth as I make my way to the closet.

I pull out another set of clothes for myself. I snatch a pair of sweatpants at the last second and spin around. She's still glaring at me, but it's easier to ignore her now.

"You hungry?" I ask, trying to keep my voice neutral as I turn to my drawers again.

She rustles behind me, but I can't force myself to leave the closet. Am I hiding? Maybe. I just know the moment I face her, I'll be reminded of her injuries. And I don't know how to process everything swirling through my head. I don't think she realizes how terrible she looks. Finding a mirror probably wasn't high on her list.

"Yes, but I want to shower."

"No."

She lets out a frustrated whine and the corner of my mouth twitches.

"You complete and utter asshole. Is it just ingrained in you? Did you fall off your bike and go through a complete personality change? Is that what the fuck happened? Because I don't remember you being so fucking annoying. Or bossy. Or—or—"

"Sexy?" The word slips out before I can stop myself.

I spin around, just to see her face. I expect her to still be glaring, but instead she's blushing and avoiding my gaze. She rolls her eyes, and I smirk.

"Cat got your tongue?"

Her jaw twitches like she's grinding her teeth. She was doing it while she slept, too. If she keeps it up, she's going to have more pain. It's most likely the reason her head aches. She kept complaining about it as I was carrying her back here. Bones didn't think she had a concussion, at least. She's probably dehydrated. And hungry. And exhausted. And I can't stop thinking about how much pain she's in. It's fucking annoying.

"I can't paralyze your tongue, much to my dismay," she mutters. "I don't even own a cat."

"What the fuck are you talking about?"

She sighs heavily as if I'm putting her out. "They don't know where the phrase *cat got your tongue* came from. Best guess is either the Middle Ages, where witch's cats were thought to either steal or paralyze your tongue, *or* ancient Egyptians."

"What'd the ancient Egyptians do?"

Her eyes meet mine and a sinister smile takes over her face. "They'd cut out your tongue and feed it to their cat. They're sacred, ya know."

"Tongues?"

"Cats. Why the hell would tongues be sacred? Especially when they're so removable."

"Cats are removable, too."

"The fuck they are. You clearly haven't spent much time around cats."

"Neither have you, genius."

She scoffs and winces when she shakes her head. "You don't know a goddamn thing about me, Storm. And you made fucking sure you never would. Now get the fuck out."

I stalk toward her, and she tips her chin up, defiance written in every line of her body, every grove of her skin, every scar marring her flesh.

"My room, sweets."

Her nostrils flare and she opens her mouth just to snap it shut again. A squeal leaves her when I scoop her up. She screams for me to put her down, then jerks in my hold. A choked sob leaves her.

"Stop squirming or I'll end up dropping you," I snap, and she stills.

"I need my backpack," she whispers. I glance down at her and find her chin tucked to her chest.

I carry her from the room and down the hall. She probably thinks I'm throwing her out, which is ridiculous. Why would I bring her back here just to toss her onto the street? I don't blame her for the thought. Unless she believes I'm moving her to headquarters. I'd let her put on pants if that was the case. Ghost would string me up by my intestines if I moved her. Especially without telling him.

"I can walk, Storm," she snarls.

"You'll fall on your face." I grip her harder as she wiggles in my arms. "Keep it up, sweets, and I'll end up giving you more reasons you can't walk."

She sputters, but at least she stops moving. Her muscles lock when I step into Ghost's bedroom. It's laid out similar to mine, but it's massive. He never did get rid of the bed we all used to share.

"Is that..." She swallows hard, her back rolling under my arm.

"Cost a lot of money," I grunt, and I turn toward the bathroom. "No use getting rid of something customized."

She cranes her neck to stare over my shoulder. I step into the steamy room, and she jolts. Gently, I lower her feet, keeping an arm around her waist. She leans into me, though I doubt she notices. I forgot how well she fit against my body. It takes everything in me to keep my mind off her curves, her skin, her heat. No matter how much I tell myself I don't want her, my cock doesn't listen.

"Thought you said I couldn't take a shower?" she whispers.

"Clearly, this is a bath."

I reach for the hem of her shirt, and she bats my hand away. "I don't need you to undress me."

I lean away from her and wait. It won't take long for her to realize she can't stay on her feet for long. I'll catch her whether she wants me to or not. My cock will be happy about it, at least.

"Get in the water."

"Why does it look weird?" she asks while she sways. I subtly take a step closer. I'd rather not have to make a call to Ghost admitting she cracked open her skull.

"It has Epsom salts in it. Just get in the fucking bath or I'll put you in there myself."

Her lip slips between her teeth, and she gnaws on the plump flesh. Even while she's sick, they're flushed a deep pink. I drag my gaze away from the sight and resist the urge to adjust myself. She'd clock me right away, and I'd rather ignore the familiarity between us. Because that's all this is—a reminder of what we once had.

She chose to blow up our lives. She chose to throw away everything. She chose to give up our futures. Which is why I shouldn't want to do anything for her. Except I can't seem to let her walk away right now. Blaming Ghost isn't working anymore.

"Time's up, sweets," I growl and step closer.

Her head snaps toward me, then her eyes slam shut. Her breath shudders out of her, and I grab her hips to steady her. I swallow hard when her palms press against my chest. When her forehead hits me, I realize how much she's trembling.

"Sorry," she breathes, trying to push away from me. "You can let me go."

"Not a chance in hell, Siren."

I pull her shirt up, keeping my eyes on the top of her head. Part of me wishes I would have kept it on instead of leaving her in just underwear. She's not even wearing a bra. She probably would've bitched about it when she was done trying not to puke. She doesn't protest when I pick her up.

"That's my ass," she whispers.

"Not the first time I've grabbed it. Just pretend it's not happening."

I lower her into the water and she gasps. She sinks down, slipping through my grasp. When she hits the bottom, she bursts into tears. I don't know what's happening and I end up on my knees next to the tub. I grip the edge to keep myself from snatching her back out. She covers her face, but it merely makes her slip down more. Her feet slide against the bottom. If she wasn't shuddering and sniffling, I might have walked away—let her have her breakdown in peace.

"Fuck it," I mutter and whip my shirt over my head before kicking off my pants.

I slide behind her and pull her into me. I wrap one arm around her waist and the other around her chest, holding her shoulder. She grips my wrist, and I expect her to shove me off her.

Instead, she clings to me. Every few seconds, her body jerks as she tries to hide her breakdown.

"Sorry," she whispers after several minutes, releasing her hold on me. "You can go."

When she tries to pull away, I resist. I should just walk out and pretend this didn't happen. I can't force myself to move, though. We could insist she shouldn't be here—for a million reasons. We could ignore the tension between us. We could imagine a world where she didn't betray us and we didn't banish her. Just for a little while, we could act like being here together was normal. It's just another night in a long line of nights we spent together. I tried for so long to let go of the fantasy of what could have been. I wonder if she did the same.

"Storm." Her voice cracks along with my heart. "You have to let me go."

No, I don't. "Why were you crying?"

Her shoulders slump and her chin rests on my forearm. "It's been a long time."

I wait for her to continue, but she doesn't. Slowly, the tension leaves her as the hot water and Epsom salts leach the tightness from her muscles. The water ripples as she swirls her hands through it. When her fingers brush my thighs, she doesn't notice, but I do. If she keeps it up, she'll feel my cock hardening against her ass and we'll be having a whole new conversation neither of us is ready for.

"A long time since what?" I finally ask gruffly.

"Since I've had a bath."

"Bullshit," I snarl, though there's no heat in my tone.

I can practically feel her rolling her eyes. She seems to do that a lot when she's around me.

She sighs. "I would have been fine taking a shower."

"If by fine you mean curled in the corner because you couldn't stand, then sure. More likely, you would have fainted and cracked your head open, which wouldn't have helped your headache."

"How'd you know I have a headache?"

"Your right eye droops when you have one. Plus, you winced whenever you moved your neck." I unravel my arm from her chest and reach over the side. "Drink this. You're probably dehydrated."

She glances over her shoulder, her nose crinkled. It's fucking adorable and I hate it. "I hate drinking water while I'm sitting in water."

"Suck it up, buttercup. After we're done here, you're going to eat, too."

She takes the bottle and mutters curses under her breath. They're probably directed at me, but I ignore them.

"I'm not hungry," she mutters after she drains half the bottle.

I snort as I slide my other arm around her waist. "You weren't thirsty either, but here we are."

"I'm allergic—"

"I know your allergies, Siren." It's a stark reminder of how well I know her, yet don't at all. "Did you have a cat? When you were gone?"

"No," she murmurs, then rests her head against my chest. Three inches to the left and my lips would be pressed to her temple. I bite my tongue and shove the thought aside. "Lived with an older woman for a couple months. She had a couple. They didn't like me. Probably because of the smell."

"You take up the habit of not showering?"

"Nah. I was cleaning houses and used a lot of vinegar. Cats don't like the smell. That's where I got these, actually. From the vinegar, not the cats, since they stayed away from me." She points to a few pinks areas on the back of her hand. Several spots mar her wrist and arm as well. "They're not as bad as they were. Most of my scars have faded."

I snatch up her hand in mine when she drops it below the water. As I examine the pale skin of her wrist, more scars become apparent. White lashes crisscrossing her skin underneath fresher ones. I've seen these types of injuries before. I've *made* these ones before.

"How many times did they kidnap you?" I ask in a low voice.

She shrugs, and I tighten my grip on her waist, my fingers digging into her flesh. "Couple dozen. As I got older, it got easier to hide. Plus, most of them were incompetent."

"They handcuffed you." I'm barely able to suppress the rage coursing through me. I thought when she left, she'd figure it out and be completely removed from our world.

"Sometimes. Other times it was zip ties. I told you some of them were incompetent. One guy used a drawstring from his hoodie. He underestimated me. Only took like an hour for me to get away from him. That was in the beginning, though." She says it flippantly, which does nothing for my fury.

Despite our past, or maybe because of it, I don't think she deserved this. She was right. I don't know what she's been through. For years, she was in the back of my mind no matter how much I tried to ignore it. With Ghost dragging her back into our life, I need to figure out a new way to live. Otherwise, we'll end up falling apart all over again.

Sixteen

Siren

Sleeping in a bathtub isn't the smartest thing I've done in my life. Then again, I've made worse decisions. Like trusting Storm to pick up my slippery body without dropping me.

I scratch at his skin, leaving red lines behind. His arm ends up between my legs and his hand grabs the back of my neck. It hurts and pulls at my stitches. I didn't even think I'd be able to get them wet, but I didn't think about it while I was begging for a shower. I have bigger issues to deal with right now. Especially since he's swinging me upright with his arm still grinding into my pussy.

"Stop fucking around, Siren," he growls in my ear as I clutch at his neck.

"You're the one who tried to kill me by throwing me on the ground."

"You're fucking slippery. And I was trying not to wake you up." As if that's an explanation.

"Just put me down," I whine, then gasp as his bone hits my clit. I shouldn't react to him, but I can't control my body. I'm not surprised. It makes sense since I was once in love with them, and I never got closure. We were entwined in each other's lives so completely it would be hard to just stop caring for or wanting them.

"I don't trust you," Storm says as he shuffles across the tile.

"Well established," I mutter.

He sets me on the cover of the toilet and slides his arm out. His fingers stroke along my wet underwear and I suppress a shudder. I swear he slows down as he does it. I wouldn't put it past him to tease me just to fuck with me.

He grabs a towel and wraps it around me. I huddle in the thick cloth as he makes his way back to the tub. I don't remember the bathroom being so large. Glancing around, I realize Ghost knocked out a wall and expanded the space into the closet. There's a large separate shower, complete with a bench. I didn't notice how big the tub was, but Storm and I fit comfortably inside.

He doesn't hesitate when he's in front of me again and rips the bath sheet away. I cross my arms over my chest, though I don't know why. It's not like he hasn't seen me completely naked before, even if it has been years. Except they did undress me when I was unconscious. Not the same thing, though. Especially after he was in the bathtub with me.

When he drops to his knees, I suck in a sharp breath. "I can dry myself off, Storm."

He ignores me, yanking off my wet underwear, then using the towel to dry off one leg and then the other. He moves to my thigh, and I stare at the ceiling. If I don't look at him, I can pretend this isn't happening. The fabric brushes between my legs and I press my lips together. The ones on my face since I'm not talented enough to move the lower ones.

He groans and my head snaps down. He struggles to his feet, his knees popping as he does. I fight a smile and fail until he scoops me up once more. A strangled cry leaves me, and he grumbles as he drops me on the long counter between the two sinks. When I try to slide off, his hands land on my thighs. He leans close and I tense.

"Stop. Moving."

"Or what?" The question pops out and I squeeze my eyes

shut, wishing I could shove the words back in. "Don't answer that."

He chuckles, then shakes his head. "I need to look at your stitches. If you keep moving, you'll rip them out."

"There's like three. I'll be fine."

"Try twelve." He ducks down and tries to push my arm away.

"Can I at least get a fucking shirt?"

"Nothing I haven't seen before, sweets. Just move your damn arms so I can see."

I shake my head, though his gaze is focused on my side. He swats at my elbow, but I refuse to move. It's one thing to sit with my back pressed against his chest in a bathtub so I don't accidentally waterboard myself. It's something completely different to have my tits shoved in his face.

He glares up at me, and a vein throbs in his forehead. I have the ridiculous urge to reach out and smooth it down. That would require me to move my arms, though.

"Give me a shirt and I'll tuck it up."

"For fuck's sake," he breathes, then grabs my wrists and yanks them away. He forces my arms behind me despite my protests. When my fists hit the counter, he snarls in my face.

"Stop being a fucking brat and keep them there."

He releases me slowly, then ducks his head to examine my healing wound. His finger pokes at the neat line of stitches, and I whimper. It doesn't exactly hurt, but the skin pulls every time I take a breath. He glances up at me and I bite my tongue, trying to plaster a bored expression on. I'm not sure it works. His gaze dips and my cheeks heat. A flush travels down my neck and I desperately will it away. I'm not turned on. Well, I am because it's been a long time since I've had an orgasm, but that's not why I'm blushing.

He reaches up and traces a scar just below my collarbone. His thumb presses into a particularly nasty bruise on my sternum and I wince. So much for not reacting. He trails his finger down my body, tracing each dip, every mark, every flaw. My skin is a map of all the hurt I've been subjected to in the years since I was banished. I've never thought much of them, but it's embarrassing.

"That's not where the stitches are," I whisper.

"Some of these are...faded. *Most* of them are faded."

"Is there a question in there?" I try to infuse snark into my words. Instead, it comes out breathlessly, as if I actually give a shit. Convincing myself I'm totally unaffected by him is a fool's errand.

"No questions." He stands abruptly, and I jerk upright to cover myself again. "Get dressed."

He stomps from the room, slamming the door behind him. I peer at the floor, wondering how I'm going to get down by myself. I don't want to call him back in. If I jump, I might end up sprawled across the tiles. The hot water was enough to relax me, but not enough to erase the ache in my bones. I'll break one if I'm not careful. I should be pissed Storm left me after the shit he pulled, except I don't have it in me.

"It's totally fine. Get me all hot and bothered and then walk the fuck away," I mutter. "I can take care of myself, and I'll prove it by getting down from here without breaking anything."

I ease my body forward, then brace my palms on the counter. My arms shake as I lift myself up. I grimace when my ass slides against the edge and my knees threaten to give out when my feet hit the ground. Rage, shame, and disappointment coalesce inside my chest, making it hard to breathe. I press my fist over my heart and double over as tears fill my eyes.

Desperately, I try to think of anything else other than how much I've failed. It doesn't even matter if I betrayed them or whether I was fucked over. I haven't done anything since then other than escape. Surviving was my only goal just to end up right back here. No matter how far I ran, fate decided to fuck with me one last time. Petty bitch.

I end up in a ball on the ground, blinking rapidly to get rid of the tears. This isn't like me, even with the kidnapping and the injuries. Those things are typical in my life. My frequent breakdowns are all *their* fault. Ghost doesn't know whether to throw my ass out or keep me locked up. And Storm can't figure out if he hates me or wants me. If it was solely up to him, I would be on a train to the other side of the country right now. Not that I could afford to go that far.

Footsteps echo through the room, and I push to all fours before crawling toward the shirt Storm removed. I shove the explosion of emotions aside, willing them away as best I can. Whatever happens from here on out doesn't really matter as long as I can escape Prophet. Maybe the Phantoms will distract the Disciples with a war, and I can slip away without anyone noticing.

The door flies open, and Storm lets out an exasperated sound from the back of his throat. "What the fuck are you doing?"

"Getting dressed," I say through gritted teeth. "Little privacy would be great since you've already ogled my body."

He stomps around and gathers the clothes. He tosses the shirt I was wearing before into a hamper tucked away in the corner. I wish I had my own clothes. Instead, I'm stuck with charity items sourced from Ghost and Storm's closets. I wonder if they share. Clothes, that is, not closets. Although they probably have their stuff scattered throughout the house. They've intertwined their lives so seamlessly it makes my heart ache. I could have been part of all this.

"I wasn't ogling your fucking body. I was trying to figure out...never mind." He drops a pair of sweatpants in front of me before stuffing my head into a new shirt.

I sit back on my knees and bite back a groan when I lift my arms. Storm doesn't wait for me to struggle my way through it and tucks my hands into the sleeves. Gently, he pushes me onto my ass and straightens my legs. I feel a little bit like a rag doll being dressed by a particularly ornery toddler. From the look on Storm's face, he's not much different from a three-year-old throwing a silent temper tantrum.

"What could you possibly be trying to figure out with your face in my tits?"

"Couldn't see your tits through all the bruises." He pushes

the sweatpants up my legs. "I was trying to figure out how often they'd hurt you."

"You can't tell that by a bunch of scars."

He glances up, and I shiver from the fierceness in his gaze. "That wasn't an answer."

I shrug, feigning indifference as I stare at my scraped knees. "You didn't ask a question."

His fingers grip my chin roughly, and he tips my head up until our eyes meet. "How much did they hurt you?"

"I wasn't keeping a list. Why do you care, anyways?"

He releases me and returns to dressing me. "I don't know."

"Sounds like you should answer that question before you start demanding shit from me."

He doesn't respond, merely tucks his hands under my arms and lifts me. He waits until I'm steady on my feet before he tugs the sweatpants up. Exhaustion swamps me while my stomach growls. I can't figure out if I want to eat first, then sleep or just fall into bed again and ignore my hunger. I might end up unconscious, face down in my plate.

When Storm drops to his knees again, I sway. He grabs me around the waist and my hands end up on his shoulders.

"Don't fall over," he growls, then folds the hem of one pant leg, then the other. "Can you walk? Or do I need to carry you again?"

"You didn't need to carry me before," I grumble.

He huffs, then scoops me up. I don't bother to protest this time. He'll do whatever the fuck he wants, regardless of my opinion. I'm done wasting my breath. The tips of his fingers dig into the side of my breast. I wonder if he even notices. From the set of his jaw, he does. Not that he'd do anything about it. And I don't want him to.

As much as his touch lights me up and reminds me of another time, I don't want to get involved with them. As soon as they decide I'm no longer useful to them, I'll be gone. If I let them back in, even for one night of fun, I'll end up with a broken heart.

One small crack in my armor and they'll seep in, infiltrating every bit of my being until they've completely taken over. They'll rewire my brain. And then they'll take it away. The pleasure. The safety. My very soul will cry out for them.

I know because I've been living in the wasteland of their abandonment for six years. If it happens again, I won't survive.

Seventeen

Ghost

Fuse yammers on about things I'd rather not think about yet. Except I've been neglecting my duties as a president. Even with years of setting up the Phantoms to run a bit without me, I still can't neglect them for long. Storm has been doing the best he can in my stead, but we're used to tackling club issues together.

Fuse seems to think my presence here means I'm ready to hear everything that's happened in the past two weeks. As if I want to hear about the latest run that went sideways or the profit counts of our restaurants.

"Ghost, I get you've been through some shit, but I need you to pay attention." Fuse leans back in his chair and crosses his arms.

"Watch it, Fuse. I can replace you just as easily as I replaced Jag," I sneer.

He rolls his eyes. "You didn't replace Jag. Man ran off to fu—"

My chair knocks back as I lunge at him. He ends up sprawled across the floor, my hand around his throat. Silence descends through the large space, but all I can hear is the heavy beating of my heart in my ears and Fuse's harsh breath rattling from his lungs. The man looks petrified under his beard. As he should.

"You want to finish that sentence?"

"No, sir," he gasps. "Sorry."

I lean in so no one else can overhear us. "Say shit about my sister again and I'll rip your dick off and shove it down your throat, then feed you to the stray dogs roaming the outskirts of town. Remember your place, Lucas."

His Adam's apple bobs under my grip, and he nods as best he can. I release him slowly and right my chair before sinking into it. Fuse coughs several times and pushes to his feet. If he knows what's good for him, he'll pretend our little interlude never happened. If he makes a big deal out of it, especially with the others surreptitiously watching us, I'll end up truly losing it. Storm mentioned a few of them were still questioning my leadership. Hopefully, my display of power was enough to get them to think twice about challenging me.

Fuse clears his throat and drains his water before glancing at me again. "The one we talked about before is still running their mouth. Disciples seem to have shored up their defenses. Our contacts have gone quiet. We don't know if they're dead or just laying low."

"Lying," I mutter as I gaze around the room.

"Huh?"

"It's lying low, not laying."

"Does it matter?"

I sigh, tapping my finger on the scarred surface of the table. Someone's been whittling away at the edges and attempting to carve the Phantom's sigil into the top. They're failing miserably. I didn't come here to give Fuse a grammar lesson. Or a lesson in decorum. Everyone should know not to talk shit about my sister. It was hard enough letting her stay in Rima. Not that I had a choice, which she was quick to remind me of.

"We need to call a meeting before everyone goes rogue," I say, choosing to focus on his first statement. I'm sure he's talking about Venom. Most of the members around us are older, and Venom is one of them. They don't go out as much as they used to unless it's to ride. I don't begrudge most of them, and I doubt they're on Venom's side in anything. They help our numbers and keep the younger ones in line. They're not looking to overthrow me.

"New recruits came through from Sandown. Brick wants up to put 'em through the gauntlet. I told him we didn't have shit set up for that, but he insisted. Said they were transplants, not homegrown."

"We're not taking anyone right now. Shit isn't sitting right here. Until we figure it out, only emergencies get through. Change the routes of all our runs. Anyone who hasn't partnered with us since I've become president, put on a list," I say, and Fuse blinks at me. "Do you need to write this down?"

He fumbles with his phone, and I knock it from his hand. He nods once, then rushes to get a piece of paper and pen from the bar tucked away in the corner. Members slide out of his way without a second glance. They're used to people rushing around. Once he's back at the table, he scribbles down my instructions. He knows if he fucks this up, he'll have to ask Storm for help, and that never goes well for him.

"What do you want me to do with the list?"

"Give it to me. I'll decide who stays and who gets paused."

"Do we need to—"

I hold up my hand and shake my head. There's quite a bit I'm willing to talk about in front of my men. His question isn't one of them. We're not going on lockdown, and we sure as hell aren't calling in reinforcements. Until we know what we're actually up against, I'm not spooking anyone. Shit goes sideways real fucking fast once they think they're about to die. Everyone ends up with an opinion and no one wants to listen. I've got enough to deal with. Including the woman sequestered away in my house.

The double doors crash open and Lexi stomps in. I slide lower in my seat, hoping the sea of others hides me. I don't have the energy to deal with her. My strength is already lagging. I check my phone and see I've been here for almost an hour. I don't even remember half the shit he said.

"Ghost," Lexi bellows across the space, and I wince.

Her boots stomp across the tiles, delivering her right in front of me. "What the fuck is wrong with you?"

"If you've got a complaint, Lexi, I'm sure Fuse can help you." I push to my feet, and she shoves me back. I glare at her, but she's unfazed.

"Are we really going to do this whole Romeo and Juliet thing?" She waves her hands around. "Did you never read Shakespeare? For fuck's sake."

I glance at Fuse, and he shakes his head with wide eyes. "Lexi, you seem to be upset—"

"Of course I'm fucking upset," she bellows, and I grit my teeth. "You're indiscriminately making decisions without thinking of the fallout for the rest of us—particularly *me*."

I stand slowly and apprehension flashes across her face. She stands her ground, though. I can respect that, but I also can't let her continue to harp on me about...I actually don't know what the fuck she's going on about. I jerk my head toward my office, then weave my way through the tables. Lexi better be following me or we're going to have problems. No one pays me any attention as I walk. They're used to Lexi flying off the handle. She's one of the few people who can talk to me like she does. I'm sure more than a couple of them assume I'm sleeping with her, which is disgusting.

I hold open the door and Lexi stomps past me. Fuse hovers at the end of hall as if I'm going to invite him in. He takes a half step toward us. I close the door, leaving Lexi sequestered inside. She squawks but doesn't come out. Thank fuck.

Stopping in front of Fuse, I cross my arms. "What do you need, Fuse?"

"Oh, uh, just wondering what else you needed me to do."

"I didn't give you enough?"

He huffs, running his hand through his light hair. "Lexi kind of interrupted us. I just wanted to make sure—" A loud thud echoes from behind me as Lexi kicks the door. "On second thought, I'll just ask Storm."

"Don't ask Storm."

The thought of Fuse rocking up to the house with Siren inside has my stomach tightening. It was hard enough to brush him off when she was kidnapped. Getting him out while Storm was freaking out wasn't easy. He's probably still trying to figure out what the hell was going on. As long as he doesn't ask me, we'll be fine.

I expect him to argue, but instead he nods and walks away. I sigh before heading to my office. Lexi is pacing across the floor, muttering under her breath when I walk in. When I point at the chair, she huffs before collapsing into it. I settle behind my desk and fold my hands over my stomach.

"Would you like to explain what the fuck you're upset about without the yelling?"

She straightens and fixes me with a glare. "We can't afford to lock down Harris."

"You don't care whether or not we can afford it. What's the real reason?"

She crosses her arms and her legs and her foot bounces with pent up energy. "Locking down would be disastrous. For everyone."

"Including you."

"Yes, including me. I'm part of the Phantoms, aren't I? I realize you haven't made us women full members, but still."

I grit my teeth. There's not much of an argument I can give her. I've implemented a lot of changes since I became president, but I haven't been able to completely change the landscape. Some put us at risk from the Disciples. Others will weaken our position in Harris. Giving women full rights as members would create an upheaval I don't think we're ready for. There are still plenty of

Snake loyalists within our ranks. Unbeknownst to most of the members, I've been riding a fine line for years. They're just waiting for one misstep on our part and then they'll strike.

"I'm working on it, Lexi. Unfortunately, I can't share everything I have in the works. Or what I'm dealing with, regardless of you being a member or not. No one is privy to what Storm and I discuss regarding the club. Now, would you like to get back on track?"

"You're fucking insufferable. I swear to...you know what? Never mind." She jumps to her feet, and I waver on whether I should stop her.

"Sit down, Lexi. I'm not locking anything down. Where did you hear that?"

She turns back slowly and eases herself into the chair. "It wasn't one person. People are talking about it. Plus, I got a text about your little meeting with Fuse just now. Perhaps you shouldn't have conversations out in public."

"And how exactly would a lockdown hurt you specifically? You work in Harris. You don't travel. You have no friends outside of the ones in the Phantoms that I know of."

"Rude," she mutters. "You don't know everything about my life, Ghost."

"So, you're telling me you're what? Sneaking off to another town? Planning a trip? Got big plans to fall in fucking love?" The last question comes out bitterly, and I glance away.

"Bitter much? You can't control my life, Ghost."

I bite the inside of my cheek. Lashing out at her won't help either of us. It's hard balancing my relationship with her. I spent most of my life looking out for Avery, my sister. When Lexi showed up, it was different.

"I'm not controlling your life, Lexi."

"You're trying. Just because we're related—" She stops when I stiffen, my eyes shooting to the door. "No one is lurking behind the fucking door, Ghost. They won't find out your dirty little secret."

"Don't make shit weird. You know goddamn well why no one knows you're my sister." I sigh, gripping the back of my neck. "I'm trying to protect you, Lex. You have no idea what the hell some of these guys will do if they find out you're..."

"A weakness." She swallows hard, then shakes her head. "I just don't want to be locked away in a cage. Are you sure you're not making decisions because of your emotions?"

"What the fuck does that mean?"

She pushes to her feet, though she's much calmer this time around. I don't expect her to actually answer. She's a fucking brat like that. Maybe I coddled her too much. She was a teenager when she showed up in Harris searching for her father. Breaking the news to her that he was dead was surprisingly easy. I didn't have to deal with tears or yelling or denial. She just said okay and tried to walk away.

Lexi pauses before she pulls open the door, and I drag myself from my memories. "I don't know how Siren showing up here affected you, but she's gone now. Maybe you should pull yourself out of the past and the what-ifs before you make a mistake."

She disappears before I can respond. Not that I'd know what to say. If she finds out Siren is still in town, she'll throw a fit and blame me. She'd never fault Storm. For some reason, she's always treated him like a delicate flower. They have a weird bond I've never fully understood. She treats him like a little brother in need of coddling, which doesn't make sense since she's younger than us. It's annoying.

My phone buzzes and I groan at the text. I just need a break. I doubt I'll get one anytime soon. With Fuse pushing my buttons and Lexi speaking in riddles, I'm becoming over-whelmed. Add in Siren's presence and Storm up my ass about her, I'm two seconds away from saying fuck it. For the first time in a long time, I'm wishing I wasn't president. It's not a great place to be.

The longer I keep Siren here, the more complicated my life will get. I should send her on her way to wherever the hell she came from. She clearly doesn't have any information we need. The only reason I want to keep her around is guilt.

If she dies because I kicked her out of Phantom territory, it'd be my fault. There are other ways to keep her safe rather than sticking her in Storm's bed. We need to make a decision about her soon. Otherwise, she'll only dig her claws in deeper than they already are.

Eighteen

STORM

"Why am I not in the hole?"

Siren's question catches me off guard, and my phone slips from my numb fingers. My head snaps up, and I find her absorbed in her food. She's on her third sandwich. I fully expect her to puke any minute now.

"You weren't even supposed to be here," I mutter and grab my phone again. Ghost isn't responding and it's putting me on edge.

"He's fine, you know. Plenty of people around to step in if he keels over."

I grit my teeth. "I know that." *Logically.* Unfortunately, my brain isn't thinking logically.

"Probably hard to convince yourself. I get that. Except he's perfectly capable of taking care of himself. Then again, I don't know how he got hurt, so maybe he can't take care of himself. Still, the other members are there so—"

"Stop," I growl. She's babbling and it's not helping my anxiety.

I don't know what transformation she went through in the bath. The thought reminds me of her almost naked body. Even with the bruises and scars scattered across her skin, she was beautiful. Maybe it's just my memories lying atop her flesh. Because when I look deeper, I see all the wounds time has wrought upon her. Gashes and marks that weren't there before. Evidence of a time we weren't there to shield her. My guilt wars with her betrayal. She threw away our protection, alleviating us of the responsibility. So why can't I convince myself each wound she received wasn't my fault?

"What's with the flowers?" she asks, jarring me from my thoughts.

"What flowers?"

She waves her half-full glass vaguely in the direction of the front of the house. "Around the porch. I mean, they're dead now that it's fall, but they were there. Who planted them?"

"Ghost did."

The water sloshes in her cup again, and I grimace.

"What kind? I thought I saw some chrysanthemums, which was a little surprising. I suppose it doesn't matter either way. Are there a lot? I'm surprised he had the time to set everything up. Especially while he's running the Phantoms. Being president probably isn't easy. I suppose he needs some type of hobby to deal with the stress. Surprising he picked flowers. Thought he'd just use fucking since that was his go-to before. I suppose it isn't all *that* surprising—"

I drop my phone on the table, and she jolts but still doesn't look up. "What the fuck is wrong with you?"

"Nothing. Just making conversation."

"Really. Just making conversation. Are you sure that's it?"

Her eyes dart up, then drop to her plate again before she mutters, "Not like you're filling the silence."

"So you decided to dig for what? Info on the Phantoms since you've been gone? Maybe find out about my relationship with Ghost? Both of us know you don't give a shit about the fucking flowers. The ones that aren't even alive right now. Stop hiding behind some bullshit excuse and just ask your damn questions."

She stares at me, her mouth open. "If you didn't want to talk, you could have just said that." She gathers her plate. "I think I'm done. Thanks for the food."

She drops her dishes in the sink, her head swiveling around as if she's searching for something. I didn't think she was really digging for info to pass onto the Disciples. Unless she's become a really good actress, she isn't working with them anymore. She's nosy, though. Even if she isn't helping them, doesn't mean they can't drag shit out of her. I've heard how they deal with snitches over there—how they get people to talk. We've even picked up a few of their victims afterward. It's never pretty.

"That's it?" I call as she starts out of the room.

"Excuse me?"

"You've been babbling for twenty fucking minutes about the most random things. Then you start talking about the goddamn flowers." I spin in my seat until I'm facing her. "I accuse you of being a fucking spy and you just...walk away? That shit isn't like you. You don't walk away when someone pushes your buttons. So, what the fuck is wrong with you?"

She swallows hard, pain flashing in her eyes, then shakes her head. A blank expression takes over her face and I know I've lost her. Whatever truth I was hoping to wring from her is lost to the void within her eyes. I doubt she'll reveal anything either way. I haven't exactly made her feel welcome.

"Why didn't you put me in the hole?"

"Why the fuck would we put you in there?"

"Stop answering questions with another question. It's frustrating," she says in a monotone voice.

"Don't seem very frustrated. You don't seem even a little bit upset." I slowly push to my feet and prowl toward her. She stiffens the closer I get, the only indication she's rattled by what I've said. "Tell me, sweets. Are you really angry at me?"

She grits her teeth, her jaw twitching, and I lean into her space. "You're not important enough to be angry at."

I raise a single eyebrow. "Is that so?"

She swallows hard and her tongue darts out to lick her lips.

What I wouldn't give to be in her head right now. After ten seconds, she glances away and sways. My palms itch to grab her, but I force myself closer instead. She stumbles back a step, then another. I keep pace with her until her back hits the wall and I cage her in with my hands on either side of her head.

"Tell me again how unimportant I am. How you weren't wet when I had you in my arms. How you didn't burrow into my bed, surrounded by my scent and dream of me. How you are completely unaffected by my presence." My lips brush her ear, and she sucks in a deep breath. "Lie to me."

"You're an asshole," she says breathlessly.

I let out a harsh laugh. "Not a lie."

"You don't know me. Not anymore."

"Pretty sure I still know how to get you hot and bothered. And leave you wanting."

I step back, and she sags against the wall. I could leave her there just like I threatened. She doesn't deserve anything from me. My mind screams to walk away while my knee tucks itself between her legs. I don't remember moving toward her once more. I'm no longer making decisions for my body.

Her palms slap against the wood. Her head does the same a second later. She glares at me when I smirk, but there's a glint of desire resting in her eyes.

"You should go," she whispers harshly.

I tilt my head, scanning her face. "Should I?"

A frustrated noise leaves her, and she slams her hands against the wall again. "Stop fucking playing with me, Storm. I'm not in the fucking mood."

"Are you sure about that? If I dipped my fingers into that pretty little pussy of yours, what would I find?" I run a single finger down her arm and goosebumps erupt across her skin.

"You'd find a fucking desert. I think you've forgotten how women are seduced. You think if you throw out a couple dirty words and crowd me against the wall I'll melt at your feet?" She lets out a harsh laugh. "You think insulting me and making demands will have me dizzy with desire? That shit might work on whatever fling you bring in, but it's certainly not going to work on me."

A smirk tilts my lips, and I shift my leg. My knee grinds into her clit, making her tense. She's trying so hard not to be affected by me. Sure, it could just be her body's biological reaction. Or it could be all the memories flooding back to her. Either way, I intend to exploit it. I haven't decided why yet. Those are questions to be answered later. When I'm alone and can hate myself in peace.

"From what I remember, you got wet no matter how I treated you. In fact, quite often you liked when I degraded you," I murmur, running my nose along her jaw. My hand lands on her hip and I squeeze. She tries to slide away from me, but my other hand traps her. Not to mention my knee between her legs.

"Too bad for you I've grown up. I've moved on. Maybe you should do the same." She tips her chin up and levels me with a stare. "Move."

"Or what?"

Her lips purse, pulling my gaze down. Her nostrils flare as I ease forward. I'm still debating whether to actually kiss her or tease her some more when her fist slams into my side. I double over, my kidney on fire. She shoves my shoulders, and I stumble back until I crash into her empty dining chair. Nausea bubbles in my stomach as pain radiates from my body.

"Whoops." Siren lets out an uncharacteristic giggle, and I grit my teeth as I breathe shallowly.

She skips away, though her steps are jerky like she's still in pain. My vision blurs and I cough, which sends bolts of pain radiating from my side.

"You should be glad she didn't have a knife," Ghost chuckles and collapses in the seat across from me. "What'd you do?"

It takes me several minutes to be able to straighten. He waits, picking at the bowl of grapes Siren left behind. I'll be sore for a while, but she didn't do any lasting damage. If she was at full strength, she probably would have ruptured my kidney. She always had bony fucking knuckles.

"I pissed her off," I wheeze.

He rolls his eyes, then sets his phone down. "We've got enough problems without you antagonizing her."

"She's being a fucking bitch."

His eyes narrow the slightest bit, and I realize I've stepped over the line. To be fair, he's been a little bitch these days, too. I don't assign gender to those who are bitches.

"We need to talk about getting her out," he murmurs.

My head snaps up, and I groan as my kidney pulses. "I thought we agreed she needed to stay. In fact, you're the reason she's here in the first place."

"We're not going to dither about who brought her here. Shit has changed, though. I have Fuse putting in some parameters to brace for whatever the Disciples have planned." He runs his hand through his hair. It used to be blond, but the older we got, the more silver the strands became. Now the color is dull and the strands are limp. He looks like he's aged five years in the last few weeks.

"If you put everything in place, why would we throw her out? Prophet will snatch her up the first chance he can get. Thought you wanted to avoid that." I cross my arms, then grunt. I drop my elbows on the table and concentrate on my breathing.

He glances over his shoulder. "If one of us takes her far enough, he wouldn't be able to reach her. Couple hundred miles should do it. Besides, you were pushing for this not too long ago. What changed?"

I bite my cheek. "I don't know."

"Doesn't matter anyway. We need her gone."

"What the hell happened with Fuse?"

His jaw twitches and rage flashes in his blue eyes. "Keep an eye on him. He's getting too familiar with us. Thinks he's one of us."

"He *is* one of us. He's been our third for a couple years now, Ghost."

"No. I mean, like we are. If you pull shit like he did today, I wouldn't knock your ass out of a chair and strangle the shit out of you."

I smirk and raise an eyebrow. "No, I get that for free."

He chuckles, then sobers. "Lexi accosted me in the middle of headquarters. She was speaking in riddles, but she was afraid we were going into lockdown. When I questioned why it would matter, she blew me off."

"You think she got into something? Does she know Siren is here? I'm guessing not, since she'd be busting down our door if she did."

"She doesn't know Siren is here. But she's definitely got something going on. Doubt it's anything important," he mutters, and I raise an eyebrow. "You know what I mean. It's not like I think she's into anything dirty."

I grimace. "Don't say shit like that."

"Like what?"

"Dirty and Lexi shouldn't be in the same sentence. She's our fucking sister."

"Technically, she's my half-sister. You're not really related to her." He sighs, scrubbing his hands down his face. "If Siren stays here, shit will go sideways. We can't do it all. If she's telling the truth about Prophet putting plans in motion, then we need to focus on that."

I nod, and my eyes dart over his shoulder. "Might as well come out, Siren."

She stomps into view and Ghost tenses. I don't know what Fuse or Lexi could have said to change his mind, but we need to hash this out. As much as she's fucking with our lives and emotions, I won't throw her out on the streets. I'd rather keep her right where I can see her. And if that excuse doesn't appease the small voice inside of me, too damn bad. I won't admit she's breaking down the walls I built up all those years ago to protect myself from more heartache. I refuse to do anything other than keep her alive.

Nineteen

Siren

This impromptu meeting can only go one of two ways. Either they pack me up and ship me off or they demand I stay. I didn't think they'd switch positions. I can't figure out which way I want to go. Do I advocate to stick around? I'd be safe for a bit. If Ghost has put enough safeguards in place, the Disciples won't be able to get in again. On the other hand, I've been trying to leave since I got here. Coming back to Harris was a mistake. Storm's little display is evidence of that.

"Have a seat, Siren," Storm says, gesturing to the chair between them, then wincing. A better person than me would apologize for hurting him. I am not a better person.

"Where'd the other table go?" I ask as I plop into a seat. My muscles scream, but it feels good to get off my feet. Crouching by the stairs while eavesdropping on them didn't do my body any favors.

"Don't bother," Storm says, cutting off Ghost. "She doesn't really care. She's in a babbling mood today."

I cross my arm, though the move stretches my stitches. "I actually do want to know. You burn it after I left?"

Ghost sighs, his gaze bouncing between us. "We just moved it. Replaced it with this one, though I'm surprised you noticed."

"Why wouldn't I? I mean, I get it looks exactly the same as the other one, but there's no nicks in it. Honestly, it looks like you just bought it." I keep my eyes on Ghost but catch Storm glancing at him as well. "So, where's the other one?"

Storm may call it babbling, and let's be honest, most of it is. He threw me off when he started touching me—when he woke the long dormant desire within me. It took me a while, but I'm finally annoyed. Before I was disoriented, so I prattled on about anything that popped in my head. It might not have been the best way to cope. Doesn't matter either way. I have a feeling no matter how I reacted, Storm would have had a problem with it— with me.

"We don't have time to discuss the furniture, Siren. Where were you living before?" Ghost asks, and I shake my head.

"Can't go back there," I mutter.

"Why not? Burn all your bridges there?" Storm sneers.

My gaze cuts to him. "Because Prophet would check there. Plus, it's hundreds of miles from here. It doesn't matter how far you ship me off, he'll find me. Unless you're willing to put me on a plane for Dublin, which I wouldn't object to."

"You're not going to fucking Dublin," Storm growls, and I shake my head.

I stare at the unblemished surface and my vision blurs. Emotions I've been ignoring roar to the forefront of my mind. I could call it nostalgia, but it feels like more than that. Being in Phantom territory, sequestered with these two, it feels like living the life I was supposed to have. Beyond Ghost and Storm, though, is something deeper. The Phantoms were my home. It was my safe space. I never thought I'd have to leave. I was born here and I expected to die here. When everything fell apart, I was lost and I never found myself again. I left most of my pieces here, embedded in this soil. Since Ghost called me back, my soul has been searching for those pieces. They're here. I can feel it in my bones. If they banish me again, I'll leave without the fragments and exist as a shell for however much longer I live. It's depressing.

I wrap my arms around my stomach and push my thoughts aside. "I just need a ride to the station. Unless you're willing to give me a bike. And maybe a sweatshirt. I know better than to ask for a jacket."

Ghost's nostrils flare, and Storm makes a sound in the back of his throat. Neither of them responds, though. If they don't get their shit together soon, we'll be in limbo forever. I can't handle living with the uncertainty of my future. I won't beg them to stay, no matter how I feel.

I clear my throat. "Backpack."

"Map," Storm says, and I glance at him. "Thought we were just yelling random shit."

"No. I need my backpack, douche canoe. I've been asking for it since you hauled my ass here."

"And if we didn't, you'd be dead."

"If you would have let me get on the damn train, I wouldn't have been kidnapped."

"Then you would have died on a fucking train instead."

"Enough," Ghost says quietly, and I snap my mouth shut. "Prophet will be too busy trying to start a war with us to go after you, Siren. We'll make sure he doesn't have the manpower either."

I shake my head but don't respond. There's nothing I can say. He's speaking like he wants me to change his mind. My shoulders slump and a heavy sigh leaves me. I'm sick of being in the middle of these two. The push and pull is too much. It always was. I spent much of our childhood and into our teenage years playing mediator between them. I finally put my foot down, claiming I was a neutral party and refused to be their referee. They fixed their shit back then. Now, it's as if they forgot how to be goddamn adults with their own relationship.

"Doesn't change the fact I need my things. I'm sure I can make it to the train by myself if you're going to throw a fit about it." I lean back in the chair.

"Surprised you're not putting up a fight," Storm mutters.

"Why would I do that? I never wanted to stay here. I made

that clear. Hell, I didn't want to come here in the first place." I glance away, ignoring the ache blossoming in my chest.

Ghost leans forward and rests his forearms on the table, threading his fingers together. "Why did you come?"

I snort dismissively. "Because Storm texted me. Or rather, *you* did under false pretenses."

"Except you had no reason to listen. I'm surprised you didn't block us, much less kept the same number. You could have ignored me."

"You could have texted back," Storm interjects.

"I did, asshole," I snap.

Ghost clears his throat, a guilty look flashing in his eyes. "It doesn't matter. Instead of ignoring us, you came. Without hesitation. Based on how much of a brat you were that first night, you clearly weren't hoping for a joyful reunion. So, why'd you come?"

I swallow and dig my nails into my arms. "Whatever answer I give will do nothing. It won't satisfy your curiosity. It won't solve some grand mystery. No secrets will be revealed. You called. I came. End of story."

"You came when you were injured," Storm says quietly. "Prophet's men grabbed you. You got stabbed. You got away. Then you came here. Almost like you needed help and hoped you'd find it here."

"Seriously? That wasn't the first time I'd been stabbed. Or shot. Or had the shit beaten out of me." I yank up my shirt to reveal the myriad of bruises scattered across my stomach. "You think this is the worst that's been done to me? You think I didn't agonize for years about my decisions? You think I was having a grand ole time out there, just living my best life, then at the first sign of trouble I came running back here? Fuck you, Storm. And fuck you, too, Ghost."

Ghost straightens. "What the hell did I do?"

I shove to my feet. "You're the reason I'm in this mess in the first place. Now, can I please get my damn backpack and my own fucking pants?"

Hysteria bubbles up my throat, threatening to choke me. Storm's sweatpants barely stay up. I've already tripped on the hems twice. If I don't get out of them, I'll end up breaking my neck. Maybe then they'd give me my pants again. Not that I could really appreciate my leggings if I was dead.

"It's in my closet," Storm murmurs, and Ghost gapes at him.

I don't wait for him to pull me back into another ridiculous conversation. He didn't care what I had to say before and he doesn't now. He just likes to hear himself talk. Which would probably surprise anyone who isn't close to him. Others think he's all mysterious. It's laughable.

I slide around the table, steering clear of Storm. When I pass Ghost, his hand latches onto my wrist. His grip is light, but it doesn't matter. I'm frozen to the spot. The rest of the world falls away. The ticking of the clock fades. Storm's presence blurs in the background. Only Ghost and I remain in this bubble. A shiver rolls down my spine when his thumb brushes the underside of my wrist.

"Sit down," he growls.

"Why?" I whisper. "There's nothing more to say."

He squeezes his eyes shut. "I have more questions."

I rip from his grasp and his hand drops. "I've answered all your questions. I have nothing else to say."

I walk away, keeping my steps quiet. I'm afraid if I make too much noise, I'll shatter. Or one of them will come after me. Harsh whispers chase me up the stairs, and I'm gasping by the time I reach the top. I stumble into Storm's room and shut the door softly, then lean against it.

When Snake banished me before, I left in a rush. I barely had time to pack a bag. I didn't even get to say goodbye to Lexi or Avery. Ghost and Storm were nowhere to be found, though my bike was left in front of my old house. I never even got to move in here. Not officially. I just needed to get out before Snake sent someone after me. He was a mean bastard and rarely kept his word. Even though his enforcer at the time said I had an hour to get out of Harris, I didn't believe him.

This time around, it's both familiar and completely foreign. There is no deadline I'm racing against. No shadows haunting my steps. I don't have to decide what to bring with me, because I don't own anything. I don't have a bike to make my getaway on. There won't be any heartfelt goodbyes either, though. It's weird, the mixing of the past with the present.

I shake my head and suck in a deep breath. No use trying to analyze my emotions. Admitting I want to stay here because I feel safer than I've felt in a long time isn't something I'm ready to do. It'll open up a flood of other emotions I'm not prepared for. If I stay here, I'll get sucked into their orbit even more and I won't be able to pull myself out. Maybe that's the real reason Ghost wants me to go. If I stay longer, they'll forget why I left in the first place. Then six months from now, or whenever they deal with the Disciples, they'd pick their heads up and remember. It'll still hurt to leave, but better now than later.

"Fuck this," I mutter, trying to get the courage to move.

It's a struggle to put one foot in front of another. Eventually, I make it to the closet. It's larger than I expected, filled with built-in drawers and a hanging rack strung along the back. My backpack sits against the far wall, tucked in the corner almost as if he was hiding it. My bag looks out of place next to the dark wood and resting on the fluffy white carpet. I specifically got a black bag so it would hide any stains. Plus, no one wants a neon green beacon slung across their back while they're running away from someone.

Even with the dark material, it looks grungy and old. Between the frayed straps and the faded fabric, it's a perfect allegory for my life. Barely held together and falling apart at the seams. I shake my head and grab the handle. As soon as I try to lift it, the whole strap comes off and the backpack tips over. The zipper pops open and spills the contents across the white carpet.

I drop to my knees and gather my meager belongings. Tears blur my vision, and I hold back a shuddering sob. I can't break down now. I don't even know why I'm crying. It's just a fucking backpack. I can get a new one.

Except this is the lowest I've ever been. I tried to play it off when they asked what happened in Stowe. Getting kidnapped and stabbed wasn't great, but it wasn't anything new. Losing everything? Yeah, that was new. Not only did the Disciples burn down the tiny house I was renting, but they wrecked my bike. The one I've had since I was fifteen. The one thing I still had from before my life fell apart. The only thing I've ever truly taken care of. The last remaining tie to Ghost and Storm—their gift to me.

"One more day. Just make it one more day," I whisper.

I swipe at my tears and shove the contents back into the bag. Whatever happens, I just need to make it one more day.

Twenty

"What's she doing?" Ghost asks, peering over my shoulder and into my room as if he can see into my closet.

"Her backpack broke." I shove my hands in my pockets. "She's crying."

His eyes snap to mine. "No fucking way. Siren doesn't cry."

"She does now. She's not the same girl who left six years ago."

"Tell me," he grunts.

I glance over my shoulder and sigh. "She broke down in the bath."

Confusion flashes over his face, and I run my hand through my hair. I wasn't going to bring it up unless I needed to. I don't expect Ghost to be jealous, but he might be pissed I got in the tub with her. He's waffling between holding her too tight and shoving her away. Both of us are. It's far from healthy and definitely unsustainable. He told Siren and me to get our shit together and I ended up throwing gasoline on it instead.

"That's what you were doing? When you told her she couldn't take a shower?" he asks, and I nod. "We're fucked, aren't we?"

"No. But we need to figure shit out before we find ourselves in too deep."

"You don't think she should leave." It comes out as a statement, but the question rests in his eyes.

"I think no matter where we send her, she'll be dead within the year. You need to figure out whether or not you can live with that." I huff and cross my arms. "Actually, you'll have to live with the uncertainty of never knowing. Until you texted her, we didn't know if she was alive or not. Can you go back to pretending she doesn't exist?" Guilt crawls across his face and he winces. "What the fuck did you do?"

He pulls me away from the door and into the hallway. "I may have been sending people to find her."

"Who the hell did you send?"

"Not physically. I was using Nemesis. Byrns's woman in Synd. Every once in a while, I'd ask her to track Siren down. She'd give me a bare-bones update, and I'd have the peace of mind of knowing we didn't cause her death."

"And you didn't think to fucking tell me? For fuck's sake, Ghost. How many secrets are you keeping from me?"

I hate this. It's like I've fallen into an alternate universe, and I fucking hate it. I understand the hierarchy within the club, but Siren has nothing to do with the Phantoms. For years, he's been getting updates about her and never once thought to tell me.

"I didn't want to admit it," he murmurs. "Even to you. Plus, how would you have reacted? Remember how you were when she was banished? You would have burned down the fucking house. Or take it out on me more than you already did."

Scoffing, I glance down the hall, not really seeing anything. "I kept my shit to myself."

At least, I think I did. I hadn't wanted Ghost to see how much her leaving affected me. He was struggling enough as it was, and he needed to focus. He was months away from challenging Snake for his position. It was more important to concentrate on where we were going instead of what went wrong in our personal lives. I blamed Siren for setting our schedule back—for putting all we'd worked for at risk. For what? Money? I assume that's what the Disciples gave her. As if we wouldn't have helped her when she needed it. If she would have just waited...

"You didn't. You lashed out at anyone close to us. Me most of all." Ghost leans against the wall as the fight leaves him. "I did what I thought was best for both of us. If I knew where she was, whether or not she was alive, I could focus on what was important. I didn't have the energy to worry about her while thinking of taking on Snake."

"She betrayed us," I growl. "Why the fuck would you worry?"

His face softens and a sad smile forms on his lips. "Because I loved her. *You* loved her. Those feelings don't just disappear because she threw us away. They didn't vanish overnight. We had to grieve her and the future that was cruelly ripped away from us."

"By her hand," I growl, and he nods.

"Yes, by her. Still doesn't change the fact that love wouldn't go away in the blink of an eye. Having Nemesis check in on her gave me the peace of mind to let her go. At least as much as I was able to."

The fire leaves me and my shoulders slump. "Then why didn't you tell me? Maybe it would have helped me, too."

"It wouldn't have. You know that. You never moved past the anger stage. Letting go of the rage she stirred in you isn't easy, and you've been holding onto it for years. And now you don't know how to act around her. You still want to choke her, you just can't figure out if it's while she's under you or..." He grins, but I'm not ready. He often jokes around when he's nervous. Sometimes it's annoying, sometimes it's helpful. Right now, it's the former.

He glances over my shoulder, and I check behind me. There's no sign of Siren, though. She's probably still crying in my closet. The need to comfort her overwhelms me again. I had it before when I was standing on the other side of the door. I ignored it then, just like I will now.

"You're not sure about sending her away, are you?" I ask, hoping to distract myself.

"No," he sighs, rubbing his fist to his chest, right over his heart. "Nemesis didn't tell me about the kidnappings. I doubt she knew, but still. If Prophet is determined to take her, she's right. It won't matter how far we send her. What did he say to her?"

"He needs her. The woman who supposedly helped her said it too. Whatever the fuck that means. Unless he thinks he's had some premonition about her?"

"He didn't. He's just delusional." Siren's voice floats from behind us, the tears still evident in her voice. When I turn around, though, her face is clear.

"How long were you eavesdropping on us?" I snarl as I slide next to Ghost.

"Just because you're unobservant doesn't mean you need to take your incompetence out on me," she says haughtily. If her hair was down, she'd probably flip it over her shoulder or some shit.

Ghost's hand lands on my arm, and I rein in the urge to snap back at her. Antagonizing her won't solve whatever shit is going on with me. I hate to admit Ghost is right, if only because I'll have to actually deal with it then. I fucking hate emotions. Life would be simpler without them. It would also be lonelier.

"Did you decide about the ride?" she asks, and I scan her body. She's in a ratty t-shirt and ripped leggings, the same clothes she was wearing the night I opened the door expecting Fuse.

"Why the fuck are you wearing those?"

She rolls her eyes. "Are we really going to get into you analyzing my clothes again? These are my clothes and I'm wearing them. Beyond that, you have no right to my business."

"I thought you threw them away," I mutter from the corner of my mouth at Ghost.

"I was a little fucking busy. I just stuffed them in her bag," he mutters back.

"I can hear you both, you know. You're like three fucking feet from me."

I glance at Ghost, and he raises his eyebrows. It's an acknowledgment and a permission all in one. A memory and a decision twisted together. She probably doesn't even realize she's berating us for something we used to do to push her buttons. She both hated and loved when we'd mutter to each other about her. We kept it up just to watch her face turn pink like it is now. He remembers just as well as I do. I wonder if the ache in his chest is the same.

"You're staying," I say, and Ghost lets out a heavy breath.

Siren plants her hands on her hips. "Excuse me? You two keep thinking you can fuck me ar—"

I snort and Ghost covers his own with a cough. I wipe away the grin that popped up without a thought. I don't know where we go from here, but it feels good to fuck with her.

"You two are assholes," she snaps and hefts the strap of her backpack over her shoulder.

She winces and Ghost growls as I step into the room to rip the bag from her grasp. Her stuff spills out and scatters across the floor. Her chin wobbles as she drops to her knees. Her hands tremble and she drops a travel bottle of shampoo once, then twice. I snatch it from her and toss it aside. Ghost mumbles something I can't hear.

"Siren, stop," I say softly as she continues to paw at her meager belongings.

She tries to grab her backpack from me, and I hand it to Ghost before crouching in front of her.

"Give it back. Just...stop. Please."

I glance back at Ghost and concern swims in his eyes. Neither one of us laughs, though under other circumstances we'd rib her about begging. She's teetering on a precipice. One wrong move and she'll plunge into a void I doubt we'd be able to save her from. It's a dangerous place to be between destruction and our mercy. It's pretty clear we're not going to leave her to her fate. Not that she trusts us.

"Siren," I whisper, reaching for her, and a tear drips from her cheek and lands on the back of my hand.

My fingers wrap around her wrist, and she stills. I pry the small notebook she's clutching from her grasp. She lunges for it.

Ghost jumps forward as Siren tackles me, screaming to give it back. My breath heaves from my lungs when I hit the floor, and I struggle as the world swims. Ghost shouts something I can't hear over the pounding in my ears. Siren straddles me, her hands straining for the book I'm still holding. Her nails rake down my arm and I drop the book over my head.

She scrambles after it and clutches it to her chest. Her weak sobs echo through the sudden silence. Ghost steps over me and doesn't hesitate before he scoops Siren up. She struggles for a second before she sinks into him. He slides down the wall and I push myself up next to him. I'm lightheaded but at least I can breathe normally. Ghost settles her on his lap and cradles her gently.

"Stop coddling me," she mutters even as she burrows into him.

"Stop spouting bullshit," he mutters back. "What's wrong with you?"

I roll my head toward him and raise my eyebrows. There's clearly something wrong. She's spiraling and I don't know whether I want her to pull out of it or hit rock bottom. If she gets her shit together, she'll bury all her emotions so deep they'll end up suffocating her. If she hits rock bottom, there's no guarantee she'll come out of it. Either way is a shitstorm waiting to happen.

"I'm fine. My bag just broke," she whispers harshly, a contradiction in tone and words.

"What's with the book?" Ghost asks, and she shakes her head.

"It's nothing. Just leave it."

Ghost's fingers cover her own, and he gently tugs them back from the notebook. It drops into her lap, and I reach around her to take it. She sucks in a deep breath, tension radiating from her. It has a hard black cover and could fit in my pocket. I run my finger along the spine and wonder how long she's carried this thing around.

Invading her privacy isn't at the top of my list. Yet I'm curious what she could possibly be keeping inside. What's so important she doesn't want us to see?

Siren jumps from Ghost's lap and staggers to her feet. She grabs her backpack and shoves everything inside, then hugs it to her chest. Indecision flashes across her face as she bounces from one foot to another. She holds out her hand and fixes her gaze on me. Ghost's arm brushes mine, urging me to give it back. I hold up the book. When her fingers graze mine, my own tingle and she jerks back. The book drops to the floor and flips open.

I glance at it and see one word repeated over and over.

I'm sorry.

Twenty-One

Ghost

"You can't come with, Siren," I growl as I yank on my pants.

She's too busy pacing back and forth to notice I've been mostly naked this entire time. Then again, her cheeks are pinker than usual. I run my hand through my hair as I stare at my reflection. A hot shower didn't fix all my problems, despite my hopes.

"Stop messing with your hair. You can't pick out grey hairs with your dye job," she snaps.

"I don't dye my hair, and you know that."

"A lot can change in six years," she murmurs. "Why can't I go? It's not like I'm asking for you to parade me out in front of the entire club. You're just going to troll the perimeter. I'll be under a helmet and I'll wear baggy clothes."

"You don't own any clothes. Which is the least of our worries right now. I'm not putting you on the back of my bike." I tug on a shirt, then pin her with a glare. "And don't even think about asking Storm. He'll say no, too."

Pain flashes in her eyes before her face shutters. "Fine. Are you sure you trust me enough to be in your house all by my lonesome? I could end up taking a baseball bat to the entire place. Fucking with Storm by rearranging his furniture might be an option. Oh, or I could just take one thing from every room and move it to another one."

She leans against the wall next to a side table. She glances down and a sly smile tips her lips as she pushes a glass figurine an inch to the left. A growl leaves me, but I don't move. Trying to get a rise out of me won't work. If she keeps pushing, one of us is going to break. I just have to outlast her stubbornness. From the set of her chin, that won't be easy. Better to run while I still can.

I grab my leather jacket from the chair and shrug it on. "Do whatever you think is necessary. But if you touch the kitchen, I won't save you from Storm's wrath."

I stalk past her and out the door. My gaze meets Storm's, and I smirk. If she takes the bait, our kitchen will be cleaner than it has in years. I don't particularly care if she rearranges Storm's room and she won't be able to find a baseball bat. Hopefully she'll be so busy with the other things she'll run out of time and won't fuck with my shit. Problem is, the threat was enough. I'll be worrying about it for the next week.

"Are you sure we should leave her?" Storm mutters as I meet him outside his door. "The men we put on duty…"

"None of them know she's in here."

"That's the problem. They don't know she's here. They don't know what they're protecting. If something happens, they won't know to get her."

I nod and sigh. "We can't tell them about the Disciples breaking in. It'll undermine our authority. Venom's already gearing up for something and I don't want to give him any more fuel."

"You think he had a hand in it? It doesn't make sense how they were able to get into Harris, much less Phantom territory. They must have had help. Otherwise, someone would have stopped them. *We* should have stopped them." He runs his hand through his hair, then grips the back of his neck.

I fight the anxiety bubbling in my stomach and the rage racing through my veins. I don't have the luxury of showing the kind of emotion Storm does. He can fly off the handle and lash out at everyone. No one will bat an eye or judge him for it. Usually, I'm grateful for the balance between us. He's the flames to my ice. Sometimes...

Sometimes I wish we could switch places. Even when I loosen the reins on my rage, I'm in control. Just once, I'd like to lose it without worrying about the consequences. When I put Fuse on his back at headquarters, there was a deliberateness to my actions. I squeezed just enough to let him know I meant business. I wanted to punch him, choke him, gut him. All the emotions I'd been holding back almost broke through the dam I'd built up. Except I was in a room surrounded by my men. I couldn't afford to do anything other than be in control.

"This is the way—"

"They broke into our house," he bellows, throwing up his hands and pacing away from me. "And you did nothing. You were so concerned with *her* and where she was, you forgot we were attacked. Disciples came into our fucking city and got into our home. They came into the heart of our territory, and you didn't even care."

I grab the lapels of his jacket and shove him against the wall. He glares at me, his nostrils flaring as he waits for me to respond.

"You think I don't give a shit? You think I put her above this club? You of all people should know better. I'm trying to keep everything together without having it all burn down around us," I hiss. His fingers wrap around my wrists.

"You have to stop doing shit alone, Ghost. We're in this together and you keep pushing me away," he whispers.

He leans his forehead against mine and I breathe in his scent, letting it ground me to the present. My eyes flutter shut, and his lips brush mine. I groan and he seals our mouths together. His tongue slips inside and I tilt my head. His hand slides up my arm and around my neck. He tugs me closer until my body melds to his.

It's been too long since we've connected—truly connected.

We've been focused on all the issues around us. Having Siren thrown back into our lives has driven a wedge between us. This right here is exactly what we need to find each other again. It won't solve all our problems, but it'll bring us closer. It sets us on a path to getting back to where we were.

I lose myself in him, relishing the peace I find within his arms. Someone clears their throat, and I reluctantly break free. No one else would have come into the house without express permission. Storm thumps his head against the wall and drops his hands to my hips.

"What do you want, Siren?" I grunt.

"Didn't mean to interrupt…" Her voice is laced with laughter, and I roll my neck to ease some of the tension already building.

"And yet you did anyway," I grumble. "What the fuck do you want?"

"Not like I haven't seen it before. In fact, I've literally been in between you two while you were making out."

I glance at her from the corner of my eye. She gnaws on her bottom lip as she gathers her hair to put it up in a messy bun. Red marks and a smattering of bruises paint the side of her neck.

"Whatever," she says when neither of us responds. "Another time and all that. Listen, I noticed some extra bikes out front and normally I wouldn't say anything—"

"In what world do you not spout off some bullshit? You've never kept your mouth shut a day in your goddamn life," Storm snaps.

I push away from Storm and shove my hands in my pockets. "What did you notice?"

"Well, Venom was down there. I didn't think he was still around, but there he was. Thought he would have been dead by now. Anyway, he seemed to be fucking with something by the back door." She crosses her arms and leans her shoulder against the wall. Her stomach contracts as if she's in pain. Her face gives nothing away.

I stalk forward and grab the hem of her shirt to lift it up. She squawks, batting at my hand. Most of her stitches are dissolved, leaving an angry red scab behind. Her skin pulls at the seams, and I grimace. We should have been keeping a closer eye on it. Bones gave Storm some salve to put on it, at least.

"Where's the cream Bones gave you?" I call over my shoulder.

Siren smacks my arm. "I don't need anything. It's fine. For two people who didn't give a shit whether I was alive or dead a week ago, you sure are fussy."

My head snaps up and I involuntarily take a step back. Storm grunts behind me, but I can't decipher it this time. Siren doesn't seem to notice either of our reactions. She's too busy tucking her shirt into her leggings. Storm probably thinks I should tell her about tracking her. It wasn't even that deep. Half the time Nemesis just sent me a thumbs up emoji to tell me she was alive. Telling Siren will only send her spiraling again.

"You said Venom was fucking with something? What was it?" I ask, breaking the tension. At least I'm hoping it does.

"If I knew, I would have said. Don't you two have shit to do?" she adds bitterly.

I glance over my shoulder at Storm, and he rolls his eyes. "Yeah, we do."

Storm stomps into his room, the only outward sign of his displeasure. He may think it's best that she come with us, but he's not going to be happy about it. Siren scoffs and turns around as if she'll walk away. She takes two steps before her hands drop to her sides and her chin drops to her chest.

I cross my arms, waiting for her to decide what she's going to do. The house isn't nearly big enough for her to hide in, though there are a few places. She probably doesn't know where they are. A lot and yet nothing has changed in the last six years.

"What happened?" I breathe, the question ripped from me without warning. I don't want to care about her answer, but I do. It doesn't matter why she turned on us. The results are the same either way. She chose money over loyalty and broke us in the process.

She spins on her heel and pins me with a blank expression. "With what?"

I swallow hard and glance away. I won't get any answers out of her. "Nothing."

Storm reappears, a black jacket in his hands, and freezes. He glances between us, then widens his eyes at me. I shake my head, not willing to fill him in. He's not ready to open up the past. He's still stuck in his anger even after our talk. It'll take more than one conversation for him to be willing to figure out her motives years ago.

Storm holds out the jacket to Siren, and she hesitates before taking it. "You got your wish. Put it on, Siren. It's getting fucking late, and I would like to actually get to sleep before the sun rises." Storm pivots on his heel and walks off.

"Just put it on, Siren. Don't ask any of the questions swirling around in that pretty little head of yours. Just get the fuck outside." I turn to follow Storm.

"Am I going to have to run after your bikes? Perhaps you'd like to attach a rope to the back and drag me?"

Slowly, I turn to face her again. "Did that happen to you?"

She shrugs, running her palms down her arms as if savoring the soft leather. "They tried. Rope broke. Shall we go?"

I grab her elbow and propel her toward the stairs. "This conversation isn't done."

"Sure it isn't," she mutters. "But you never answered my question. Thought you didn't want me on the back of your bike?"

Storm waits by the front door, a helmet in his hand. He shoves it over her head, cutting off whatever nonsense she's about to spout. I guide her outside with a hand on her lower back, the silent street greeting us. Storm must have told the others to clear out until we're gone.

"Mind the stairs," Storm says, and grabs her arm.

"I can get down the fucking stairs by myself. For fuck's sake, you two are driving me up a damn wall." She rips her arm away from Storm and rushes down. Her head knocks into the post holding the awning up and she stutters to a stop.

"Do not say a fucking word."

Twenty-Two

Siren

I hate wearing a helmet. Logically, I know it could save my life, except it makes my head feel like it's twenty pounds heavier and sitting on a toothpick. Every time I lean even the slightest bit back, my chin tips up, and I struggle to right myself again. Ghost isn't helping. I've knocked into his ear seven times. Not that I was counting. His reactions have escalated from merely a tightening in his stomach to him pinching my knee.

"Ow, fucker," I yell. "I can't help it."

He doesn't hear me. Because of course he doesn't through the helmet and over the rumble of the engine. Storm weaves around us and I turn my head too quickly. My helmet smacks into Ghost again and his fingers dig into the muscles right above my knee. I yelp, but don't kick him even though I want to.

He pulls into a dirt parking lot, the gravel kicking into the trees as he parks. I slide off the bike before he cuts the engine and hop to keep my feet. It's harder with all the aches and pains plaguing my body. My side burns, and no matter how I twist, there's no relief for my back. I yank the helmet off and drop it next to me. Storm snarls as he snatches it up and places it on his seat. I resist the urge to stick my tongue out at him.

Ghost waves Storm over, and I leave them to plan. They won't want my input. Not that I have anything useful to say. The longer I stay here, the deeper I fall into the familiar patterns of the past. As soon as my muscles relax and my mind forgets, I'm jarred back to the reality of my situation. I can't afford to forget they hate me. Sometimes they make it really difficult, though.

I should have left when I had the chance. To hell with my injuries and the threat of the Disciples. Ghost and Storm wouldn't have come after me. They may be treating me marginally better than they were, but it doesn't change our past. The pity they feel for me will dry up. The guilt plaguing them will run out. And I'll be left alone. The way it's supposed to be.

Wandering closer to the tree line, I scan the forest. We're on the far west side of Harris, as far as we could get from Disciple territory. They weren't taking any chances with me being along. Storm steps next to me and we sit in silence while Ghost mutters into his phone behind us. I can't make out his conversation.

"Ask me," Storm murmurs.

I glance at him from the corner of my eye. "What am I asking you?"

He huffs, pinching the bridge of his nose. "Your reappearance is...hard. It's influencing how we make decisions. And we can't afford that right now."

"I know," I whisper. "You're not the only one struggling, Storm. Then again, unless it was Ghost, you never really noticed anyone else's suffering, did you?"

I walk away before he can respond. I don't need to hear his rebuttal or excuses. He probably doesn't even know what I'm talking about. I know he loved me once. He told me often enough. And he took care of me just like Ghost did. We had each other's backs.

Except when I needed them the most. They believed everyone over me. No, they didn't even do that. They just believed whatever lies they were told. I became a burden—a liability. I stood in the way of all their plans. It's why I didn't try harder to get them to listen. Nothing I said would have changed the path I was on. I couldn't exonerate myself. All the evidence was stacked against me. I'm now a traitor by proxy no matter how much I wish otherwise.

Knowing everything hasn't given me any peace. I'm still pissed they didn't truly love me when it mattered most. I'm still sick of living to survive. I'm still scared of Prophet and his plans. Most of all, I hate that I'm still caught between these two.

They're toying with me. It's the only explanation I can come up with. Ghost wanted me to stick around so he could use me for information. Storm wanted me out at all costs. Then they flipped. Then they flipped again. They may seem to be on the same page right now, but that'll change. I can't keep living in this grey area. Earlier I was too tired, too injured, to make a rational decision. Coming out here tonight, I know I need to leave, regardless of the consequences.

Ghost meets my gaze and raises an eyebrow. I wrap my arms around my waist and wait for him to finish his call. He hangs up and slips his phone in his jeans pocket. My mouth waters as I follow his movements. He just *had* to wear the tightest pants I've ever seen. How the hell did he even get in them? Did Storm use a spatula to help? Maybe he sewed them on.

"Did you pick up sewing?" I blurt out, still staring at his crotch.

"What the fuck?" he mutters.

"Never mind." I clear my throat. "What exactly are we doing?"

"Walking the line." He presents the way and gives me a little bow.

I bite back a groan and settle for wrinkling my nose. Storm chuckles as he passes me, and I stomp after him. Walking the lines is one of my least favorite things in the world. It's boring and takes for fucking ever. Nothing ever happens on this side of Harris. Even if we were on the east side of town, this would still be torture. Trudging through the dark, searching for anything out of place, freezing my fucking ass off—there's literally nothing about it to like.

"Why are we walking the line?" I grumble. "And do I get a gun?"

Storm snorts and Ghost falls into step next to me. "If you think Storm is going to give you a weapon, then walk in front of you..."

Storm glances over his shoulder. "She wouldn't shoot me."

"Might stab you," I mutter. "Why are we going tonight, though?"

"Because we need to make sure the Disciples aren't pushing from this way. One of our scouts thought he saw some sketchy shit around here," Ghost says as he scans the forest. "We won't do the whole line, though."

I breathe a sigh of relief. The boundaries around the territory are broken up, but this stretch is the longest one, extending for a couple miles. There's no way I'd make it to the next line much less all the way back. Already my right calf muscle is cramping. My left ankle will be screaming tomorrow. My nostrils flare and I glare at Ghost.

"Spit it out, Siren," Ghost snarls. Asshole doesn't have a right to be nasty to me.

"You're the reason my ankle aches when it rains."

"I'm not the one who dared you to jump off the cliff. Blame Storm for that one."

Storm spins around and walks backwards. "She didn't sprain her ankle jumping off the cliff. She hurt it when she tried to run out of the lake afterward. It was your fault, Siren."

He turns around again and saunters on. I scoff, but I can't argue. I was pissed at myself when I hit the freezing water. I was even more pissed when I slipped on a rock on my way to the shore. Ghost, Storm, and Lexi lost it, and I refused to tell them I was in pain. I'm still blaming them.

"I wouldn't have been up on that cliff in the first place if it wasn't for you guys. I was supposed to be working. Not only was

I on crutches for a whole damn month, but I almost lost my job at the garage."

I loved my job at the shop. I wasn't particularly good at fixing up bikes back then. What I lacked in skill, I made up for with enthusiasm. Once I left Harris, I never went to another garage again. Not that anyone would have hired me. I barely did more than wipe down and change the oil in the bikes. Most of the time I worked the desk. I didn't bother going back after Snake banished me. None of them would have stuck their necks out for me. I don't blame them. Turns out, there's only one person I blame. Except I can't take out my anger on a dead man.

"Was a fun night before that, though," Ghost says quietly. "Breaking into headquarters. Stealing those beers and drinking them by the tracks. Egging Kiwi's house. And as I recall, you were more than willing to go skinny dipping."

His fingers brush mine, sending a bolt of electricity up my arm. He lengthens his stride to catch up with Storm. I fall farther behind them while I try to get my shit together. The last thing I need is a walk down memory lane. Their casual touches don't help either.

I glance up and find them a good twenty feet in front of me. A streetlamp above them illuminates their figures. I take a snapshot in my mind, hoping I can remember them like this—their heads tilted toward one another, hands brushing with every step. A sigh leaves me and an ache builds in my chest. It's just another reason why I shouldn't have come here. There's no space between them. No room for me anymore.

A twig snaps to my left, the small sound filtering from the trees. I freeze and peer into the woods, trying to see between the thick trunks. I really wish I had a gun or a knife. Literally anything would be better than my half-broken body.

I'm not incapable of defending myself, but with my recent injuries, I don't know how long I could hold my own. I glance at them still walking, then back into the darkness. Nothing moves, not even the wind. It's as if the entire world holds its breath.

I swallow hard and take a step closer. A shadow flits from one trunk to another, and I stop. It could be an animal. They're used to living on the edges of civilization. The wind picks up and the dry leaves shiver overhead. I shake out my hands before slipping under the canopy of branches crisscrossing above me. Darkness envelops me and I blink rapidly, trying to force my eyes to adjust.

I drop into a crouch when something rustles not ten feet in front of me. As I inch forward, Storm shouts my name, and I whip around. Whoever's hiding takes off deeper into the woods. I shoot to my feet and catch sight of a figure weaving through the underbrush. Ghost curses and their pounding feet drown out the person's retreat. Just as the darkness swallows them, I see a flash a green, and a grin spreads across my face.

Reluctantly, I trudge back to the dirt road. Ghost and Storm skid to a stop in front of me, matching thunderous expressions plastered on their faces. Storm grabs my shoulders and shakes me, yelling nonsensical words. I knock his arms away and snarl.

"What the fuck was that?" Ghost demands, and I roll my arms.

"Heard a noise. Stopped to see what it was." The less I say, the better. I'm sick of being interrogated by them.

"You heard—" Ghost throws up his hands and spins away, only to face me a second later. "What the fuck is wrong with you?"

I open my mouth to respond, then snap it shut when Storm shoves me away from him. It's not hard, but it's enough to get his point across. It doesn't matter what my reasonings are. It doesn't matter what I found. I'm not capable. I'm not an ally. I'm not trusted.

"Did you find anything?" Storm growls. "Or were you just a fucking fool who wandered off without backup?"

I pull in a deep, calming breath and pull a mask over my features. "Guess I'm just a fool."

Twenty-Three

Ghost grabs my elbow and shakes me a little as he mutters, "Calm the fuck down."

Easier said than done. I rip away from him and stalk toward the next checkpoint. I can't stop myself from glancing back every few seconds to make sure Siren is still there. My palms itch to grab her again. My heart still pounds in my chest. Everything in me screams to throw her over my shoulder and make sure she doesn't run off. Add in the fact I know she's lying and I'm about ready to blow.

She saw something in the forest, and I can't figure out what. Why lie about it? It's either something embarrassing or she's hiding shit. For someone with her past, I'd think she'd do everything she can to instill trust in us. Yet here she is, lying to our faces.

I'm pissed she's lying, yet terrified she'll disappear. I want her where I can see her, but I want her to leave. I want to fuck her and strangle her and hold her and stab her. I have half a mind to put her over my knee. She always bitched when I'd do it, yet her pussy was drenched by the end. I shake my head, wondering where the hell that memory came from. Ghost is right—I need to calm the fuck down.

Ghost stomps past me, grumbling under his breath. I glance behind me for the umpteenth time and find Siren frozen in the middle of the road. I stop and my head swivels back and forth from Ghost to Siren. He doesn't even waver as he turns the corner. Sighing, I swing around and make my way to Siren. Her hands come up as if to ward me off, and I wonder if she's going to take off.

"Don't even think about it," I murmur.

She tenses and I surge forward. She yelps, trying to run, but I get to her first. I tip her over my shoulder and ignore her shrieks. I spin around and follow Ghost. She twists, screaming at me to put her down. Before I can think better of it, my hand connects with her ass, and she squeals. Her fists pound into my kidney, and I swat her again.

"Keep it up, sweets. We can do this all fucking night," I say and she howls. "Keep it down. Someone might be watching."

It's a low blow, but it gets her to stop. I expect Ghost to have vanished once more. Instead, he's leaning against a fence butted up against the tree line, talking on the phone. He raises an eyebrow when he spots us, and I shake my head. I assume I don't have to explain to him what she's like.

"I envy those who haven't met you yet," she taunts. It takes me a minute to decipher her insult. I roll my eyes and decide to let it go.

I turn my head, though I can't see her face. "You going to take off again if I put you down?"

"I didn't take off," she growls and slams her fist into my ass. I smack her in return.

"You were about to. I'll put you down if you promise you won't run. I'm tired and I don't want to chase you." I grit my teeth when she stills. "Don't."

I can practically hear her grin, and I brace myself. Her hands slide around my sides, caressing me, and I hold my breath. Ghost smirks and I squeeze my eyes shut. She slips one hand under my jacket, then my shirt, and grazes my stomach. I swear I'll dump her ass on the ground if she tries to grab my cock, her injuries be damned.

She braces her palm against my gut, her thumb slipping under my waistband, and I exhale. Fire races through my veins and I tighten my grip on her thigh. My brain short circuits as her nails dig into my skin. Her other hand slips to my jean-covered ass and part of me wishes I'd put on something else, if only to revel in the feeling.

The thought distracts me long enough for her to make her move. Because of course she was plotting this entire fucking time. She rams her stiff fingers into the crease of my ass, hitting my tail-bone instead of the hole. It's enough for me to fling her over my shoulder once more and she ends up sprawled on the ground, wheezing. She curls into a ball, body shaking as she laughs at my expense.

"You'd think you'd have anticipated that move, Storm," Ghost calls as he slips his phone in his pocket.

"Fuck you," I groan, rubbing the wound. I swear she poked a new hole when she rammed her fingers up there.

"If you two are done fucking around, we have a lead."

Siren pushes upright, her legs kicked out in front of her. If I wasn't watching her, I'd miss her wincing. A second later and she's bounding to her feet and flipping me the bird. I probably shouldn't have dropped her with the still-healing injuries. Then again, she hasn't given any indication she's in pain until now. We're going to need Bones to come by and check her out when we get back.

"What's the lead?" I ask, pulling my gaze away from her.

"Fuse said there was a disturbance about a half mile from here. We're going to check it out instead of sending someone else." He turns and makes his way between two buildings.

Siren falls into step with him and shoves her hands in the pockets of the leather jacket I gave her. I had to dig in my closet for it. I doubt she realizes it's hers. Snake refused to let her take anything with her other than her bike. I'm surprised he let her take that, actually.

We weren't allowed in the room when they were questioning her, and Snake wasn't one to explain his reasonings. Maybe he told her she could take her jacket if she removed the Phantom's patches. Except she left it at our house, and we didn't let her inside. Guilt curls in my gut when I remember how she stood on the front lawn with pleading eyes. Tears streaked down her face, but she never begged. I don't know what we would have done if she had. I doubt she even knew we were inside.

"Pay attention, Storm. I'm not walking into this while your head's in the clouds," Ghost calls over his shoulder.

I shove the memory away and catch up to them. "What exactly is the disturbance?"

"He didn't say. From the tremor in his voice, I think it might be a fire. Probably a small one."

"Wait," Siren says. "Why do you think it's a fire from his reaction?"

"Fuse doesn't do well with fire. Just one of those things," Ghost murmurs as we turn yet another corner.

The outskirts of Harris aren't very populated. A few businesses here and there popped up after we took over. Helped that we actually gave a shit whether the town died around us or not. Snake never did understand the balance between an MC and the city they were in. He thought he could run roughshod over everyone and bully them into complying. We modeled a lot of what we built after the mafia families and the MC in Synd. Harris isn't nearly as large as Synd, but the concept rang true.

Usually, I love being out here at night. The darkness reveals more than the light ever could. When the world is plunged into shadows, the true nature of things is exposed. Nefarious plans and evil schemes are whispered when they think no one is listening. I'd much rather hide in the night than saunter through the daylight.

We pass a park. The swings creak in the soft breeze and a

sheen of dew covers the play equipment. As much as I like wandering the dark streets, the playground is a little creepy. A chill runs down my spine and I slow to a stop. I turn in a circle and scan the area intently.

Ghost's usually the one who gets these types of feelings. He's the one who has the sixth sense. I'm merely along for the ride. Except something is swirling through the air—something sinister. The breeze dies out and I hold my breath.

"Storm?" Ghost calls and our gazes meet. "What's up?"

I open my mouth, but nothing comes out. I don't even know what to say—how to describe what I'm going through.

"Is this what you feel like?" I murmur and his brows pull low. "Never mind."

Muffled shouts echo from a few blocks over and his head whips around. Silence descends once more, and Ghost grabs his phone to call for backup. A scream splits the night, then abruptly cuts off, and I lunge toward Siren. She takes off and I follow, despite Ghost's orders to stop. I don't know if she planned this. Maybe whoever she met in the forest was giving her instructions. She's always been one to run headlong into trouble regardless of the risks.

"Siren," I bellow as she disappears around the corner of a building.

I make it two blocks, catching the barest glimpse of her with each turn. A gust of wind blasts through the alleyway and more shouts ring through the air. I push myself harder, the pit in my stomach growing. When a pop ricochets off the building, my heart nearly stops. The sky lights up, flashing orange, before the boom.

My knees hit the ground, and gravel digs into my palms as I shove my body up again. Ghost yells from somewhere behind me, but his cries are drowned out by another explosion ripping through the sky. I can't wait for him. I have to get to Siren. Regardless of her involvement in this, I can't watch her die.

I skid around the building and slam into someone frozen on

the sidewalk. I wrap my arms around Siren and twist my body as we fall. My back hits the concrete, forcing the breath from my lungs. Siren screams over more explosions and fights against my hold. The heat from the blast blisters my skin. At least it feels like that's what's happening.

"Shit. Fuck. God-fucking-dammit," Ghost snarls as he grabs Siren.

She flails her arms, reaching for the fire. Her sobs trail behind them as Ghost runs away from the flames. I push to my feet with a grunt and squint into the burning building. It's a small apartment building, though I don't know anyone who lives there. I'm rarely on this side of the city. No one moves through the streets, but sirens blare in the background. I wonder if Ghost called them or someone who saw the blaze.

I limp after them, using Siren's cries as a beacon. He's struggling to keep hold of her under an awning of a closed restaurant. Dozens of bikes rumble in the distance. We don't have much time to calm her down and get her out of here before they show up.

"Just breathe, sweets," Ghost says as he locks his arms behind her back.

"S-she's dead. S-s-save her. Have to s-save her," she sobs.

Ghost's concerned eyes meet mine and I press my body to her back, trapping her between us. "Who, Siren? Who do you have to save?"

"No," she mumbles. "No, no, no, no."

The fight leaves her, and she buries her face into Ghost's chest, trembling. I duck my head, and my lips brush her ear.

"Who," I breathe.

"Avery. Please," she gasps softly. "Help her."

She breaks down again, mumbling nonsensical words. She pleads with us to find her, but we already have.

Ghost threads his fingers through her hair. Her ponytail came out somewhere along the way. He presses her closer to him and I grip her waist, trying to keep her upright.

"Siren, listen. Avery's fine. She's in Rima with Jag. She wasn't in the fire." Ghost tips his head back.

"No. She's dead. She's dead and I didn't do anything," she moans. "I froze. I froze. I froze."

"Siren, she's fine. I promise."

Her body sags and I struggle to hold her up. She shakes her head, barely able to move at all we have her pressed so tightly between us. I don't know why she thinks Avery is in there. Siren hasn't seen Avery in years, since she left. Avery told us she cut off communication after Siren was banished. Avery was never in a fire. She'd take off when Ghost got too protective, but she was never in any danger. Usually, we'd send Jag to tail her just to make sure she didn't get into trouble.

"I don't trust your promises," she whispers, and my heart cracks.

I shouldn't be surprised. We probably broke her just as much as she broke us. I blame her, but I can't imagine what it was like to have everything she knew ripped away from her in a few hours' time. She went from having a future to nothing in the blink of an eye. She must carry the guilt around with her.

"We can prove it. We'll call her right now," I say, and Ghost tightens his grip on her.

I pull my phone from my pocket, realizing we don't have time for this. Avery's name flashes on the screen and I put it on speaker while it rings once. Twice.

"Storm? Everything okay?" Avery's voice fills the night, and Siren breaks down again. "What's going on?"

"Just checking in. Everything good?" I ask, trying to keep my voice steady.

There's a pause and I grit my teeth. "Uh, yeah. Everything's good. What's—"

"Thanks." I hang up and tilt my head to scan Siren's tear-streaked face. She swallows hard and nods.

Ghost clears his throat lightly and I glance up. "We have to go."

"You carrying her, or am I?"

He passes her over to me, her limp body curling into mine. As I run back to our bikes, her blank eyes stare at the night sky. Whatever happened between her and Avery goes a lot deeper than either of us realized. Once she snaps out of this, we'll need to finally have a conversation, whether we want to or not.

Twenty-Four
Siren

Every time I close my eyes, images flash across my lids. My body reacts against my will. Muscles tense. Fingers tremble. Gut twists. They're not new feelings. Over the years, I've hidden these episodes from everyone around me. I know when they're going to hit me.

Except this time.

Of course I had to fall apart in front of Ghost and Storm. I don't remember most of what they said. I did hear Avery's voice when Storm called her. Trusting it is something else. Logically, I understand Avery's fine. She's off somewhere doing something with someone. The details are fuzzy and not important. My mind doesn't believe them. Until I see her face, talk to her myself, hear the safeword from her own mouth, I won't calm down.

The ride back to their house is a blur. It helps being stuffed in a helmet. The rest of the world is cut off, leaving me to deal with my emotions alone. I should have worked through all my trauma a long time ago, but I didn't have the energy. Between trying to survive and constantly being kidnapped, I didn't exactly have time for therapy. Besides, what would I say? *I grew up in a criminal enterprise and knew how to kill a man when I was six, but it's totally fine. I'm cool with that part. It's these pesky flashbacks and horrendous nightmares I get. Oh, and the panic attacks when someone sneaks up on me.* I'm sure they'd be super happy to help me and totally wouldn't call the cops.

I keep the helmet on when I slide off Storm's bike. Wrapping my arms around my waist, I wait for one of them to make a move. Neither of them gets off their motorcycles, choosing to stare at the back of the house. I wonder if they've changed their minds again. They've been waffling so much, I wouldn't be surprised. I dig my fingers into my sides, hitting my wound. The pain clears my head enough to move my feet.

They still don't move as I make my way up the stairs. No one says a word when I open the door and slip inside. There's no pounding of feet when I tiptoe past the empty rooms, then upstairs. I expect them to follow me by the time I step into Storm's room, yet it's utter silence around me. My heart calms and I finally can pull in a full breath.

I stare at nothing for fuck knows how long before I shake my head. I stomp to Storm's nightstand and rip it open. My phone sits innocently on top. It's probably not charged, but at least it's here. It's not worth it to ask Storm where he found it. None of it matters anymore. I slip the device in my pocket. I stumble on my way to the closet and wince. My adrenaline wanes, highlighting the aches from my antics tonight.

I grab my backpack and make it two steps before I realize this isn't my bag. It looks remarkably similar, but definitely not the same. When I unzip the top, though, I find all my stuff neatly tucked inside. Where the fuck did they get this? And on such short notice?

"Doesn't matter," I whisper and crouch to close it up.

"Going somewhere?" Ghost says from the doorway, and I groan.

"Time to go," I mutter. "I've overstayed my...well, my stay. Whatever."

I glance at him from the corner of my eye and find him

leaning on the doorframe. "Running. It's what you do best, isn't it?"

I huff and stand, throwing the strap over my shoulder. "I didn't run before. I was banished. Which you know pretty fucking well since you had a hand in it. Listen, I appreciate you made sure I didn't, uh, die. You were right before, though. Leaving is probably best for everyone."

"Except leaving will get you killed. Maybe not today or tomorrow, but soon. No matter how far you run, you can't outrun the Disciples."

"Been doing it for over five years. They were *gracious* enough to leave me be for the first year. Besides, it'll be easier for you to deal with all the shit they're bringing without me here," I say, then bite my cheek. "Storm'll agree with me."

He smirks and steps into the room, revealing Storm. I should have anticipated that. They're the same height, two sides of the same coin. From their hair to their eyes. Even their personalities. Ghost runs cold, hiding his emotions until he detonates. Storm lives hot, a heartbeat away from exploding. Only their builds are similar. And the way they made me feel—safe in a world that did everything it could to kill me, wanted when no one else cared to even remember I existed, loved me when I was unlovable.

"Turns out I don't agree with you, sweets." Storm takes Ghost's place, leaning against the doorframe. "I think it's about time we had more than a few of the conversations we've been putting off."

The bubble of anxiety bursts in my chest, making it hard to breathe. Somehow my voice comes out steady. "What's the point? You won't believe me either way. I'm a traitor. Or did you forget?"

Storm's nostrils flare, but Ghost chuckles. If I can push Storm enough, he'll blow up, and Ghost won't be able to stop him. I'll be able to leave without ripping open any more old wounds. Flaying myself alive in front of them isn't what I call a good time. Especially when it won't matter in the end. Nothing matters in the end.

My phone vibrates in my pocket and my breath hitches. I pull it out and my knees almost give out. Avery's text notification flashes across the screen—the safeword we set up when we were kids. I've had enough time to calm down, but I still needed the reassurance. I wonder if she called Ghost back. Maybe he told her I was here. I tuck it away again and find them watching me with matching expressions.

"Can I help you?"

"Nope. Let's go." Storm steps aside and presents the way to me with a small bow.

I clutch the strap tighter and march past him. There's no way I'd be able to run out of here without them catching me. Might as well get this over with. Storm's hand grips my elbow, and I shrug him off. He doesn't care, just grabs me again as if he's worried I actually will run. I could tell him I won't. Except the heat from his body seeping into mine is comforting. Not that I'd admit it to him.

He leads me down the stairs awkwardly, then into the living room. Ghost snatches my backpack, and a cry of protest leaves me. He sets it next to the loveseat, then takes his place on the couch across from me. Storm sits next to him, and I have a flash of déjà vu from the first night. I'm not nearly as nervous as I was. I think I covered it well with an egregious amount of confidence, but who knows.

"Well?" I cross my arms over my chest to hold myself together.

Storm jumps up and takes off for the kitchen. Ghost sighs as he tracks Storm's movements. I tuck one foot under my leg and tip my head back. I'm exhausted yet wired. When Storm reappears, I roll my eyes. He tosses a water bottle next to me and it rolls into my thigh.

"Better drink up. This'll be a lot," he says as he collapses next to Ghost.

"Let's just get this over with."

Ghost leans forward, resting his elbows on his knees. "You had a flashback."

"That's a statement, not a question." If they want to pull information from me, they're going to have to work for it. I'm not about to offer up everything I've been up to since I left the Phantoms. Spilling everything would hurt me more than anything else. Especially since I don't know how they'll react.

"What happened with my sister?"

"Which one?" I smirk when he scowls.

"Avery. Although maybe I should ask about both." He sits back and crosses his arms. His gaze is too much like he's attempting to peel back my layers and expose me for a liar, a fraud, a thief. My heart clenches and I resist the urge to rub the spot.

I pull my eyes away from him and glance at Storm. His expression isn't much different and I stare between them instead.

"Few years ago, she called me, said she was in trouble and needed help." I hold up my hand when both of them open their mouths. "She wasn't about to call either one of you." I point at Ghost. "You would have lectured her and made her feel incompetent." I switch to Storm. "And you would have told *him*, defeating the purpose of her calling you in the first place."

"I wouldn't have," Storm mutters, but I ignore him.

"She told me it was urgent, so I left that evening. By the time I got to where she was staying, she wasn't answering my texts. I called when I got there, but it wouldn't connect." My vision blurs and I fight against the images threatening to take over. "I went to the spot she told me to meet her at. She wasn't there. Then I got a text..." I swallow hard and press my nails into my palms, then whisper, "It just said *help*. I got to her apartment and it was on fire."

I bite my tongue and wait for their reaction. When I can't take it anymore, I peek at them. Ghost's face sits in his hands and Storm looks like he's about to blow up. Red cheeks, blazing eyes, and hands curled into fists—all the classic signs.

I tuck my chin to my chest and focus on my breathing. Convincing myself their opinions don't matter isn't working anymore. I spent a lot of time building up my walls and emptying my heart. All it took was a tiny amount of time with them and they've chipped away at those barriers. They reminded me I wasn't as devoid of emotions as I strived to be.

"Was she inside?" Ghost whispers harshly.

I shake my head, though he doesn't notice. "No. I tried to run into the building. Some neighbor stopped me."

"Where'd you find her?"

"She was at a cafe about ten minutes away, hiding in the bathroom. That's why I had a flashback. Because I thought she was dead, and I wasn't quick enough."

"Who?" Storm growls as if I didn't take care of the threat already. I snort, though he doesn't seem to care for my response.

"Doesn't matter. He's dead."

Ghost's head whips up. "You kill him?"

I nod, then pull in a deep breath. "Any other questions?"

"You didn't fucking answer me."

I roll my eyes, wishing he'd just fucking drop it. I'd rather not relive more of that night. "Some guy who couldn't take no for an answer. She worked with him or something. I don't know. Doesn't matter since I buried him in the middle of fucking nowhere. Can I go now?"

"Abso-fucking-lutely not. You think the only thing we want to know is about some bullshit that happened two years ago?" Storm snaps.

"It was four years ago, but who's counting."

Ghost explodes to his feet and looms over me. "You've been in contact with my sister for four fucking years?"

I struggle to wipe my expression clean. I'm not afraid he'll hurt me. Doesn't mean I like when he flies off the handle. Especially when I'm pretty sure he's about to blame me for whatever shit Avery got into. He knows she's a grown-ass woman who can take care of herself, which doesn't change a damn thing. It'll be my fault. Everything's my fault according to them. At least from what Avery's told me. They may not have done it publicly, but privately? Yeah, they blamed me.

"No," I murmur when I realize he's not going to give up. "She's been messaging me since about a month after I left."

His lips part and something flashes across his face. It takes me a moment to pinpoint it.

Betrayal.

Avery and I staying in touch isn't something he ever anticipated. He won't hold Avery responsible for it, even though I never reached out to her. When I needed help, I didn't call her. Not because I didn't want to, but because of this right here. Because of Ghost.

No matter how they've been waffling lately, it all comes back to what I did to them. They'll never see me as anyone other than the girl who sold them out for a fistful of cash.

Twenty-Five

Ghost

Avery has had more contact with Siren than I have. She knew whether or not Siren was alive. Yet every time I asked my sister if she'd heard from Siren, she denied it. She lied straight to my face without a second thought. It doesn't matter if I had Nemesis keeping tabs on the woman I loved. Avery should have told me.

"Did she ever ask you?" I croak out, and confusion flashes across her face before she ducks her head.

"Ask me what?"

"Don't fuck with me, Siren. What did you tell her about your banishment?"

Storm's hand lands on my elbow, and I jerk away from him. He yanks me back until my calves hit the couch, and I sink onto the cushion. He mutters at me to calm down. Bold coming from him. He's usually the one who can't keep his shit together.

"We never talked about it. I told her she shouldn't be contacting me. She didn't care," she whispers, pain lacing her voice.

I grit my teeth and Storm shifts in his seat. "What happened?"

She lifts her head, the same stubborn expression on her face. "You're going to have to be a bit more specific."

Anger bubbles inside of me again. She's back to being a

fucking brat. I wish there was a way to wring the truth from her. Or slip her some type of serum to make sure she's being honest with us. I might have to see if someone in Synd has anything. We've spent too long believing one thing, if she comes out with something completely different, I won't know what to do. Trusting her used to come easily. Not anymore.

"Why'd you betray us?" It's as if the question is ripped from Storm against his will.

He doesn't want to have this conversation any more than I do. We can't trust her answers. We can't trust our own emotions. Therein lies the issue. No matter what she says, we'll always wonder if she's telling the truth. The doubt will be there, waiting, and based on the pain in her eyes, she knows it.

"You're not ready for that conversation, Storm," she whispers. "Pick something else."

"No. You don't get to dictate how this goes. You're the one in the wrong." He leans forward, stabbing his finger at her. "*You* betrayed us. *You* threw everything away. *You* sold us out. Just fucking admit it."

Her face softens the slightest bit, losing some of the defensiveness. "Is that what you want? For me to spread all my mistakes out? Perhaps I could flay myself alive. Would that make you happy? Or better yet"—she stands slowly—"I could just disappear again."

"Sit your ass down, Siren," I growl, then turn to Storm. "You done, or do you need to yell at her some more?"

He glares at me. "Don't pull that shit with me. You're just as pissed. Just because you're better at hiding it doesn't mean it isn't there."

Siren inches toward the door as if we won't notice. "Sit the fuck down, Siren. We're having this out whether you like it or not. This shit has been a long time coming."

She sighs as she drops onto the loveseat and crosses her arms. "Fine. Go ahead."

My arm shoots out and I block Storm from jumping to his

feet. He mutters curses at me. I don't fucking care. We've all got shit to deal with and being at each other's throats will only get one of us killed. Siren's mistakes all those years ago might have changed our futures, but the sharp sting has faded into a dull ache. I can work with that, though I doubt Storm can.

"When did it start?" I ask, keeping my tone even.

"You're asking shitty questions. I don't know what you mean."

I grit my teeth. "When did you start taking money from them?"

"I didn't."

Storm throws his hands up. "She's not even willing to admit she betrayed us. She'll lie to us like she has been this entire time."

"Then kill me," she snaps, and my head whips around. "I told you this was a bad fucking idea. You two can't see past your own egos enough to think maybe you might have been wrong. You don't trust me. You never will. You'll always be looking over your shoulders, wondering if I'll pop up and fuck you over again. Except this time, you have more to lose. So, kill me. Solves a lot of problems."

"We're not going to fucking kill you, Siren," I grunt. "Stop spouting bullshit you know won't actually solve anything."

"Then I'll leave. Then you won't be responsible for whatever happens. Which solves everything." She glances away, and I swear there's a sheen in her eyes.

"Why the fuck are those your two solutions to fucking everything? Death or running. Hell, I'm surprised you didn't suggest Snake kill you." Storm laughs humorlessly and shakes his head.

Her jaw twitches. "Oh, he threatened to. At least according to Banner. I never actually saw Snake."

My head pops up. "He didn't talk to you?"

She gives us a rueful smile. "No one talked to me. Including you two. The only person who ever asked if I was in trouble was Avery."

"What did you say?" Storm whispers.

She swallows hard. "Nothing. It was before I was dragged in, and I didn't want her to get sucked into whatever was going on."

I sit back and my vision blurs. It's been a long time, but that whole night is seared into my brain. My timeline of events clearly doesn't match with hers. Hell, Storm was missing for an hour. I never asked where he went. Everything happened so fast and when we found out what she did, I lost track of the details.

Now, all the things I missed, all the questions I never asked, swirl around me. If I could pluck one out and give it a voice, maybe it would ease a bit of the anxiety building inside of me.

"Walk me through it," I murmur. I'm determined not to interrupt her once she finally starts talking. *If* she starts talking. "What happened that night?"

"No," she answers with conviction, and I level her with a glare.

"It wasn't a request, Siren. Tell me what the fuck happened that night."

"I can't." She holds up her hand when Storm sputters. "I can't because I don't remember a lot of it. I remember Avery coming by and I remember...uh, walking into headquarters. I thought it would be empty, but it was almost full."

"They confronted you in front of the whole club?" The question pops out before I can stop myself.

"Uh, no. Not exactly. Banner. He, well, he..." She pulls in a deep breath. "It doesn't matter. Point is, I didn't get a chance to defend myself. They'd made up their minds long before I walked into the hole. Just like you did when you heard. And you know what? I understood. I *still* understand. I get why you had to cut me loose. My mere presence threatened everything you'd worked toward. I thought you would have let me explain, but I understood why you didn't."

Silence descends over the room, a heavy weight of memories pressing down on me. Storm's fingers brush mine, lending me the strength I need.

"The hole." My throat contracts as I force out the words.

"I'd rather not talk about that. It won't change what happened and I'm not keen to relive that particular memory. Especially after tonight. Anything else?"

"Why?" Storm breathes. It's a plea ripped from the depths of his soul. "Why didn't you come to us? We could have helped you."

She explodes to her feet. "You think I didn't try? You think I just took my beating and skipped off into the fucking sunset without a fucking thought in my head? I came here. I walked right up to your goddamn door and you two couldn't even be bothered to tell me to fuck off to my face. Like fucking cowards, you pretended you weren't home. You don't get to sit there and scold me like a damn child, Storm. You didn't care whether I lived or died. You didn't care whether I was guilty or innocent. You threw me away the minute I was no longer useful to you."

She stomps away and I tense. Instead of running out the door, she races up the stairs. A minute later, a door shuts softly. I glance at Storm and rest my hand on his thigh. He jolts and his Adam's apple bobs.

"He beat her," he murmurs. "Did we fuck up?"

His eyes meet mine and my throat closes. I wanted him to move on from being so angry at her, but not like this. I've lived with the guilt of my actions for almost six years. I thought I'd worked through them and came to some semblance of peace over what happened. Now? Now I'm drowning again. Storm won't be there to yank me out of this. And it isn't Siren's job to make us feel better. I don't understand how she turned everything around on us. How is she the one who gets to walk away?

"She still lied. She still manipulated us. She worked with our rivals—"

"Did she?" Storm shakes his head. "We never asked her. She's right. We threw her away the second she threatened our plans. We assumed she betrayed us, but we never talked to her."

"You're forgetting we had a source. We had someone we trusted who had proof of her actions. Maybe it was a mistake.

Maybe she didn't do it on purpose, but the results were the same. Intent doesn't erase the hurt."

He nods yet doesn't look convinced. I can admit the details Siren's given us pull at a long-forgotten heartstring.

Storm clears his throat. "She never apologized. Not once. Even if we didn't open the door, she could have sent a text, called, something. Yet she never did. She fed the Disciples info about the Phantoms for months. Even if she didn't embezzle thousands of dollars." His head swings around. "Did we ever know who she was blabbing to? Did they catch him?"

"Nope. He disappeared."

"You don't think..." Pain lances through his eyes and I grit my teeth.

"No. I don't think she cheated." It's one of the few things I clung to for months to get through the hurt. Regardless of the betrayal, she never gave her heart to anyone else. She never slept with someone else. She wouldn't.

"We need to find out what her motivations were. If she was in trouble, she should have told us. Instead, she thought she could fix everything herself."

"Nothing was broken." Siren's small voice echoes down the stairs. "There was nothing to fix."

Storm's hands curl into fists as if he's fighting not to look over his shoulder at her. I spin on the couch until I'm facing her. Part of me wishes she'd come down and we can finish this. The other part knows I need to be next to Storm and he's one confession away from strangling her. Or provoking her to punch him. Maybe he needs to be hit, though. Fighting or fucking are usually the only two ways to calm him down.

"Then why'd you do it?"

She sniffs, resting her elbows on her knees, and she threads her fingers together. If she leans much farther, she'll tumble down the stairs. She might not care anymore.

"I didn't meet with anyone. I didn't embezzle any money. I didn't give anyone information." Her eyes meet mine. "But that's not what you want to hear. Which is fair. Like I said before, your minds were made up long before I ever walked into headquarters. Instead of me trying to convince you, why don't you explain why you're so certain of my guilt?"

Storm shoves to his feet and twists to glare at her. "You're not a victim, Siren. We saw the pictures. Stop fucking lying."

I grip the back of my neck, wishing I could slap some sense into Storm. He's giving me whiplash with how his emotions are bouncing back and forth. He never has been able to regulate and process her leaving. One minute he would fly off the handle and the next he'd be begging me to find her. Then he just shut down, refusing to talk about her at all. Everything he bottled up is coming out and I don't know how to help him through it.

She straightens and tilts her head. I can practically see the gears turning in her brain. I wish I could reach in and pluck out her thoughts—sift through them until I understood where her mind has gone. Maybe then we'd finally get somewhere, because at this point we're just going around in circles. None of us wants to concede.

One night changed everything. We used to be able to deal with our issues together. We worked through them even if shit was hard. It wasn't always easy, but we grew together. Then everything came crashing down. Back then I could read her. Apparently not anymore.

"Where'd you get pictures?"

Storm snorts. "Looking for someone else to blame?"

Her nostrils flare, but she keeps her voice even. "Show me the photos, then."

"As if you need proof of your own betrayal." Storm sneers.

I move to the trunk tucked in the corner of the room. We probably shouldn't keep this shit out in the open, but once we threw everything in here, we didn't want to think about it again. Someone could easily break the combination lock. Not that they'd find much. It's not like Siren's actions were kept a secret. Snake bitched about it for months afterward. He even taunted me with her betrayal when I challenged him for the presidency. Except he didn't know about the photos. We kept those to ourselves.

It doesn't take me long to find the prints. They're one of the last things we put in here before we closed it for what we thought would be forever. Storm suggested we burn it. I said no. I knew he'd regret it at some point.

I stand and hold them out to her. She hesitates before pushing to her feet. Storm kicks the couch before stomping past Siren as she reaches the bottom of the steps. I'm surprised he doesn't shoulder check her as he passes. Siren watches him go, then makes her way over to me. She doesn't grab the pictures, just stares at them in my hand.

"Take them. Might jog your memory."

Her brows pull low, and her fingers barely pinch the corner. Her gaze bounces over the print. I don't want to be here while she comes up with some excuse. It's clearly her and some asshole. She can't refute the fact she's talking to him.

Slowly, she flips to the next one. A five-year-old could tell she's passing the man papers in this one. She'll be hard pressed to find a reason behind her laughing with him in the picture she's looking at now.

"I don't know who this is," she murmurs more to herself than me.

"He's one of the Disciples. The one you spread info to that allowed them to sabotage us. We assume it's the same one who helped Prophet orchestrate a raid against the Phantoms. And the one who shot Jag and tried to kill a bunch of our men. He was your handler."

Twenty-Six

"She didn't know?" I ask, then I hit the bag again.

The makeshift gym we installed in the house isn't the best, but it has enough for us to work off excess energy. Which is exactly what I need right now. I've been harboring more tension than usual.

Sweat rolls from my temple to my cheek and I swipe at the droplet. Ghost swallows hard and I fight a smirk. Between shit with the Disciples and Siren waltzing back into our lives, I haven't been able to relax. Except for when I was holding Siren in the bath, which freaks me out more than anything.

I tried to hold on to my anger, thinking it would help keep Siren at bay, or at least my feelings toward her. It didn't work. Now I'm just confused. After the way she reacted when we started questioning her, I'm no longer so sure about her role in things. I'm still convinced she fucked us over. I'm no longer sure she did it on purpose.

"No," Ghost says, pulling me from my thoughts. "She wasn't aware Jag was shot. Nor the hit they put out on our men. I thought she'd ask Lexi after she got banished, but apparently, they didn't keep in contact. I thought it was because Siren knew Lexi was the one who took the photos and gave them to us. She genuinely doesn't know why they were taken."

"How'd she react when you told her? More excuses and lies?" My fist flies through the air, sending the heavy bag swinging around. He waits until I've worn myself out and I collapse onto my back. He looms over me with crossed arms. His muscles bulge and my mouth waters. If I don't get my shit together, I'm going to end up bending him over the bench press.

"I didn't tell her about Lexi. When she found out about Jag and everything else, she shut down. Wandered off in a daze. Probably hiding in a closet."

I let out a humorless laugh. "She always did like to hide, huh?"

"I truly don't think she's seen those pictures before. Doesn't seem to know anything about them at all. Which makes me wonder..."

I give him a look. "You wondering about shit is never a good thing. Especially when it comes to Siren."

He drops next to me and stares at the ceiling. "You asked if we fucked up. I wonder if we did. Maybe there's an explanation for the photos."

I lace my fingers with his. "Even if it wasn't her passing info, she still met with a Disciple. Her actions had major consequences for more than just her."

"I don't want to talk about her anymore. Not right now. I'm exhausted mentally. We should have waited to have that conversation."

I roll my head toward him, and he does the same. His lips brush mine and some of the tension leaves me. My eyes flutter shut as I breathe in the silence. He's not the only one who wishes we would have dealt with this some other time. If we would have talked to her all those years ago, maybe things would be different. Maybe we would have been able to work through things.

"I missed her," I say quietly. He doesn't respond right away, and I wonder if he heard me.

"Me too."

"Why do I feel this way?"

He sighs and I realize he won't let me pretend nothing's changed. Not with my question. She morphed our lives into something unrecognizable once before and she's doing it again. I recoil from the thought of letting her go.

If we don't get things sorted soon, we won't be able to deal with all the other issues we need to deal with. We've been neglecting the MC, and we're going to have more problems than the Disciples on our hands if we let it go much further. The enemies lurking in our ranks will strike when we're at our weakest. And right now, I'm feeling pretty weak.

"Why did you miss her?" he asks with a light laugh. The sound makes my chest tighten. "Because she was everything. She was the glue that kept us together when we were young. She was the constant when nothing felt like it would last. She was the only one who didn't judge us."

"You're getting sentimental."

"You asked. Did you want me to tell you it's because you miss fucking a pussy?"

I chuckle and turn to stare at the ceiling again. "I do miss fucking a pussy sometimes."

"Nah. You miss fucking *her* pussy."

I lick my lips, remembering her body pressed against mine in the tub. I close my eyes and the image of her tits in my face has my cock hardening. He's right, though I wish he wasn't. I could explain my body's reaction to her away if it was a woman. Except I haven't desired anyone besides Ghost since she left. Found others attractive? Sure. Imagined being deep inside them? Not once. As soon as I found Siren on our doorstep, I've been dreaming about her under me—riding me. Whatever way I could get her. I swear I woke up with the taste of her pussy on my lips this morning.

I glance at him from the corner of my eye. "You miss it too."

"Never said I didn't."

I rip my hand away from his. "I'm offended. Am I not enough for your insatiable needs?"

He rolls his eyes, then moves and straddles me. My hands land on his thighs and his fingers dig into my chest. I was already hard, but with the pressure of his body on mine, my cock strains against my shorts. He leans closer, his nose brushing against mine.

"You miss having her in between us. Admit it," he demands, and I swallow hard. "You deep in her pussy and me slamming into her ass. Or are you imagining what it was like to fuck her while her lips were wrapped around my cock, hmm?"

I wrap my fingers around the back of his neck and seal my mouth to his. When his tongue licks along my lips, I force him away.

"Actually, I was remembering your cock sliding against mine while we fucked her together."

His rasping breath fills the space between us as his length presses into my stomach. I groan, giving away how affected I am. He buries his face into my neck and sinks his teeth into my skin. I tilt my head and run my hands under his shirt. I lose myself in touch, letting it wash away the last of my anxiety.

"Imagining someone else when I'm about to fuck you is a bold move," he growls.

My hands stall on his waistband, and I pull in a deep breath. Since Siren left, our relationship grew without her. I don't want her coming between us. Not like that. I don't even know if I actually want her here with us. It's one thing to fantasize about being with her again. It's another to bring it up while in our current position.

"Get out of your head, Storm. Lose yourself in this," he murmurs as his hand slides down my stomach and dips under my waistband. I grunt when his fingers wrap around my cock and squeeze.

He strokes me once before pulling back, and a low whine escapes me. He sits back on his knees and grabs my shorts. I lift my hips, and he slips the fabric down my thighs. My cock springs free and he chuckles. When he stands to rid himself of his clothes, I kick off my shorts and take off my shirt, then grip my shaft to ease some of the pressure. A rumble erupts from him, and he leans over me. He grabs my wrist and his nostrils flare.

"Let go," he growls.

I smirk, refusing to do as he says. He's not going to deny me tonight, as he sometimes likes to do. I'll let him be on top and come first, but I need to be in control today. He'll just have to get the fuck over it.

He raises an eyebrow. "So, that's how you're playing it tonight?"

I nod slowly and continue to stroke myself. I expect him to argue or try to wrest control from me. Instead, he stalks away, and I narrow my gaze. I swear if he leaves me here, I'll end up throat punching him in his sleep.

I track his movements as he walks to the table set up in the corner and rummages through the drawer. When he spins back, he's clutching something in his hand. He saunters back to me, a smug expression stamped on his face.

He kicks my legs open, then drops between them, and I pull my knees up. With his eyes fixed on me stroking myself, he flips the top of the container, and a shudder runs through me. I tip my head back and brace myself for the cold gel to hit my skin. My grunt echoes around us and my lids flutter closed.

"Relax," he murmurs. "You're so goddamn tense."

I unclench my muscles, and he pushes one finger into my ass, then another. I spasm around him and my hand runs up and down my cock. He's murmuring something, but I can't hear him over the blood rushing in my ears. My mouth waters as I watch his shaft twitch. He's too focused on his hand between my legs to notice.

I let go of my cock and prop myself on my elbow to grab his throat. His eyes snap to mine, desire flaming in the depths.

"Careful, Storm. You're playing with fire," he murmurs. He thrusts his fingers deeper and I swallow a moan.

"I'm done playing. Fuck me or get the fuck out."

His eyebrow rises and a smirk plays on his lips. He curls his fingers inside my ass and my back arches off the floor, an involuntary moan leaving me. He adds another one, determined to work me into a frenzy. We've been abstaining while he was recovering. It's been torture to refuse him. Now he's punishing me for it and probably so many other things. He's always been an asshole. I can't complain. If he keeps it up, though, I'm going to turn the tables on him. He'll be the one on his knees.

Ghost's free hand lands on my chest and his nails dig into my skin. "I know that fucking look. Don't even fucking think about it."

A wild grin takes over my face. I grab his wrist and force him deeper. He curls his fingers and I clench around them. We stare at each other, both vying for control. I loosen my grip just enough, and he pulls his hand away. I wince and he pinches my nipple, distracting me from the sting. This is exactly what I need. I squeeze my cock, then let go before he catches me.

He tugs his fingers out, and a delicious, familiar burn rolls through me. An ache fills me at the emptiness he leaves behind. Thankfully, he doesn't make me wait. After all we've been through the last couple days, hell, the last couple weeks, I don't think I'd be able to stand it if he took his time. He pushes inside my ass, my groan joining his own.

He winds his hand around the back of my neck and tugs me up. The move has me clenching around his hard length, forcing a grunt from him. He slams his mouth into mine and our tongues fight for dominance. Something hard hits my back and I rip my face away to glance behind. Somehow he's pulled the incline bench to the side. He wraps his fingers around my throat and forces my back against it.

The new angle makes my breath catch and I struggle to fill my lungs. He pulls out slowly, then buries his cock in me. He fuses our mouths together and his tongue sweeps in. My eyes flutter closed, heightening the sensations coursing through my body. If he doesn't move faster, I'm going to flip us and take over. I don't take control often with him. I rarely have the need or desire to truly dominate him. It's happened more often since Siren was banished, though.

She didn't submit easily, resisting my dominance every step of the way. She always was a brat like that, and I loved it. I had to fight for her submission, which made it all the sweeter when she finally gave in.

"You're thinking of her," Ghost whispers harshly, punctuating the statement with a hard thrust. "Reliving her being between us, aren't you? Taking her together, both of us driving into her."

I moan in response, my fingers digging into his back. He'll keep bringing her up, using our shared memories to egg me on. Or maybe he's punishing himself. His teeth graze my neck as his cock fills me. His words flow from my mind like sand through a sieve, but the emotions left behind etch into my heart.

"Answer. Me." His growl rumbles through my chest.

"Yes," I gasp as he pushes deeper.

A deep chuckle reverberates around me, and he stops moving. "Should we invite her in? Bring her to the edge, then fuck her just like we used to. We can play out every fantasy we've had since she left."

"I want you," I growl.

"You already have me," he breathes.

I glance over his shoulder as he slams into me over and over. My eyes meet Siren's as she leans against the doorframe. Heat curls in my gut when her tongue darts out and runs along her bottom lip. Her gaze narrows, but she's not fooling me. She's probably soaking through her panties while she watches us.

I fixate on her while I stroke my cock. My eyes dart to Ghost, expecting him to notice her. He's too busy watching his length drive into me. I push my hips up and the new angle has me taking him deeper. A deep groan rumbles from his chest.

His movements become erratic as he chases his orgasm. I fight against my own, though it isn't easy with her gaze fixated on us. Between Ghost's reminders and my memories flaring to life, I might lose the battle. Except if Ghost was serious about fucking her and she's as willing as she looks right now...

Desire blazes in her eyes as Ghost groans, his entire body shuddering above me. I clench around his cock and he flies over the edge. It takes everything in me not to follow him. I drop my chin to my chest and hold my breath as his pleasure crashes over me. Ghost's lips flutter over my pulse, words of affection he rarely utters washing across my skin.

When I look up again, the empty doorway mocks me, and I wonder if she was ever there to begin with.

Twenty-Seven

I shake out my hands as I hurry down the hallway. I knew they were still fucking, but I didn't expect to see it. Nor did I expect how much it would turn me on.

There's nowhere for me to run in this damn house. I spent the last forty-five minutes holed up in a closet upstairs. I'm surprised Ghost didn't come searching for me. He had enough questions swimming in his eyes to justify one of them slipping out. Instead, he let me walk away. I make my way back to my hideout and grab the photos. I could retreat once more. Not that Storm will come for me. He's too busy getting railed.

I clutch the pictures and make my way to Storm's room. It's practically mine now, anyway. Storm's been staying...somewhere else. I assume in Ghost's room, though half the time I've woken up, he's posted up in the chair next to my bed. I kick the door shut and try to lock it. Except there isn't one.

"Seems like an oversight," I mutter.

I drop the photos onto the nightstand and collapse onto the bed. Studying the pictures didn't help. I couldn't tell who took them or why I was in them. My memories from right before I was banished are hazy, overrun by later events.

A shiver rolls through me when I remember Banner's fists hitting my flesh. He screamed a lot of things while he was beating me, but I couldn't really comprehend his words. All I knew about was the money. Thousands and thousands of dollars hidden in my walls, in my mattress, in my closet. No one asked if I knew where it came from. I didn't. No one asked if it was my father's. It was. No one asked if I was at fault. I wasn't.

They didn't care if the money was mine or not. The massive amount of cash didn't really matter. I'm surprised they didn't kill me. I thought they let me off with a banishment because they didn't have proof I stole anything from the club.

My father had access to the accounts and the motive to embezzle. He was a drunk, a womanizer, and a gambler. I'm pretty sure if he stayed sober long enough, he would have taken all the money and disappeared. He certainly wasn't staying for me. Snake and the others knew it was him. They needed someone to blame and there I was, a ready-made scapegoat.

The pictures, though, create a whole new story. At least when it comes to Ghost and Storm. It explains why they abandoned me after I was banished. I pick one up and study my profile. I don't remember this at all. Not a flicker of recognition. I can't even figure out where it was taken, though it looks like a restaurant. One I can't place. I wish I would have asked Ghost some questions about them.

Huffing, I drop it back on the pile and stare at the ceiling. An image of Ghost thrusting into Storm flashes through my mind. Storm refused to look away from me the entire time. I wonder if he'll tell Ghost I was standing there. I couldn't have walked away if I wanted to, even if Ghost would have noticed. Heat flashes down my body and settles between my legs.

When I was in the bathroom with Storm, I was able to explain away the feelings. I can't deny the desire I felt while spying on them. It has nothing to do with my dry spell. I've been living the last six years without sex. It's not anything new for me. Which means it must be them. Being around them has woken a longing in me I haven't felt since I left.

I hate it.

And I love it.

I thought I was broken. I thought *they* broke me. Or rather, their rejection. I wasn't interested in anyone else. No one randomly caught my eye. I could blame it on my focus on surviving, except I knew it wasn't. Picking up a random one-night stand wasn't appealing and dating was out of the question. Truth is, I never wanted anyone else. Whenever I touched myself, I closed my eyes and pretended it was one of them. It was the only way I'd be able to orgasm. It broke my heart when the high vanished. All it did was remind me of their absence.

I close my eyes and curl my fingers into two tight fists. I should *not* touch myself while in Storm's bed. Either of them could bust in here at any moment. I slide under the covers and flip onto my side. I'm not tired and I doubt I'll be able to fall asleep anytime soon. My body is practically vibrating, especially when I press my thighs together.

Distracting myself with the photos doesn't help. Planning my escape from Harris isn't interesting enough. Mostly because I know I won't be leaving just yet. I've been lying to myself, thinking I'd take off in the dead of night. Even when I was certain the best thing would to leave, I knew I wouldn't. Not until they told me to go. Then when one of them did, I was pissed. Actually, I was hiding my hurt behind the rage.

"This is ridiculous," I mutter, and burrow farther under the covers.

Darkness envelops me and I feel like I'm in my own world. I'm cut off from everything—everyone—and it's glorious. My hand ends up under my shirt and my thumb flicks across my nipple. I do it again and bite back a moan. They might not be coming to find me, but I'm not going to give away what I'm doing.

I roll onto my back and prop my knees up, one hand playing with the hard nub and the other snaking under my waistband. Of course I'm soaked. Why wouldn't I be? I heard what Ghost whispered to Storm about me being in between them. I saw Storm's arm flexing while Ghost fucked him. I smelled their pleasure, a thick perfume of lust and desire and everything I'd been missing.

I shove the thoughts away and concentrate on the sensations building within me. I circle my clit, then slide my fingers to my core and back again. A moan leaves me, and I cut off the sound. I close my eyes and strain for any indication they're about to walk in. I press my lips together and my legs fall open. My arms aren't quite long enough to get deep like I want. I need a toy, but I lost the last one in the fire and didn't have time to get another.

Biting my lip, I pinch my nipple as I slip two fingers inside once, then twice. Images both old and new flash behind my lids as I move to my clit. I rub the sensitive bud harder, faster. I can't keep up the pace with both my hands and I abandon trying to give myself the full experience. Nothing will compare to what I once had. My fantasies will have to do.

The familiar tightening in my gut makes me whimper, and Ghost's voice floats from my memories, commanding me to come for him. It's not enough, and a frustrated sob leaves me as my fingers slow. Bastards. This is all their fault. If they wouldn't have been fucking with the door open, I never would have stumbled on them. If they would have let me leave—hell, if they wouldn't have texted me in the first place, I wouldn't be in this position.

Tears fill my eyes, and I swipe at them furiously. The covers fly from over me and I gasp. Storm stands there in only his boxer briefs, his eyes traveling down my body. Ghost stops me when I attempt to pull my shirt down. I suppose he doesn't want to be the only one naked.

"Someone got a little hot and bothered while watching us, wouldn't you say?" Storm says with a smirk.

"Sure looks like it. Then again, one can never be too sure without proof."

"Should we ask? Or..."

Ghost slowly pulls my arm away and forces my hand over my head. I don't resist, mostly because I'm really fucking frustrated. Storm hooks his finger in my waistband, and I bite the side of my tongue as my gaze darts from one to the other.

I want to come. No, I *need* to come. I want to pretend this is normal. To imagine nothing has changed between us. Or maybe I just want to know whether or not I'm broken. If I am, then so be it. I've survived this long without truly feeling satisfied. If this is all I get, at least I can use the memory for as long as I have left on this earth.

A shudder rolls through me and Ghost chuckles. "I doubt we need to ask. Do we, sweets?"

I shake my head, then swallow hard. They exchange a glance and I hold my breath. If they walk away, there's no going back for me. I'm already fighting back the feelings of being unwanted. They never fought for me. Not when it really mattered. I shove away the thoughts, desperate to stay in this moment.

Storm runs his finger down my side, leaving goosebumps in his wake. His jaw twitches and he walks away. My eyes slam closed and I drop my hand to my shirt. Ghost's growl echoes around me, making me wince. He seizes my wrist and forces it over my head once more. I open my mouth to protest or cuss him out or even look at him, but nothing comes out.

I peek at him as he grabs my other wrist. At the same time, Storm grips my pants and yanks them clean off me. My emotions ping-pong in my chest, making my heart race. I thought he'd left. It was pretty clear how pissed he was. It doesn't make any sense why he'd stay. Unless he wants to punish me. From the look on his face, though, he's not walking out anytime soon.

Storm grabs my ankles and forces my knees up. I bite my lip, waiting for their next move. Maybe I can get away with not saying anything. I can pretend this is all a dream and we won't have a messy aftermath. I'll fall asleep and they can sneak out. Then we'll never speak of it again. Mentally, I shake myself. I'm already fifteen steps ahead when I said I'd live in the moment. I'm shit at this. I thought sex would be like riding a bike.

Ghost's lips brush my ear, and I startle. "What's going on in that pretty little head of yours?"

I shake my head, and he hums. Like hell am I going to spill all my insecurities to him. He lost that right years ago.

"Close your eyes, sweets." Ghost waits until I comply, then murmurs, "There's a good girl. You're going to let us make you come. Before your body's done shaking, we'll do it again."

Storm eases my knees open, and I peek at him. He licks his lips as he stares at my pussy. Despite my brain refusing to shut off, I know I'm wet. My body vibrates in anticipation as he brushes his fingers up my calves to my thighs and stops short of where I really want him.

"She's not a very good listener, Ghost," Storm says, and I close my eyes again. His light touch up and down my legs is almost too much.

"Unfortunately, I don't think we can punish her just yet."

Ghost flicks my nipple, and my eyes fly open. He doesn't scold me again, just tweaks my other nipple. My back arches when he pinches the hard nub. Before I can recover, Storm buries his tongue in my pussy. A moan leaves me as he sucks on my clit. I don't know what to do with my hands and they end up fluttering around Storm's head. Another chuckle from Ghost has me gritting my teeth.

He clicks his tongue as he drops to his knees next to the bed. He throws one arm over my stomach and the other traps my hands above me once more. Storm wraps his own arms around my thighs, preventing me from closing my legs. It's both the best and worst thing to happen—to be completely at their mercy.

It's been so long since I've been caged by them, I almost forgot how it felt. My mind skips from one question to the next. Why are they here? Do they want to bring me to the edge, then abandon me? Should I have shaved my legs? Not that I had access to a razor. When was the last time I trimmed?

I should be focused on the pleasure they're lavishing on me, but with Storm's face getting up close and personal with my business, it's a genuine concern. I doubt shaving or showering or hell, even fighting them would change what's about to happen.

Heat flashes through my body and a flush travels from my chest, up my neck, and to my cheeks. How would they react if I fought them? We had discussions before, complete with safewords and boundaries. We knew how far to push each other. With just a look, Ghost would know what mood I was in. Storm demanded words—clear and complete communication. All those plans died when I left, and I no longer know the rules. It's a limbo I don't particularly enjoy.

Ghost's breath brushes the shell of my ear, and I shiver. "Get out of your head. Focus on my hands, teasing your body. Concentrate on Storm and how his tongue moves."

An unbidden moan leaves me, and my eyes flutter shut as I whisper, "Don't stop." I don't know which of them I'm talking to. Or maybe it's for me. To not stop whatever's happening right now.

"Not until you come," Ghost murmurs.

Storm teases me with his fingers, then thrusts them inside, and my yelp turns into a whimper. He doesn't wait for me to urge him on, merely curls his fingers every time he drives them into me. His tongue flicks my clit, and my orgasm takes me by surprise. Ghost's mouth covers mine in a brutal kiss and he swallows my cries of ecstasy. Waves of pleasure crash over me again and again while Storm attempts to wring every last ounce of euphoria from my body.

"Such a good girl," Ghost murmurs against my lips.

He lifts his head as Storm pulls his fingers from my pussy. My thighs are drenched, and my cheeks heat again. When I try to close my legs, though, Storm grabs my knees and forces them back to the bed.

"No hiding, Siren," Ghost says, then sinks his teeth into my neck. He'll probably leave a mark behind.

It hasn't escaped me how silent Storm has been. No, not silent. He just hasn't spoken to me. He's barely looked at me. Sure, he buried his face in my pussy, made me come, but our eyes haven't met at all. It's like he's here, yet not. Like if he pretends this is a fantasy, a dream, he can dismiss what he's doing. Pain lashes through my heart, making it hard to breathe.

Storm's head whips up, and finally our gazes clash together. I try to fix my face, to pull on the mask I've spent so long perfecting for moments like this. Ones where feeling anything is too much. He licks his lips and his eyes darken.

Ghost drops his hand to one of my knees and Storm holds the other, as if they practiced this a million times. Like they know exactly how to keep a woman where they want her—open and waiting for them.

I wonder how many other—

I cut the thought off before it can take root. I don't care. I *shouldn't* care. They didn't owe me their loyalty. They didn't belong to me while I was gone, just like they don't belong to me now. It's a sobering thought which only makes me spiral more.

Storm swipes his finger along my pussy, then holds it up for me to see. "Still soaked. Did you need more, sweets?"

I stare at him, not sure where to go from here. My thoughts weave into a tangled tapestry of longing, anticipation, and insecurity, creating a disjointed canvas draped in desire. He tracks every emotion as it flits across my face and an understanding enters his eyes. I don't need his words. He would only sound like he was placating me. Apparently, he doesn't need my words either.

He shoves his sweatpants down and kicks them to the side. He grips his cock and strokes it once before kneeling between my legs. Ghost growls and my head snaps to the side. If he stops Storm, I might cry. There was no jealousy between us when we were together. From the look on Ghost's face, there isn't now either. His gaze is fixed on Storm, or rather, on his cock. I swallow hard, then suck in a shuddering breath.

Storm's fingers dig into my inner thighs, but I keep my focus on Ghost and the desire dripping from him. I gasp as Storm buries his cock in me and my back arches off the bed. Ghost keeps my hands locked above my head. A delicious burn rolls through me as I stretch around Storm. His groan rolls through the air as he pulls out and slams into me again.

Ghost grips my chin and forces my head forward. "Look at how well you're taking him. What you're doing to him."

A spasm hits me and Storm grunts as I squeeze his cock. I pant as my pleasure coils tighter with each thrust. Ghost runs his hand over my nipple, then down my body. When his fingers find my clit, a shockwave hits me. Ghost keeps up a steady stream of whispered dirty words as Storm embeds his length into me harder and faster. My vision blurs and needy noises fall from my lips.

"Next time, we'll both be inside you," Ghost murmurs.

Memories and fantasies burst in my head, and I cascade over the edge. Storm either doesn't notice or decides to fuck me through it since he never slows. He grunts every time he's fully inside me. Ghost's fingers circle my clit, the sensitive bud practically vibrating under his touch.

Another orgasm builds within me before the last one is done. Storm's movements become erratic, and he moans my name as he throws his head back. I follow him into oblivion, stars bursting behind my lids. I didn't even realize I'd closed my eyes.

Our sharp gasps fill the room and I'm floating in a weightless darkness as I shudder out the last of my release. I hum as I feel Storm pull away, my pussy clenching as if to keep him inside me just a little bit longer. Ghost's lips brush against mine, but I'm barely able to react. I'm too busy floating in a sea of contentment. They exchange whispered words. I can't make them out. I don't want to know. Knowing usually leads to hurting and I'm not ready for it to hurt yet.

I don't know how much time passes, but eventually my lids flutter open to an empty room. Tears fill my eyes, and I curl on my side. Expecting them to stick around afterward was a fool's dream. Did I really think they'd cuddle? Of course they wouldn't crawl in next to me. They got what they wanted, which wasn't even sex. They don't need me to fulfil their desires. This was something else —pity or guilt. Maybe it was merely to assert dominance over me. To show how much control they could exert with a few touches. And I failed. At every fucking turn, I failed at keeping my heart safe. And now it's breaking all over again.

Twenty-Eight

Ghost

My vision blurs as I wash my hands. Snapshots of Siren writhing on the bed flash through my mind. Couple the memories with having Storm underneath me and I'm already hard again. I feel like we've opened Pandora's box. We'd successfully stuffed all our emotions dealing with Siren away, then ripped it open as soon as she came back into our lives.

I sigh, shutting off the water and grabbing a towel. Gazing around my bathroom, I catch sight of her leftover towel hanging over the edge of the large tub. Shaking my head, I toss the fabric on the counter and prowl into my bedroom, only to freeze in the doorway.

"What the fuck are you doing?" I snap at Storm.

He finishes pulling my sweatpants over his hips before answering. "I'm putting on pants. What's your problem?"

"Did you tell her? She was practically comatose when I left to clean up."

"Still sleeping," he says, then pulls a shirt on. "We need to figure out how we're moving forward. And how much we trust her."

My eyes dart to the doorway, then back at him. "You fucking left her alone? And didn't say a word? She's going to think—"

"Think what? That we used her? That she's nothing more than a convenient plaything?" Storm props his fists on his hips. "It won't matter what we say. She'll either think we were using her or...I don't know. Fucking her over while we fuck her?"

I run my hand through my hair, then grip the back of my neck. "We should've—"

He snarls, cutting me off. "Don't. Don't fucking start. We can't afford to be distracted."

The bedroom door creaks open and I groan. I can't tell how long she was standing there from the look on her face. She's a blank mask, hiding everything she might be feeling.

"Hey, distraction here. Just wondering if I can shower and if you converted another room to a bedroom like you did the gym."

Storm gapes at her, and I bury my face in my hands. We're never going to get on the same page. There's too much past and not enough trust between us, and I don't know how to fix it. Every time I make a decision or Storm opens his mouth, shit goes sideways.

"Only other rooms we have are at headquarters," I say after dropping my hands to my sides.

She nods as she stares off into space. "Okay. What about my old house? I could get out of your hair. Stay there until things die down here."

"No," Storm snaps, then turns to raid my closet for a sweatshirt.

"What Storm means is there's no way for us to protect you when you're there. Plus, most of the floorboards are missing, along with part of the roof. You'd die from sepsis long before things with the Disciples settle down."

She tilts her head, eyes narrowing on me. "You don't get it, do you? This isn't something that will settle down. You set in motion things that can't be stopped. Prophet's been planning this for ages. Probably long before you took over the Phantoms. He's had *years* to put everything in place. You've had, what, weeks? You can't protect me and deal with the war that's coming. Oh, and I wouldn't get sepsis from staying there."

She turns and Storm lunges forward to snatch at her arm. Slowly, she looks down at his hold on her, then back up.

"You'd do well to remove your hand," she murmurs.

For a second, I don't think he'll listen. I take a step toward them when he rips his hand away. She crosses her arms and I wince. I know that look. I've seen it a thousand times and it's never good.

"Why'd you meet with him?" Storm whispers, desperation bleeding into his voice.

Her brows pull low. It's the first emotion I've seen from her. "I don't know."

The veins in Storm's neck stand out, and I take another step forward. "Do you remember where the photos were taken?"

She shakes her head, and Storm curls his fingers into tight fists as he asks, "How can you not remember?"

"How the hell should I know? It was years ago. I don't know who the guy is. I don't know where they were taken. I don't know why I was there. I have no recollection of any of that. And just for your peace of mind, which you won't fucking believe anyway, I didn't pass any info to the Disciples. If I *did* say anything to anyone, it would have been a flippant comment about Snake. Because I was a shit talker who didn't know when the hell to keep her damn mouth shut."

"Exactly," I murmur, and her gaze snaps to me.

Her nostrils flare as she takes me in. "Let me ask you something, *President*. What critical information could I have possibly had at the tender age of twenty-one? Someone who wasn't even technically a member of the club and wasn't even allowed in headquarters anymore. Who the hell would even look at me and say, *you know, she seems like a good person to exploit. Maybe we can turn her into a mole.* For fuck's sake. It's like as soon as you got your damn feelings hurt, all your common sense fled for the hills."

"We assumed you told them our plans," Storm says, though he doesn't sound confident anymore.

She lets out a sharp laugh. "Your plans? Why the fuck would I do that? Besides, would Snake have really gone after me if I had exposed your secrets? You know, the ones indicating you were about to kill him and take over his goddamn club? If that's what it was, he would have thrown me a fucking parade. You two would be six feet under, that's for damn sure."

"Back then, we didn't have a lot to go on," I cut in before Storm starts yelling. "We were more worried about the funds. You revealing our plans was one of the hypothesises. Not the only one."

"Hypothesises isn't a word," she huffs, and wraps her arms around her waist. "Whatever. It doesn't matter."

I step closer, crowding into her space. To her credit, she doesn't flinch or retreat. She never was one to back down from a fight, which is why it's so weird she's piecemealing what she knows. Then again, we've given her very few chances to trust us. I need to talk to Avery. She's the only one who's had any contact with Siren. She'll be able to figure things out much better than I will.

"It does matter. Right now, though, we don't have time to unpack all the goddamn trauma," Storm says bitterly.

"Or we could just not unpack anything." She drops her hands and slips the mask over her features once more. "I go to my old place and you two stay here to deal with the bullshit. I'll check in and everything like a good little girl."

Storm steps up next to her, his chest brushing her arm. "Do you even remember what it's like to be a good girl?"

She tenses and her cheeks hollow, implanting images of her on her knees with my cock in her mouth. I'm sure she knows exactly what she's doing. Too bad for her we're much better at punishing her than she ever was at teasing us.

"We're not doing this. You two had your fun and now we can

pretend it never happened. No more of this." She waves her hand limply at her side, almost hitting Storm in the dick in the process.

Storm slides behind her, whether to protect his assets or sandwich her between us, I don't know. She stares at my chest, refusing to meet my eyes. I hook a finger under her chin and force her gaze to mine. I raise an eyebrow, and her lip slips between her teeth. I glance at Storm, and he nods.

"Listen, sweetheart, we might not have everything worked out, but the last thing we're going to do is let you out of our sight. You're too valuable to let go. Besides, you need more than your hand can provide. So, there will be no pretending." I grip her chin when she tries to look away. "Say you understand."

Storm leans his face next to her ear. "Unless you'd rather lie and say you didn't come. Twice."

A gleam enters her eyes, and a smirk tugs at the corner of her mouth. "It wouldn't be a lie. I didn't come twice."

Storm snorts, sliding his arm around her waist. His hand splays on her hip and I lean closer, our lips almost touching. She sucks in a sharp breath and my cock twitches. She needs to accept her fate. I'm not one to play around when it comes to the universe. Things happen for a reason, whether I understand them or not.

She rips her chin from my grip and slaps me, then drives her elbow into Storm's stomach. It happens so fast I don't have time to react. I grab for her arms, but she spins around and nails Storm between his legs with her knee. He doubles over and she shoves his shoulders. I snatch at her ponytail and the strands slip through my fingers as she dances away. Storm groans, falling in slow motion toward the floor. He grips my ankle, preventing me from going after her.

She glances over her shoulder when she reaches the hallway. "You two lost the right to demand anything from me. Ask all the questions you want now. Just remember you should have asked me then. And when you figure out you were wrong and failed me, don't expect an apology to make anything better." Her eyes glisten, yet she tips her chin up. "I owe you nothing. Remember that."

She disappears and I close my eyes. Storm wheezes, then coughs. He rolls on his back, clutching his dick. I have the irrational urge to bury my foot in his side. He always pushes shit to the extreme. She wouldn't have popped off if he hadn't touched her. I don't know what he was thinking.

"Don't say a fucking word," he grunts.

"You brought that on yourself."

"I'm sick of being in this grey space. I'm sick of wanting her. I'm sick of trying to convince myself I don't. I just want to be done with everything."

I hold out my hand and help him up. "You're going to have to be more specific. What do you mean by everything?"

"Hit the Disciples, make them think twice about attacking us. Clean out the ranks and get rid of those we don't trust." He tucks his chin to his chest and whispers, "Stop fighting with Siren."

"So, you suddenly trust her? Two orgasms and a half-ass conversation is all it took?"

He shrugs, rubbing his crotch. "I'm tired of being angry."

"Well, I'm about to piss you off again. Got a text from Fuse. Venom's on his shit again. I want to deal with him now rather than give him the opportunity to fuck us over when we're knee deep in shit with the Disciples."

He shakes out his leg, and I roll my eyes. She didn't even hit him that hard. I cross my arms and wait until he's done.

"Fuck. I feel like she pinched one of my balls. Maybe we should send Siren after him. She'd probably take care of him with just her fucking elbow." He chuckles lightly, then winces. "We need to figure out what happened, though. You should set up a meeting with Lexi."

"I want Venom dead. No banishment. No second chances. He needs to die, and it needs to look like an accident. I'll figure it out."

"He's had it coming for a long time."

He limps to my bed and collapses onto it as he pulls out his phone. I run my hands through my hair. I need one day. Just one day where we're not on a goddamn rollercoaster. I doubt I'll get a reprieve anytime soon.

Twenty-Nine

Siren

My body vibrates as I raid Storm's closet. I wish I had my own things to choose from, but beggars and all that. Pinching Storm's clothes makes me feel things I definitely shouldn't—nostalgia for one. I keep reminding myself it's just fabric.

I have more pressing matters to think about rather than pining over his sweatshirt. At least I have my own pants. I can't imagine trying to sneak into some place. I'd probably trip over the damn hems and faceplant. Not exactly conducive behavior for killing someone.

My rough plan might get me killed. On the off chance it doesn't, though, it might help Ghost and Storm. Selfishly, I hope my taking down Venom will have them trusting me more. From what I overheard, they want him gone. He's a creep and I'm surprised he's still around. Killing him will help everyone and they'll thank me for it. Then again, sneaking out after I slapped one and ball-checked the other might not help my cause. I'm surprised they didn't come after me right away, if only to put me in my place.

I pull one drawer open after another, searching for a weapon. I used to have a gun and a knife in my backpack, but they're missing. Probably Storm trying to keep me here. I smirk when my knuckles hit the back of a built-in cubby and it rings hollow. It takes me a minute to figure out where the latch is, but eventually I get inside. There's not a lot to choose from, but that's fine. Hopefully I won't even need the gun. Or the knife. I'd rather choke Venom with my bare hands. The hard part will be dealing with the body afterward.

With a small revolver and a switchblade tucked in the front pocket of Storm's sweatshirt, I slip out of the bedroom. I close my eyes and listen for their voices. After a minute, there's a thud from Ghost's room at the end of the hall. I might be able to get away without them noticing. Hell, maybe I'll even be back by the time they figure out I've left. Then I won't have to come up with an excuse. Despite wanting to be covert, I take my phone with me. If I get into trouble, I'll have to call them.

It's been years since I've had to think about anyone other than myself. Whenever I thought about being part of the Phantoms, I imagined it would be hard to fall back into things. Yet here I am, taking care of their problem with Venom and making plans for if things go sideways. I'd rather not have to involve them, but this is their club. Protecting the MC is the most important thing. At least that's how I was raised, though my father didn't exactly live by the rules he taught me.

When I slip out the back door, I breathe a sigh of relief. It takes me longer to get to headquarters than usual. I blame the still-healing injury in my side. Bones came by and took the stitches out that didn't dissolve, though she wasn't gentle about it at all.

We never did get along, but I thought she'd gotten over her crush on Storm. He never gave her any indication he was interested. I might have been too absorbed with my own relationship to really care what she was feeling. Which seems selfish except we weren't friends. She was on the fringes of things, especially when we were kids. I suppose Bones won in the end. She's a member of the Phantoms and I got banished. I'm only here temporarily, so I don't know why she cares so fucking much.

"That bitch will get what's coming to her." Venom's voice

filters down the alleyway. I tuck myself into the shadows of headquarters.

"What'd she do?" a man I don't recognize asks.

Venom snorts. "What didn't she do? All I did was tell her to go to dinner with me. She's definitely a slut. Slept with half the club, but her going out with me? Apparently, that was too much. Didn't even have the decency to just say no thanks. Bitch decided to call me out in front of a bunch of members."

"Bet we could teach her a lesson."

They both laugh, the sound grating on my frayed nerves. Even if I didn't know Ghost wanted him dead, I'd want to kill this man. He was always hitting on Avery and me. It was subtle back then. I wonder if Avery ever told Ghost about him or if he just figured out what type of guy Venom is. From what I recall, Venom was tight with Snake despite not being very high in rank. Last I heard, he was an enforcer, pretending he was keeping members in line instead of just beating those he didn't like.

"You think I'm going to let you anywhere near her? No offense, Hornet, but fuck no. Lexi's mine to punish."

"How you going to get around Prez? Or Storm? She's tight with them." A rock skitters toward me, and I shrink back, though there's nowhere to go. I'd rather not have to kill both of them. At least not by myself in an alley right next to headquarters. I'm much more likely to be discovered, and I can't afford that.

Venom snorts again, and I wonder if that and laughing annoyingly is all he does. From what I remember, he had a big-ass nose slapped onto his blotchy face. I'm not surprised Lexi turned him down. Ignoring, well, his entire personality, he didn't have much to offer. Plus, he's at least two decades older than her.

"Neither of them will care. Ghost was close to beating her the other day. He'll probably thank me for putting her in her place. I'll have my fun with her before I do."

Hornet mutters something I can't hear, and they laugh again, but I'm no longer listening. I don't put much stock in Venom's statement. The idea of Ghost hitting Lexi is preposterous. If they did have an altercation, it must have been here. Lexi hasn't been by the house as far as I know. She probably doesn't even know I'm still in town. I told her I was leaving as soon as I could.

"Okay, but what if they do care? You can't afford to have them up your ass," Hornet says. "Not with your plans."

The sound of fist on flesh echoes through the chilly night. "Keep your fucking mouth shut, Hornet, or you'll be the one I'm teaching a fucking lesson to."

Internally, I groan as Hornet mutters an apology. My job just got a whole helluva lot harder now that Venom has *plans.* Why can't shitty men be shitty without having ideas? It's not enough for them to be assholes. They think they're smart enough to have schemes. It's annoying as fuck. Prophet probably started the same way. He had a dream of terrorizing people and being in control. He thinks he's entitled to rule over others.

"Hey," Hornet calls, and I tense. "Where you going?"

"Home. Then to deal with the bitch. I'll let you know when you can have a turn at her."

Venom's boots click on the sidewalk, and I slip around the back of the building, hoping Hornet goes inside instead. The last thing I need is to get ambushed by one of them. I make my way by the edge of the forest toward where Venom used to live. He's a creature of habit or at least he used to be. I'm banking on him not having moved in the last six years. He was only on the periphery of my attention.

Once Ghost started his bid for a higher rank in the club, I kept an eye on the inner workings of the Phantoms. It was hard, though, since I had to get all my information secondhand from him. He wasn't as forthcoming back then. Which is why it was so laughable that they thought I'd given Snake their secrets. I didn't have anything to give. The only reason I knew who the enforcers were was to steer clear of them. Most of them were exactly like Venom, using their fists to solve any perceived problems they encountered.

The rumble of a bike splits the night, and I peek around a

building. A second later, Venom comes into view, and I duck back into the shadows. I really hope the guys haven't figured out I've left and are searching for me now. Not only will it be really hard to explain if they find me before I've dealt with Venom, but I won't have as much time to force him to tell me his plans. I probably should have thought this through better. I'm not used to doing this anymore. Hell, I didn't before, really.

Storm made sure I knew how to use a gun. Ghost taught me how to use a knife. Then they made Jag teach Avery and me how to defend ourselves. I didn't have an opportunity to test the skills when I was younger. Once the Disciples started showing up, I learned pretty quickly. It was a sharp transition—too sharp. I cried for days after I shot the first man who came after me. I don't know if he died or not. I've heard the first life you take is the hardest. They were wrong. It's all hard in a bizarre way. And Venom's won't be any different.

I make it to the corner and stop. The lights from a gas station pierce the darkness and I wince. Venom lives in the apartment across the street right next to the business. He slips through the front door of the building, and I lean against the bricks to wait. Ambushing him in his apartment might not be the best idea. I could have jumped him on his way home and staged it as a robbery gone wrong. Except anyone could have come along. I'm not about to hurt an innocent person who's only trying to help. An assassination will have to do.

My phone vibrates and I pull it from my pocket. Avery's message flashes across the screen before disappearing. I bite my lip, wondering if I should deal with her now or after. I unlock the phone and peek at what I can see of the text in the notifications. She's spouting something about her brother calling her. I put it away and pull in a deep breath.

It takes me longer than I want to get into the building. I didn't grab any gloves, and the fire escape attached to the back is partially broken. By the time I make it to the fourth floor, I've already cut my palm and bruised my knee. No one investigated the noise, though. Small miracles. Venom's shadow passes across the curtained window. When the light flips off, I test the sash and grin as it gives easily. There isn't even a squeak.

I tap down on the adrenaline coursing through me as I slip inside. It's a fucking mess with a mattress on the floor. I wrinkle my nose as I take in the stains on the fabric, because of course he doesn't have sheets. Dirty dishes are scattered across the space, and I end up tiptoeing around them. I slide on a black ski mask I swiped from Storm. It's a little too big, but I wasn't about to go without in case shit went wrong.

A laugh track filters through the door I inch open. Apparently after he threatens to hurt a woman, he watches sitcoms. The sound will drown out his screams. I pull the gun out of my pocket and peer into the living room. Venom hums while he mixes himself a drink in the attached kitchen. He didn't even bother to turn on any of the other lights, leaving the flashes from the television to illuminate the small space. I'm surprised he didn't move out of this hovel. Then again, he probably lost a couple ranks when Ghost took over.

Venom swings around and freezes when he spots me. I don't know what I expected, but it wasn't for him to laugh, then down his drink and throw the glass against the wall. Shards ping across the tile and settle at his feet.

"Well, get on with it. Make sure you don't miss, though. One shot is all I'm going to give you," he sneers.

I train the gun on him. "Want to reveal all your evil plans first? This is your opportunity to go full villain. I'll even let you monologue."

He laughs again and my nose wrinkles, which makes it itch. I resist the urge to scratch it. "You're a girl? For fuck's sake, they're really scraping the bottom of the barrel, huh? Who sent you, baby girl?"

He saunters toward me, and I resist the urge to back up. I'm slightly terrified I'll trip over the pile of takeout boxes, and that would be embarrassing.

"I don't have a lot of time to chitchat. Answer my questions and I'll make it quick."

He smirks and his gaze travels down my body making my skin crawl. "Definitely not Lexi. Can't be a Disciple. You from Rima?"

I shake my head slowly, then clear my throat to cover the sound of my phone vibrating. "You were talking a big game earlier. What plans did you have?"

"Sorry, sweetheart. Unless you're going to ride my dick... maybe suck me off, I'm not saying shit to you. Will say, you got some balls breaking in. You even know who I am?"

"Oh, I know exactly who you are," I say softly, and the grin drops from his face. "I knew when you took that girl from the club. I knew when you killed Mist and called it an accident. I knew when you burned down the laundromat and that man's house."

The longer I speak, the paler he gets. Half the shit I'm talking about happened years ago. He probably thought he got away with a lot of it. At the time, he did. Snake never cared what crimes he committed as long as he was loyal to the club. Now that he isn't, there's no reason to keep him around. I don't know what he did to make Ghost want him dead, but it doesn't matter. He's lower than scum and deserves to die.

"Who the fuck are you?" he whispers, giving away his fear. It's a tangible thing weaving through the air—pungent and sour. It assaults my senses and turns my stomach.

I shrug, glancing around at the filth he's living in. "Justice. Retribution. Vengeance. Take your pick."

"How about bitch?" he sneers.

I shrug again. "You can call me whatever you want. Won't change the fact you'll be dead."

He takes another step forward, his boots grinding the shards of glass into the carpet. "I don't think you're going to do a fucking thing. I bet this type of shit turns you on, doesn't it?" He grabs his crotch, a lascivious grin spreading across his face. "If you wanted to fuck, all you had to do was ask, baby girl. I'm nothing if not generous."

I gag and the barrel of my gun dips. "Gross. You've got ten seconds to start talking or I shoot."

"If you were going to shoot, you would have done it right away." He stalks forward, weaving his way around the various piles of garbage and clothes. I'm forced to turn with him or expose my back.

"Or, and hear me out, I could just want to know what your plans are. Were you going to betray us?" It's the only thing I can come up with.

I doubt he'd challenge Ghost for the presidency. He's older and has at least twenty pounds more than Ghost packed around his middle. He knows he wouldn't win in a fight to the death. Unless Ghost did away with the tradition.

He pulls a wicked-looking knife from behind him. I kick myself for not noticing he was carrying one. It's hard to hide my surprise when he throws it. Not at me, but at the opposite wall. The dull thud barely twangs over the show still playing on the television. I half expect him to pull out a gun next, but he just spreads his hands wide.

"He sent you? Well, you can go back and tell him I'm still loyal. He doesn't have to worry about me. I want to see them fall just as much as he does."

I raise an eyebrow, not that he can see through the mask. It sounds like he's working with the Disciples, which isn't surprising. I planned on framing them, anyway. If he keeps talking, maybe I can figure out how deep in their club he goes.

Is he working directly with Prophet? How many of the Phantom's secrets has he handed over? I wonder if Ghost suspects him and that's why they want him dead. Even if he isn't working for the Disciples, Ghost still wants him six feet under. It's the least I can do.

"Prove it."

Venom's spine straightens and panic flashes in his eyes. "I already did."

"He wants more." I drop the gun to my side, hoping he takes it as a sign I'm willing to listen.

"I could...I could..." He runs his hand through his thinning hair. "I don't know what the fuck else I could do." His eyes narrow. "How do I know you're with them?"

I roll my eyes, then dip my hand in my front pocket and finger the coin I found in Storm's closet. I have no idea if the Disciples use these to prove they're on the same side. They usually show up when the Disciples have taken someone out. They scatter them around businesses they've burned to the ground or hide them in places that are supposed to be secure to fuck with whoever they're going after.

Using the coins to identify themselves, though? Fuck if I know. Most of the men who came after me weren't very forthcoming. I never thought to interrogate them. I was too busy trying to get away from them. We didn't have a lot of time for chitchatting. I stayed as far away from Prophet coins as possible. They always gave me the creeps, like they held a piece of Prophet within them. Even now, having it in my pocket is freaking me out a little.

If I wait too long to answer Venom, though...

"I don't owe you shit," I sneer. "Last chance to prove you're loyal. And it won't even be that hard. Tell me what you're planning, and I'll bring it back to him. Can't guarantee it'll be enough, but it'll at least be a slight reprieve."

"This is bullshit," he mutters as he eyes me.

He tenses and I jolt, knowing he's about to attack me. I trip over a pile of clothes, and he lunges forward. A yelp leaves me, but I manage to raise the gun and get off a single shot. Venom's body crashes into me and my head slams into the thin carpet. Stars burst across my vision and glass ricochets around us. If my ribs weren't broken before, they probably are now.

I fight against his weight, a frustrated cry leaving me. It takes me a minute to figure out he's not fighting back. In fact, he's not moving at all. I wiggle my arm out and drop the gun. My breaths come out in gasps as I attempt to roll him off me. It takes way too long to squirm enough to get out. I wince when my wrist gives out as I push myself to my feet.

As I stand over him, panting, I wonder how the hell I got away with this. I dig my toe into his shoulder to make sure he's actually dead. Which doesn't make sense, but I'm giving myself grace. When I peek at his face, I realize I shot him right between his eyes. This is not how I wanted this to go.

When the guys find out, I'm fucked.

Thirty

Storm

Leaning against the fence across from the apartment building, I wait for Siren to appear. I have no idea why she's here. It's not like she knows anyone in Harris anymore. Lexi lives across town, as far away from headquarters as possible. Avery's been gone for a few years now between randomly disappearing and then moving to Rima. Bones has a house a couple blocks from here, but I doubt Siren would try to visit her.

She's either meeting a contact or trying to connect with someone. Some of the older members, including Venom, live around here, though I doubt she remembers that. Either way, she's been lying.

I shouldn't be as surprised as I am. Or hurt. Ghost wanted me to march in there and drag her ass out. I told him to go home. He needed to deal with shit at headquarters, anyway. The last thing we need is him more riled up. He's always been consistent, confident. He knew what he wanted and what steps to take to get there. I've met a fair amount of people in my life and Ghost is by far the most steadfast in his convictions.

Until her. Until now.

Her reappearance threw him off his axis. He's not as sure of himself. He's ignoring the club. He's waffling between shoving her away and holding her closer. I'm not much better. Except I'm the volatile one. I rarely know what I want, and my emotions override my better judgment half of the time. When I follow Ghost, I know he won't lead me astray. I don't know where the fuck he's leading us now, and I hate it.

Curtains flutter in the fourth-floor window, and I cross my arms. I don't want to believe she's conspiring against us, especially after our interlude this evening. I smother a snort behind my hand. Interlude doesn't exactly cover what we did. It messed with my emotions, dredging up the devotion and loyalty I once felt for her. It broke through the rage and betrayal, reminding me of what we had. It's the only reason I'm calmly waiting for her to descend from the broken fire escape instead of ambushing her—instead of killing her. I'd never be able to pull the trigger, anyway. I can admit that now.

Her feet hit the pavement, and she crouches, glancing from side to side. The light from the gas station illuminates the side of her face and I straighten. She presses a hand to her side where her stitches were and winces. I tighten my grip on my feelings and clear my throat. Her head whips around and her hand dives into her sweatshirt. No, *my* sweatshirt.

"Out for a midnight stroll?" I call, thankful for the steadiness in my voice.

Her shoulders slump and the tension leaves her. At least I think it does. She's half hidden in shadows. "Clearly not. Did you follow me?"

I shrug, though she probably can't see me. "Does it matter?"

"Well, what are you going to do?"

I step into the light. "Why don't you tell me why you're coming out of a random apartment building?"

She swallows hard and glances away. "I was taking care of a problem."

"Bullshit."

Her eyes meet mine and I finally notice the trembling. It's in her hands, her limbs, her head. Her entire body vibrates. And the blood. It's matted in her hair, flecked across her face, and covering her hands. Questions crowd my mouth, almost tripping off my tongue to demand she tell me what happened. Her body sways and her chin trembles.

"Is the blood yours?" I demand, stepping closer and she blinks at me. "Dammit, Siren. Who?"

She bursts into tears and her body crumples to the ground. I catch her before she hits the pavement and haul her into me. She attempts to push me away, but it's halfhearted at best. I run my hands down her arms and to her waist. I grab the hem of the sweatshirt and expose her stomach, searching for a wound. When I don't find anything, I lift her easily and press her face into my chest. She clings to me, her muffled sobs echoing around us.

"You're okay," I whisper into her hair, not sure if I'm convincing her or myself. "You're okay."

Her legs wrap around my waist, and I walk us back into the shadows. No one comes to investigate and all the lights in the apartment building stay off. Small mercies are all we're afforded these days, and I'm going to be thankful for every one of them. I don't know if she's running away, if she killed them, if I need to call someone to clean up her mess. Focusing on those issues instead of whether or not she's injured doesn't help.

My phone vibrates as I make my way back to my bike. If Siren fully breaks down, there's no way she'll be able to ride. I'll have to get a car, which means we'll have to wait for Ghost to go home, get the vehicle we rarely use, then drive his ass over here. With her being hysterical and possibly hurt, we don't have time to wait.

"Shh, we're going home," I murmur as my bike comes into view. Usually, I wouldn't hide it away in a dead-end alley, but I wasn't taking chances tonight. Not while I was tracking Siren.

"I'm—" She gasps. "I'm f-f-f-fine."

I slide to the ground and lean against the wall as I settle her in my lap. She doesn't fight me, nor does she push me away. Her fingers dig into my neck, and she shakes her head over and over. I sigh and hold her closer. I feel like she's cried more since she got here than she did the entire time we were growing up. Her shuddering subsides and she gulps in deep breaths.

"Sorry," she breathes as she tries to push away. I hold her tighter and she stops.

"Are you hurt?" I ask, and she shakes her head. "Is any of the blood yours?"

She shakes her head again, then rests her forehead on me. "I miscalculated is all. You can let go now."

"Tell me what happened." I attempt to tip her chin up, but she buries her face into my chest again. "Siren, you just fucking broke down and are covered in blood. And don't think I missed the gunshot. So, start talking or I'm going back to the apartments and figuring it out myself."

She swallows hard, then clears her throat. "I took care of Venom. I think he was working for the Disciples."

"You..." I don't even know what to say. She must have been eavesdropping.

My phone vibrates again, and she leans back, then scrambles off me. This time, I let her go. She paces around my bike, shaking out her limbs. I grit my teeth and pull up Ghost's texts. He's given me a play-by-play of his movements as if I couldn't just pull up the tracking app we have. I type out a message quickly and push to my feet.

"Let's go," I grunt, and she swings to face me. I swing my leg over my bike and settle on my seat. "Get on."

She takes a step back and wraps her arms around her waist. "I can walk."

"Like fucking hell you can. Get on the goddamn bike, Siren."

Pain flashes in her eyes, so quickly I almost miss it. I can't explain what's going through my mind without yelling. If she pushes me, I'll explode. And we can't afford to do that while out here.

If she's right and Venom was working with the Disciples, he's probably got accomplices. Maybe even within the Phantoms. She put herself directly in the line of fire without a fucking care in the world. She didn't think any of this shit through.

She shuffles closer and climbs up behind me. I grab her wrist and yank her against my body until she loops her arms around me. I don't have an extra helmet. To be honest, I was going to make her walk home while I trailed behind her. Ghost thought I was ridiculous. I didn't give a shit. Now I wish I would have made different choices, which is a recurring theme when it comes to Siren.

"He's dead," she whispers a split second before the engine rumbles to life.

I don't know why she cares enough to cry over him. Venom was an asshole. He was an asshole when Snake was in charge, and he was an asshole when Ghost took over. He just got better at hiding it. We heard the rumors surrounding him. We never had concrete proof of his misdeeds. I'm sure Siren saw even more than we did since Venom liked to hang out at the garage. I used to think it was because he liked fixing bikes, but maybe he was there to watch the girls Rivet took under her wing. A shudder rolls through me at the thought, and I take off for home.

The cold wind whipping past centers me. Ghost will meet us, and Siren can explain exactly what she did. We'll call in a crew to get rid of the body and make an announcement at the next meeting. If Venom was working with the Disciples, we'll say his betrayal caught up to him. I'd rather not set him up as a martyr for the Phantoms. And if we say he was killed by them without cause, it'll be a declaration of war. We're not ready for that yet. Not nearly ready enough.

By the time we pull in front of the house, I've got a dozen scenarios in my head, along with alibis and ways to placate Venom's friends. He's not as popular as he was when Snake was president, but there's at least a handful of the old crew still hanging around, biding their time. For what, we could never figure out. Venom seemed to be their little leader, though.

I kill the engine and peel my hand from Siren's thigh. I didn't even realize I was holding on to her while we rode. She doesn't say a word, just slides from behind me and hops away. The move is so familiar, an ache rips through my chest. I reach out if only to steady her, but she's already shuffling for the stairs.

"Siren," I call, and she freezes, refusing to turn around. "You shouldn't have—"

"I know, okay? I don't need a lecture," she says bitterly.

She starts walking again and I rush after her. My foot gets caught on my bike and I almost faceplant but recover just in time. I glance up to find her horrified gaze on me.

"Stop running away from me," I wheeze.

"I wasn't running. I was walking." She rolls her eyes. "Besides, I'd like to take a shower. I don't know if you remember what it's like being covered in someone else's blood, but it's not pleasant."

I whip my head around and scan the shadows rolling between the trees. They dance as if they're sentient. I don't know what I heard, but something's out there—or someone. Watching. Waiting. I hurry to Siren and guide her quickly toward the house with a hand on her lower back. She mutters something about assholes and shiny objects, but I'm too busy trying to get us in the house.

Once inside, I lock the door and take a framed picture off the wall revealing a keypad and display. We rarely use the security system Nemesis had put in place. It's extreme and overkill, in my opinion. I set it for the lowest possible security, which is still ridiculously loud in my opinion. We've been using it since the Disciples got in.

"Do you know who took you before?" I ask, hoping I don't set her off. "Not who they brought you to, but who actually took you?"

"I told you they drugged me. Didn't see faces. Just flashes," she mutters as she stares at the photo in the frame.

I take it gently from her hands and hang it back on the wall. I'm not ready to delve into the memories the picture holds. *We're* not ready. Despite her breakdown, she's still closed off. I realize it's mostly because of me, but it doesn't make it any easier to deal with.

"Could it have been our members? Maybe Venom? Did you question him?" I ask.

She shrugs, her gaze still fixated on the photo. "Don't think so. Venom smelled. Patchouli and sweat. He wasn't there. That night, I mean. Can't say who it was. Maybe Phantoms. Dunno."

"You still do it," I mutter.

"Do what?"

"Shorten your sentences when you don't want to talk, but think you have to. You give the bare minimum for info." I shake my head. "Ghost will be home soon. I'm going to make food and you're going to eat it while I tell you exactly why I'm pissed."

"I'd rather not," she says haughtily.

"Too bad, you don't have a choice."

Thirty-One

I never should have killed Venom. Yet I don't regret it.

"Why'd you kill him?" Storm asks as he stirs some boiling pasta on the stove. It's a familiar scene. He was always the cook in the house. He used to make sure I was fed and always seemed to know what I was craving. My heart aches while my stomach growls. At least he let me take a shower before he forced me into this conversation.

"Ghost said he wanted Venom taken care of. I took care of him."

"And you just took it upon yourself to do our jobs. Without informing us. Without thinking we might be worried. Without considering the consequences."

I roll my eyes and my mouth waters as he dishes up the food. "This isn't the first time I've killed someone."

His head snaps around. "You—"

"How the hell did you think I got away from some of the Disciples when they came for me? You thought I just asked them nicely?" I plaster on a simpering expression. "Oh, please Mr. Biker man. Don't take me."

He glares at me, a growl stuck in his throat. "At least something I taught you got through that thick head of yours."

I lean back and cross my arms. "Thought you said I had a pretty little head?"

"I think he meant you give pretty good head, sweets," Ghost says, and I jolt. He drops a kiss on my neck, then settles in the chair next to me.

Storm pulls more bowls from the cupboard. "You want to know where she snuck off to?"

I peek at Ghost from the corner of my eye. He sighs, a slight smile playing on his lips. I don't know what happened between when I left and now. He's acting like we're fine, like nothing's happened in the last six years. It's freaking me out. We're supposed to be at odds, not acting like we're dating. Yet here he is, waiting for Storm to finish dinner and smirking at me like we're embroiled in an inside joke.

"I assume she was going for a run?" Ghost says, pulling me from my thoughts.

"Actually, she overheard you saying we needed to off Venom. She was kind enough to step in." Storm drops a bowl in front of Ghost, then slides another one across the table to me.

Steam wafts into the air, and I breathe in the scent of garlic and alfredo. My mouth waters and my shoulders drop. I didn't realize how tense I was. Who knew a simple home-cooked meal would relax me. It's like a warm hug, something I've yearned for. I sniff, blinking back the sudden tears. What the hell is wrong with me? I swear I've never cried this much in my life.

Ghost taps the back of my hand with his fork. "He dead?"

"Uh, yeah. I put one of those Prophet coins in his mouth."

He nods, but Storm isn't about to let me off as easily. "Where the fuck did you get a Prophet coin?"

I take my time to answer, spinning my fork in the pasta. I shove it into my mouth and my lids flutter shut as the flavors explode across my tastebuds. An involuntary moan leaves me. It's not like I was starving when I lived on my own. After the money I had saved ran out, it was a bit dicey, but I always kept myself fed.

This is different. This isn't a greasy bag I picked up in a drive thru or a pathetic sandwich I made.

Storm's fist slams into the table, and Ghost bursts into a fit of laughter. My eyes fly open and meet Ghost's twinkling gaze.

"I think he's dreaming about that pretty awesome head you give, Siren. Might want to tone it down before he throws you on the table. You wouldn't get to finish your dinner then." He dodges Storm's hand with another laugh and starts eating again.

I clear my throat. "I got the coins from your closet. Along with the gun, a knife, and your sweatshirt. There was only a little blood on the hood, and I washed it off. You want to tell me why you have them?"

Storm grunts and I realize he won't confess. Of course he won't. Talking to me would require him to reveal Phantom business I'm not privy to.

"We take them off the bodies, just in case we need them later. Except Storm should have kept them locked away. Clearly, our house isn't as secure as we thought it was," Ghost says.

My muscles are tense again as I hunch over my bowl and take a small bite. I'm the threat to their security. Any way I look at it, I'm the problem. Either I'm the thief within their midst or I've led the Disciples into their home.

I feel myself retreating into the small creature I was when I was slipping through the world like a shadow. I never made myself big, never drew attention to myself, never made my presence known. The moment I did, the Disciples would sniff me out like rabid bloodhounds. I flew under the radar for survival. Every time I feel myself sliding back into who I was before—who I truly am —I'm yanked violently back to reality and forced to cower once more.

Ghost forces my chin up. "Don't hide, Siren. That's not who you are."

My mouth drops open, yet he goes back to eating like he's being completely normal. As if any of this is normal. We shouldn't be sitting around having dinner at two in the morning.

We shouldn't be doing any of this. I should be long gone by now. In fact, I never should have been here in the first place.

"Siren," Storm growls, and my mouth snaps shut. He turns to Ghost. "She snuck out. Broke into Venom's apartment. Shot him. Then broke down."

I ignore Ghost's eyes on me. "Venom also threw a glass against the wall, I tripped over a pile of clothes, and I'm pretty sure he broke one of my ribs."

"How the fuck did he get close enough to break one of your ribs?" Storm asks softly, which is scarier than when he was bellowing.

I doubt I'll get out of actually telling them what happened. Plus, they've already called me out on giving them the bare minimum. It didn't work anyway. I thought if I kept my thoughts, my decisions, my past hidden, I'd come out on the other side with my heart intact. I forgot it was already shattered and has been lying in pieces inside my chest all these years. Hell, I don't even know if I have all the parts necessary to put it back together. I've resigned myself to a life half lived.

My gaze drops to my bowl. "Why don't we finish eating first?"

Silence descends around us, broken only by the occasional clink of silverware on porcelain. Part of me wants to ask for a second helping. Not only because it's fucking delicious, but it would prolong this short reprieve. I'm tired and don't particularly want to have a heart-to-heart tonight. Except the tension keeps growing the longer we sit here, and I might lose it if we don't.

Storm takes my bowl and I press my lips together. He rinses the dishes off in the sink and methodically loads the dishwasher. Ghost swipes at his phone, probably calling in a clean-up crew. I should tell him not to. If he wants it to look like the Disciples took care of Venom, then he technically shouldn't know yet. Someone else will have to discover Venom's body and call it in. I reach out without fully thinking things through. He jolts when my hand brushes his arm, and I yank my fingers away.

"Sorry. You, uh, you shouldn't call Al," I mutter.

He gives me a curious look. "I wasn't calling in a crew. What's with the apologies?"

"What do you mean?"

"You're acting like you're at fault for every little thing. I don't like it."

I cross my arms, using them as a shield against his criticism. "Well, I don't like how you're acting either, so how about we call it even?"

His brows pull low, and he presses a hand to his chest. "Me? What the hell did I do?"

I roll my eyes and huff. "Acting like a doting—You're behaving as if this is normal. We all know it's not. This is like some story you'd read on the internet and assume it was made up."

He sets his phone down and eyes me. "Expand."

I should heed the warning in his voice. He always speaks in one-word sentences and makes demands instead of requests. I don't envy what he does when someone doesn't give him what he wants. I've never pushed the limits when he gets that look in his eyes.

"You think I betrayed you while I think you gave up on me. You reel me back into this bullshit, and we do this little dance trying to figure out where we stand. After one small encounter, suddenly you're acting like nothing ever happened and everything's peachy keen—kissing me when you come home." I gesture to Storm, who's putting the leftovers away. "He's cooking dinner like we're a happy little family and this is something we've done a thousand times before."

"We have done it a thousand times before," Ghost murmurs.

I throw my hands up. "Not like this. Not when we're adults and at each other's throats most of the time. Not when you've made it clear you don't fucking trust me. And the thing is, I don't even fucking blame you." My anger vanishes and I slump in my chair. "I'd blame me, too."

Ghost nods, then glances at Storm. "You want to take this one, or should I?"

Storm drops into his chair across from me. He searches my face for...I don't know. It's not like I can magically make myself more trustworthy. Now that I've had some time, I can admit I went after Venom to impress them. I thought if I took care of a problem, they'd trust me more. I knew it wouldn't miraculously make everything better, but I deluded myself into thinking it would help. We could be okay. Not what we used to be, but more than we are. It was a fanciful notion. I should have known better. I got caught up in the fantasy I built in my head, brick by brick. Now it's tumbling down on my head, crushing me under the weight of each wasted dream.

"No one's taking anything. It's fine. Let's get on with these questions, Storm. You wanted to know what happened at Venom's. Well, I tracked him to headquarters. He was chatting with some asshole named Hornet." They exchange a glance, but I forge onward. "They split off and I followed Venom to his place, crawled through his window, and decided to have a little chat." I hold my hand up when Storm opens his mouth. "He said he had plans, but also he was planning on teaching Lexi a lesson. Apparently, she embarrassed him."

Silence descends again, this time broken by Storm's fingernail tapping out a sequence. I'm surprised Ghost didn't explode when I revealed that last tidbit. It took everything in me not to shoot Venom as soon as he started talking shit, and I haven't seen Lexi in years. Ghost is protective of her in a way I've rarely seen. I suppose I didn't have a lot of examples of healthy relationships growing up. Ghost and Lexi may not have had much time to figure out how to be siblings, but he fell into the role seamlessly. Helped that he already had Avery.

"You tried to get him to spill all his evil plans?" Storm asks finally.

"Even gave him a chance to monologue. He, unfortunately, declined."

"Did he actually say he was working with the Disciples?"

"Not in so many words. He was talking about being loyal and he wants to see their downfall, too. Said he already proved himself. I assumed he wasn't speaking of you two." I pull in a deep, calming breath. "I broke down because I was overwhelmed. I've only sought out one other person to kill. Dealing with the men Prophet sent after me was easier to explain away. I could handle defending myself, even if it meant they were dead. So, while Venom may have deserved it, the aftermath was still jarring."

I don't mention my nerves being frayed from them fucking me, then leaving. It's not what they want to hear. Besides, I told them I'd pretend like it didn't happen. No matter how much it hurts, I'll keep my end of the bargain.

Ghost drops his chin to his chest, a look of concentration on his face. Storm seems to be grappling with something. I'm done trying to guess what they're thinking. And I doubt they'll reveal anything to me. It used to hurt. I thought if I ignored it long enough, eventually I'd be okay. I'm not.

I'm definitely not okay.

Yet I can't tell them. The moment I reveal too much will be my downfall. I'd survive, but it wouldn't be a life worth living. If they knew how much they hurt me, they'd be able to do it again. And again. And again. I'd willingly put myself in a position to be hurt over and over, because despite the pain, I can't let go of them.

"Bullshit," Storm finally says.

"You realize you can't just say bullshit and expect me to know what you're talking about."

"I can and I will. But you and I both know you're spouting bullshit. You broke down because of us. Because you're back here."

"Not everything is about you, *Storm*. Are you so fucking conceited you think my breaking down has anything to do with you? It doesn't." The half-truth sits between us as Storm glares at me. I'm exhausted at trying to make up for decisions that weren't my fault.

Ghost sighs and I'm pretty sure he kicks Storm under the table. "Siren, we're on the same side now. And I think we all want the same thing here."

"And what's that?" I ask bitterly.

He smirks, then pushes to his feet. I track him as he walks deeper into the house. I have no idea what the hell he's talking about. We want the same thing? I doubt it. Hell, I don't even know what I want from them. My emotions are so tangled, they're threatening to strangle me from the inside out. They're just as mixed up as I am, it seems. I doubt we can get to a place where we all get what we want—even if it is the same thing.

Thirty-Two

Ghost

I lean against the wall at the top of the stairs and count. It'll take under a minute before Storm comes after me. A smirk spread across my face as his footfalls filter up to me. When Storm's dark hair comes into view, I duck my head. We need to finish getting on the same page before we can deal with Siren.

"What exactly do we want?" Storm asks as he stops in front of me.

"Her. It's always been her. We've been fucking around, worrying about whether or not she betrayed us when the truth was staring us in the face. If we don't rein her in, she'll keep doing shit like going off on her own, and she'll get herself hurt."

"Or killed," he mutters, glancing over his shoulder. Not that he can see the kitchen from here.

"Exactly. She'll get into a situation we can't get her out of. We won't be able to fix what's between the three of us. And all the while, the Disciples will be gearing up to hit us where it hurts. They'll attack when we're too busy fucking with our personal lives. I'm not about to lose it."

He sighs and runs a hand through his hair. "Lose what?"

"Her. The club. You. Take your goddamn pick. I'm done

going back and forth about this, though. I don't know what the hell happened to us back then, but we fucked up. We should have talked to her after she was banished."

Regret slams into me, making it hard to breathe. I knew something was off, but I was too angry to think clearly. With time and clarity, the fog is lifting, leaving only shame behind. But regret and shame won't help us. Only action will.

"We were kind of in the middle of a hostile takeover."

My lip curls at the slight whine in his voice. I realize it's a defense mechanism on his part, but it doesn't help. He either needs to get on board or...I don't know. I'm just sick of waiting. She's endgame for us. She always was. I let everything else blind me to that fact. Storm may not have come fully around, but he will. I'll shove him over the line if need be.

"Why were our ambitions more important than our love for her?"

His nostrils flare and he sputters, then sighs. "Because it wasn't that simple. It wasn't just us trying to take over. It wasn't just the embezzlement. Hell, it wasn't even her supposed betrayal. It was everything all at once. It was the photos and the pain and the uncertainty. We had too much all at once. How the hell were we supposed to know who the enemy was when we were surrounded by them?"

"By trusting what we knew. We knew Siren was ours. We let everything else distract us from the truth. She wouldn't have betrayed us. Not without a very good reason."

"And then what? She was banished," he snaps. "What could we have—"

"We could have helped," I bellow, and he leans back, the anger bleeding from him. I clear my throat and murmur, "We could have kept in touch, then brought her back when we were in charge. Once we weeded out Snake's supporters and were stable, we could have...we should have begged her to come back to us."

He shoves his hands in his pockets and nods slowly as he stares at his feet. "You really think she's a victim?"

"I'm not answering that." I can't answer that for him. He has to come to that conclusion himself. "Why were you pissed about Venom?"

"She put herself in danger. She didn't think anything through. What if she would have been killed?"

"Didn't care about that when you were kicking her out of Harris with a stab wound in her side," I mutter, and his fist flies out, catching me on the chin. I stumble into the wall.

He didn't hit me that hard, but it's enough to get his point across. His hands clench, then relax at his sides, over and over while he gasps, like he can't pull a full breath in. He grits his teeth, practically vibrating with emotion. He won't apologize and I don't expect him to. We'll figure it out like we always do.

"I deserved that," I say.

He doesn't answer, just spins on his heel and stomps down the stairs. I rub my jaw, trying to ease the ache. It'll smart for a while, then blossom into a bruise—a reminder of when I let my mouth speak before my brain could think. As long as it gets Storm back on track, it'll be worth it.

I saunter after Storm. When I come to the kitchen, he's pacing back and forth. Siren hasn't moved, probably waiting for an answer to her question. Or maybe she just doesn't believe we want the same things. Taking care of Venom wasn't what convinced me of her innocence. It was a series of steps she took, the way she held her body, the pauses between her words. While she was attempting to shield herself from us, she revealed much more than she intended. I doubt anyone else other than maybe Storm would have picked up on it. He was too angry. I'm kicking myself for how long it took me.

"You can't go running headlong into situations because you think it'll help us," Storm says, and I lean against the counter.

Siren's eyes meet mine and I smile. Her gaze zeroes in on the mark Storm left behind. The house isn't big enough to hide anything. I'm sure she heard both of us yelling. I'm sure it didn't help my cause to get her to drop her guard with us.

If Storm and I don't seem like we're on the same side, how will we convince her to stay? We won't. She'll assume she's coming between us and will slip out in the middle of the night. Then one of us will have to go after her and we don't have time for that. Not with the reports I'm getting from Fuse about the situation with the Disciples.

"Storm, I think she gets it."

Siren's gaze narrows on me. "What's the thing?"

I raise an eyebrow. "You didn't tell her, Storm? No, I suppose you didn't. You were too busy venting out your frustration about her trying to help us."

"That's not the fucking point," he bellows, throwing his hands up.

"Except you've told her the point several times now. So, why don't you tell her what the real problem is?"

Siren straightens. "I took care of the problem."

Storm's mouth parts, his eyes glittering with an emotion I can't name. For once, I don't know what he's going to do or say. I trust him not to do something foolish. Then again, when it comes to Siren, he gets a little unpredictable. He's been teetering on the edge of an epiphany for quite some time. I've been waiting for the breakthrough.

I had my own issues to work through when it came to her. He had to do it on his own as well. I just hope he doesn't push her away again. I don't have it in me to start at the beginning. We have more pressing matters to attend to and I'm sick of being in a fog. Now that I've sorted my feelings out for her and made my decisions, my head has cleared. I can see the future we should have had.

"You didn't. You may have killed Venom, but you didn't think about why. Or you're not ready to admit why you went after him," Storm says, and I hide a grin behind my hand.

Siren narrows her gaze and her nostrils flare. "You keep saying I didn't think shit through. I didn't have a reason. I put myself in danger. Did it ever occur to you I knew exactly what the consequences were, and I just didn't give a damn?"

Unshed tears make her eyes, and I sober. "Siren?"

She shakes her head. "Don't give me that fucking look. It's fine. I'm fine."

"Are you?" I ask softly.

"What the fuck do you care?" she yells, jumping to her feet. Her fists slam on the table. "I'm only here so you can get information. Use me as goddamn bait if the need arises. And the minute I take matters into my own hands, you freak the fuck out. So, I'll just be a good little girl and stay in the house. Will that make you happy?"

"No," Storm and I say in unison. She snorts and her lips twitch, though she covers her reaction with a scowl.

"Then I don't know what you want from me." She spins on her heel and marches toward the stairs.

Storm doesn't move, but I do. I catch her long before she makes it out of the room, wrapping an arm around her waist and hauling her into the air. She squeals as she kicks her legs, then curses me out when I haul her back to the table. Storm rounds the table, and she tenses as he approaches. He snatches her up and I let her go. When he plops her on the top of the table, she immediately tries to hop down.

I slide in front of her as Storm slips to the side. Gripping her thighs, I keep her in place so she can't run again. I step between her legs, and she leans back. She braces her hands behind her yet still seems wary.

"Why don't you tell her what we want from her, Storm?"

"I'd like her to admit why she went after Venom first," he murmurs, tucking a piece of hair behind her ear. Her thighs jump in my grip, belying the disinterested expression she's plastered on her face.

Siren opens her mouth, then snaps it shut. Indecision swims in her eyes as she stares at me. I nod and she swipes her tongue across her bottom lip, pulling my gaze down. My cock hardens and I shift my stance. If she doesn't start talking, I doubt I'll be able to walk away. Storm will end up edging her until she's a sobbing mess. He'll demand an answer from her before he allows her to come. She knows how this works.

"Better tell him, sweets," I say, and I run my nails up and down her leggings.

"Or else?" she asks, mockingly.

I lean in, my lips brushing hers. "You know the consequences. They haven't changed."

"You wouldn't," she breathes.

"Oh, we will. Don't push your luck, Siren," Storm says.

"Fine. I went because I wanted you two to trust me again. I wanted to be useful. I wanted to at least do something worthwhile before I..."

I rest my forehead against hers. "Die? Leave? Vanish?"

"All the above?" she whispers. "I'm tired. In my bones. Exhaustion has infiltrated my soul, and I can't get rid of it. No matter where I go or what I do, it never leaves me. I just want to—"

She glances away, and I slide my hand to her back. I force her upright, pressing our chests together. I haven't held her this close in years, at least while she was conscious. Storm's held her while she cried. For all his arguments and indecision, he's been comforting her since she came back. His body knew long before his mind accepted that she belonged with us.

"I told you, Siren, we want the same things."

"I want to not be lonely." Her voice is muffled and low, almost as if she hopes I don't hear her.

Storm runs his hand down her hair and some of the tension leaves her. "Then you stay here, and we'll make sure you're not."

We still have things to work through. I'll have to talk to Lexi about the photos. We need to deal with the fallout from Venom's death. Rooting out the Disciple sympathizers won't be easy. They've clearly been ingrained into the Phantoms since Snake was president. Above all, we need to handle the Disciples themselves.

Most of their members will follow Prophet into battle without a second thought. It won't be easy to find those who just want to live their lives.

And above all, we need to build trust with the woman in my arms. Healing what's broken between us won't be easy, but I'm determined not to let her go again.

Thirty-Three

For the first time in six years Siren is sandwiched between us in Ghost's bed. They're both fast asleep, but I can't get my brain to shut off. Every scenario runs through my head. Venom, the Disciples, Siren, the Phantoms, the smaller clubs under our rule—it's all too much. Everything's intertwined, leaving a tangled mess behind, and I'm stuck trying to unravel it.

Ghost called a meeting for tomorrow night, or rather, tonight since it's after midnight. I don't know what he plans on doing with Siren. He said we'd figure everything out beforehand. I trust him to tell me what I need to know when it comes to club business. We've been neglecting a lot of things we usually keep a closer eye on. Thankfully, we have enough protocols in place for things to run with minimal interference from us.

Except certain things are falling through the cracks now. The massive number of unanswered texts waiting in my messages attests to that. I sigh and slip from Siren's side. She murmurs in her sleep, then rolls toward Ghost. His arm wraps around her back, and she throws her limbs over his body. My heart aches, wishing I could shut down my mind.

I toss the blanket over them and swipe my phone from the nightstand before slipping from the room. Sometimes I wish we'd put an office in the house instead of a gym. If we moved closer to headquarters, we'd be able to find one with more bedrooms. Ghost said he wanted the distance, especially after he took over.

It was a volatile time back then, and I didn't blame him. I also knew it was more about giving up the house he grew up in. We made this place into our home and giving that up was too much of a sacrifice even for the Phantoms. This place is as much mine as it is his. After my father was killed in a raid when I was fourteen, I lived here. Ghost's dad spent all his time at headquarters, anyway. Until he died two years later.

I'm sure if we lived in any other place, we would have been picked up by some well-meaning person until we were of age. I imagine we would have been separated and neither one of us would have survived that. I snort, remembering Siren saying she'd build us a fort in the woods to hide out in. A bigger one than the one we had. She had it all planned out.

I collapse on the couch and go through my messages. I dismiss one after another until I find a problem I can solve easily. It takes three rings before someone picks up.

"Boy, do you know what time it is?" Rivet's deep voice echoes through the room, and I chuckle.

"Actually, no."

She sighs and my stomach tightens. "Couldn't sleep?"

"Nope." I run my hands through the fringes hanging off the edges of the pillow next to me. I don't even remember getting this thing, but it's an ugly green. The feel of the threads sliding through my fingers helps calm my thoughts, though.

"What's on your mind?"

What's not, I want to say, but I press my lips together. I shouldn't have called Rivet. She's too perceptive for her own good. No matter what I tell her, she'll suss out whatever is actually eating at me. And I won't be able to stop myself from spilling everything. I don't think Ghost would want Rivet to know Siren is back in town.

"I need a ride. Smaller bike if possible."

"Okay." She pulls out the one word, infusing it with a healthy amount of suspicion. "Who's it for?"

"Doesn't matter. Just get one and drop it here. In the back." I can practically hear the gears in her head turning through the speaker.

"You need a helmet?" she asks after the silence stretches.

She was probably waiting for me to crack. I'm not about to put Siren at risk because I want to talk through my issues. Not that I think Rivet would deliberately hurt her or us. She's loyal to the Phantoms but will choose us every time.

"No, I've got one," I say absently, then immediately kick myself. "I mean, I can—"

"I know what you meant, boy. Don't treat me like I ain't smart just because I'm old."

"You're not old, Rivet. You're experienced."

She lets out a sharp laugh. "Flattery will not get you out of this. She's back then?"

I wince. "Who?"

"Fine. Keep your secrets. Just remember, they're bound to come out, eventually. They always do. Secrets are like vines creeping under the soil. Before long, they'll emerge, seeking the sun, then overrun your lawn. Hard to dig out after that. And killing them? Forget it."

I'm sure her words will haunt me long after we've hung up. It's always like this with her. She never just has a conversation. Never just leaves well enough alone.

"Thanks for the sage advice—"

"Call me grandma and you'll regret it. Now, tell me why you can't sleep."

I settle for the one thing I can talk to her about. "Shit's going down with the Disciples. They're gearing up for something big."

She hums, then sighs. "War?"

"Looks like it. We're having a meeting tomorrow to get a read on things."

"You want me there?" Rivet's one of the few women we have

in the Phantoms, and it was a bitch to get her in. Too many of Snake's supporters were left to get anything to really change. Ghost was laying the groundwork to open things up, but then he got his ass blown up.

"Up to you. Might be good to have you there, though. We're going to need all the eyes we can get. Plus, the support."

The line falls silent, and after a bit, my mind wanders. She'll speak when she's ready and not before. I wish I could tell her to hurry up, though. The longer the quiet stretches, the more my thoughts spiral. I can't always handle it. I thought sleeping next to Siren would calm the chaos threatening to overwhelm me. Obviously, it didn't.

Soft footfalls reach me, and I glance over my shoulder. Siren, her hair mussed and sleep heavy on her face, shuffles across the hardwoods. She lifts the hem of her white shirt, nearly exposing her pussy, and scratches her upper thigh. I lick my lips as the fabric drops back into place. She sinks next to me and yawns.

"I'll get what you need. Don't fuck this up, boy. It won't be your ass you'll lose if you do," Rivet says, jarring me from my thoughts. She hangs up without a goodbye, and I drop the phone next to me.

"Why're you up?" I ask Siren, my palm itching to thread my fingers with hers lying innocently next to me.

She shrugs. "Had to pee and saw you weren't there. You still have insomnia?"

"Nope. I just like getting up in the middle of the night. Oh, and not being able to fall asleep. Also, feeling both tired and weirdly wired. It's fucking great." I tried to keep the bitterness from my voice, but it slips through.

She lifts her hand as if to comfort me, then hesitates. I thread our fingers together and relax when she doesn't pull away. I have other things to do, but sitting here in the dark living room with her next to me seems like a better idea. This feels different from the other times we've been together lately. Peaceful. Except she's still yawning.

"You should go back to bed," I murmur, brushing my thumb across her skin.

"Except if I go back to bed, I'll just be there with Ghost muttering in his sleep and thinking about where you are."

I chuckle softly. I've learned to ignore Ghost's sleep talking. Most of the time it's not bad, a few words here or there. When I'm actually sleeping, I don't wake up. Sometimes, though, he has full-on conversations with himself. Most of the time it's ridiculousness—yelling at little green men, complaining about ice cream on the stairs...and crying out for Siren. I don't think I should tell her about those times. Ghost doesn't even realize he's doing it. I sure as hell haven't mentioned it.

Still, I don't think Siren sitting here with me and wallowing will help anyone. "I'm not going anywhere. I'm just going to take care of a few things. Go back to bed."

"Are you ordering me around?"

"That's exactly what I'm doing." I untangle our fingers and cross my arms to keep myself from pulling her onto me. If I do, I might never let go. My emotions haven't settled, but Ghost was right. She belongs with us.

Siren sighs and pushes to her feet. I swallow hard and try to set my face when she stands in front of me. Our knees brush and I'm wishing I would have put pants on. Sitting here in my underwear doesn't do much to hide what she's doing to me. Especially when she leans down and grips my thighs. Her face hovers in front of mine and she searches my eyes.

"Why are you trying to get me to leave? What are you really doing out here?"

I roll my eyes. "I told you what I was doing. You know why I'm out here." I straighten, my lips almost brushing hers. "And if you don't leave now, you're going to end up riding my cock."

She smirks. Not exactly the response I was looking for. Honestly, I don't know what I thought she'd do. Siren isn't the type of person to run from a challenge. From the way she dealt with Venom, that clearly hasn't changed. Doesn't mean she's ready for the new dynamic between us. I thought she'd be resistant, demanding us to grovel for all the shit we put her through—me, in particular. I didn't treat her the way she deserved, no matter her betrayal that wasn't really a betrayal.

"Ask nicely," she whispers, then runs her tongue along my bottom lip.

A shiver rolls through me and my cock twitches. Her gaze darts down as if she can sense how hard I am. When her thumb grazes my shaft, I grip her wrist.

"You're playing with fire, Siren."

"Good thing I'm not afraid of getting burned. Ask. Nicely."

"Would you like to ride my cock, Siren?"

She shakes her head, huffing out a laugh. "I meant...fuck it."

She crawls onto my lap and her shirt rides up her thighs. My hands settle on her waist to keep her from rubbing herself on my length. I've been craving her for too long. One taste wasn't enough to slake my desire. I won't last if she attempts to tease me. I'm hanging by a thread as it is.

Her nails drag up my stomach to my chest before finally settling behind my neck. She rests her forehead against mine and sighs. My lids flutter closed when she rubs her nose along my own. She uses my distraction to settle her pussy fully on me and I groan. Once, twice, she rocks back and forth, grinding into me, then lifts onto her knees.

Her breath caresses the shell of my ear, and she whispers, "Take them off or I'll make you watch while I make myself come."

"You're bossier in the middle of the night," I say, yet hook my thumbs in my waistband and lift my hips to shove them off. It takes some finagling, but they finally drop to my ankles, and I kick them to the side.

When she drops once more, I tip my head back and let out another groan. "The entire fucking time, Siren?"

She rubs herself along my length, coating me with her slick. "You didn't ask."

"I didn't think I'd have to specifically ask if you were wearing underwear."

She buries her face into my neck and says, "I rarely wear them these days."

I'm sure she's trying to be sexy, but the reality is she probably doesn't have any panties. At least not enough to get her through the week. I make a mental note to buy her more. She needs her own things, mostly so she stops stealing my clothes just to get blood all over them.

"You going to take care of this?" I jerk my hips into her, and she sucks in a sharp breath.

She drops her hand and grips my cock. A breathy moan leaves me when she strokes me once, then holds me tightly while she lines me up with her core. I glance between us and watch with fascination as she sinks slowly, enveloping my cock. A whimper leaves her, and her nails dig into my neck. I grip her waist once more and lift her up before slamming her down. I do it again, just to hear the needy noise she makes when I bottom out inside her.

I don't think I'll be able to let her fully take charge. Not tonight. I surge into her, and she meets me thrust for thrust. She's intoxicating with her head thrown back, her hair cascading over her shoulders, pleasure splashed across her face. Our harsh breaths echo through the room, coupling with the occasional moan.

When I let go of her and grab the hem of her shirt, she keeps bouncing on my cock, pushing me closer to the edge. I whip the fabric over her head, and my mouth waters as her tits bounce while she rides me. I grab her again and pull her nipple into my mouth before flicking the tight bud with my tongue. Our hips move in unison and my stomach tightens. I fight off the orgasm, needing to watch her fall before I do.

"Play with your clit, sweets."

She obeys immediately, dropping her hand between us and finding the sensitive nub. Her pussy clenches around me, and I grit my teeth. I surge into her, whispering all the ways I want to fuck her. She jerks in my grasp and quivers around my cock.

Her eyes meet mine, and I see the exact moment she tumbles into oblivion. I dig my fingers into her hips and bury my length into her again and again, fucking her through her orgasm. My name is a cry on her lips, resonating in my soul, and a piece I've long been missing slots into place.

A long groan leaves me as I erupt, spilling inside her. She collapses onto me, and I wrap my arms around her. We sit for a long time, linked together in so many ways beyond physically. I cling to her, finally at peace.

Thirty-Four

Siren

I shouldn't be here.

The thought runs through my mind like a mantra. Ever since Ghost told me I'd be attending the meeting tonight, it's been at the forefront. He didn't want to hear my protests. He walked away when I brought up the dangers. Storm wasn't any help. I thought he'd see how ridiculously foolish this plan was. They somehow think parading me out in front of the entire club will distract everyone. From what, I don't know.

Storm's fingers brush my wrist, and I jolt. "It's not everyone, you know."

"What?"

"Tonight. The meeting. It's not the whole club. It's just the central members who are in Harris."

He hands me a shirt that definitely wouldn't fit him. I don't know where he's pulling these clothes from, but they're not mine. I don't want to wear what his old fling left lying around so I drop it on Ghost's bed. Storm's eyebrow shoots up. I'm not about to explain it to him. It's not worth it.

"I have no idea what you're talking about."

He sighs, scooping up the shirt and sauntering back into

Ghost's closet. He's probably not actually sauntering, but with the way his hips sway, I'm calling it like I see it. When he reappears, he's clutching another shirt with a deep vee neck. He tosses it on the bed when I refuse to take it.

"Ghost spread the club out. Or rather, took some smaller clubs under his wings, I suppose. They were scattered around the smaller towns. Some of them only had a couple members, other had a few dozen. He brought them under the Phantoms' protection. They pay us dues and we help them." He enters the closet again and comes out with a pile of clothes, most of them black, and dumps them on the bed.

"You talk like he did it all alone and you weren't involved at all."

I paw through the mess. Shirts, jeans, leggings, even underwear and bras make up the pile. My fingers lands on a leather jacket and I yank my hand away. I wore one the other night when we walked the line, mostly because I didn't care. I thought I'd be gone in a bit. With the way they're talking, though, I'll be here for quite a while.

I can't fully trust their words. It's not that I think they're lying, I've just lived so long shielding myself from disappointment that I don't know how to truly believe them. I remind myself it's only been twenty-four hours. Maybe less. I doubt tonight's excursion will help, though.

"He's president. I'm not. Vice presidents are vital, but not important, if that makes sense."

"Don't talk to me like I don't understand how an MC works, Storm."

"Do you know how clothes work? Because you've been staring at them like you forgot what a bra is for."

"Bras are a social construct made up by men. Sure, they help some women hold their tits up, but mostly they were designed by a man so he could ogle a woman's body. I wouldn't be surprised if the whole of women's fashion was designed around a bra. Except for the shirts meant to expose skin. And then they turned around and punished us for them."

He crosses his arms and stares at me like I've grown a second head. "I'm pretty sure a woman invented the bra, but go off."

"Then men stole it from us in order to both praise and punish us." I don't actually have such strong opinions about bras. Sometimes I wear them and sometimes I don't, depending on my mood. I don't particularly like the looks from creepy men when my nipples stand at attention. As if theirs don't do the same damn thing.

"How the fuck are you punished for wearing a bra?"

I snatch up a lacy number with half-cups barely capable of containing an apple. "This thing would offer no support. It was designed to be looked at. Not practical at all. Yet, if I wore it in public, I'd get catcalled to high fucking heaven. And don't even get me started on how they punish girls in school. The two most tempting things on a girl's body are apparently her shoulder and an exposed bra strap. At least according to men."

"Alright, why are you deflecting?"

I drop the piece with a curled lip. "I don't like double standards. What's wrong with that?"

"Nothing. But you don't give two shits about bras. Hell, you never cared about fashion at all."

"I care about women's rights."

He throws his hands up. "We all care about women's rights in this house, but you—" He points his finger at me, his thighs leaning on the bed. "You are deflecting from something you don't want to talk about. Is it the meeting or the clothes?"

I shrug. "Why can't it be all of the above?"

"You're going to the meeting because we don't need anyone trying to accost you in the street or think you're a spy for the Disciples. The clothes are yours, so fucking pick something to wear. We need to get going." He walks toward the bathroom.

"I'm not wearing someone else's clothes, Storm. It's disrespectful." It's not. At least, that's not why I don't want to put them on. Just the thought has my skin crawling—like wearing someone else's flesh. It's probably not that serious, but I don't want their ex-lover's castoffs.

He turns slowly and leans against the door frame. "I said they were your clothes, not someone else's. Whose did you think they were?"

My chest tightens as I gaze at the pile again. "I don't know."

"Lexi's? Avery's? Or some random woman we were fucking?"

My head pops up and I glare at him. "You don't have to be a dick about it."

"Oh, I'm not, sweets." He smirks. "Forgot how cute you are when you're jealous, though."

My mouth drops open as shock hits me. I sputter out a denial, but he just chuckles as he spins back to the bathroom and kicks the door shut. Seconds later, the shower turns on and I'm still left with questions. He said they were mine, but there's no way they're *actually* mine. There's no tags. They didn't have time to buy them, anyway. I dig through the clothes and find a soft t-shirt. It's old and worn, tugging at a thread in the back of my mind. I glance at the bathroom door, then smooth out the fabric.

It's an old band shirt. I haven't listened to them in years, but I used to. Their songs were on repeat, and Ghost used to complain. He wanted me to expand my musical horizons, but this band spoke to my soul in a way I'd never felt before. Once I left, I stopped listening to them. Not because they were suddenly terrible or no longer relevant to my life. Every song reminded me of a life I no longer had access to. I couldn't handle the heartache.

I swallow hard, then strip before pulling on the shirt. It feels like I'm reclaiming a piece of myself. Which seems ridiculous. It's just a top. Except I can't shake the feeling like I'm slipping into a role I'm no longer suited for. I might have been an adult, but I didn't feel like one. Even now, I'm far from an adult, at least one who knows what the hell they're doing.

"Wear these," Ghost murmurs from behind me and I jolt. His hand grips my hip to hold me steady as he leans over me. He snatches up a pair of leggings and the leather jacket. I take them automatically, and he presses his lips to my neck before moving toward the bathroom.

"What the fuck just happened," I breathe. I swear he chuckles as he closes the door after him.

I end up putting on the clothes in the end and before I know it, we're on our way to headquarters. My jaw hurts from clenching my teeth just to keep all the questions I have from blurting out. Instead, they crowd my brain and there's a throbbing behind my ears now.

"You're quiet," Ghost murmurs from beside me. Why he decided to sit in the backseat with me is beyond me. I don't even know why we took a car in the first place. Storm muttered something about safety, but it probably has to do with me. I haven't figured out how, though.

"You know we'll protect you, right?" he says.

"What an odd thing to say," I mutter as I gaze out the window.

"Why's that?"

I glance at him from the corner of my eye. "Well, you're the president of the Phantoms. They're your men. You shouldn't have to protect me from them."

"We don't know who's loyal and who was working with Venom," Storm says from in front of me. He's taking forever to get there, and I wonder how long it's been since he's driven a car instead of a motorcycle.

"I'm not concerned with someone jumping me." My finger taps out a tempo on my leg as I contemplate whether or not to ask. "Do you let women join now, or will I be the only one?"

Ghost clears his throat. "Um, Rivet will be there."

"Lexi? Or are you hoping her and I don't cross paths?"

I finally face him fully to gauge his reaction. I'm met with a stony expression, devoid of emotion. He probably thinks I'm going to beat the shit out of her the next time I see her. I have no intention of doing that. He knows something went down between us that first night I came back. I've kept my mouth shut about her comments, though. Her and I need to have a conversation later. I'm just not ready yet.

"Rivet is the only one allowed in full-member meetings," Ghost mumbles.

I tilt my head. "Is that so? How progressive of you."

"You're in a fucking mood," he grumbles. "Want to tell us what's your fucking problem before we get there? I'd rather not get bitched out in front of my men."

"Oh, I think I'll just let you stew. A little wait and see." I give him a sweet smile and glance out the window again.

Despite my words, I'm terrified. The last time I was at an MC meeting, I could fit in the cupboard of the bar lining one of the walls. We used to play with the beer caps dropped on the floor. Avery used to braid my hair. She let me practice on her, but I was shit at it. I never paid attention to what the adults were talking about. Storm would cover my ears when someone would start yelling. I doubt Ghost lets kids in headquarters these days.

Ghost's fingers brush the back of my neck, and he whispers, "Did you have fun with Storm? He told me how you rode his cock. Do you need another round to take care of that attitude?"

I swallow hard and glance at the rearview mirror, meeting Storm's eyes. He obviously didn't hear Ghost, or he'd be egging him on, going into detail about everything we did. They always did like to compare notes. I wouldn't be surprised if they pick right up where they left off.

Storm clicks his tongue and regains my attention. "We can't afford for anything to go haywire tonight, Siren. I need you—"

"On my best behavior." I salute his reflection.

"Not what I was going to say. We need you to watch our back. You being nosy won't draw attention. Plus, you'll be the distraction we need to see if anyone acts out of character."

Ghost's phone vibrates and a minute later he huffs. "They found Venom's body. We'll have to address it tonight."

"What's the story?" I ask.

"Disciples most likely took him out. Retaliation will be discussed later, pending investigation," he says slowly as he swipes at his phone. I nod, not that he's paying any attention. "Fuck, Siren. You shoved one in his eye socket?"

I shrug, feigning nonchalance. In reality, my throat tightens as I remember the squelching sound his eyeball made when I popped it out with a dirty spoon. I wasn't going to do something so disgusting, but I needed it to look like there was more than one guy doing the job. If it was just one, the Phantoms might think it was a vendetta. Anything to make it more believable.

"How the fuck did you get a coin in there?" Storm calls.

"Uh, I just kind of angled it? I don't kn—"

"You carved a shepherd's staff into his chest? What the fuck, Siren." Ghost makes a gagging sound.

"I had to make it look professional."

"The bullet between the eyes wasn't enough?"

I roll my eyes. "Didn't realize you two were so squeamish. I did what I had to do to make it look like it was a Disciple job."

We pull into the alley next to headquarters. The same one I hid in while eavesdropping on Venom and Hornet. I wince as I climb out. The rumble of dozens of bikes fills the night. I should have asked how many were coming tonight. If there's a crowd here, I'll be overwhelmed more than I already am. Shit, I should have asked what exactly they wanted me to look for, too. This whole night is going to be a fucking disaster.

I grab Storm's arm and he swings around. "Do the others know you and Ghost are a thing?"

"Do they know we're fucking? Probably. Do they know we're together? Yeah. It's not a secret. Why?"

"No reason," I murmur as a shadow flits past the mouth of the alley. Storm turns to gaze in the same direction, but they've gone.

I shake my head and drop my hold on Storm only for him to link our hands together. He tugs me around to follow Ghost around the corner of the building toward the back entrance. I straighten my spine and tip my chin up. These two might not know it, but tonight might change everything. And I don't think I'm ready for the possible fallout.

Thirty-Five

Ghost

This is the last place I want to be tonight. Usually, I enjoy this part of leading the Phantoms. Most of the club runs itself. We have protocols and deliveries that need little oversight from me.

These meetings are reserved for the bigger things we want to tackle. It's how I was able to set up a makeshift orphanage for the kids whose parents died or abandoned them. It's how I was able to expand our reach beyond Harris. It's how we were able to implement many of the programs throughout our territory and help our community.

Now, it's as if everyone is collectively holding their breath. They're waiting for shit to go sideways. We've already heard reports from our road captain, a wiry fellow ironically named Bear. Fuse hasn't made a peep, mostly eyeing the enforcers from the edge of the room. We put a lot on him the last couple weeks, but I feel like he's hiding something.

When our treasurer steps up, I bite back a groan. He always goes on and on, spewing numbers no one truly understands. I keep telling him to meet with me privately instead of droning on in a meeting like this.

"Digit, I'm going to have to cut you off," Storm calls from behind me. I'm surprised he was paying attention. Siren's been stuck to his side for most of the evening, whispering about how boring this is. I can't fault her. This is really fucking boring.

Digit sputters and adjusts his glasses. Fucker doesn't even need to wear them. He thought people would respect him more if he started. Newsflash, they didn't. It did help him get some attention from the women who hang around. Other clubs call them bunnies, but I got rid of that term when I took over. The label reminded me of my mother. Outlawing it might have been selfish, but I've never regretted it.

"Fuse," I bark, and he straightens. "Report."

He nods, though his nostrils flare the slightest bit. I glance at Storm, and he subtly raises an eyebrow. Venom being a spy didn't surprise me. Hornet being his accomplice didn't either. If Fuse turns out to be a mole for the Disciples, that'll shock the hell out of me. Not to mention hurt. We may not be as close as we were to Jag, but still. He's been loyal and exactly what we needed when Jag stayed in Rima.

"Venom's dead."

I close my eyes and swallow a groan. Asshole could have delivered that news a little more delicately. The club erupts into chaos. A group in the back jump to their feet, sending several of their chairs skittering across the tile floor. Bear's gaze meets mine and he shakes his head. It's a fucking bitchfest. I let them yell for another minute before I lift my hand. No one seems to notice, which only serves to piss me off more. I pull my gun from my back and point it at the ceiling. The shot echoes through the space. Half the members hit the floor and the other pull their own weapons. No one shouts or screams, though.

"If you're all done bitching, perhaps you'd like to hear what we know. Fuse?"

He waits while the members settle in their seats. Several men in the back slam their chairs upright, their grumbles rumbling through the air. Hornet's among them, rage and terror warring on his face. We'll have to bring him in. A night in the hole will have him cracking in no time. I step back while Fuse tells them what we know.

"Note the people at Hornet's table. We're going to need to bring all of them in," I murmur to Storm.

"Already done. Siren's got quite a few she's pointed out, too."

My gaze skips to her. She's still pale and there's a tightness around her eyes giving away how stressed she is. I'm sure no other than Storm and me would notice. No one said anything when she walked in, though there were a couple people who did a double take. Rivet didn't even blink and I'm starting to suspect Storm said something to her.

"We need to keep an eye on Rivet. They'll target her and her shop next," Storm says.

He opens his mouth, then snaps it shut when shouts drown him out. I whip around and scan the crowd. Two tables are squaring off as if they're going to fight right in the middle of the fucking room. Every damn time it's something. For as much control as I have over the MC, they're still men used to their independence.

I reach for my gun again, but Storm stops me. He shakes his head, then sits back. We can't just let them go at each other's throats. I feel like I'm slowly losing control over the Phantoms. If I don't cut out the traitors soon, we'll rot from the inside out. The Disciples won't have to do a damn thing. They could sit back and watch us destroy ourselves.

"Ghost," Siren whispers harshly, "just walk out there."

I give her a look over my shoulder. If she thinks I'm going down there to get caught in the crossfire...

Her brows pull low. "I'm serious. They'll stop if you get off this damn pedestal. You've put yourself up here on a goddamn stage. They need to remember who you are. So, fucking show them."

I sigh heavily. "Get the ice packs ready."

I hop off the raised platform, ignoring the stairs, and weave my way through the tables. Several members scoot out of my way.

We're supposed to have dinner after this, but I doubt it'll happen. Not unless people get their shit together real quick. Then again, we paid the local Mexican restaurant to cater.

I thought food would help get everyone on board for the plans I've half mapped out. We need to hit the Disciples before they come after us out in the open. I almost wish they would get it over with. Uncovering the tendrils they've threaded throughout Harris isn't easy. I'm sure they've infiltrated more than we've discovered. The uncertainty and waiting are the worst in these situations.

"Careful, boy," Rivet mutters as I pass her. I don't bother answering. I think this is a foolish plan, which makes me wonder why I'm listening to Siren. If I get shot, I'm blaming her.

No one notices as I approach. The two tables are too busy screaming in each other's faces, spittle flying in all directions. I'm surprised no one's pulled a gun, though Hornet's hand rests on the weapon attached to his hip.

I nod to Widow, one of my enforcers, and he pushes from the wall. He'll be able to take Hornet down before he can get a shot off. He's been with us since the beginning, and I trust him. At least, I did. Now, I'm questioning everyone's loyalty and I hate it. I don't trust all my members equally, but now my mind is muddled. Falling back on my instincts might get me killed.

Bracing myself, I step between the two factions and cross my arms. They all fall silent, their harsh breaths the only indication they were fighting not ten seconds ago. I lock eyes with each of them, noting those who duck their head to glance away. When I get to Hornet, he glares at me.

"There a problem here?" I ask calmly as I scan them all again. There's only a dozen of them, yet it's still hard to stand here in between them.

"No problem, Prez. Just a misunderstanding," Ranch, a member, mumbles, avoiding my gaze.

"Is that so? Why don't you tell me what it is? I might be able to help." I turn to Hornet. "Well?"

He scowls, finally tucking his chin to his chest. If he has something to say, he's going to have to do it in front of everyone, and I doubt he will. I don't know how deep he was in with Venom. Maybe he just knew surface-level shit and he's tore up about his death.

"I want proof he's dead," he grunts.

I raise an eyebrow, though he doesn't notice. "Proof. You think I'm lying?"

The men around him who were so quick to defend him not minutes ago tense, then back away slowly. Perhaps Siren was right after all. For all the mistakes I've made lately, how absent I've been, they still have the good sense to be wary of my wrath. Standing before them, I'm no longer the leader who tried to force us into the next century. I'm no longer the boss who withholds their salary when they fuck up. I'm no longer the figurehead making decisions they don't understand.

I'm the one who took out Snake—who crushed his windpipe with my bare hands. I'm the fucking president of the Phantoms. The one other clubs whisper about. The one others fear, as my own members should. I may not have picked my name, but it suits me well. My enemies know what I'm capable of. I can't afford for those underneath me to forget, either.

It's the only way I'm able to survive in such a cutthroat world. I hold on to my position with an iron fist, lest someone else rise up to rip it from me.

"He was my friend," Hornet finally whispers. I almost believe him.

"We're all brothers here, Hornet. At least, the rest of us are. Does your friendship override that of the brotherhood?"

He blanches, shaking his head vigorously. "No, Prez."

"I suggest you not forget who your loyalty lies with, Hornet. Or you'll find yourself alone when it matters most."

I pivot on my heel and saunter back to the stage. No one speaks this time. No fights break out. I seem to have cowed them into submission, for now. This time, I take the stairs and am met with Siren attempting to hide a grin. She's doing a terrible job. My nostrils flare and she sobers. I smirk, hoping she's imagining the same things I am. Her gloating will only lead me to put her over my knee.

I spin around to face the crowd. "Now that you're all paying attention, we can get to the important issues at hand. Storm?"

I don't miss Hornet's sour face when I deliver that line. He'll find out soon enough how much we know of Venom's involvement with the Disciples. Storm steps forward and begins his spiel about reduced shipments and dirty product.

When he starts talking about Oracle bleeding into our city, there's another uproar. It takes a minute for them to settle down, and Ranch raises his hand like we're in school. He just became a full member, though he's lived in Harris for most of his life.

"Sorry." His voice cracks and he clears his throat. "What's Oracle?"

"Nasty drug that ran through Synd a while back. Bled over into Rima, though it didn't take hold as well there. It was produced by the Guild to fund their operation."

"Another MC?" Ranch interrupts, and his buddy smacks him in the back of the head.

"No, the Guild had everything from brothels to dog fighting rings. All of that was just a way to funnel funds into their central objective. Trafficking. They somehow made a new drug they called Oracle. It's highly addictive, comes in many forms, and users often have no memories after the high wears off. It's flammable in some cases."

Fuse's head snaps toward me. "The fuck?"

"Synd's river was on fire at one point. I'm told it was...interesting. That's besides the point. The attempted hit a few weeks back? The truck was holding Oracle. It wasn't fully processed yet, except we have found out it was mixed with an accelerant that made it explode. We've reached out to our other factions and put them on alert. Touch base with your own members and find out if they've seen anything and make your reports to Bear."

Storm runs through the protocols of how to deal with shipments, then what will happen if we need to go on lockdown. Most of them have no idea what it would look like. They've never experienced our entire MC shutting down our territory, much less the whole of Harris. Our small police department wouldn't be able to handle the upheaval, and our main priority will be to keep the citizens safe. It won't be pretty.

"One more thing," I call when Storm is done. "The Disciples. They're gearing up for something. Until we have more info, we'll be watching things. In the meantime, stay away from their territory. If you come into contact with a Disciple, don't engage and inform whoever's above you."

I don't like leaving everyone in the dark. Until we know who's infiltrated our ranks, we can't give anything away. Storm thinks we should bring some of the members on board, but until we know more, I'm loath to do it. This meeting has gone on long enough anyway, and I want to get home.

"If there's nothing else..." I scan the crowd, daring someone to speak up. "Great. Food'll be here in a minute. Don't burn the place down."

They cheer as I turn to gather Siren. I was sure someone would be an asshole and point her out. Most of them ignored her. Usually, we'd stay and eat with them. I refuse to put her in danger, though, and from the tension still resonating through the room, she'd definitely be a target. I gather her up and slip my arm around her waist. As we walk out the back door, I breathe a sigh of relief. We just need to get through this season, and everything will go back to normal.

Thirty-Six

Ghost doesn't sit in the back seat with me on the way back to their house. I wonder if he's punishing me for speaking up in the meeting. Storm told me it'd be best if I just kept my mouth shut. Except Ghost was about to start an all-out war. He may be the president, but shooting one of your members because they're yelling at each other isn't a good look. Then again, I don't really know how meetings are run. Maybe that's what he actually does. One chosen sacrifice is fed to his inner beast by way of a single bullet.

"Ridiculous," I mutter, then glance at them. They're too busy talking about the intricacies of the meeting. I swear they're going to get into people's facial expressions next.

Storm pulls into the small driveway and parks. I reach for the handle, but neither of them move. I sigh and rest my head against the seat. For some reason, I don't want to go inside by myself. I've spent enough time being alone. Plus, going in there without them will probably feel like I'm breaking and entering. Irrational, but there it is.

I roll my head to the side and stare out the window. A shadow detaches from the darkness, and I tense.

"Uh, guys?" I murmur, focusing on the spot. They don't hear me or they're ignoring me. "Guys."

"What, Siren?" Ghost snaps.

I grind my teeth together, wondering if I should let him figure it out himself. Logic wins out in the end. "Might want to see who's lurking on your front porch."

Ghost's head swings around, and Storm leans to gaze out the windshield. I sink into my seat, wishing I had a weapon. Storm rudely took the ones I borrowed from him, saying I wouldn't need them. As if they'd actually be able to protect me in a firefight. I'm not used to relying on anyone else. It's strange how much I've changed, and I don't know if I can go back to the way things used to be.

"For fuck's sake." Ghost shoves open his door.

"Stay here," Storm says as he follows.

Neither one of them sound particularly worried. I count to ten, then crawl from the car. Storm scowls at me from over his shoulder, and I resist the urge to stick out my tongue. Just because we're...whatever we are, doesn't mean I have to listen to them. Still, I lean against the door as they approach the house. I should probably ask what they think we are. Except they have enough on their plates without me demanding to define our relationship. I doubt this is my happily ever after.

I'm holding my breath, waiting for them to remember why they threw me away in the first place. It wasn't because of the banishment. Or the photos. If they truly thought I'd betrayed them, they wouldn't have just let me leave. They wouldn't have refused to talk to me. There must be something else, some reason they were so quick to cut me off. Which makes me wonder what changed. What made them flip back to wanting me around? Sex? Because they could have gotten that from anywhere. I'm sure they've been propositioned at some point since I've been gone. None of it makes sense and I'm just waiting for the other shoe to drop.

Now isn't the time to deal with any of my feelings. My heart doesn't factor into the equation. Not with the Disciples and the dissent within the Phantoms breathing down their necks. My heart and future aren't as important as them dealing with all that. I'd be a bitch if I forced them to deal with my problems first. They might deserve it for the way they've treated me.

Huffing, I push from the car and stomp toward the porch. I don't want to wait around for them to acknowledge me. Whoever they're talking to will just have to handle it.

Once I get to the bottom of the stairs, though, I freeze. Lexi and Ghost are in a heated argument. I doubt it's about me, but my mind still goes there. Part of me wants to run. From the way Lexi acted when I stumbled upon her, I don't know what her reaction will be and that scares me. It was almost like she believed everything Snake said about me. Which hurts almost as much as Ghost and Storm's assumptions. We used to be so close and then nothing. I turn, intent on going back to the car or maybe just walking the streets of Harris until they're done.

"Didn't make it far, did you?" Lexi calls, and I close my eyes before spinning back to face her.

"Not exactly." I don't know what else to say, so I stand there, letting her scan me from head to toe.

"Well, you don't look like you're two seconds away from the reaper coming to snatch your soul anymore." She wanders to the edge of the porch and raises an eyebrow. "You the reason we're going into lockdown?"

My gaze snaps to Ghost, and he rolls his eyes. Storm buries his face in his hands. I didn't realize they'd gone into lockdown. At the meeting, they talked about it, but nothing happened on the way home to change that as far as I know. Either Lexi has bad info or she's just jumping to conclusions.

"Wasn't aware we were in a lockdown. I'm not exactly privy to information."

"Yet you were at a meeting. No women are allowed in those. Except you, apparently." Her expression twists with jealousy.

I cross my arms. "Rivet was there. Why don't you go ask her

about this instead of subtly accusing me of influencing the way the Phantoms are run? I don't have any sway over what they do."

Pain flashes in her eyes and I wonder if I've gone too far. I didn't say anything against her, but I wonder how long she's been asking Ghost to include her in things. And he'll have denied her under the guise of protection. He always said he wouldn't put her in danger, so no one was told they were siblings. It only ended up hurting her. He thought the end justified the means. Apparently, Lexi never got over it.

"Could you give us a minute?" she whispers to Ghost.

Ghost glances at me and waits for me to nod before he grabs Storm's arm and they disappear inside. Lexi noticed from the tightening in her shoulders. She sighs as she sinks onto the porch swing. It creaks as it rocks gently back and forth.

"Well, you going to join me or was I too much of a bitch?" she calls, and I force my feet to move. I'm not scared of her, but I was hoping to avoid this conversation a little longer.

I drop next to her and send us swinging once more. She props her feet on the railing and gazes out at the street. We stay that way for a while, and I take the time to study her profile from the corner of my eye. She certainly dressed to blend in with the shadows from her black ballet flats to the dark sweatshirt, complete with a hood. The streetlight a block down barely illuminates her face, and I wonder how much she's actually changed. She looks basically the same, minus the plump cheeks she had in high school. I wonder if she still blushes at the merest hint of sex. Probably not.

"You going to tell me why?" I ask, breaking the silence.

"I didn't know what else to do," she whispers. "I'd say you can't blame me, but I suppose you're entitled to. I did what I thought was right. And yeah, a lot of it had to do with jealousy. I just...I don't have an excuse."

I have no idea what she's talking about. I was asking about lockdown and why she cares so much. Asking will allow her to lie to me, which apparently she's done before. Unless she's upset about how we left things a few weeks ago.

"I'm going to be honest, I'm hella confused. What the fuck are you talking about?" I face her, hoping I can catch her fumbling.

"Wait, what were *you* talking about?"

I shake my head slowly. "I think yours is a little more important than mine. What did you do, Lexi?" I don't mean it as a threat, but it comes out like one.

Her eyes widen, and I wonder if she'll try deflecting again. "They didn't tell you? Shit. Um, okay." She drops her feet and leans away from me. "Ghost said he showed you the photos. I figured he told you."

My muscles tense. "Told me what?"

I already know the answer. I need her to admit what she did. Questions flood my brain, and I almost blurt them out. Who gave her the photos? Why didn't she come to me? Was it really jealousy that made her destroy my entire life? Still, I wait.

She swallows hard, then sucks in a deep breath. "Listen, I admit I gave Ghost the photos out of jealousy. You were so much closer to him than I was. Not romantically, 'cause ew, but he always turned to you. No matter what I did, he didn't see me because you were standing right there. And I understood, which made it so much worse. I just wanted to be like you, yet nothing I did was ever good enough."

She pushes to her feet, and for a second, I think she's going to stomp off. Instead, she paces in front of me. My hand twitches, and I resist the urge to grab her.

"I don't regret taking the pictures—"

"What?"

She clears her throat. "I know that sounds bad, but you have to understand. All I saw was you meeting with that guy. At first, I thought you were cheating, and it pissed me off. I was going to ask you who he was and what the hell you were doing. Then I found out he was a Disciple, and well, I did what I thought was right. So no, I don't regret giving them the photos I took. I was trying to protect Ghost. He's my brother. He was the only one who gave two shits about me after Mom died. Can you blame me?"

"Why didn't you come to me? Why didn't you ask me what the fuck I was doing?" I cry and shove to my feet. The swing catches me on the back of my knees, almost sending me tumbling. Lexi stumbles back and clutches the railing for support.

"I did. Sort of. I mean, I asked you what you were doing that night, and you said you were hanging out with Ghost and Storm. Then you went to that restaurant instead. You lied to me." Tears fill her eyes, and she holds her hands out as if I'll take them—as if I'll comfort her.

"So you have one half-ass hidden conversation with me, then follow me to take photos of a situation you knew nothing about. You assume the worst, then you assume the second worst scenario and bring the 'evidence' straight to the two men I loved the most. And you did it because you were jealous? Am I getting that right?" I'm holding on by a thread and only her answer will keep me from snapping.

"I'm sorry," she whispers as tears streak down her face. "I'm so sorry."

Nodding, I pivot and head for the front door. I need time to process. I need time to think. I need to talk to...someone. Maybe. The thought of approaching Ghost or Storm with this has my skin itching. My chest and neck are hot under my shirt, and I tug at the collar. I probably have stress hives. Lexi's footsteps scuffle behind me and I freeze. If she tries to stop me from leaving, she's not going to like what I turn into.

"Lexi," a woman's voice calls in warning. It takes me a minute to place who it is, but then I realize it's Rivet. I wonder if she followed us home or if Ghost even knows she's here.

I glance over my shoulder and catch Lexi's scared expression before she turns away. Rivet stands at the bottom of the stairs and gestures to her.

"Time for you to go home, girl." She waits until Lexi reaches her. "Give her time, Lexi."

Lexi nods, then disappears into the dark. Rivet climbs the stairs and points to the swing. My feet move before I've made the decision to sit. Not surprising.

She was one of the few adults who gave me a chance despite my relation to my father. She gave me a job, taught me more than I ever learned in school, and kept my ass from falling into a life I'd never be able to drag myself out of alone. She saved me and I'll never be able to repay her.

Once she's settled next to me, she hands me a key. "Brought you your bike."

"Uh, I don't have a bike. Lost my last one in a crash, then it burst into flames. I doubt even you would be able to put her back together." I try to hand them back to her, and she wraps her fingers around mine.

"I brought your bike. It's parked around back. Here are the keys. You will take them and use the bike as needed. Please don't run away with it. Never did you any good before. At least talk to them first. They didn't do so well when you left the last time." She says it gently, but my chest tightens.

"I didn't run away last time. I was banished. And they did nothing to stop me. Neither did Lexi. Or you, for a matter of fact. You don't have a right to lecture me about sticking around." My voice vibrates with barely suppressed rage. Between Ghost and Storm, Lexi, and now Rivet, I just can't fucking do this. I need a goddamn break.

"Not what I was talking about, Siren."

"Then what the hell *were* you talking about?"

"You didn't fight. You didn't defend yourself. You just left, making yourself look guilty."

"They didn't fight for me. Isn't that what people who love you are supposed to do?" I say bitterly.

She nods slowly, gazing out at the dark street. "They should have. I figured you three had a heart-to-heart and worked your issues out. I suggest you deal with that, then deal with Lexi. Just know, her heart was in the right place. She brought those photos to the one person she trusted."

"Don't talk to me about trust, Rivet. I respect you, but I'm not doing this. Her actions fucked up my entire life. She torched my future and ripped away the two people I loved more than anything else in this world." I push to my feet and stalk toward the front door.

"Just don't let your rage consume you, Siren. It's a sad way to go."

Thirty-Seven

Ghost

"Shit is tense, right? Like it's not just me?" Storm asks me at breakfast three days after the meeting.

"It's not just you. I knew she'd need time to deal with Lexi's role in everything, but I didn't think she'd take it out on us," I mutter, then shove a spoonful of oatmeal in my mouth. He glances away, his throat contracting as he tries not to gag. He never did like oatmeal, but usually he doesn't have such a reaction.

He pushes his scrambled eggs around his plate. They've gone cold, but he doesn't leave. It's late in the morning, yet Siren isn't up. She's been sleeping more and more the last few days. I kept thinking she'd come to one of us to talk. I told Storm to leave it, but I'm starting to question my judgment. We're going to lose her again if we don't figure shit out. I thought we'd settle things, then Lexi had to show up and blow it all up.

I'm sick of being in this grey area. I just want everything to be settled between Siren and us so I can focus on everything else. Fuse keeps texting me, trying to keep me up to date on the Disciples movements. Problem is, they've gone dark. Even his contact inside the club is quiet. Part of me thinks we'll wake up to an attack and we won't be ready. It's not easy being in this holding pattern, especially with so many smaller clubs under our protection. One of these days, the dam will break and I'm afraid we'll be swept away with the onslaught.

"I keep thinking we'll wake up and she'll be gone," Storm says softly, pulling me from my worries.

I snort, twirling my spoon around. "That why you took her keys?"

"I didn't take her fucking keys. I *tried* to, but she hid them." He scowls at his cold eggs.

"Surprised she's still sleeping in the same bed as us," I mutter. "Not that you're in there much."

"We've got a lot to do and most of our members are working at night. Not all of us have the luxury of a full night's sleep." He glances over his shoulder, and I follow his line of sight, but Siren's nowhere to be seen.

"Yeah, sure, that's why you're awake. It's totally not because you're stressed about her skipping town and think if you fall asleep you won't catch her before she does."

He sighs heavily, unwilling to admit I'm right. He laces his fingers behind his head and stares at the ceiling. What he doesn't realize is I haven't been sleeping either. Oh, I get a few hours here or there, but I always wake up. There are too many things to deal with. I don't have time to sleep. Every night I've been immersing myself in the issues within the Phantoms. Shipments are being rerouted. Our contacts are ghosting us. Two MCs in towns closer to the Disciples have stopped communicating with us. They're all small problems we could deal with. Stacked on top of one another? Maybe they're hoping we'll be too overwhelmed to fight back.

"What if we reached out to Prophet?" he mutters.

"Why?"

He drops his elbows to the table and shoves his plate away. "It's not like he'll back off and we'll become besties, but it might get him off our backs."

"The last time I met with Prophet, he tried to bless me." I give him a look. "With poison. You remember that, right?"

"I wasn't saying you waltz into their headquarters with a fruit basket. He might reveal something. It's not like we usually call for a conference. At least not with the Disciples. They might be caught off guard. We'll find a neutral location far enough away from both our territories. And we could send someone if it comes down to it."

"Suppose that's why I'm still here, huh?" Siren says as she breezes into the kitchen.

If she was hoping for a reaction, she'll be sorely mistaken. We're not actively keeping anything from her. Not anymore. It'll take more than a few days for her to realize that, though. Not that I'm in a sharing mood right now. Between too little sleep and her silence, my fuse has shortened considerably.

I kick out the chair between us when she approaches with a banana. It's still mostly green and my nose wrinkles. She peels it carefully as I study her. Dark rings rest under her eyes. Her hair was just gaining some of its shine back. Now the strands lay limp around her shoulders, dull and lifeless. A slight frown plays on her lips, though I doubt she realizes.

"You're not going anywhere near the Disciples. Especially Prophet. If that man wants to come for you, he'll have to kill us first," I snarl, then shove from my seat. I stomp around the kitchen, cleaning my bowl and aggressively attacking the piles of dishes from breakfast.

"I could do it. He'd probably tell me more than anyone else you send," she murmurs, and I glance over my shoulder as she takes a bite of her banana.

It's been a long time since I saw the act of eating as sexual, but it's like she's purposefully deep-throating it. Especially when her eyes meet mine. I swear she fucking smirks. For someone who's been actively avoiding us, she sure is being flirty. She tips her chair back and rests her feet on the table. The wood creaks as she rocks on only two legs.

"Not smart, Siren," Storm mutters, and his gaze darts to me.

I turn back around, trying not to freak the fuck out at her

disrespecting the furniture. It's why most people aren't allowed in the house. I've shoved Storm to the floor more than once when he's sat on the arm of the couch. He calls me grandma afterward.

I move to wipe down the counters to keep an eye on them both. If she pushes her luck, I'm going to kick those legs out from under her, though she'd probably bust her head open, and I'd have to deal with the blood.

"Woo bont ooh ind ur oh isess," she says around the banana.

"I have no idea what the fuck you're trying to say, but you can definitely keep trying while you deep-throat that banana. And if you need something else to fill your mouth..." Storm smirks, grabbing his cock through his athletic shorts. The move has my own cock throbbing, but I push down the zing of desire.

"If you two are going to eye fuck each other, fine. At least wait until I'm out of the fucking room," I sneer, and Storm grimaces.

"You're in a mood," Siren says to me.

"As if you haven't been?"

She waves her hand around dismissively. "I was working through some things. I'm fine now. Except for possibly wanting to punch Lexi in the throat."

I slam the dishwasher shut and spin around. "That's it? You shut us out for three fucking days, and we're just supposed to fuck your bad attitude away."

"If you're offering..." She tosses her peel toward the garbage can and misses, and I scowl. She has the good sense to scramble to her feet to toss it away. I take my seat again and kick her chair before she can sit down again.

Storm pats his leg and says, "Got a seat here if you want."

She rolls her eyes and marches toward me. "What's your problem? Let's get it all out in the open so we can move on."

Storm clears his throat. "Maybe we should take a breather."

I glare at her, then drop my gaze to the table. I don't want to deal with this now. Actually, I don't want to deal with this at all. If I had it my way, we'd skip all this pain and hurt and everything would be fine. We'd deal with the Disciples and pretend the past six years didn't happen. There were no betrayals, no lies, no mistakes. We would just live our lives. We'd be in love and running the Phantoms together like we always talked about.

Except I can't erase those years. Or the pain. Or the guilt. Or the shame. Nothing can change the past and I fucking hate it. Usually, I know exactly what to do. If I fuck up, there's a reason. I apologize and move the fuck on. Except I can't. Siren won't let me. We might be able to pretend for a while, but it'll always come back and bite us in the ass. It'd be in the background of everything we do and every decision we made. It would haunt us until we either fix it or fracture completely.

Still, I want to avoid it all as long as possible. "We don't have time to hash this all out, Siren."

"Then making fucking time," she snarls.

I explode to my feet and gesture wildly. "We fucking loved you. You think we just stopped when you were banished? You fucking destroyed us."

"And you think you didn't destroy me? You think it was easy? Not only did I have to leave behind everything I knew with almost nothing to my name, but I had to deal with you two shattering my fucking heart. I was completely alone in this world, and you didn't give a shit. You didn't care if I was alive or dead or worse. So, excuse me if you jumped the goddamn gun and now you're having some regret."

Her fingers curl into fists over and over as she glares at me. I feel like she punched me in the gut, which I suppose she sort of did. I barely register as Storm stands slowly and makes his way around the table. I'm too focused on Siren. Storm's fingers brush her back as he passes, and her shoulders slump. It's as if he's taken all the fight from her.

He glances at me, disappointment shining in his eyes. As if he has any room to criticize me. He's been flip-flopping the entire time she's been here. One minute he wants her and the next he wants to strangle her. I refuse to be judged by him. Neither of them knows how to fix this. Hell, I don't know how to fix this either.

"He knew," Storm whispers to Siren and her head snaps up. Bastard. "Ghost knew you were alive. Not the specifics, but he knew. While you were surviving, we were shadows of ourselves. Blame us. Scream at us. Forgive us. It's up to you, but we're doing the best we can."

She snorts, though there's no heat behind the noise. "When did you become the voice of reason? And so damn corny?"

"Punching Ghost helped me. You want to punch him? Might help."

Her gaze slides to me and I straighten, accepting my fate. I'll let her hit me, just like I let Storm. It's what he needed at the time and if it'll help Siren, so be it. It might help me, too. Usually, I know what the hell to do. It's what makes me good at leading this club. The sixth sense I have for spotting trouble has served me well until now. When it comes to Siren, that intuition has abandoned me.

Storm seems to have dealt with all his feelings toward her. He's worked through his anger and came out on the other side, his devotion to her akin to before. I thought I was the same, that I'd let go of my resentment and her role in things. The last three days have been hell, though, dredging up old hurts I thought I'd long since buried.

"No, I don't want to punch him. I want this feeling to go away," she whispers.

"Which one?" I growl.

"I don't know. I'm just..." There's a heaviness in her sigh. "Mad. I'm fucking furious. I'm mad at Lexi for not talking to me. I'm mad at Rivet for not sticking her neck out for me when she told me she would. I'm mad at Banner for beating me—"

I flinch and she freezes. The image of her being in the hole, his fists pounding into her, flash through my head. I don't know which one of the many scars I've noted on her skin was from him. I don't know how to take that pain away. Or the guilt of not being there to protect her. She had to leave town by herself without any help while she was hurt. I don't even know how many injuries she had.

"What else are you mad at?" Storm asks when I can't.

"You," she spits and glances at Storm. "Him. This whole damn club. The Disciples. Prophet. I'm so fucking pissed at Prophet. I don't know why I'm on his radar—why I've been on his radar for years. And I don't fucking care. I just want...I want to be okay. And I don't know how to be okay. The thought of being on my own again is terrifying. I learned how to be on my own, to be alone, and now I don't know how to do that. You fucking broke me. Then you left me. Then broke me again. How do I fix that?"

Storm tugs her toward him, and her forehead hits his chest. "We fix it. We helped break it, so we help fix it."

"Sappy son of a bitch," she mumbles. "People don't talk like that."

My stomach flips and my palms itch. I don't know what she said that tipped me off, but something isn't right. I glance around the kitchen, then out the windows. Nothing moves other than the air shivering the leaves through the tree out front. Storm whispers to Siren, his face buried in her hair. I can't hear him over the blood rushing in my ears. I grit my teeth, fighting against the rising tide of dread hitting me.

"Ugh," she groans, then shoves away from Storm. "You two are fucking assholes."

Her outburst snaps me out of it. "We're assholes? You're an asshole."

"Fuck you, Ghost. I didn't do shit to you."

"Still met with a Disciple," I mutter, rolling my eyes, hoping the move lessens the blow of my accusation. While I'd like to know what the hell was happening in those photos, I no longer think she was passing info. Like she said, it doesn't make sense.

Her palms slam into my chest, and I rock back. "Who was he, huh? If you're so fucking smart—kept those photos all these years, then tell me who he was. You don't know, do you? Because it's some random fuckass I probably ran into while getting dinner. Food for us." She shoves him again. "It was your favorite. Bet you didn't know that, did you?"

My mouth parts and clarity hits me. All this time we've been asking the wrong questions. We just thought the Disciple was a random member, maybe a prospect who wanted to score some points within his club. We barely even looked for him. We were so focused on Siren and what her banishment meant, we completely disregarded him. We need to find him. He's the key to this. I don't know how he fits in with everything going on now, but for some reason, it does. I can't explain it. I just know.

"I...I...yeah. Okay. You two make up or whatever. I gotta check something." I lean in and kiss her forehead. Her mouth drops open as I pull back.

Storm snatches my arm as I turn away. "Ghost, what's—"

I grab the back of his neck and yank him toward me. His mouth smashes into mine, and I let him go just as suddenly. I walk away before I change my mind. If I stood there any longer with Siren between us, we'd end up fucking her. We'd lose the entire day, which would be amazing in the moment, but wouldn't help us in the long run. I'll leave Storm to take care of her while I find some answers.

Thirty-Eight

Storm

Storm

My arm slips around Siren's waist, and I pull her back into my chest. She melts into me for a minute before she sighs and pushes away. She wanders around the kitchen and opens the fridge twice, then finally closes it and turns to me.

"What do you think that was about?" she asks, leaning against the counter and crossing her arms.

"Dunno. Maybe he's going to find the mystery man. He had that look in his eye." I shrug and grab my plate. My nose wrinkles as I dump the cold eggs into the trash.

"Wait, what look?"

I sigh and drop back into my chair. I thought we were going in an entirely different direction. Her mind seems to be fixated on Ghost, who is currently walking out the front door. Siren's brows pull low as his bike roars to life and slowly fades as he takes off.

I clear my throat. "He didn't really talk about it when we were younger, but he thinks he has a sixth sense. He knows when shit is about to go down. He had it before you were banished. Again when he was in Rima a year ago. When the truck blew up right before you got here? Yeah, bad feeling in his gut, something in the air, weird look in his eyes. Could be nothing, though."

"Nothing? He stumbled out of here and took off. You don't even know where he went, and you don't seem worried even a little bit."

I tilt my head and smirk. "Are *you* worried about him, sweets?"

She throws her hands up and rolls her eyes. "You're impossible."

Her spine straightens when I push to my feet and slowly round the table. "Impossible. Asshole. Wonder what's next?"

Her throat bobs and she presses her lips together. My fingers grip the edge of the counter, trapping her. Her bottom lip quivers as desire flashes in her eyes.

"Thought we were talking about Ghost and the possible trouble he could be getting into?" she says, her voice trembling.

I could say I'm just following Ghost's orders to take care of her or I'm distracting her from her worry. In reality, I just miss being close to her. I miss being inside her. Having her next to me in bed may have healed something broken within me, but I'm barely in there.

Most of the time I sleep a few hours, my arms wrapped around her, then I'm wide awake. I've been using the time to deal with club issues. There never seems to be enough time to do everything. Half the time I'm waiting for Siren to come find me again.

"Ghost is a grown man who can take care of himself. You, on the other hand, definitely need help taking care of your needs."

"I can make myself come, Storm. I don't need you for that."

I raise a single eyebrow and her body trembles. "Is that so?"

Her eyes narrow and she nods once. I grab her waist, and she squeals as I swing her around. She clings to me when I plop her ass on the table. When I shake her off and step back, her nostrils flare. If she wants to make claims like that, she's going to have to prove it. Whether or not I'm able to contain myself long enough to watch her come has yet to be seen. I lean against the counter and smirk. Her palms slap the table behind her, and she kicks her legs back and forth.

"There a reason I'm on the table? You realize people eat here, right? Unless you've got something else planned..."

"Are you offering me second breakfast?"

"It's closer to elevensies, wouldn't you say?"

My mouth drops open as her peals of laughter fill the room. I shake my head, unable to fight a grin. So much for me being in charge. With just a couple words, she's derailed all my plans. I stalk forward and throw her over my shoulder. Her giggles chase us down the hallway as I thunder up the stairs. Her joy fills in the cracks I've been living with for years. I'd successfully ignored the fractures, or at least I thought I had.

I toss her onto Ghost's bed, and she squeals, scrambling back. Her mouth parts, a smile playing on her lips and laughter dancing in her eyes. This might be better than what I had planned. I take one step and she tenses, leaning to the opposite side of the bed.

"Thinking about running, honey?"

Her nose wrinkles. "Don't call me honey. I'm not a bee and you're not a cowboy."

"Only cowboys are allowed to use honey?"

She shrugs. "And bees, though I doubt they can talk. Wait, don't they dance? I forgot about that. It's fucking adorable."

"They buzz, so maybe they're singing to each other about the joys of honey," I say, then tip my head back and groan. "You're fucking distracting me."

"Now, why would I do that?" She glances to the side, giving herself away.

I walk slowly around the bed, then grab her wrist. She tugs, her heels slipping against the silk sheets as she tries to scramble away. A giggle escapes her, and I unearth the restraints from under the mattress.

In her quest to get away, she's worked herself down the bed and onto her back, putting her in the perfect position. This might be easier than I thought. When the cuff snaps around her skin, she freezes. Her head turns slowly, and she stares at the black fabric encasing her wrist.

Her mouth drops open. "You cuffed me."

I drop my hold, then trail a single finger down her body as I make my way around the bed. "I did. Problem?"

"When the hell did you get these? No, *where* did you get them?"

She's too busy examining the makeshift bracelet to notice me getting the other restraint. She doesn't even fight me when I hold her hand still and snap the other one on. There's enough slack for her to move freely for now.

I contemplate tying up her ankles as well but reject the idea. All that would take a longer conversation. I don't know what she's been through in detail. A part of me was worried I was going to trigger something in her when I cuffed her wrists.

I watch her carefully as I yank on the strap hanging off the bottom of the bed. She gasps as her arms straighten and her fingers brush against the headboard. Her tongue darts out and runs along her lower lip. When she rubs her thighs together, I breathe a sigh of relief. Things might change, but we'll cross that bridge when we get to it.

"Do I need to cuff these, too?" I ask as I encircle her ankle. "Guess we'll have to see. You're going to need a safeword."

"What?" A slight waver enters her voice, the first sign of anxiety.

"The restraints are magnetic and custom made. There's a button you can reach. You can get out at any time." I nod toward her hand and her thumb brushes over it but doesn't engage it. "Still, you need a safeword. Pick one."

She sucks in her cheeks, and I bite my tongue to keep from

laughing. If I open my mouth, I'll end up making a joke about fish or some ridiculous shit like that. This is supposed to be my way to regain control, to connect with her, to distract her from everything going on. Except she's making it very hard. I could pull out the drawer at my shins and get one of the scarves to gag her. I'd rather be able to hear her, though.

Her eyes meet mine, laughter dancing in their depths. "Potatoes."

My lips twitch and my nostrils flare as I attempt to stay calm. "That's..." I clear my throat as she smirks. "Are you sure?"

"Oh, I'm sure. They're versatile enough to fit every situation if need be."

I hold up my hand, closing my eyes. "Don't. Just...don't."

"What? Is it not sexy enough?"

"Safewords aren't supposed to be sexy, Siren."

"You know, you should have taken my shirt off before you put these one me." She tugs gently at the restraints.

I crawl onto the bed and straddle her, my cock hardening as my gaze runs along her body. She presses her lips together, all traces of humor replaced with desire. Her hips jerk and I swallow a groan. It's a good thing she's tied up or I'd have a hard time staying in control. If she touched me right now, I might explode. While I like fucking her hard and fast, I'd rather take my time with her.

I trace her collarbone and she shivers, the strap snapping when she tries to move. I drag my nail between her tits to her waistband, then grip the edges of her shirt.

"This is Ghost's, isn't it?" I murmur.

"Yes," she breathes.

"Good."

I rip her shirt, the fabric tearing easily under my hands. She squeaks, her hips bucking underneath me. I drop onto her and grind my cock into her. A moan slips from her, and I do it once more just to hear it again.

"I swear to fuck all, if you edge me, I will punch you in the throat," she wheezes as she strains against the bonds.

I run my nose between her tits, then sink my teeth into the plump flesh. Her breath hitches and I grin. "Hard to punch me when you're tied up, sweets."

She lifts her head and our eyes meet. "I'll figure it out."

"I have no doubt you'd bide your time, then strike when I least expect it." I flick her nipple and it hardens. "Unless you'd prefer me to stop." I prop myself on my elbows on either side of her head and smirk.

Her nostrils flare. "Don't you fucking dare. Although, I could just call Ghost and have him take care of me. Perks of having two men at my beck and call."

"Is that so? Sounds like you're trying to make me jealous. But you and I both know we don't get jealous. Competitive, perhaps, but not jealous."

"Oh, I remember," she whispers. "Now take off my pants and fuck me."

"Yes, ma'am," I whisper back and crawl off her.

I grab her pants and underwear and rip them down her legs. I shuck off my own shorts and boxer briefs. She licks her lips, her gaze fixed on my cock. I grip my length and stroke it lightly. Her knees drop, opening herself up. My mouth waters as I stare at her glistening pussy and I realize I'm not going to be able to take it slow. As soon as I'm inside her, I'll lose all control unless I can rein myself in. Except I don't want to. There'll be plenty of time to romance her later.

Even with the threat of the Disciples and dealing with the issues in the Phantoms, I don't regret her coming back. We were missing a piece of our family, though we didn't realize it. We don't have to find a place to fit her into our lives. She's merely filling the hole we ignored for too long.

"Storm?" she whispers, and I squeeze my eyes shut.

I lift her foot and press my lips to her calf as I meet her gaze. Her ankle ends up on my shoulder and I kiss behind her knee. My eyes never leave hers as I travel to her inner thigh. My nose brushes her clit and her pussy clenches around nothing. I could give her what her body is begging for. Instead, I work my way down her other leg until both of them are propped up in the air. They tremble as soft whimpers fall from her. I run my tongue along her skin, then sink my teeth into the plump flesh of her thigh.

"Do you know how much I missed this?" I murmur, skimming my nose over her clit. I breathe in her scent and it fills my lungs.

"My pussy?" she gasps as she attempts to push her hips into my face.

I hum and flick the sensitive bud with my tongue, then move to her hip bones. "I missed this."

I nip at her stomach, her ribs, the underside of her tit. "And these."

"Can't forget about these," I purr, then give each nipple the attention they deserve. Her chest heaves the more I tease her. Maybe taking her slowly is still possible.

I bury my face in her neck and her nails rake down my back. I shudder at the burn as I settle between her thighs. My cock throbs as I rub against her, coating my length in her essence. When my tip slips inside, she moans and the sound vibrates in my chest. Her hand grips the back of my neck. I slip deeper, then jerk my hips away. Propping myself on my forearms, I glare at her.

"What?" she gasps, digging her heels into my ass in a desperate attempt to bring me back.

I reach around and grab her wrist. Slamming it above her head, I raise an eyebrow.

"Found the safety, did you?"

She grins, biting her lip. "Whoops."

"Whoops? You never planned on keeping them on, did you?"

She huffs, though her eyes are still filled with desire. "If I tell you the truth, are you going to walk away?"

"Not a chance in hell," I growl, then nip at her lower lip. She smirks and I narrow my gaze. "Punish you, though? Yeah, that's still on the table."

"You wouldn't."

I lean in close to her ear and whisper, "Watch me."

I push to my knees, then grab her ankles. She squeals as I flip her onto her stomach. She scrambles to get away, but I grip her hips and force her ass in the air. Her head hits the headboard, rattling the wooden frame, and I pause. Her fingers wrap around the slats.

"Ready to be a good girl and take your punishment?"

She mumbles something I can't hear with her face smashed into the pillow. Still, she wiggles her ass. I slip my hand into her hair and grip the strands, then force her head to the side.

"Would you like to use your safeword?"

She whines out a no, and I chuckle. I skim my hands along her sides, then dig my fingers into her hips. She moans, but I've barely touched her. I wish we had more time in the day and less problems facing us. It would give us time to connect more.

At least I have this—a way to tie us together, strengthen the thread between us. I line up my cock with her weeping pussy, and a noise I haven't heard in a long time echoes through the air. I trace her spine with one finger and her back arches. I do it again, then slam into her.

I only give her a few seconds to adjust before I pound into her hard and fast. She meets me thrust for thrust, shuddering underneath me. When I ease my grip on her, she whines and smacks my wrist. I didn't want to leave more bruises on her body, but I'll give her what she wants.

A familiar ache blooms in my chest, pleasure and longing weaving together as she clenches around me. I mourn the fact I won't last longer. Having her here and willing, begging me to fuck her harder, drives me onward.

"Please, Storm. I c-can't," she pleads.

Despite our years apart, I know exactly what she needs. I slip my hand around her waist to her clit. She explodes underneath me and I fuck her through her orgasm. I surge into her once, twice, then follow her into oblivion. I groan, my vision going black. Or maybe I've closed my eyes. It doesn't matter. None of it matters other than this right here—the completeness I feel when I'm with her. With both of them.

I drape my body over hers and hold her close. Whatever the future brings, this is what I need. Only Siren. Only Ghost. Everything else we'll deal with together.

Thirty-Nine

Rocks skitter across the parking lot, and I kick another one. It disappears into the dark and I wish I could disappear as easily. Most of the last week has been a waiting game. I fucking hate it. I'm used to having something to do during the day. I'm always planning my next move, my next job, my next kidnapping. Now, I'm useless.

Most of my time is spent eating. I swear Ghost thinks I've been living in squalor. It may not have been the most glamorous of existences, but I did fine. I just wish I had something to do. When I asked Storm to give me something, he said he'd look into it. Which is utter bullshit. Every time I walk into a room, they stop talking. They're keeping shit from me. Their words aren't matching their actions. They say they trust me, but it's clear they don't.

Now I'm stuck playing lookout while they poke around an abandoned gas station. At least I'm not stuck in the house anymore. Hell, we're not even in Harris. From what I could glean mostly from eavesdropping, they got a tip this was being used by the Disciples. I doubt it, but I'm not going to say anything. I'm pretty sure this place hasn't had any humans near it in the last ten years. It's probably haunted.

I'm surprised the single streetlamp still works. It's close enough to light half of the building, which means I'm tucked away in the shadows of the front door. Not that it matters since everything's boarded up. I thought they'd have to take an axe to one of the windows. Apparently that was a ridiculous suggestion. They failed to tell me there was a door in the back being propped open with a piece of wood.

I wish they'd stop looking at me like I'm incapable of doing shit. If they're not going to tell me what's going on, though, I doubt they'll assume I'm competent enough to do, well, anything. At least they gave me a knife. When I asked for a gun, Ghost looked at me like I grew a second head. Bastard.

It's like now that they've accepted me back into their lives, I've reverted back to being a twenty-something. I'm no longer an adult who's probably dealt with more shit than they could comprehend. Despite the fact I've kept myself alive for over six years, I'm not able to protect myself. It's annoying as hell.

A shadow detaches from the corner of the large shed across the street. I don't bother moving since they know I'm here. I've been watching them for the last ten minutes, waiting for them to finally reveal themselves.

As I kick another rock into the dark, I sigh. Ghost and Storm won't be out for a while. They told me not to bother them for at least thirty minutes. If I find out they decided to have a quickie in there while I kept watch, I'm going to stab one of them. Maybe both.

"Long way from home," the woman says when she gets closer. I still can't make out her features, but I recognize her voice.

"Suppose. Gonna tell me why you're following me? Or why you blew up that apartment building, what, a week ago?" I lean against the stucco wall, letting the roughness ground me to the present. The days have bled together, and it feels like a lifetime since I saw her last. I almost forgot about it in the aftermath. Having flashbacks of burning buildings doesn't help either.

"First of all, I'm not really following you. Second, I didn't blow that place up. I *do* know that it was empty when it went. Oh, and why they targeted that particular place." She stops by the concrete post marking where the front walk should have been. It's a crumbled mess now and I'm half expecting to break my ankle any minute.

I bite my cheek, trying to organize my thoughts. My understanding of the history between the Phantoms and the Disciples isn't helpful since it's so out of date. Bits and pieces aren't enough to construct an entire picture of what's happening. If Ghost and Storm weren't gatekeeping shit, I'd be able to have a conversation with this woman.

"What's your name?" I ask, and she leans closer, leaving half her face in shadow, giving me a look. "Make one up if you'd like, but I can't keep calling you the woman with green hair. It's weird."

She straightens with a light laugh. "Fair enough. It's Rogue. You can share with your...men. I'd appreciate it if you didn't spread it beyond that. Unless you choose to have me killed. Then I suppose it won't matter."

"Well, since you haven't done anything to me, I guess I can do that."

Rogue nods, an understanding forming between us. We'll keep shit to ourselves unless the other fucks up, then all bets are off. If she was actually a Disciple, she wouldn't have helped me escape. She could be playing the long game, doing Prophet's dirty work. It's not unheard of to insert someone to play the rescuer just to gain a rival's trust. My gut's telling me that's not her way. I've been wrong before, though.

"The Disciples didn't burn the apartment down. That was one of yours. I believe it was a setup, but I don't have proof of that."

I want to say I'm not part of the Phantoms. None of them are "mine." I don't bother correcting her. There's no point. I'm with them right now, so that's enough.

"A setup for what?" I ask.

Her shadow shrugs and she wanders closer. Her green hair shimmers, though it's duller now. I bite back a gasp when I actually see her face. One eye is practically swollen shut and bruises litter most of her skin. The gash above her eyebrow might need stitches. She must be in pain, but she doesn't show it until she presses a fist to her side.

"Some of your members have been compromised, as I'm sure you know." She smirks, then winces, and her hand flutters by her side. "One of them was just found dead. Prophet wasn't very happy about it, but it doesn't matter. Not really. He's got others to take over, though they're not as high up."

"You're saying Venom blew it up?" It's not outside of the realm of possibility.

She shrugs, glancing around. "Maybe. Or one of his minions. Either way, the call came from him. Since he's dead, you can't really question him about it." She taps the side of her nose, and I tense. "Might want to look at his buddies, though."

"You still haven't told me anything I don't know." I flip the knife and the blade pops out, then flip it again to hide it.

"What the fuck are you doing with a butterfly knife? That shit will get you killed," she spits out.

I slip it into the front pocket of my sweatshirt and grab the dagger from the holster tucked in my back. "How about this one?" I put it away. "I just like having something to do with my hands. Usually I have a fidget cube, but I keep losing them. Doesn't matter. Why are you supposedly helping me?"

"Our goals align temporarily," she murmurs, her eyes still bouncing around.

"And when they no longer align?" I ask, though I already know the answer.

She smirks, the move pulling at the wound and blood seeps from the gash. "I suppose we'll just have to reassess our goals, then. Won't we?"

She turns and I resist the urge to call after her. I want to know if she knows about Oliver and why he was on the street. I want to know if she knows Lexi. I want to know about Prophet and how deep she's embedded with the Disciples.

She didn't really tell me anything I didn't know before. I could have figured out Venom was behind the fire. We already knew no one was inside and he wasn't working alone. With one conversation, I found out Venom was in with the Disciples. I wonder if she knows Hornet was in Venom's pocket as well.

"Hey," she calls from the darkness, and I squint to find her. "Prophet thinks you're his destiny—divine will. He won't stop until he owns you."

She disappears, not that I care. I'm too busy trying to remember what Prophet said. None of it made any sense at the time. I thought it was because I hadn't eaten and was on the verge of death. I didn't think he had a reason for obsessing over me. If he actually thinks I'm the key to some prophecy, he's clearly deep in his delusions. I'm not some mystical creature capable of fulfilling—

"Oh, shit," I mutter, knocking my head against the wall.

"Something the matter?" Storm asks, and I jolt. "You really are the worst lookout."

I clear my throat and wipe my palms on my jeans. "As if there's anyone lurking in the shadows. This place is in the middle of nowhere. If they were out there, they'd attack when I was alone, then ambush you two inside. They'd blow the place up or something."

"Whatever. We didn't find anything. Now what's wrong?"

I could keep everything from him, but then I'd be no better than them. I'm not about to tell them about Rogue. They'd freak out, and it would solidify the misgivings they clearly still have. Neither of them would ever trust me again. We'd never get over that final hurdle and I'd end up alone. I won't survive if that happens.

"I was thinking about what Prophet said. He said he needed me."

"Because he wanted to fuck you," he says dismissively.

"No. He didn't say he wanted me for sex. He wasn't jealous or anything. He didn't even touch me." *Prophet may want me, but he doesn't want to fuck me. At least, I don't think he does. I don't know how else to explain it, and I doubt Storm would understand.*

He glances around, probably searching for Ghost. "Then it was us."

I glare at him, not that he notices. "That makes no sense. Him kidnapping me didn't have anything to do with the Phantoms. He brought up 'my friends' in the beginning, but abandoned that line of questioning without me even doing anything. I'd spent all of what, a day, in your house? Plus, he's been sending men after me for years. What information would I have to give them?"

He huffs and I resist the urge to smack him. "What does it matter? It doesn't change what we're going to do."

"Because he said he *needed* me. What would he need me for? It's not like I'm a valuable member of the Phantoms. For years, he's been playing this game of hide and seek with the goal for me to join them, but for what? It doesn't make sense unless he thinks there's some...I don't know, divine reason." I press my tongue to the roof of my mouth, hoping he doesn't dismiss me again. If I push this too hard, he'll shut down or start questioning why I'm so invested in it.

"Divine reason," he murmurs. "You know why he calls himself Prophet?"

"Uh, the same reason all bikers have nicknames? Other than me, of course."

"Yeah, your mama didn't really think that one through, did she?" Storm grins at me and I smack his arm. "Most of the time, it comes from someone else, right? Beast named Ghost after he vanished during that game of capture the flag. Remember when Avery was Sweet Pea? She lost her shit."

I rub my temples as a headache builds behind my eyes. "What does this have to do with Prophet?"

"He picked his own name. No one remembers when he came

in. We don't know how he took over or how he came to Rose-wood. It's like the Disciples are a legit cult more than a motorcycle club. I hear he even has a pulpit he runs services from. Because he doesn't call them meetings."

"Like a narcissistic asshole."

"Like a cult leader. It's weird, and trying to get any information out of the members is like pulling teeth. Even under duress, they don't crack. They're fanatics." He runs his hand through his hair. "Either way, it doesn't really change anything. So what if he thinks you're some mystical goddess? Where the fuck is Ghost?"

I straighten and realize we've been out here a long time. "What was he doing?"

"Rigging a trap. He said he knew what he was doing," Storm mutters, and I scoff as I stomp around the corner.

Storm calls after me and then his footsteps follow. As I round the back of the building, strong hands grip my arms, and I scream. I'm herded around until my back hits the wall and a hand slaps over my mouth, cutting off the sound. The sweet smell of honey-suckle hits me, and I instantly relax.

"Try not to alert the entire county of our location, hmm?" Ghost whispers.

He replaces his hand with his mouth and kisses me hard. He pulls back before I can respond. His warmth leaves me, and I swallow the whimper.

As pissed as I am at their inability to trust me, I still crave them. I could blame being sex-starved or even touch-starved. Whenever the opportunity to be with someone else arose, I couldn't do it. Regardless of how we left things, I still felt like I was cheating, as ridiculous as that sounds.

"We need to get out of here. I've got a feeling we're being watched," Ghost says to Storm.

This is my chance to tell them about Rogue. Instead, I trail after them to their bikes. Whatever Rogue is planning, I want to see it play out. The moment they find out, they'll interfere and possibly fuck things up.

I'm fully aware I'm keeping shit from them and the fallout will be disastrous. It's not any different from what they're doing to me. I'm sure they won't see it that way. They'll explain away why they couldn't tell me anything, denying it has anything to do with me. I'll be expected to give them grace, but I have a feeling they'll freak out once they discover my secrets. Hopefully, I'll survive their wrath and they'll give me a little grace, too.

FORTY

GHOST

My fingers trail down Siren's soft skin, tracing the goosebumps popping up on her side. Her lashes flutter against her cheeks and I pause. She sighs and I start up again. I don't want to wake her in the middle of the night. We've been running on fumes the last few days.

For weeks I've been holding my breath, waiting for the Disciples to make their move. We've been gathering information, setting up contingencies, separating the members who might have turned on us. We're on the cusp of making decisions that'll alert Prophet and I'm hesitant to move forward. Not without concrete proof we're about to be attacked. The minute we go into lockdown or shut down our shipments, he'll know. It'll tip his hand and we're not ready. If we wait too long, though, we'll be blindsided, and I'll lose more men. It's an impossible position to be in.

Siren whimpers in her sleep, and I loosen my grip on her hip. Gently, I roll her onto her back and smile when she flings her arm over her head. I brush my fingers across her stomach, then up to her chest. Her breath catches when I circle one nipple, then the other. I thought we'd worn her out earlier, but apparently not.

I didn't realize how much I missed this until I walked in on her riding him. With her head thrown back, hair cascading over her shoulders and ecstasy stamped on every inch of her skin, she was the most exquisite thing I'd seen.

I ended up leaning against the door frame, unable to look away. Siren didn't notice me until Storm flipped her around on her hands and knees. She gasped, desire dripping from every line of her body, as Storm filled her from behind. My cock ended up between her lips, despite my resolve to stay put.

My shaft hardens at the memory, and I cup her tit, brushing my thumb over her nipple. I warned her before she fell asleep that I wasn't done with her yet. I told her I'd be playing with her body while she was off in dreamland. She merely smiled and said to do my worst.

Her breath catches again when I pinch the bud and roll it between my fingers. I glance toward the door, wondering where Storm is. He snuck out at some point with his phone. I could text him to come help me wake her up, but I'm content to let him stumble upon us, just like I caught them.

The more I think about it, the more I realize I need this. I need time with just her. She's still wary of me and what I truly want. The longer she's here, though, the more I can't imagine her being anywhere else. I'll probably carry my guilt with me forever, but I can make up for abandoning her.

I'm still determined to find the answers to what happened all those years ago. Right now, though, I need to prove to her I want her—every piece of her, shattered or not. I'll work on putting those pieces of her back together.

My hand skims down her stomach to her leg. She shifts and I fixate on her face while I ease her knee over my hip, opening her up for me. A shiver rolls through her body when I trace the crease of soft skin and my knuckles caress her pussy. My nostrils flare and I bite back a groan.

I lean closer, my lips brushing against her temple as I whisper, "So wet for me, sweets. Even while sleeping, your body knows exactly who you belong to."

Her lashes flutter and I pause again. Another sigh leaves her, and I smirk before dragging my finger lightly along her pussy. When I reach her clit, a whine escapes. I'm surprised she hasn't woken up yet especially with how wet she is.

Her chest heaves as I stroke her, and I wrap my lips around her nipple and flick the hard nub with my tongue. When I release it, she cries softly and I push inside her, then drag my soaked fingers out. Fixating my gaze on her face, I do it again. As much as I'd like to see if I can make her come before she wakes, I won't last that long. Even now, my cock aches, pressing against her hip.

Carefully, I pull my hand away and lick the evidence of her desire from my skin. Her essence explodes across my tongue, and I swallow a groan. She tastes exactly how I remember, like temptation and sin and home. I contemplate waking her up with my face buried between her legs, but I quickly reject the idea. There'll be plenty of time in the future for that. Tonight I need to be inside her, to feel her pussy clenching around my length as I fill her up.

I ease away, and her leg slips off my hip. She burrows her face into the pillow and tries to roll over. I stop her with a hand on her stomach. Her muscles jump under my touch. I bite my bottom lip as I settle on my knees. She barely reacts when I push her feet up. With one hand on her waist and another gripping my cock, I line myself up with her core. I could inch into her slowly, giving her just enough to rouse her. Except she told me to do my worst, and I never said I'd be gentle.

I surge into her, and she gasps, her back arching off the bed. Our eyes meet as I bottom out, letting out a low groan. I grind my hips into her and a needy noise falls from her lips. Her chin quivers and her tongue darts out, pulling my gaze to her mouth. Her fingers grip my forearms when I pull out slowly.

"Please," she moans, and I slam into her again.

My fingers slide into her hair and grip the back of her neck. I force her head up. "Look at how well you take me. How wet you were for me before you were even awake."

Her nails dig into my arms, eyes fixed on where we join. She meets my every thrust and my heart stutters. I haul her upright, still buried inside her. She plants her feet, and I wrap my other arm around her waist. Our breaths mingle and our gazes clash as I fill her over and over.

"Harder," she breathes.

"Demanding little thing," I groan. "Do you want me to put you on your hands and knees? Fuck you with your face buried in the pillows? Maybe I'll fuck you against the wall so hard the pictures crash to the floor. I could bend you over the bed and fuck your tight little ass."

With every image I plant in her mind, she whimpers as she bounces on my cock. "Yes. Fuck yes."

I grip her waist and pull her off me. She cries out as I toss her onto her back. "Turn around. Hands on the headboard."

She scrambles to obey, and my skin tingles in anticipation. She glances over her shoulder, knuckles turning white as she grips the slats. Need rests deep in her eyes—a need only I can fulfil. I crawl toward her and run my palms up her legs, her thighs, her waist, then around to cup her tits. I pinch her nipples and roll them between my fingers. She bucks under my hold, but her hands never leave the headboard.

I grip my cock and push myself between her ass cheeks. "I know you want me here, don't you?" She nods, a desperate plea on her lips. "You're not ready to take me there again. Soon, sweets. Soon enough I'll be here"—I push just enough for her to feel me in the tight hole—"and Storm will be deep in your pussy. Tonight, I'm going to make you come all over my cock."

I bury my length into her pussy, and she clenches around me. She pushes back, trying to take me deeper with each thrust. I grip her hips hard, her cries driving me toward the edge. A peace steals over me while my orgasm builds. This is exactly what we needed. It might not heal everything between us, but it's a good start. And I'll keep fucking her, keep taking care of her, until nothing else remains except the three of us together. Storm and I may have been content with just the two of us, but something was missing. We both knew it was her, though we never said it.

"Come for me," I grunt, and her head drops as she jerks in my grasp. Her pussy spasms around my shaft, forcing a growl from deep within me. She chants my name as she wades through the pulses of ecstasy racking her body. I never slow, fucking her through it all. I drop my hand to her clit, and she jerks in my grasp.

"Another," I demand through gritted teeth.

"I can't," she gasps, and I wrap my fingers around her throat. She groans as her back hits my chest. My movements become erratic as she flies into oblivion once more, and my stomach tightens.

My heart hammers, blood rushing in my ears as I erupt. Stars burst behind my lids and satisfaction seeps into my bones. My fears quiet, drowned out by a completeness I haven't felt since she left. This is exactly where she's meant to be. In my arms. In my bed. With us. Nothing else will do. If she left, we'd spend the rest of our lives searching for her. We'll do exactly what we should have done years ago.

I slip from her and she slumps. Easing her down, I attempt to control my breathing. I tuck her under the covers, then crawl off the bed. She mumbles something as she reaches for me. I smile as I make my way to the bathroom. When I get up, she's sitting up, clutching the sheet to her chest.

"Down, Siren," I murmur, and she flops back.

Her disheveled hair fans out on the pillow and her lids droop. I tug on the sheet until it slips from her fingers and ease her knees open.

"I can't," she whines.

I chuckle and use the warm washcloth to clean her up. "Go back to sleep. I won't wake you again."

"See that you don't," she says through a smirk.

I toss the rag toward the bathroom and climb in next to her. She rolls on her side and fits her body against mine. Warmth blooms between us, seeping into my skin. I smooth her hair away from her face, then press a kiss to her neck. She tilts her head, and I grin.

"For someone who wants to sleep, you're giving very mixed signals."

She's quiet for so long, I think she's fallen asleep. My palm runs down her body, hoping to soothe her.

"I missed you," she whispers, and my heart cracks.

"I missed you, too."

She shuffles onto her back and her eyes meet mine. "You had Storm, though."

"I may have had Storm, but you know you completed us. You were the missing piece. And we felt that every day you were gone," I say. She opens her mouth, then snaps it shut. "No, don't do that. Tell me."

She shakes her head. "I'm sick of fighting, of blaming you two. I mean, I still think it was your fault, but we were young." She presses her lips together as her brows pull low. "A couple years ago, I met a woman. She was like me. Not really, though. She had this fiery red hair and didn't take any shit. She never stayed in one place for long. I suppose that's the only thing we had in common. She was so confident and snarky. I swear I want to be her when I grow up."

"You're pretty bitchy when you want to be."

She narrows her gaze. "I said snarky, not bitchy, though she could definitely be a bitch. The point is, she was searching for her best friend who went missing years ago. She never gave up."

"What was her name?" I don't know where this is going unless she's talking about searching for something—a home, a purpose, a will to survive. My mind shies away from the thought.

"Sienna, but I'm pretty sure that was an alias. I used to do that, too. The thing is, she was both running from something and searching for someone. I don't know all the details, but it felt like I finally had someone to talk to about what happened. She didn't judge me. She did call my ass out, though." She sucks in a deep breath. "Told me I was an asshole for not confronting you two. I would never know how you guys would have actually responded."

"I don't know what we would have done. Now, though, we'll fight for you. We'll protect you." I try to put as much conviction as I can in my voice.

She shakes her head. "I don't need you to fight for me or protect me. I need you to pick me."

I bury my face in her neck and pull her closer to me. "I will. I'll pick you every time."

"Prove it."

Forty-One

Siren

When I wake up, I'm alone. It's not as jarring as it was when I first got here. I've gotten used to sleeping in Ghost's bed. It's normal to be living here, and that terrifies me.

I thought I'd hold out longer, make them grovel a little more. I don't know what I want from them, though. How do I know when they've suffered enough? Punishing them doesn't really work for me. Besides, I'd rather test them later. I suppose it's not really testing them if I'm just waiting for them to prove themselves. It's probably fucked up, but I've spent a long time waiting for shit to go sideways.

I grab my phone from the nightstand and check my messages. A text from Storm tells me they're off on a run and wanted to let me sleep. I send him a quick message bitching him out and add a robot emoji to throw him off. He'll be thinking about that for the rest of the night. This is why I've been fighting them every time they tell me to take a nap. I knew they'd leave me behind when shit came up.

"Siren?" Lexi calls from the other side of the closed door. There's a light knock, but I don't have it in me to respond.

A text from Ghost pops up, telling me Rivet is going to stop by, and I grind my teeth. I wouldn't be surprised if Rivet sent Lexi instead, hoping we could make up. I've been avoiding this conversation for too long. Either we figure shit out and move forward, or I beat the shit out of her and we still move forward.

I toss the covers back and grab Ghost's sweatshirt from the floor. I tug it on before I rip open the door. Lexi swings around, wringing her hands with a contrite look on her face.

"I didn't mean to wake you. Rivet had to take a call and sent me instead. I'm sorry. I didn't—"

I hold my hand up and she presses her lips together. "It's fine. We should get this over with anyways."

I step around her and make my way downstairs. The last thing I'm going to do is have her sit on Ghost's bed like we're at a freaking sleepover. We used to do that when we were younger—when we were on the same side. Now it feels like we're on opposite sides of a battlefield, each waiting for the other to charge. I hate it. I just want to know where I fit in. I still act like I have one foot out the door.

She drops onto the loveseat, her back facing the large picture window. A soft rain hits the glass, not that I can see it with the thick curtains in the way. I plop onto the couch across from her and tuck my feet underneath. I wish I had something to do with my hands. Sitting here with only pillow fringes to play with sets me on edge.

"Well, go ahead," I say.

She nods once, then again. "I—I don't actually know what to say. I already told you I was sorry. I explained why I did it. We were practically kids."

"Who was he?"

Confusion flashes across her face. "I—what?"

"The man in the photos with me, who was he?" I know Ghost was trying to figure it out. I overheard him telling Storm he couldn't find Lexi, but he didn't seem that worried.

"I...uh, I don't know."

My eyes narrow and I tilt my head. "You're a shit liar, Lexi."

"Okay, fine. I may know who he is, but he isn't a bad guy. He doesn't want to be in the Disciples, but he can't get out."

"You know who he is? And you never told anyone? You could have gone to Ghost or Storm at any time and told them he wanted to defect. You could have cleared my fucking name, and you didn't?" I'm desperately trying not to yell at her. She already looks like she's on the verge of tears. If she breaks down, I won't be able to get anything out of her.

"What was I supposed to tell them? That I went after the guy you were meeting with because I was so ashamed? I didn't know he was part of the Disciples until after you left." She rocks back and forth, her eyes staring off into the past. It's a lie, but I don't call her on it. "By then you were in the wind. No one knew where you were and if they did, they weren't talking to me. I fucked up, Siren. I know I did, but you have to understand."

"Understand? You expect me to understand what? That you became friends with him? He's a fucking Disciple, Lexi." My voice raises the longer I talk until I'm yelling. I don't even remember standing, much less leaning over the coffee table toward her. It's probably a good thing I didn't have a fidget. I'd be whipping it at her head right about now.

Tears track down her face, devastation in her eyes. "He's different. Siren, please. I love him."

My mind blanks, and numbness floods my system. I sink onto the couch and stare at her. Her words echo in my head over and over.

I love him. I love him. I love him.

How do I argue against that? I know what it is to love with every fiber of your being. I know what it is to be so desperately and hopelessly captivated by another. I know what it is to be so smitten nothing else exists beyond them.

"How?" I whisper.

She pulls in a shuddering breath. "I don't know. How did you fall in love?"

"Why is he still there? You said he was different, except he's one of them. He never left. If he loved you—"

Rage blazes in her eyes. Gone is the devastation and guilt. "If you loved them, you never would have left. You would have fought for them—for yourself. Do you hear how that sounds?"

She's right. I hate how fucking right she is. We were so young back then. The world outside considered us adults. Growing up in a motorcycle club, we grew up faster than most. It doesn't mean we were smart. We didn't have it all figured out. We made mistakes. We were insecure and self-absorbed. Yet we thought we were so mature and had everything figured out. It wasn't until I was banished and out in the real world instead of in this bubble that I understood how underprepared I was.

"Still doesn't explain why he didn't leave in the past six years."

Lexi jumps to her feet, and I track her as she paces. "At first, he didn't realize how bad it was. Being raised in that environment... it's not easy. Things we think are common sense? They don't get. They're taught something completely different, and everything is warped to fit their narrative. It's not as simple as presenting them with information and having them believe it. Prophet's taught them that everything they're told is a lie unless it comes from him."

"So they're brainwashed. How did he get out of that way of thinking, then?"

She picks at her fingernails, a nervous habit she had when we were teenagers, then stops and stares at me. "You. He met you at the restaurant where he worked. He wasn't supposed to work, but he needed money to help his sister. She was sick, so he got a job far enough away from Disciple territory and hoped no one would find out. Apparently you came in a lot."

"I don't remember him at all, though. If I went in that much, don't you think I would remember having full-on conversations with him?"

She swipes at her cheeks and sniffs. "No. I don't. That was just the person you were. You talked to everyone. Smiled at them, helped them. It didn't matter who they were, you were just *nice*."

I sit back and press my thumbs into my temples. My eyes close as I try to remember what it was like to be nineteen with no real responsibilities. I suppose I was nice.

Lexi didn't start coming around until she was fifteen or so. She didn't grow up like us so she was shy, reserved, constantly trying to prove herself. Ghost and Storm had to be tough, though it means something different now than it did then. When I got older, I thought I was naive and a doormat, but maybe I was just kind.

She clears her throat, and I glance up. "When I came after him, he was so confused. Creed didn't know about any of what happened."

"First of all, Creed?" I ask with a raised eyebrow, and she blushes. "Second, I thought you said he didn't tell you he was a Disciple right away, but you confronted him?"

"I may have accused him of cheating with you." She waves her hand around dismissively. "Doesn't matter. The point is, he wants to get out, but he can't. His sister is still in and she refuses to leave. He thinks she's planning something, but she won't tell him what."

"What do you think she's planning?" I watch her carefully for any indication she's keeping shit from me. If she's protecting them, we might have a bigger issue. The Lexi I knew wouldn't have turned on Ghost. She wouldn't have been sucked into Prophet's fucked-up teachings.

"Honestly? I think she's trying to—" She glances around as if she'll find some hidden camera, then drags her finger across her throat. "Creed won't leave without her."

I nod slowly, not ready to burst her bubble. Could there be someone trying to bring down the Disciples? Sure, but it hasn't happened yet. From what I know about their inner workings, they're mostly cut off from reality. I could be wrong, though, since I don't know much. I don't even know if I believe Lexi's story. I'm sure she thinks Creed is a good guy. I wouldn't put it past him to play the long game. If he thinks she can be manipulated, he'll use her. She's so deeply in love, she won't accept anything else.

"I don't know what you want from me, Lex," I say softly.

She crumples onto the loveseat and buries her face in her hands. Her voice is muffled when she finally speaks. "I just wanted you to understand what I was doing. *Why* I didn't tell anyone afterward. Everyone seemed to have forgotten you, and I just got in too deep. I'd already fallen for him and then you came back, and I thought you were leaving again, but then you didn't and Ghost was talking about lockdown and—"

"Whoa, calm down." I lean forward and reach out my hand. I pull back before I touch her. "I get it."

She lifts her head. "You do? Or are you just trying to get me to stop crying?"

I huff out a laugh. "No, I really do. Everything spirals and you don't know how to get out. I had plenty of opportunities to clear my name. Hell, there were a few times when the Disciples took me that I could have spilled everything about Ghost or Storm. I could have given them up, but I didn't."

"Because you're better than me," she whispers harshly. "I chose myself instead of you. But you chose them every time. You protected them even when they didn't deserve it."

"Maybe. It's complicated. The minute I got that text from Ghost, I was running here. I told myself I wanted to face them and rub it in their faces that I wasn't dead. I wanted them to see their rejection didn't break me. But really, I just wanted to come home." I sigh as I run my hand through my hair. "What are you going to do? If Creed's sister really is going to take out Prophet and he won't leave her, then shit is going to hit the fan there."

"I don't know. Creed doesn't want me to get involved." She straightens and presses her lips together. "I'm going to confess to Ghost when he gets back."

"Uh, the hell you are," I growl. "You tell him everything you just told me and he'll call you a fucking fool. He'll call it all bull-shit and demand you set up a meeting with Creed so he can kill him."

"He's not going to do that. He might with *you*, but not me. He doesn't care that much."

I let out a harsh laugh. "Bitch, you think it's about how much he *cares*? Ghost isn't going to shoot him because you fell in love with a Disciple. He's going to put his ass six feet under because he *is* a Disciple. He'll say Creed's playing you. He'll ream your ass out for getting taken. A silly girl who got conned into falling in love with the enemy."

I push to my feet and settle next to her. She tenses, then melts into me when I put my arm around her shoulder. I don't know if I forgive her for being the catalyst in blowing up my life. I do know I'm sick of living in the past. Carrying around this rage and pain hasn't helped me. If anything, it's made my life infinitely harder. It's exhausting and doesn't help. It doesn't fix the past. I could keep blaming Lexi for taking the pictures, and Ghost for putting his ambitions above me, and Storm for not fighting for me. All I'd have then is a mess of emotions I don't know what to do with.

"I missed you," Lexi whispers.

"I know. I missed you, too."

"Are you going to stab me? I'd let you, if that's what you needed."

I smile and rest my chin on top of her head. "Not today. Maybe later. We have bigger problems to deal with and I don't want to listen to you whine about stitches."

"Please don't tell Ghost about Creed."

"I won't. For now."

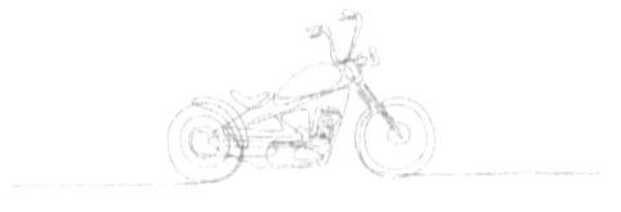

After Lexi poured her heart out, I thought she'd leave. Instead, we ended up eating Storm's secret stash of ice cream and catching up. For once, it didn't feel like there was a blade hanging over my neck. We didn't talk about my banishment or her role in it. We didn't talk about my kidnapping or the Disciples. We talked about my many jobs and the time she had a one-sided prank war with Ghost.

It's one of the few times I've felt at ease since I've been here. I'm not waiting for someone to grab me. I'm not waiting to be thrown out on the streets. I'm not waiting for bad shit to happen. We're just two friends catching up. From how relaxed she is by the end, I'm not the only one who needed this. Maybe this could be our new normal.

The idea takes root, a stranglehold on my psyche. It persists when Lexi falls asleep on the couch. And as I text Storm, then Ghost, and get no response. And when I wander upstairs to shower. By the time I'm back downstairs, it's become a mantra.

Letting go of the past, looking to the future—it sounds fucking ridiculous. I'm not an optimist. My life hasn't been filled with rainbows and unicorns. I don't fuck with idealistic and fanciful notions. The rose-colored glasses fell from my eyes long ago. I prefer to drown myself in realism. Then I'm never disappointed when I end up in a hellhole.

Which begs the question, why am I so enamored with the idea of a promising future? A pint of ice cream and a few laughs doesn't morph someone's personality completely. Except I can't shake the feeling this is a turning point in my life. Shit might get bad, but as long as I hold on during the coming war, I might have a chance at something beyond merely surviving.

I shake my head as I make my way down the stairs. Whatever happens will happen and I'll deal with my strange, new outlook then. I peek into the dark living room. Lexi probably won't wake up for a few hours. The nap I took earlier is the only reason I'm still upright. After all the emotions we went through tonight, I'm oddly energized. And fucking hungry.

I turn toward the kitchen, wondering if I could bribe Storm into bringing me food instead. My feet stutter to a stop when my brain catches up. Spinning around, I hold my breath and scan the dark room. Something's off, but I can't figure out what. I creep closer to the couch, glancing at the windows. They're still covered, muffling the pitter-patter of rain.

My eyes catch on the lump on the couch. I rip away the blankets, already knowing I'll find nothing. Lexi must have slipped away when I was in the shower, but why wouldn't she tell me? A stark white piece of paper flutters to the ground at my feet and I stare at it. A wave of nausea hits me and my mouth fills with saliva. There's no reason to think it's anything other than a note saying she went home. No reason except my gut screaming at me to run.

Before I can lose my resolve, I snatch up the paper and unfold it with trembling hands. Lexi's shaky script covers the page. Most of the words are ones of apologies and regret. Despite our conversation, she still doesn't feel like she did enough. A string of curses leaves me the more I read. My feet are moving while my mind tries to fully understand what she wrote.

Just know I'm doing this for me, too. I need to end this like I should have done years ago. Please help Creed get out. He deserves more than what he's been handed. He'll help you if I don't make it out. Just know I'm trying to fix this. I love you and I know you'll be fine. I'm going to fix it. I promise.

"Fuck," I yell. "Fuck, fuck, fuck."

I don't have time to wait for Ghost or Storm to get home. A text will have to do. Hopefully, I can catch Lexi before she gets anywhere near the Disciples compound. At least I'm going to try. I won't let her die alone.

Forty-Two

Storm

I step up next to Ghost and nudge him with my elbow. He glances at me from the corner of his eye, and I tilt my phone toward him. Siren's text isn't much, but I can't make sense of it. It might be worse than the weird-ass emoji she sent me when she woke up. I know she did it on purpose to piss me off. Except there's a small part of me that wonders if there was a reason.

This new message, though, doesn't make a lick of sense.

"What the fuck am I looking at?" Ghost mutters.

"No idea. Any guesses why she's going to the Sizzle Griddle?"

He shrugs, focusing on the men unloading the box truck. I didn't realize how many supplies he called in. Bear, our road captain, usually sets everything up. He wasn't happy when Ghost added more runs and expected him to figure it out. One of the prospects drops the box he's carrying, and I wince as the top pops off, spilling the contents all over the road. Bear smacks him in the back of his head.

"First aid supplies?" I ask quietly. "Thought we were getting weapons."

"I'm not buying more crossbows. I don't care how fucking cool they look. They take forever to reload, and no one knows how to fucking aim with them."

I hold my hands up with a grin. "I'd rather have a flamethrower, but I wasn't going to push my luck."

Ghost rolls his eyes, mumbling, "You and fucking Alex King."

"Why first aid shit?"

He gives me a look, then sighs. "It's one of the few things we needed more of when I went to Rima to take down the Guild. Lot of injuries what with shit blowing up and firefights breaking out. It was a shitshow they weren't prepared for. Aelia sent us this to help out."

"You told them?"

He grabs my arm and leads me away from the others. "We can't trust our lower clubs to come help us. Most of them aren't equipped to handle this type of war. If Prophet really is planning on attacking us, we'll need all the help we can get. From the info Widow brought to me, the Disciples outnumber us five to one. They'll overwhelm us without a second thought. Frankly, I don't know what they're waiting for. So, yeah. I told Raines and Helms. I gave Ryker the go ahead to tell the Kings and Byrns as well."

"Are we really asking them to send people?"

"No, but Roman Drake kindly offered his wife to come help. I declined. I'd rather not have her burn down any more buildings. We have enough problems without adding that—"

"Careful. She's probably hovering in the shadows waiting to hear you talk shit." I grin, but he doesn't seem in the mood. He's been on edge since we left. "She's fine, Ghost."

He shakes his head. "I'm not worried about Siren. This is something else. Did we hear from our contacts in the Disciples?"

"No, but that's not surprising. Their check-ins are sporadic at the best of times. If what Prophet told Siren is true, he's sealing shit off. I never fully trusted them anyway."

Bear walks over, his nostrils flaring. Thunder rumbles through the night air as if announcing his arrival. "Fly called. There's an issue down at the Bog."

"What kind of issue?" Ghost asks. Shouting breaks out by the truck between one of ours and the driver. Ghost grumbles under his breath as he stomps over to them.

"What's the problem, Bear?"

He hands me his phone. "He's freaking out. Thinks Disciples are there."

I squint at the screen. Fly's messages are only one or two words with no context at all. "Candles? What the fuck is he talking about?"

"I think there's candles surrounding the Bog. I tried calling him, but it wouldn't go through."

"Fine. I'll go down there and check it out."

"Bring Prez. Him being here doesn't do us any good," Bear grunts, then rejoins the others. They're almost done anyway.

Another bout of thunder echoes in the distance. I doubt we'll have to worry about the candles. As soon as the skies open up, the flames will be wicked out. I'd rather get home to Siren instead of chasing an obvious ploy to distract us from something bigger. Ghost stomps back to me, mumbling under his breath.

"We need to go down to the Bog. Fly thinks they're under attack by way of tea light candles." I snort, then send a quick message to Siren.

Ghost sighs heavily. "He should be better at handling his shit. He's been an enforcer for five years now. How many guys he bring down there?"

"Dozen or so. They're only supposed to be stocking the guns in the basement. I don't think Henry even shut down the bar for it like he usually does."

"He did. Said he'd open when they were done. Let's go."

We make our way to our bikes, leaving Bear to finish the job. He'll make sure the supplies make it to headquarters. If the Disciples do attack us, headquarters will end up being our makeshift hospital. Most of us have some first aid training, but Bones will be busy if shit goes down. It takes us at least twenty minutes to get to the Bog. The closer we get, the more on edge I become.

A soft glow around the bar isn't unusual. The extreme quiet

is, though. No music blasts from the outdoor speakers. No bikes rumble in the distance. No shouts of laughter split the night. When we round the bend, gravel kicking up from our tires, I curse. Fly had every right to be freaked out. Ghost swerves off the road and cuts his engine before I've even pulled up next to him. He's halfway across the parking lot when I catch his arm.

"We don't know what they put in there. Slow down."

"How the fuck did they get thousands of candles out here without anyone noticing?" Ghost snaps as he skirts around them.

A single shepherd's staff with a note fluttering in the breeze is stuck in the middle of them. I crouch and examine the flickering light.

"These are electric," I call to Ghost who's edging closer to the building. "They must have set them up, then turned them on all at once with an app or something."

Ghost prowls back to me when he can't find a way to the front door. "If they can wire them up like that, what else are we going to find in there?"

"Doubt it's a bomb. It would defeat the purpose of a note on the staff."

Ghost looks at me and his jaw sets. "Don't fucking lose it."

He sprints toward the staff before I can stop him, kicking candles as he goes. He rips the note from its perch and runs back. It takes everything in me not to burst out. He's practically pinwheeling his arms in his haste to get away from absolutely nothing. When he gets back to me, he doubles over, hands on his knees while he gasps for breath.

"Hope someone was taking a video of that shit. Siren will be delighted to watch it," I say, fighting a grin.

He gasps for breath. "Siren's never been delighted a day in her life."

"You really should work out more. We have a gym in the goddamn house. You really have no excuse."

"Shut the fuck up and read it," he wheezes.

My grin drops from my face as I scan the opening. The words

blur as I read it again. The thin paper creases and I loosen my grip. My heartbeat thrashes in my ears, drowning out Ghost's rasping breath. While he regains control of his body, I'm slowly losing mine.

His voice cuts through the pounding in my head. "What's it say?"

I clear my throat. "I don't...I can't..." Lightning flashes overhead, illuminating the Disciples insignia at the bottom. I swallow hard and he rips the paper from my fingers. The words are etched in my mind's eye. I doubt I'll forget them anytime soon.

My little lamb,

How I've missed you while they've locked you away. While you may not feel the ache as acutely as I, fear not. I've suffered enough for the both of us. It's time to accept your destiny. Keep watch and know I'll forgive you for your past transgressions. We shall begin anew. Those who would strive to keep you from me shall see their end soon.

Until you're where you belong.

Acknowledgments

Thank you so much for reading Ghost, Storm and Siren's story!

Ready for another adventure?

Check out the other works available by Emilia Abraham.

If you'd like to hear about the other stories that have been living in my head, sign up for my newsletter (including extra scenes & epilogues), visit my website, or follow me on social media visit:

emiliaabraham.com

Special Thanks:

K.B. Barrett Designs - Cover Artist and Formatter
Dragon Smith Publishing, LLC - Emily Michel - Editor
Erenee - Beta Reader
Krysten - Omega Reader

About the Author

After many years of dreaming of becoming a full-time writer, Emilia Abraham took the leap, bringing her words to print. From sweet contemporary romance to spicy why choose and everything in between, she focuses on the happily ever after.

Emilia lives in the Upper Midwest with her husband (who's probably sick of listening to her expound on fictional men) and three kids (who try to steal her post-it notes). When she's not writing, she enjoys reading, playing video games, and consuming copious amounts of energy drinks.

Also by E Abraham

Other Works:

Also by E. Abraham:

Shadows of Synd:
Under the Shadows-Book 1
Between the Shadows: Novella
Running From Shadows-Book 2
Becoming Shadows-Book 3
Shadows Within Us-Book 4
Beyond the Shadows-Book 5

Ruins of Rima: Spin-off Series
Chasing Darkness-Book 1
Charmed by Darkness-Book 2

Novella:
Cadence of the Xylophone

Available on Newsletter:
Extra Scenes,
Bridging Epilogues (Shadows of Synd-Book 1 & 2)

Also by Emilia Abraham:

Stuck at Sundown

Write on the Edge

The Cryptid Chronicles:

Bewitched by Bigfoot

Seduced by the Sliver Cat